FELLOW AMERICANS

Como was fighting to keep his anger under control. "Get the airborne dropped," he barked.

"The drop zones have not been laid out, Sir," Krigel replied.

"What?"

"Sir, the Pathfinders went in last night, but they all deserted and joined the Rebels. To a man. They said they won't fight fellow Americans, and anyone who would is a traitor."

"Goddamn it!" Como yelled. He pointed a finger at Krigel. "You get the airborne up and dropped. Start the push. Right now!"

This was the moment Krigel had been dreading. "We have a problem, Sir. Quite a number of the residents of the Tri-states were . . ."

"Paratroopers, Rangers, marines, SEALs, AF personnel." The CG finished it for him. "Wonderful. How many are not going to follow my orders?"

"About fifty percent of the airborne have refused to go in. No Rangers, no Green Beret About thirty percent of the marines infantry refuse to go in. They said, Sir, the gates of hell for you, with only spit to fight with, but they say the Americans, and they haven't done an They are not criminals."

OUT OF
THE ASHES

WILLIAM W.
JOHNSTONE

PINNACLE BOOKS
Kensington Publishing Corp.
http://www.kensingtonbooks.com

PINNACLE BOOKS are published by

Kensington Publishing Corp.
850 Third Avenue
New York, NY 10022

All Kensington Titles, Imprints, and Distributed Lines are available at special quantity discounts for bulk purchases for sales promotions, premiums, fund-raising, and educational or institutional use. Special book excerpts or customized printings can also be created to fit specific needs. For details, write or phone the office of the Kensington special sales manager: Kensington Publishing Corp., 850 Third Avenue, New York, NY 10022, attn: Special Sales Department, Phone: 1-800-221-2647.

Pinnacle and the P logo Reg. U.S. Pat. & TM Off.

ISBN-13: 978-0-7860-1953-3
ISBN-10: 0-7860-1953-0

First Pinnacle Books Printing: August 1996

10

Printed in the United States of America

To Danielle Dubois

This country, with its institutions, belongs to the people who inhabit it. Whenever they shall grow weary of the existing government, they can exercise their Constitutional right of amending it, or their revolutionary right to dismember or overthrow it.

Abe Lincoln

PROLOGUE

Louisiana, 1984

"Are you nuts?" Ben Raines asked, fighting back an urge to laugh in the man's face. "I mean, honest to God, fellow, have you got both oars in the water?"

The sarcastic slur and intellectual insult was lost on the visitor. "I assure you, Mr. Raines, I am in full command of all my faculties. You came highly recommended to me. To us."

"By whom?"

"I cannot divulge that information. Not just yet. I am sorry."

"How do you know I won't go straight to the FBI with this . . . scheme of yours?"

The man pointed. "There is the phone. Call them. You can't prove a thing. But we can—about you." He smiled.

"The FBI knows damned well I was a mercenary back in '69 and '70. So does the State Department. I made that very clear in several of my novels. Blackmail won't work with me."

The man shrugged. "It was worth a try."

"Look," Ben said, "I don't like the way this country is going any more than you do—believe that, or not. But violent overthrow—even if you people had the men and

7

equipment, which you don't—is not my forte."

"But we do have the men and equipment, Mr. Raines."

"You say. I don't want any part of it."

"You're certain?"

"As certain as the sun comes up in the east."

"Then we badly misjudged you, Mr. Raines."

Ben shook his head in disagreement. "No, you didn't. If you had approached me just a few years ago, back in '80, or even '82, I probably would have gone along with you. But now . . . no."

"May I ask why not?"

"Because for the past few years I've been very comfortable. And getting fatter all the time. My books are selling well; no bill collectors calling every night; everything you see around you—including the house— is paid for. I have no reason to rock the boat."

"If you are so happy, why do you drink yourself into a stupor every evening?"

Ben smiled. "You have been investigating, haven't you? I didn't mention happy, did I? Comfortable was the word I chose."

"Has it not occurred to you that we may be privy to . . . matters concerning the situation in the world that . . . you are not aware of, sir? I beg you to reconsider your stance."

Ben shook his head no.

The man sighed. "Well . . . you will not be contacted by us again, Mr. Raines. Thank you for your time." He hesitated, then said, "I . . . may be making a mistake, Mr. Raines, but everybody is entitled to one. So here is mine: Bull Dean and Carl Adams are still alive. They're running the show."

Ben came out of his chair. He stared at the man. "I

don't believe it. Hey! I saw the bodies, buddy."

The man's expression did not change. "If you reverse your position, Mr. Raines, just run an ad in the local paper that you'd like to buy a Russian wolfhound. You'll be contacted." He turned and was gone into the night, the door closing softly behind him.

Ben sat down. He looked at the half-full glass of bourbon and water on the table. He picked it up and emptied it without taking the glass from his lips.

Bull and Adams alive? No way.

Ben Raines laughed and put the mysterious visit out of his mind. He put on a symphony and got drunk while listening to it. The next morning, the visit was hazy in his mind. After a week, he had forgotten all about it.

PART ONE

PART ONE

Washington, D.C., 1988

"Maybe historians will treat me in a more humane fashion than the press has for the past eight years," President Fayers remarked to his wife. "But sometimes I wonder."

"You've done a lot of good things over the years, Ed." She smiled at him, patting his hand. "SALT 5 was only one of them. It's taken you time, and you didn't win all the battles, but you certainly didn't lose the war."

"Then why, for the past several months, have I had this . . . uneasy feeling in my guts that . . . oh, hell, honey—I don't know. I've been a politician all my life. And I *know something* is going on. I can't put my finger on it, but . . . some *thing* is crawling around the gutters of this city. Some . . . secret I should know."

His wife studied him. She knew only too well the sixth sense career politicians develop over the years, and knew it was not to be taken lightly. Her husband had had his finger on the pulse of the world for more than forty years, for the past eight as President of the United States. If he believed something was amiss . . . it was.

"Ed, this unknown . . . quantum bothers you that much?"

"Yes, it does, honey. Ever since that gun-control bill went through, the unrest in this country has been building. Baby, citizens of this country—not criminals—have been beaten, jailed, and *killed*, simply because they clung to the belief—a correct belief, I might add—that they had a right to own a gun. Damn that Hilton Logan for the son of a bitch he is! He and that pack of liberal bastards really stirred it up with that gun-control bill."

"You didn't sign it, Ed. Don't forget that."

"It still became law."

"The law of the land, Ed," she reminded him.

"But," the president stared hard at his wife of fifty years—more than his wife: his friend, his confidante. "Is it really the law of the land? Of the people, for the people? Is it constitutional?"

"The supreme court says it is."

"Five to four," President Fayers grunted. "Not exactly an overwhelming majority." He walked to the window and looked out at the night. "I cannot forget the news film of that fellow down in South Carolina. That man never had so much as a traffic ticket in his whole life. And agents—federal agents—employed by the very government his taxes help support, shot him *stone damned dead!* And for what? Because he wanted to keep a .38 pistol in his house. Ah, hell!" The president waved his disgust.

"The country is becoming prosperous once again," she said, attempting to change the subject.

"What's the matter?" He grinned at her. "You worried about my blood pressure?"

"Somebody has to. You won't."

"After all the social blunders of the '60's and '70's . . . I'll be goddamned if we're not heading down the same old road. Just look at that new pack of liberals in Congress."

"It's the will of the people, Ed."

"No." He shook his head. "No, honey, that's the shame of it—it isn't. It's the will of pressure groups, lobbyists, so-called Christians." He poured a drink under the frowning gaze of his wife. He downed it neat, then sighed. "Something's in the wind. And it stinks. I just don't know what it is." He sat down. "God, I'm tired. I'm seventy-five years old. I'm tired. I just want out."

Ben Raines sat on the front porch of his home in Louisiana and for the first time in a long time thought about Vietnam and how, during the quiet moments after patrol, unwinding, but still too keyed up to sleep, he would sit with his buddies and talk of home, women, movies, and politics—as well as other topics.

Two decades had passed since that exercise in futility had ended for Ben. He didn't think about it often. The nightmares had dimmed into occasional dreams, without substance, the blood in them no longer red and thick and real. The screaming faint night sounds now had no meaning, and the smoke from the burning villages was no longer acrid, did not burn his eyes or leave a bitter taste on his tongue.

It was just a fading memory. Nothing more.

He wondered, now that SALT 5 was two years old and the nuclear weapons around the world had been greatly reduced, at least for the major countries, if there would ever be another war.

He felt there would be, and he also wondered if Russia and America were living up to the terms of the agreement.

He doubted it. Both sides still had missiles tucked away, hidden, ready, and aimed. Each side knew the other too well. Only the doves in America truly believed in all the terms of SALT 5. Ben wondered if those missiles aimed at Russia and America were nuclear or bacteriological types. He thought probably the latter, for SALT didn't cover germ-type warheads . . . that came under a different agreement.

"Come on, Ben," he muttered. "Why are you thinking like this tonight?"

He tried to think about the new novel he was planning, but his thoughts would not jell. Then he suddenly recalled the words one of his long-dead buddies had spoken to him, so many years before, during one of those long bull sessions.

"How would you change our system of government, Ben? I mean, we all agree the system isn't working. But how would you correct it? If you could?"

And that had sparked hours of debate and sometimes heated arguments that turned into fist fights. The debates had lasted for days.

He recalled the legendary Col. Bull Dean listening to his men argue and debate. The Bull had smiled. Then, when they were alone, Bull had said to Ben, "Keep your dreams, son. You have good thoughts for one so young. Keep them alive in your mind, for someday, probably sooner than you might think, you just might have a chance to see them spring to life. Hell, son! You might write a book!"

Ben had grinned, thinking the Bull was kidding.

On this soft night in Louisiana, Ben remembered Bull's words as they had waited to lift off from Rocket City, heading into North Vietnam, to HALO in: high altitude, low opening. They would jump at twenty thousand feet, their chutes opening automatically when they got under radar.

"We're losin' this war, son," Bull had said. "And there is nothing that guys like you and me can do about it—we can only prolong it. Back home, now, it's gonna get worse—much worse. Patriotism is gonna take a nose dive, sinking to new depths of dishonor. There is no discipline in schools; the courts have seen to that. America is going to take a pasting for a decade, maybe longer, losing ground, losing face, losing faith. That's when the military will be forced to step in and take over. And God help us all when they do that."

"Why do you say that, sir?"

"Remember that line about absolute power?"

"Yes, sir."

"The military leaders—those with enough sense to pour piss out of a boot, that is, and we do have a few of them in uniform—realize the truth in that line. They won't want to take over the country—but they might be forced into doing it. For a time. It will be a bad time for you all."

"For *you* all? Not including yourself in that, Colonel?"

The Bull had smiled.

"Sir? Why are you telling me all this . . . now?"

The Bull shook his head. "I haven't told you as much as you might believe. But in the years ahead of you—two decades, more than likely—you'll understand."

Ben stirred uncomfortably on the porch. It had been two decades, almost. The strange visitor of several years back suddenly popped into his mind. He shook away those memories.

And just before that leap into the rushing night, so

17

many years ago, as the Bull stood in the door of the plane, he screamed at Ben: "Bold Strike, son. Remember it. Bold Strike. Say it to no one."

A few weeks later, Col. William "Bull" Dean was supposedly killed, his mutilated and unrecognizable body found days later by a team of LRRPs—Long Range Recon Patrols. Then Adams was reported missing. He was MIA'ed; then, finally, listed as KIA.

A month later, Ben had been wounded and sent home.

After he recovered from his wounds, he found he could not tolerate the attitudes in America toward her Vietnam vets. He was restless, and missed the action he had left behind. He had been sent home to a land of hairy, profane young men who sewed the American flag on the seats of their dirty jeans and marched up and down the street, shouting ugly words, all in the name of freedom— their concept of freedom.

Ben left the country and made his way to Africa, signing on as a mercenary with anyone who wanted and appreciated fighting men. For two years he fought in dozens of little no-name wars, just drifting, becoming hardened to death and blood and suffering.

One day he told a visiting American writer—whom he had met in a bar—he thought he might write a book. The writer questioned Ben closely, then told him to do just that, and when he was through with it, to send it to his agent. He'd tell the agent it was coming.

The more Ben thought about it, the more he liked the idea. He went home, back to Illinois, to his parents' home, and wrote his book.

He'd been writing ever since and had lived in Louisiana for almost fifteen years.

He stirred from his misty memories and realized the

phone was ringing in the den. He walked from the coolness of the front porch and picked up the phone. Two words were spoken, and they caused his heart to pound and a dizziness to spring into his head.

"Bold Strike."

Then the line went dead.

Ben sat down hard in a chair. He had not heard those words in years. But what the hell did they mean? A warning? A cue for him to do something. What in the shit had the Bull meant by them?

Ben turned on the TV set and caught the last of the nightly news. Fresh outbreaks of race riots in Newark and Detroit. The government was worried about the resurgence of the KKK and the American Nazi Party—and the fact that they had joined hands, to jointly spew their hate. White robes and black uniforms.

"Bold Strike," Ben muttered. "What's going on? Bull Dean is dead. And so is Carl Adams. I saw the bodies."

No, he corrected his thoughts. You saw *a body*. Someone said it was Colonel Dean. You later—much later—saw pictures that someone *said* was Adams.

Then the words of the news commentator numbed Ben. "Certain military units have been placed on low alert. No reason was given. But it's nothing to be concerned about, the Pentagon says. Just testing security."

"What units, you son of a bitch!" Ben shouted at the TV set.

A commercial for a female hygiene spray greeted his question.

Ben turned off the set.

Something dark and elusive darted around the shadowy corners of his mind. He fixed another drink and

19

sat down by the phone. He jerked up the phone, consulted an address book, and dialed the number of a friend over at Fort Stewart, Georgia. His wife answered the phone.

"No, Ben, he's not here. No. I can't tell you where he is, 'cause *I* don't know where he is. It hasn't been this tight around here since the Iran thing."

They chatted of small things for a few moments, then Ben said good night. The wall of secrecy was closing. Ben knew it well.

He tried his old outfit, the Hell-Hounds. Probably less than five percent of Congress knew of their existence. Maybe not that high a percentage. Certainly no member of the press knew of them. In times of trouble, they would be gearing up in Utah, at an old AEC base. The Hell-Hounds had no permanent base, being constantly on the move. The nearest thing they had to a home was that desolate, deserted spot in Utah.

Col. Sam Cooper, CO of the Hell-Hounds, was blunt with him. Blunt, but not unfriendly. He simply had his orders, and that was that.

"I don't know what's going down, Ben. But it's good to hear from you. I enjoyed your last book. Good stuff."

"Honestly, Sam? You really don't know what's happening?"

"I'm leveling with you, Ben. To tell you the God's truth, I can't find anybody who knows what's going on. Or at least who will talk about it."

Ben felt a chill move around in his belly. "Take care of yourself, Sam."

"Will do. You hunt a hole, partner," the Hell-Hound said. "Keep your head down." He broke the connection.

Or somebody did it for him.

*   *   *

"It's firm, Hilton," the senator's chief aide told him. "The military is up to something. Lots of moving around and quiet talk. And I can't even get in the front door at Langley. Certain units of the military are on some kind of low alert."

"Why?" the senator demanded.

"I don't know."

"President Fayers?"

"He's fat, dumb, and happy."

"You mean *he* doesn't know what's going on?"

"Apparently not."

"Jesus Christ!"

TWO

A fishing lodge in the Missouri Ozarks

The banquet hall of the lodge had been cleared of all furniture not essential to the meeting. The building had been electronically swept for listening devices. Long tables had been placed end to end, side to side, forming a huge square, capable of accommodating fifty people in comfort. Pitchers of water, drinking glasses, pads and pencils, and briefing books were placed on the dark blue cloth, the items neatly arranged before each chair. A shredding machine stood silent in the corner.

Tension, heavy and ominous, hung in the huge room as the room filled with men in groups of two or three. Although no nametag designated individual place, there was no confusion; each man seemed to know exactly where to sit. There was no unnecessary chatter, few social amenities were exchanged. The men looked at each other, nodded, then sat down.

All of the men were military. That would have been evident to even the most uneducated in military bearing. Neatly trimmed hair, out of style; eyes that gave away nothing; erect bearing; no wasted motion.

To the more knowledgeable, the men were line officers

and combat-experienced sergeants and chiefs. All career men.

The Army general and colonels, had they been in uniform, would have had Airborne/Ranger/Special Forces tabs on their shoulders. The generals and colonels of the Marine Corps are Force Recon—trained—Raiders. The general and colonels of the Air Force are combat pilots and Air Force commandos. The Navy men are UDT, SEAL, pilots, ships' captains. The Coast Guard men are all career; they have all seen combat. There were fifteen sergeant majors and master chiefs making up the complement.

During the past twenty-four hours, the men, all having arrived at night, had traveled various routes to get to the lodge. The real-estate agent who had rented them the lodge knew only that he was renting the place for a top-level think tank.

"Keep your mouth shut about this and we'll be back next year. A handsome bonus for you. And don't disturb us."

"Yes, sir," the agent had replied instinctively. Guy looked like his old drill sergeant.

Guards were sentried about the two hundred acres. They were in civilian clothes and their sidearms were out of sight.

Cigars, pipes, and cigarettes smoking, water glasses filled, the men waited for someone to open the ball.

"Who ordered this low alert the press is talking about?" the question was tossed out.

"Came out of the Joint Chiefs. It's confused the hell out of a lot of units and caused several hundred thousand men to be shifted around, out of standard position.

Goddamn, it's going to be days before they get back to normal. We not only don't know who issued the order, but why?"

"Maybe to get us out of position for the big push?"

"I thought we had more time—months, even."

"Something's happened to cause them to speed up their timetable," Gen. Vern Saunders of the Army said. "That means we've got to move very quickly."

"Hell, Vern," Gen. Tom Driskill of the Marine Corps said, "what can we do . . . really? We're up against it. We all *think* we know where 'it' is. But we're not certain. Do we dare move? If we do, what will be the consequences?"

Admiral Mullens of the Navy looked around him, meeting all eyes. "I don't think we dare move."

Sergeant major of the Army, Parley, stirred.

"You got something on your mind, Sergeant Major," the admiral said, "say it. We're all equal here."

"Damned if that's so!" a Marine sergeant major said.

Laughter erupted.

Parley said, "I don't believe we can afford to move. But if we don't, what do we do—just sit on our hands and wait for war?"

"I think it's out of our hands," Admiral Newcomb of the Coast Guard said. "We're damned if we do, damned if we don't. If we expose the location of the sub—where we *think* it is—we stand a good chance of a war. A very good chance. I think we're in a box. If we expose the traitors, they'll fire anyway. And we're not supposed to have that type of missile."

"Which is a bad joke," Sergeant Major Rogers of the Marine Corps said in disgust. "Russia's still got us outgunned two to one in missiles of the conventional nuclear type. God only knows how many germ-type warheads they have." He forced a grin. "Of course, we have a few of those ourselves." He shook his head. "Jesus! Thirty damned guys control the fate of the entire world. Even worse than that, if our intelligence is correct, it's a double double cross."

Master chief petty officer of the Navy, Franklin, looked across the table, disgust in his eyes. "Admiral? Do you—any of you—know for sure just who we *can* trust?"

The admiral shook his head. "No, not really. We don't know how many of our own people are in on this . . . caper."

"You mean, sir," a colonel asked, "one of *us* might be in on it?"

"I would say the odds are better than even that is true."

"I wondered why I was jerked out of Italy so fast I didn't even have time to zip up my pants," the Ranger colonel smiled.

"Well, you'd better zip 'em up, Pete," a SEAL laughed at him. "You don't have that much to brag about."

"How the hell do you know?" A marine chuckled. "You two guys queer for each other?"

"I ain't free,"—the Ranger grinned—"but I'm reasonable."

An AF commando laughed. "He bends over in the shower a lot, lookin' for the soap."

The rough humor touched all the men. After the laughter had died, the men seemed more relaxed, able to talk without constraint. A Special Forces colonel said, "General? You think some of my men are involved in this?"

"No," General Saunders said. "Our intelligence people"—he waved his hand—"all services, seem to agree on one point: no special troops are involved. But"—he held up a warning finger—"this touches all branches of the service, not just in this country, but *all* countries. Russia included." He smiled grimly. "I take some satisfaction in that. Those men in that sub have friends all over the world. That's why they've been able to hide from us for so long."

"The Bull and Adams are really alive?"

"Yes. I talked with Bull. It came as quite a shock to me."

"I . . . don't really understand what they have to do with this . . . operation," a master chief said, as much to himself as to the men around him.

"Really . . . neither do we," an admiral replied. "But we do know these facts, one of which is obvious: Bull and Adams faked their deaths years ago; we know they are both superpatriots, Adams more than Bull when it comes to liberal-hating. All right. We put together this hypothesis: Adams and Bull had a plan to overthrow the government—if it came to that—using civilian . . . well, rebels, let's call them, along with selected units of the military. Took years to put all this together. But . . . the use of civilian rebels failed; couldn't get enough of them in time. We know for a fact that many ex-members of the Hell-Hounds turned them down cold."

"How many men do they have?"

"Five to six thousand—at the most."

"That's still a lot of people. And knowing Bull and Adams, those men are trained guerrilla fighters. How have they managed to keep that many people secret for so long?"

The admiral allowed himself a tight smile. "You didn't know the Bull, did you?"

"No, sir."

"If you had known either of them, you wouldn't have asked."

"I knew both of them," a Ranger colonel said. "If they even suspected a member of any of their units was a traitor, they would not hesitate to kill him—war or peace."

"I see," the man said softly. "So . . . Bull came up with the sub plan?"

General Saunders shook his head. "No. It wasn't his plan. We believe it was Adams' idea. But I couldn't discuss this with Bull. I only had two minutes with him. Besides, he and Adams have been friends for twenty-five years. But I did manage to plant a seed of doubt in his mind. Yes, we believe Adams has lost control; he's slipped mentally. Mr. Kelly of the CIA shares that belief."

"There is something I don't understand," a Coast Guard officer said. "Obviously, this plan has been on the burner for a long time—years. To overthrow the government, I mean. Why have they waited so long?"

"That's what we don't know. And we've got dozens of computers working on the problem right at this moment." The general rubbed his face with his hands. "I didn't get a chance to ask the Bull that. So many questions I wanted to ask. Men, I don't think we have a prayer of stopping those men on the sub. I think we're staring nuclear and germ warfare right in its awful face and there isn't a goddamned thing we can do about it."

"I gather," a Marine officer said, "the Joint Chiefs don't know about this?"

"We don't know if they do or not," Admiral Mullens said. "But we can't approach any of them for fear one of them is involved."

"One or more. And which ones?"

"That is yet another point to consider."

"And we can't do to them what we're about to do to each other," General Driskill said, as an aide, as if on cue, wheeled in a cart with a machine on it.

No one had to ask what it was; all the men present held the highest security ratings in America. They had all taken these tests before. The machine was the most highly advanced of the psychological stress evaluators. PSE. The same type the Bull and Adams used to ferret out informers.

"Each of us will submit to a PSE test. Sergeant Mack is the best around." General Driskill smiled as he laid a pistol on the table, in front of him. "This won't take too long."

A few seconds ticked past. An Air Force colonel tried to light a cigarette. His hands were shaking so badly he finally gave up the effort. He looked into the hard eyes of the Marine general. "Save yourself the trouble, General. I don't know where the sub is; I don't know who on the JCs—if anyone—is involved in this operation; and I don't know anyone who does know."

"You damned fool!" General Driskill snapped at him. "Don't you people realize—or care—you're bringing the world to the brink of holocaust?"

"Oh, the hell with that!" the colonel said. "Let Russia and China fight it out. Let them destroy each other. We'll pick up the pieces and be on top once more."

"So that's it," a man muttered.

The Air Force colonel smiled.

"I don't believe that's all of it," General Crowe of the Air Force said. He pulled a pistol from his waistband and pointed it at the colonel. "You traitorous son of a bitch. Which one of the Joint Chiefs is it?"

The Air Force colonel was suddenly calm with the knowledge that he would never leave this room alive. He was not going to give the men in the room the pleasure of seeing him squirm. His gaze touched each man, then he lit his cigarette with steady hands. "I don't know. And that's being honest. I think it's an aide, but I can't be sure. You can test me; I won't fight the machine."

He was tested. He did not know the name of the man on the Joint Chiefs, and his hunch that it was a top aide showed positive. He did not know the location of the sub, and had no further knowledge of it.

"Explain it all!" General Crowe snapped. "I've seen men tortured before, sonny." He still held the .38 in his right hand.

"General, I don't know much about the operation. That was deliberate on the part of the top man, or men. Not even the men in the sub know who the architect is. Least I don't believe they do." No one in the room believed him. "My orders are to report what I heard here, that's all."

"He's lying!" a master chief said.

General Crowe said, "Colonel, make it easy on yourself. We can do this one of several ways. We're not savages, but the fate of the world may very well rest in this room."

The Air Force colonel glanced at his watch. A smile tugged at one corner of his mouth. He gave the general a Washington, D.C. phone number.

"Trace it," Driskill told Sergeant Major Rogers.

The colonel's eyes hardened.

"Let's tighten up all the loose ends, Colonel. Too many

ropes dangling, flapping in the breeze."

He looked at his watch once again and said, after a slight smile and a deep breath, almost a sigh of relief, "We—those of us in the operation—knew that Brady would eventually put things together and go to Fayers."

"Harold Brady of the CIA?"

"Yes. We had hoped he wouldn't put it together until after the elections." He glanced at his watch.

"Why are you always lookin' at your goddamned watch?" an Air Force commando asked. "You takin' medicine?"

"He's stalling!" a SEAL said. "Playing for time."

The Army Ranger hit the colonel in the mouth with a short, hard right, slamming him out of his chair. General Driskill kicked the man to his feet and shoved him back in his chair.

"Now, speak!" the general barked.

The Air Force colonel shook his head to clear away the cobwebs and wiped blood from his mouth. He smiled.

"What do you find amusing about all this?" Admiral Mullens asked.

The colonel's smile broadened.

"Because," Admiral Newcomb said quietly, "there aren't going to be any elections—right, Colonel?"

The man's smile faded. "That's right, Admiral."

"Why?"

He again glanced at his watch. "Because it's 1207, that's why."

"What?" Driskill barked. "What the hell has the time to do with anything?"

"Brady put it all together much sooner than we expected. I should have received a phone call before 1145 hours. I didn't. That means our computers have concluded that no one can beat Hilton Logan in the fall elections. It—they—have concluded that even if it's close, too close, no clear majority, it'll be thrown into the House. Logan will come out on top, and that liberal son of a bitch will find out we've built new nukes and order them destroyed."

"Son,"—General Saunders leaned forward—"don't do this. Don't do it to your country. Logan is just a man. Not much of one," he grimaced, "but still a man. He's not going to dismantle the nation. We'll weather it."

"No, General. No, we won't. This country's had it." His eyes were sad, his voice low when he spoke. "We've had eight years of conservatism, but everything Fayers has pushed through has been a battle. People aren't interested in the long run; they're only interested, concerned, with *now*. The gun-control legislation proved it; we're moving back to the left, and we can't allow that to happen. This way is the only way we can get back on top. China will give Russia every missile she's had hidden for years, then pour half a billion troops across the border. They'll destroy each other. The two-bit countries will blow each other off the map once we start the dance. Africa will go up like a tinderbox, the Mideast with it." His eyes grew wild with fanaticism.

"And what of America, Colonel?" General Crowe asked.

"Oh, we'll take casualties," he admitted. "Somewhere in the seventy-five- to ninety-million range; you all know the stats. But we'll come out far better than any other major power. And when we're back on top again, this time, by God, we'll stay there."

"You're crazy!" Sergeant Major Parley blurted. "My God, man—think of all the innocent people you're

31

killing. You people are fucking nuts!"

Rogers came back into the room. "I used the mobile phone in the car, General, just in case the phone here has a long-range bug on it. The phone company in D.C. got a disconnect order on the number he gave us. Got it about two hours ago. What's happening here?"

"Holocaust," a buddy informed him.

Driskill looked at the colonel. "I believe the colonel is about to give us all the details, aren't you, superpatriot?"

The Air Force man laughed in his face. "Sure, I'll tell you. Why not? There isn't a damned thing any of you can do about it."

Only blow your fucking head off when you're through flapping your gums, General Crowe thought, his hand tightening on the butt of the .38.

"There won't be any elections," the colonel said. "Not for a long time—a very long time. The military is going to be forced into taking over the country: suspending the constitution and declaring martial law. That's all we wanted, all along. All we were doing, once we learned Brady was onto us, was buying time. Getting set. We're five days from launch."

The men in the room, to a man, sucked in their guts. One hundred and twenty hours to hell.

"I should have gone to the president when my intelligence people first stumbled onto this . . . treason!" General Saunders said.

The Air Force colonel laughed. He lit a cigarette. His last one. "Well, General, I'll salve your conscience a bit. It wouldn't have made any difference. You couldn't have stopped us. You didn't really know what was going down until today. You couldn't have gone to the Chinese to tell them the Russians were going to launch against them. No proof. Big international stink would be all you could have accomplished. Same if you'd gone to the Russians. It all boils down to this: an American sub will launch the missiles—*American* missiles. Both countries would have turned on you. And . . . I think most of you know what type of missiles we're going to fire. Missiles so top secret not even the President knew of their existence. You clever boys got too clever, that's all. We used your cleverness against you."

"What type of missiles are you using?" a master chief asked.

"Supersnoop missiles," Admiral Mullens answered the question. "Thunder-strikes. We started building them on the QT when we realized SALT 5 was becoming a reality. Yes, the Russians knew we were going to build them—before SALT was signed. That's the main reason Russia agreed to SALT 5."

"The president and/or congress know of them?" he was asked.

"No," he said tersely.

"The lid is being slowly nailed on our coffins," a Navy officer said. He looked at the Air Force colonel. "What about him?"

General Crowe jacked back the hammer on the .38 and shot the colonel between the eyes, knocking him backward, out of the chair.

"Good shot, Turner," General Driskill observed.

THREE

Saturday—five days to launch

General C. H. Travee, chairman of the Joint Chiefs of Staff sat quietly in his office. He sat for a long, speculative time, drumming his fingertips on the polished wood of the desk top.

Too many rumors being whispered in this city. Entirely too many to ignore. Whispered rumors of a power play. Among the military? Too incredible to believe. Still . . .

Travee had tried to reach his old friend, Vern Saunders, just that morning—couple of hours ago, after Vern failed to show for their regular Saturday morning golf game. Travee had tried to track down his friend, but had hit a stone wall in every direction he turned.

Odd.

Then he heard rumors that General Crowe was seen climbing into the cockpit of a fighter and taking off for parts unknown. Odd. Crowe was entirely too old to go roaring off into the wild blue yonder like a young buck, cutting didos in the sky.

And General Driskill always worked in his office for a couple of hours on Saturday mornings. But not this Saturday morning.

Travee punched a button on his desk.

"Yes, sir?"

"Get me Major Bass from ASA. Tell him I want him in my office in thirty minutes."

"Yes, sir."

The Army Security Agency major was standing in front of the general's desk in exactly twenty-nine minutes. There were questions in his calm eyes.

"What's going on, Major?"

"Sir?"

"Come on, Major—you're in the know. You've heard the whispers all over the town. Now *you* tell *me*."

"I . . . don't know, sir. We can't even pinpoint who gave those low-alert orders."

"But yet it came from the Joint Chiefs?"

"Yes, sir. Sir? We think it was an aide. But the one we have in mind has . . . disappeared."

"I won't ask you who you suspect. Just this: why would he do such a damned fool thing?"

"I don't know, sir."

Travee nodded, then said, "I want you to do me a personal favor, Major. Find out where Gen. Vern Saunders was this morning. Pronto. And report your findings *only* to me."

"Yes, sir."

Sunday—four days to launch

President Fayers looked out the window of his office, wondering why any man would want the thankless job of President of the United States.

"It's such a lousy job," he said to his chief aide and good friend. "Damned if you do, damned if you don't.

The massive responsibility for running a country this size should not be dumped onto the shoulders of one man. It's too much."

"Yes, sir," the aide agreed, not really knowing what his boss was talking about. The president hadn't been himself lately. He'd been depressed, complaining of sleeplessness, and the aide was worried the press would discover it and blab it all over the nation. Not that it was any of their goddamned business. No—the president is supposed to be perfect. Can't ever be sick in private. Can't be a human being. No, the president has to be superman.

"Ed," the aide said, "are you all right?"

"Yes, of course I am. No, I'm not. Hell, I don't know. I'm getting old, that's what." He sighed heavily. "What is on the agenda for this afternoon?"

"The meeting with the analytical and statistical chief of the CIA's overseas intelligence operation."

"Hal Brady, you mean?"

"Yes, sir."

"Titles. Everybody has to have a title," Fayers muttered. "When is the meeting?"

"Right now."

"Send him in."

Harold Brady limped into the oval office, carrying a thick briefcase jammed with papers. His limp was the result of his days with the old OSS during World War II; a leg broken during a jump into France and never properly set.

Brady glanced at the aide. "In private," he said shortly, as was his manner. Abusive-sounding until one got to know the man.

The aide left the room.

"You look exhausted, Mr. President," Brady said. "I thank you for seeing me on Sunday afternoon. I know you like to rest on this day. Are you feeling well, sir?"

"As well as could be expected," Fayers replied, pouring them coffee. "Hilton Logan is privately saying he is unbeatable; he is our next president. God help us all, for he's probably correct. The unions are bitching and striking—as usual. Every minority group in this nation is complaining—loudly—that I am discriminating against them . . . and my wife has had a headache for three weeks. At night. Calls me a horny old goat." President Fayers smiled. "And you think *you've* got troubles."

Brady laughed along with his boss. "Well, sir, at least you've managed to keep your sense of humor."

"Only by straining, Hal. And by keeping in mind that in a few months I will be out of this office. Now then, what glad tidings have you to offer?" He lifted his coffee cup to his lips.

"I believe certain factions within the U.S. are preparing to start a war between Russia and China."

Fayers dropped cup and saucer to the carpet. "That's a rotten joke, Hal!" He knelt to pick up the broken bits of chinaware.

"It isn't a joke," the CIA man said, opening his briefcase, spreading papers on the president's desk. "You'd better sit down, sir."

Behind his desk, his face ashen and suddenly shiny with sweat, Fayers asked, "When is . . . all this supposed to occur?"

Brady shrugged. "I don't really know, but I would guess within a week. Maybe less. I just put together the remaining bits and pieces of evidence and supposition this morning."

"Do you want the secretary in on this?"

"Not just yet. You listen first, sir."

A half-hour later, President Fayers told his aide, "I don't want to be disturbed the rest of the evening. I'm going to Camp David to rest and to spend the night. That's all anybody needs to know."

Sunday evening—Camp David

"Begging your pardon, Mr. President," General Travee said, after recovering from his initial shock, "but I . . . just can't believe it."

"You'd better believe it, C.H.," Brady said. "I've been working on this for months. In total secrecy. I just didn't know who I could trust—not even you. But when the computers turned out this new evidence, I . . . had to come to the President."

"Why didn't you come to me before this, Hal?" Fayers asked.

"Because . . . I believe your staff—a few of them—are part of this. I don't know which ones. And the secret service; there again, I don't know which ones."

The secretary of state, Rees, had flown to Camp David with Fayers. The Joint Chiefs had joined them an hour later, arriving by car. Barry Ringold, director of the FBI had driven in, followed by Kelly of the CIA and Hal Brady.

"I resent the fact you did not come to me with this information, Brady," Kelly said.

"There, again, sir," Brady replied. "Who to trust?"

The two men glared at each other. But Kelly dropped his gaze after only a few seconds. Kelly was a political appointee; Brady was a career snoop with a lifetime spent in the shadows. Kelly was just a bit afraid of the man.

"Now, let me get this straight," Ringold said. "You want us to believe there are some five to six thousand rebels—organized and trained and armed—in the U.S., ready to move against the government?"

"That is correct," Brady said.

"They will be working with certain breakaway units of the armed forces?"

"That, too, is correct, sir—as far as it goes. But please bear in mind that many of those units—if not all of them—are not traitorous; they have been misinformed. They do not know the full scope of the story. Only bits and pieces. That is my theory."

Ringold nodded. "All right. Now, Bull Dean and Colonel Adams are both alive and well, working with the rebels and the maverick units of the military? Goddamn it, Harold! Dean and Adams are buried out there in Arlington. What kind of fairy tale is this? What have you been smoking?"

Brady flushed, opening his mouth to tell the FBI director to go fuck himself, then thought better of it.

Ringold said, "And China is going to declare war on Russia . . . you say. But you haven't, as yet, explained how or why that is going to occur."

His composure restored, temper in check, Brady said, "May I do so at this time?"

"Please do, sir," Ringold replied, with greatly exaggerated courtesy.

The two men did not like each other, had never liked each other, and would never, in the time left to them, like each other.

Brady looked at each man in the room before he replied, "Because I believe agents, posing as Red agents, will assassinate the Chinese premier and every member of his party when they visit the town of Fuchin next week."

"And you believe that will prompt a nuclear war between the two countries?" Kelly asked.

"That will be the start of it. Yes. A missile will then be fired from a submarine lying just off the coast of Russia." He limped to a huge wall map of the world and thumped a spot. "From right here. The sub will fire its missile, or missiles, probably, from just off the coast of Zapovednyy. I have reason to believe there will be more than one missile, single- or multiple-warhead type. I also believe the cities of Harbin, Mutanchiang, and Haokang will be destroyed."

"Why would Russia want to launch a nuke attack against China?" Ringold inquired. "Half the world might well be wiped out."

"There are many reasons they'd like to," Brady said. "But just as it will not be Red agents who kill the premier and his party—it will be Americans—it won't be the Russians who fire the missiles. They will be American missiles fired from an American sub."

General Travee had been studying the huge map. He said, "Fired from a Stealth-equipped sub, pulled in so close to the coast it would appear the missiles came from Russian soil."

Brady sat down. "Correct."

Admiral Divico had been unusually quiet, his eyes studying the map. "We're in a box," he said. "We're in a damned box, unable to do anything about it."

"What do you mean, Max?" Secretary Rees asked.

Ringold looked angrily at the admiral.

Brady smiled grimly.

40

"The small-class experimental sub that supposedly sank last year during a test run," the admiral said.

"What about it?" the president asked. "That was one of our best-kept secrets. All civilian personnel on board. High-paid volunteers with no family, picked by . . ." he paused. "Who did pick that crew?"

"We did," Kelly said glumly.

"Several members of the agency who," Brady said, "have quietly and mysteriously left the city over the past thirty-six hours. No answer at their homes."

"That doesn't answer my original question," Fayers said.

The admiral locked eyes with Brady. "I believe Mr. Brady is about to tell us that sub didn't sink."

"That is correct, Admiral. It was spotted last month by one of our operatives. He couldn't be one hundred percent certain; but certain enough to report it to me. I had had strong suspicions about it all along. The agent was killed just hours after making that report. The sub was taking on supplies, from a ship belonging to— quote/unquote—a friendly nation."

"Goddamn it!" Ringold said. "What small-class experimental sub?"

"It was top secret," the admiral said. "Very few people knew anything about it."

"Well . . . thanks just a whole hell of a lot!" Ringold blurted.

The admiral shrugged his total indifference as to what Ringold thought. "You didn't have a need to know." The admiral then added, "Shit!" Then he put together a string of expletives that made the Watergate tapes sound like children's nursery rhymes.

"Where in the hell could a sub hide for this long?"

Ringold asked.

"This sub could hide anywhere it wanted to hide," Travee said. "It's invisible. Sonar can't detect it. But God, it was expensive to build. Greatest weapon invented in the past fifty years. Came along much faster than its airborne counterpart. For all the good it's going to do us."

"All right," Secretary Rees said. "Do we or don't we notify the Russians and the Chinese? Do we tell them what we know—what we suspect? Take a chance?"

"What do we know we can prove?" General Dowling of the Marine Corps asked.

"We have nothing we can prove," Brady said. "No hard evidence to present to them. And," he said softly, "do we have the time? The Chinese—and this is my personal opinion—would, I think, behave in a decent manner. The Russians I wouldn't trust as far as I could spit. Their minds would work this way: the sub is American; the missiles are American; the crew is American—the fault is ours. They'd drag us right into a war. We don't know where the sub is; we can't stop it. No,"—he sighed—"I think we have to chance this and hope we take minimum casualties. And the American people *must not* learn of this. The instant we assume a public defensive posture, the sub will fire its missiles. The American people won't have time to do anything. Besides, we don't know how many missiles will make it through our screens."

"That's a damned cold-blooded attitude!" Ringold said.

"But a necessary one." Brady defended his statements. "Better the people are surprised—if it comes to that—than have several days of pure panic. And"—he held up a finger—"the Russians have a very good civil defense system: bunkers, food, water. The U.S. has shit for CD. Let the Russians get the message the same time our people receive it. More dead Russians and less U.S. casualties."

"I'll go along with that," Divico said. The other members of the Joint Chiefs nodded in agreement.

"Let me say this," Fayers said. "Mr. Brady believes the launch will be made within a week. All right, we'll stay with that hypothesis. We don't know where the sub is, but we'll assume it's in position to fire. Now, according to Ringold, his bureau has never heard of the rebels. Fine. As far as I'm concerned the rebels—if they exist—are of little concern at this moment. I'm not sure how we would go about breaking up a group we didn't know existed—again, if they do—until a couple of hours ago. We don't know what military units are involved in this, or where they are located. We don't know what commanders we can trust. For that matter, I don't know if I can trust any of my staff, and you don't know if you can trust me. I don't know if I can trust any of you!"

Fayers' gaze swept each man. Words of protestation formed on each tongue, then died before being sounded, each man knowing there was nothing he could do to convince the others of his innocence.

Fayers continued. "So we have to assume we can trust each other. That is the only way we can possibly deal with this."

"How is the sub armed?" Ringold asked, feeling a bit less left out.

The admiral sighed, cutting his eyes to General Travee. "With Thunder-strikes," he said.

"Oh, hell!" Hyde of the Air Force and Dowling of the

Marine Corps spoke in unison.

"What is a Thunder-strike?" Ringold asked. The feeling of being left out once more struck him.

"Yes." The President leaned forward. "I'd like to know that myself. I've never heard of anything called Thunder-strike." He glanced at each of the Joint Chiefs.

General Hyde said, "The . . . ah . . . president before you . . . ah . . . authorized them, sir. Before our tenure on the Joint Chiefs, I might add," he said, a bit defensively. "The code name is 'Supersnoop.' It is not a large missile, but it is very powerful . . . and practically unstoppable. Like the sub, it's Stealth-coated. No one will pick them up until it's too late. Hugs the ground."

"How very interesting," President Fayers said dryly. "How very informative. I can but assume construction continued even after the latest SALT was signed?"

Divico cleared his throat. "Yes, sir."

"And they are not included in the breakdown of our nuclear arsenal?"

"That is correct, sir," Divico admitted.

"Well, isn't that marvelous?" the president said. "That sure as *hell* lets out telling the Russians anything, doesn't it, gentlemen?"

No one said anything in rebuttal.

Fayers' tone was sharp. "How many of these Thunder-strikes do we possess?"

"One hundred and fifty," General Dowling replied.

Fayers swung his gaze to the marine. "You all knew of these missiles?"

"Yes, sir."

"The weapon is very powerful?"

"Yes, sir. Some are equipped with germ-type war-heads."

Fayers slammed his hand on the table top, startling the men. "Well, that is just dandy. Yes, indeed. That is just fucking wonderful!"

And the president seldom used profanity.

Divico defended his missiles. "We had to have the edge, sir. Had to stay ahead of them. Without the missiles, the Russians would have never signed the new SALT. We talked of telling you, but . . ." His voice trailed off.

"Where are the Thunder-strikes stored?" Fayers asked.

"California."

Fayers pointed a finger at Divico. "Admiral, you will—personally, tonight—transport yourself to that depot and count each Thunder-strike. Report back to me as soon as possible. Within hours. Understood?"

"Yes, sir."

"I'm certain that all one hundred and fifty will not be at the depot," Secretary Rees opined. "But of those that are, do we ready them for launch?"

"Yes," Fayers said.

"I may take that as a direct order, sir?" Divico asked.

"Yes," Fayers said.

"Dear God!" Ringold whispered.

FOUR

Monday morning—three days before launch

"You know this for a fact?" the Russian asked.

"I know it for a fact." The man spoke from the shadows of the room.

"The Chinese have developed a low-level missile, capable of sliding through our defenses undetected?"

"That is true, sir. Our mole in the Pentagon reported this to me."

"I find it most difficult to believe," the Russian agent said. "I find it incredible that Chinese technology in the field of nuclear weaponry would surpass ours, much less that of America."

"They were working together, sir."

"China and America?"

"Yes."

"That I can believe. So these reports, rumors, we've been hearing for months—they are true?"

"Yes, sir. I am afraid so."

"These missiles . . . we thought were solely American . . . Thunder-strikes—how many do the Chinese possess?"

"Hundreds."

"No! Hundreds?"

"Yes, sir. Our mole said several hundred, at least. All armed and aimed—at us."

"And many are of the germ type?"

"Yes, sir."

"I'd like to see one."

"I know where one is stored, ready for shipment to China."

"Message coming in, sir," an aide informed the president.

Fayers jerked up the phone. "Speak!"

Admiral Divico's voice was calm. "You wanted the count on the missiles, sir?"

"I didn't send you out there to pick cantaloupes!" Fayers was angry, his angry mood made worse by the dizzy spells he'd been suffering all night and most of the morning. His head ached, throbbed with pain. He had said nothing about it.

"One hundred, sir."

"*One hundred?* You said we had a hundred and fifty."

"One hundred, sir."

"How many does the sub carry?"

"Twelve, sir."

"Thank you very much, Admiral." Fayers spoke through the pain in his head. "That only leaves thirty-eight unaccounted for." He broke the connection.

Major Bass stood before Travee's desk. He thought the general looked tired . . . haggard. Maybe worried about something. "General Saunders was fishing with the CG of Fort Leonard Wood, sir. On the morning in question."

"Fishing? Vern hates fishing. Where were they fishing?"

47

"Missouri, sir."

"Vern flew eight hundred miles to go fishing?" In a pig's ass, he did. "You're sure of this, Major? No room for any doubt?"

"None, sir. I'd stake my life on it."

Or mine, Travee thought. Or the entire world.

"Something else, sir."

"Say it, Major."

"Driskill of the Marine Corps and some of his senior sergeants were in Missouri, too. As were Admiral Newcomb, some special troop commanders and senior sergeants, and General Crowe and some of his people."

"I have to ask, Major. Are you sure of this?"

"Yes, sir."

"Thank you, Major."

"Yes, sir." The ASA man wheeled and left the office.

Travee phoned General Fowler, head of Army Intelligence. They arranged to have lunch that day. The two men had graduated from the Point together. Their paths had gone in different directions after that, but they remained friends. Or so Travee thought . . . until today.

Who do I trust? he mused.

"You're picking at your food, C.H.," General Fowler noted. "Don't you feel well? Have something on your mind?"

How about holocaust? Travee looked at the food on his plate. Or treason? He lifted his gaze to his friend.

The men sat in the rear of the plush Washington restaurant, in a private dining area where they could not be heard or seen.

Unless Fowler is wearing a bug, Travee thought.

"Monk." Travee used the general's nickname. "I want

48

you to tell me something."

"If I can, C.H., sure. Shoot."

Travee took a small sip of coffee, glanced around him, then shot straight, the words pouring from his mouth. Monk Fowler dropped his fork in his lap. Two minutes later, his face ashen, he tried to take a sip of water. His hands shook so badly he spilled water down the front of his shirt.

Travee finished by saying, "Don't tell me you haven't heard the rumors, Monk. Don't insult my intelligence by saying you haven't seen bits and pieces of this crop up in reports. And don't tell me you haven't put it all together—or you're not a part of it. Talk, Monk. And make it good."

"C.H.! I . . . ah . . . I don't know what you're—"

Fowler heard the almost inaudible click of an Army-issue .45 automatic pistol jacked back to full cock, under the table. He looked into his friend's eyes. Cold.

"God, C.H.! Don't let that thing go off."

"I ought to kill you right here, Monk. You're a treasonous snake. Damn you! You were my friend. *Were!* As head of Army Intelligence, you have to be involved in this up to your butt!"

"Please put the pistol away, C.H."

"You're a part of it, aren't you, Fowler?"

General Fowler's eyes were wide with fright. "I don't want to die, C.H."

"We're all going to die in a matter of days, you son of a bitch! My God—who can I trust?" Travee stood up, shoving the pistol back into his belt. "Get up, you slime, and don't get hinky or you're dead. And I'll gut shoot you, Monk. Takes a lot longer to die that way. Painful." He dropped money on the table for the meal and shoved

Fowler toward the rear door. "Move!"

"Where . . . are we going?"

"To the White House."

Behind them, Washington diners ate and gossiped and flirted, unaware that nuclear and bacteriological horror lurked only hours away.

"And that's all you know?" Fayers asked, speaking through the roaring pain in his head.

"Yes, sir," Fowler said. "I don't know all the details, but I do have suspicions."

"Bull Dean?"

Fowler shook his head. "No, I don't believe so. I haven't been able to contact him for several days, but the Bull fronts up the rebels, that's all. Adams said he'd never go along with something like this."

"Is it world-wide, Fowler?" Travee asked.

Fowler hesitated. "I . . . can't say, C.H."

"*General* Travee, Fowler. Sir. With a sir. Put a sir on it when you speak to me."

"Yes, sir. I won't say, sir."

"Oh, yes, Monk—you'll say, all right."

"I will say I'm glad it's over."

"It isn't over, Fowler," Travee said, then knocked the general out of his chair with a short right punch. "You're going to tell us all you know, or you're going to die hard." He turned to General Hyde. "Put a pistol on that warrant officer in the hall. Don't let him get gone with those codes. We've got to buy us some time . . . if we can."

"Good Lord, General!" Fayers said. There was an odd look in his eyes. The president laughed out loud.

Hyde paused at the door to glance at the president. He

50

lifted his gaze to Travee. Travee shook his head slowly, sadly.

"God! My head hurts." Fayers rubbed his temples.

General Hyde stepped out into the hall and motioned the young warrant officer inside. The W.O.'s mouth dropped open at the sight of Fowler, struggling to get to his feet, his mouth bloody.

"What's . . . sir?" He looked at the president.

Fayers looked at him. "Beware the ju-ju bird, son."

"Sir?" The W.O. stared at his commander in chief.

Travee held out his hand. "Give me those codes, Mr. Anderson. And please bear in mind General Hyde has a .45 aimed at your back."

The W.O. did not hesitate. He stepped forward and handed the briefcase to General Travee. "Has it hit the fan, sir?"

"Yes, son," the general replied. "*It* most certainly has."

Fowler was sitting in a chair, holding his head in his hands. "Don't hurt me, C.H. You know I have a low pain tolerance."

Travee's smile was ugly. "I'll bear that in mind— traitor."

Monday afternoon

In a warehouse on the waterfront in New York City, the Russian agent looked at the gleaming shape of the Thunder-strike, lying in its long crate, marked: AXLES.

The Russian shook his head. Leave it to the Americans, he thought. The most secret weapon in the world, and they dump it in a wooden crate, mark it AXLES,

51

and stick it in an open warehouse.

The missile did not look dangerous; it looked beautiful and sleek. It was minuscule compared to a huge ICBM. But when the warhead was placed inside the nosecone, it became the most advanced missile in the world. Even God—if He existed, thought the Russian—would need clearance to view this missile. The agent knew he was looking at the reason his country signed SALT 5.

The Thunder-strike suddenly appeared very ominous. The Russian began to perspire, knowing he was looking at, in all probability, the object that would be the cause of his death. Very soon.

He nailed the lid back on the crate, sighing as he looked at the markings on the crate. DESTINATION: MAINLAND CHINA.

"Little yellow bastards!" he muttered.

"Hey, you!"

The Russian turned. A man dressed in jeans and hard hat stood with his hands on his hips, glaring at him.

"What the hell you doin' in here?"

"Waiting for a man."

"Yeah? Well, wait somewheres else. You ain't supposed to be in here. Git outta here!"

The worker had apparently not seen him place the hammer back on the workbench. "Of course. I beg your pardon. Is there a place where I may wait, nearby?"

"Yeah. Right down the pier. A little beanery. Move!"

When the Russian had gone, the man walked to a phone, quickly dialed a number, and said, "He bought it; everything is go."

President Fayers looked in disbelief at the body of General Fowler. He was dead! Fayers could not believe this was happening. Not here! Not in the oval office. His head hurt. He felt reality slipping from him; he was sliding through the most intense pain he'd ever experienced. Through his daze and pain, he could hear the military people talking, but their words were incomprehensible; he didn't even know who those men were. He began to hum, very quietly.

"When they learn Fowler talked," General Hyde said, "we won't have much time."

Fayers looked up and for a moment ceased his humming. Who were these men? Where had they come from?

"World-wide," Dowling said. "Fowler must have named a dozen or more countries. Including Russia. I can't believe they are planning armed revolt in Russia."

"C.H.," Admiral Divico said, "we can't just carry a body out the front door. There must be a dozen press types hanging around."

"Did anyone see or hear you waste Captain Bingham?" Travee asked Divico.

"No," the admiral said, the taste of betrayal bitter on his tongue. "A traitor on my own staff. I left the son of a bitch sitting in his chair, behind his desk, with half his head gone." He had locked the door and put a "Do Not Disturb" sign on the doorknob, Bingham's own signal that he did not wish to be disturbed.

"This thing is growing like a cancer," Travee said. "Touching all branches. I've been in contact with Saunders and they confirm they were at a special meeting Saturday, all branches present, trying to decide if *we* were behind this mess. Our own men didn't even trust us. God!"

"Can you blame them?" Dowling asked. "Hell, C.H.,

put it out of your mind—we've got to buy some time. It's getting precious.''

Fayers' intercom buzzed. The president looked up, glanced at it, then giggled.

"He's out of it," General Hyde looked at Fayers. "Why do I envy him his bliss?"

Travee punched the "talk" button. "Yes?"

"Ed? You sound funny. Look, I've got to tell the press something. They want to know why all the brass are here."

Tell them it's none of their goddamned business, Travee thought. He glanced at the Joint Chiefs. "Get in here."

"Who is this?" the aide questioned.

"Get your ass in here!" Travee snapped.

The aide, James Benning, came to a sliding halt on the carpet, his eyes wide as he looked at the body of General Fowler. The man's fingers were all broken, twisted into grotesque shapes. He looked at the president. Fayers returned his gaze, but it was an empty look, void of any understanding.

The room stank of sweat and of urine from a suddenly relaxed bladder.

"That man's been tortured," the aide said lamely. "There is a gag in his mouth. My God—he's dead!" He put his hand on Fayers' shoulder and gently shook him. "Ed?"

"He's out of it, James," Dowling said. "Get the VP."

"I . . . uh . . ." The aide shook his head. "I can't. He is right now"—he looked at his watch—"approaching the Mideast. Conference that was set up months ago."

"Damn!" Dowling said. "Where's the Speaker?"

"The Speaker's on a junket. President pro tem of the

Senate is in the hospital, recovering from surgery."

"Goddamn it!" Travee roared. "Then get Secretary Rees in here."

The aide picked up the phone, then looked at Travee. "Did you do that to General Fowler? You're an American general, sir. What in the hell is going on?"

"Get fucking Rees in here!"

"Yes, sir!" The aide snapped to, punching out the number, contacting State.

Fayers sat in a chair in the corner, out of the way. He was softly humming his old college fight song.

"Rees is on the way," James said. "I'll get the secret service in here. General, sir, what is going on?"

"There is a coup attempt going down, son. Among other . . . issues. Can we trust the secret service?"

"We have to," Dowling said.

Travee turned to the young W.O. "Who relieves you?"

"Myers, sir."

"You know him well?"

"I don't know him at all, sir. Sir? This is America. This can't be happening here!"

"Well, it is happening, and not just here. Why don't you know this Myers?"

"He was just assigned this duty." The W.O. paused. "And that's odd, too, sir. All the guys who normally handle this job have been replaced over the past few months. I'm the only one of the original bunch left. Their orders came in so fast, and there just wasn't any reason for them."

Travee handed him his briefcase full of war codes. "Sit down, son—out of the way. If anybody other than the men in this room attempt to take that briefcase . . . shoot them. You're armed. Understand?"

"Yes, sir."

The chief of White House Secret Service walked in. He stood in shock for a few seconds. "What in the *hell* is going on?"

Travee told him, bluntly and quickly. "Get all your older men in here. I don't give a damn where they are or what they're doing. Just get them."

"I don't take orders from you," he was informed by the secret service man.

Travee lifted his .45, cocked it, and pointed it at the man's head. "You have five seconds to obey my orders."

"Yes, sir," the secret service man said, walking stiffly to the phone.

Travee looked at Benning. "Where is Mrs. Fayers?"

"In California, sir. Speaking engagement."

"All right. Get the White House doctor in here." He used another line to call the Pentagon. "This is General Travee. The code word is Blue Tango. I'm going to say this only once, so you'd better listen. I want these orders sent out immediately, top priority, scrambled. They are as follows: every military base in this country is to be shut down tight. Tight! Every leave is hereby canceled. Get those personnel back to base. You understand me?"

"Blue Tango, sir?" the rustle of paper. "Blue Tango! That's . . . hell, that's insurrection within our borders, sir."

"I am fully aware of that, Colonel. Just do it."

"I can't, sir. I need more code designation."

"Red Fox!"

"That has to come from the president, sir."

"Goddamn it, I know that. The president is . . . incapacitated."

"The VP, then, sir."

"The VP is out of the country. Do what I tell you to do!"

"Sir," the colonel protested, "I'm only following orders—the chain of command."

"Goddamn you, Colonel—I am giving you a direct order!"

The phone buzzed in Travee's ear. He looked around in astonishment.

"That son of a bitch hung up on me," Travee said.

FIVE

Monday evening

"I cannot believe the Americans are doing this," the Russian ambassador said. "Unless . . . unless those rumors within our country have some validity to them. Yes. That must be it." The Russian agent sat before him in the embassy.

"I have seen the Thunder-strike with my own eyes. By now it is on its way to mainland China. To join the several hundred others they have."

"Aimed at Russia," the ambassador said. "Things were going so well—we thought." His hands were shaking.

His secretary buzzed him. "Sir, President Fayers has just been rushed to Bethesda Hospital. He's had a massive stroke. Not expected to live. The vice president cannot be located. His plane and everyone on board have vanished somewhere in the Mideast. There are fears that Fayers' wife has been kidnapped."

"Thank you. Keep me informed. Send a message of regret and sympathy to the White House." He told the agent what had just been relayed to him. He lit a cigarette with trembling hands. "Too much is happening too quickly for it to be mere coincidence. I think the world is about to explode in our faces. We have much to do, Fyodor. So let's get busy doing it."

Premier Su listened to the colonel from Chinese Intelligence. His face remained impassive as the colonel talked . . . and talked. Finally, Su interrupted.

"You have seen these missiles?"

"With my own eyes, Premier."

Su sighed. "With who else's eyes—a goat? We have nothing in our arsenal that would stop them?"

"No, Premier. Nothing."

"The Russians were going to assassinate me at Fuchin?"

"And your wife."

"Barbarians! What of the Americans?"

"Our intelligence reports they have nothing to do with it. The Thunder-strike is theirs, true, but the plans were stolen from them—by the Russians. Of course, neither side could mention any of this at the SALT talks."

"Naturally. Some deviousness was to be expected. From both sides of the table."

"The fox does not tell the hound of its exit," the colonel said.

Premier Su sighed heavily. "Colonel, please spare me your pearls from the Orient. I was never an admirer of Charlie Chan."

"Yes, sir. There is also something going on within America's borders, sir."

"I know, I know. President Fayers is quite ill. I have sent wishes for an early recovery."

"More, sir. The vice president is missing, as is the president's wife. Military chain of command is . . . well . . . confused."

"Confused? What kind of briefing word is that— confused?"

"I'm sorry, Premier. All outgoing traffic has gone to a new type of scramble system. We haven't, as yet, broken it."

"Keep trying." Su smiled. "Perseverance keeps honor bright."

The young colonel's face brightened. "Confucius, sir?"

"No, Shakespeare."

Premier Su covered his mouth with his hand to hide his slight smile at the colonel's crestfallen expression. "Oh," the colonel said.

Su said, "You and your people are certain the Russians will attack us—beyond any doubt?"

"Yes, Premier. We have broken several of their coded messages from the base at Zapovednyy. This one confirmed it."

Su looked at him, sighed, said, "I'm waiting, Colonel."

"Sir?"

"Read the message!"

"Yes, sir. 'Operation Dragon-Die into effect at 2359 Monday. Wipe the yellow horde from the face of the earth.'"

"Dragon-Die." Su shook his head in disgust. "How quaint. How like the Russians. Yellow horde. Barbarians! Four days," he said softly.

"To hell," the colonel added. "If there is one, I mean."

General Sun, commander of the Chinese Army, spoke for the first time during the meeting. "When do we strike, sir?"

"Tomorrow." Premier Su glanced at him, then at the colonel. "Noon." He smiled. "The early bird gets the worm, you know."

*   *   *

The White House resembled a besieged command post. Outside, the grounds were calm, but inside, controlled chaos. The press was screaming for information— receiving very little. Travee had received word that the Speaker of the House, upon hearing of the tragedy in America, had suffered a mild heart attack and relinquished his succession to the presidency to Secretary of State Rees.

Secretary of State Rees, now Acting President Rees, was showing signs of coming unglued. The presidency was the last job in the world he wanted. He had been, prior to becoming secretary of state, president of a bank in Des Moines.

Following the news that Ed Fayers had died on the operating table, after a massive cerebral hemorrhage, a message came in that the VP's plane, and the press plane, had been shot down over the Mediterranean Sea. No survivors.

Reports were conflicted as to just what had happened to the two planes. The Israeli Air Force spokeswoman said an American fighter-bomber had downed the planes.

Where had the fighter-bomber come from?

They didn't know.

The PLO screamed they didn't do it. Libya said they were delighted it had happened. The rest of the Mideast countries said they certainly didn't do it. Nothing was coming out of the Russian Embassy. The Chinese ambassador expressed profound regrets.

"Mr. President," Sen. Hilton Logan said to the harried Rees, "I believe we should do something, immediately."

Hilton Logan had never been known for his grace under pressure—or under anything else, for that matter—especially water.

Rees frosted him with a look. "Well, Senator . . . that is just brilliant. The UN is running around in circles, screaming threats at each other. The world situation is deteriorating hourly. I am anticipating panic in the streets of America once the press learns all that is happening—and will, in all probability, happen. About twenty percent of the military is unresponsive to General Travee's commands; and mine, I might add. Now, Senator, with all that in mind, what would you have me do that is not already being done? Without your help, sir. And by the way, how in the hell did you get in here? You certainly were not invited."

"Mr. President, I did not mean to be impertinent. But *I* might add that I have spoken again and again about those special troops being overtrained and being nothing more than animals. I—"

"Oh, shit, Logan," General Travee shut him up. "Close your mouth. The special units are all right. Thank God," he added. "*They* are all responding to my orders. I've got SEALs coming into the city from Camp A P Hill now, just in case the police need a hand. But that is not the immediate problem." He waved a piece of paper, just handed him by an aide. "This is."

"What is it?" Rees asked.

"China has ordered all troops ready for full-scale war. Massive build-up along the Russian border. Our snoops say Russia is gearing up for war. Silos ready. And," he said, looking straight at Logan, "I have ordered ours to do the same."

"I must protest that order!" Logan said. "I would like to convene Congress to discuss this."

"Yeah, that's all we need," Dowling growled.

"Then Brady was right," Rees said.

"Brady who?" Logan flapped his arms.

"Sir?" An aide spoke to Travee. "The press is screaming for information. They're already on the air with a bunch of shit from overseas bureaus. What do I tell them?"

"Where is Fayers' press secretary?" Logan demanded.

"Gone," Dowling said. "He was one of the other side."

"What other side?" Logan almost screamed the words. He was ignored.

The general smiled. "Tell them . . ." His smile broadened. "Tell them with all the heartfelt sincerity you can muster, that General Travee is leveling with the members of the fourth estate when he says: 'GO FUCK YOURSELVES!' " He roared.

The military in the room grinned—to a person. Someone among them finally got to convey to the press what they really felt about them.

"We must tell the American people what is going on," Logan said. "We must."

"Time," President Rees said. "We have to buy a little more time."

"Why?" Logan demanded.

"So the military can get set up in a defensive posture," Travee said. "Clear the bases of all those men not loyal to the government."

A colonel, in civilian clothes, walked into the oval office. "Sir, I've got General Graham from Fort Campbell on the horn."

Travee grabbed up the phone. "Go, Mike."

"I've had a little trouble here, C.H." The sounds of gunfire were faint in the background. "But it's just about under control. Not too many men involved in the rebellion. I just spoke with Harrison down at Bragg, and

63

Huval out at Carson. They're secure. Same with Lewis and Stewart. Fort Knox is a hot spot, C.H.—bad over there. You want my boys to go in?"

"Don't strip yourself bare, Mike. You got my message. You know the balloon is going up."

"Yeah, I know. O.K., we'll secure Knox. I got some Green Bennies coming in from Bragg, along with the Rangers from the First, Seventy-fifth. Take care, C.H."

"Luck to you, Mike." Travee hung up. He wondered if he'd ever see his friend again.

Admiral Divico said, "I've got one carrier and several destroyers out of pocket, C.H. Oh, we know where they are; they're just not responding to orders."

"I've had some trouble," General Dowling said, a grim look in his eyes. His jaw was set like a hunk of granite. "My men put it down—hard. I have ordered any rebel survivor shot. Goddamn a traitorous marine!"

"I've got some pilots missing," General Hyde said. "And their planes. A few silos that aren't answering."

"Are the planes armed?" Rees asked.

"Yes, sir. All the way. I have given orders to have them destroyed if they don't set down and surrender."

"The silos?"

General Hyde shook his head. "We can only hope they will listen to reason and come around."

Logan said, "General Dowling? Did I understand you to say you ordered your people to *shoot* any marine involved in this uprising?"

"You damned sure did, Senator."

"But that's unconstitutional, sir! Those men are entitled to a trial."

"Oh, they'll get a trial, Logan," the marine assured him. "The shortest judicial proceeding in history." He turned his back to the senator.

President Rees glanced at Divico. "Admiral, was it . . . some of your people who brought down the VP's plane?"

The admiral's face was gray with exhaustion and tight with anger. "Yes, it looks that way, sir. From the maverick carrier."

"And . . . ?" Rees pressed him.

"I've given the captains one hour to acknowledge my surrender orders and begin steaming to the nearest port. Or"—he sighed—"I will have the ships blown out of the water."

"All the men on those ships may not be a part of the coup attempt," Logan said.

"Yes, Senator." Divico's gaze was hard. "Believe me, I realize that far better than you."

"General Travee?" an aide said. "We finally found out why the secretaries of the services have not responded to our calls."

"Let me have it." Travee spun around.

"They're dead, sir. All of them shot to death."

"Secretary of defense?"

"Still no word, sir."

Another aide walked into the oval office. "The press has put some of the story together, Mr. President. CBN just broke the news of a revolt within the military. Another network added a bit more to that and brought up rumors of a nuclear war. Missing missiles and so forth. It gets worse as it goes along."

"How are the American people reacting?"

"Just as we expected, sir. Panic. Riots starting in some of the cities; many trying to flee the cities."

"Where in the hell do they think they're going?"

The aide shook her head. "They don't know, sir. They're just running scared."

President Rees shook his head in frustration. He glanced at his watch. "Do we have the secret service clean?"

"Yes, sir. That's positive."

"Then the White House is secure?" he asked.

"Until the birds fly," he was told. With that, President Rees puked all over the carpet.

Ben Raines sat in his den and watched the TV news. Regular programing had been abandoned. Ben drank his whiskey and was sourly amused at the panic building within the U.S.

He arrogantly toasted the TV newswoman with his whiskey glass and said, "I always wanted to screw you, honey."

Then he rose from his chair, turned off the TV, and put on a symphony. Wagner's Ring.

The pistol in Bull Dean's hand never wavered. The hammer was jacked back to full cock, the muzzle pointed at Adams' belly. "I should have put it together months ago, Carl," he said to his longtime friend. "You've been playing me for a fool. Worse than that, Carl—you've been playing God."

"You're wrong, Bull!" Adams protested. He kept his hands at his side. He made no quick moves; he knew the Bull too well to try to jump him. The Bull was an old man, but still as deadly as a black mamba. "It was now or never, Bull. The only way."

"You gave the orders for those units to revolt—knowing they would be killed."

66

"I had to start it rolling, Bull!"

"You gave the orders to shoot down the VP's plane. Leak the Thunder-strikes to the press."

"I had to!"

Bull Dean shook his head. "You fool—you poor misguided fool. You didn't really think the special troops would fall in with you, did you? Commit an act of treason?" He shrugged, but the pistol never wavered. "Well, it's over. Hours to go. Worse than being a fool, Carl, you're a traitor. Since three o'clock this afternoon, I've been in contact with more than ninety-five percent of the rebel commanders. They're out of this; keeping their heads down."

"They'll follow my orders!" Carl screamed.

Bull shook his gray head. "No, they won't, Carl. They're Americans, not traitors. Their only reason for rebelling was for this nation—we saw it going back to the left. They were doing it for their country, not for you or me. You don't have an army."

"Maybe you're right, Bull. O.K., so you are. But I've won, Bull. Even though I'm seconds away from being dead—I've won after all."

"How do you figure that, Carl? We've been underground for eighteen years. Lost our families, everything. How have you won?"

"Out of the ashes, Bull. This nation will be stronger than it's ever been in its history. The survivors will be tough. They'll never let it go left again; never again go soft on criminals and punks. Discipline will be restored, and citizens will once more be armed—and they'll never—*never!*—give up their guns again."

"It might go the other way, Carl. Ever thought of that?"

"No way."

Bull smiled sadly. "We've started a world war, Carl. A horrible war—the worst this world has ever seen. But maybe we can stop it. Tell me how to stop the men on that sub from pushing the button."

Adams shook his head. "They can't be stopped." He smiled. "No verbal orders. They've shut off their only link to the outside. They're prepared to die for their country, Bull. It's too late."

"Yes," the old sailor said with a sigh. "I suppose it is." He pulled the trigger, the heavy .45 automatic jumping in his hand, the slug punching a hole in Carl's chest. The slug shattered the heart. The man slammed backward, dead on the floor.

Bull Dean stood over the cooling body of the man he had called friend and fellow warrior for more than thirty years. He shook his head.

The phone rang. Bull picked up the receiver. It was the commander of the eastern-based rebels. "I have my people in position, sir, ready to move into the shelters. Same with all the others. I wonder what the civilians are going to do?"

"If they're smart,"—the old soldier smiled grimly— "they'll put their heads between their legs and kiss their asses good-by."

He hung up.

Bull sat down in a chair by the phone and thought of calling Ben Raines, down in Louisiana. He shook his head. Last he'd heard Ben was somewhat of a drunk. Best damned guerrilla fighter Bull had ever seen. A drunk. Shame.

He reviewed the facts in his mind. Carl had left the Adirondacks twice during the past month, traveling to

New York City. Bull had followed him, slowly putting it all together. Carl was playing footsie with both the Russians and the Chinese, using the Thunder-strikes as bait. A double double cross that had worked. Then Carl had instructed his people in NATO to rig a message, letting it fall into the hands of the mainland Chinese, informing them of the strike against them. And he had set up the Russians. It had all worked to perfection.

Now it was too late for anything except prayer.

"We both should have died in 'Nam," he said aloud. "We were two good soldiers gone wrong."

No. He shook his head. We weren't wrong. Not at the outset. It was basically a good plan, restoring America to her constitutional roots.

He sighed as he looked at the cooling body of Adams. You got too big for your boots, partner. Went off the deep end. I think, toward the end, you were crazy.

He picked up the phone, telling the operator, "Get me the White House, miss. Tell whoever answers that Col. Bull Dean wants to speak with Crazy Horse Travee." He laughed. "That should get his attention."

Only hours before the press broke the rumors of a nuclear war looming world-wide, in almost every state in America, people who knew how to survive, were ready for war, were vanishing.

Prof. Steven Miller disappeared from the campus of USC. The quiet, soft-spoken professor of history, a bachelor, could not be found. His apartment was unlocked, but nothing appeared to be missing or even out of place. An associate professor thought it strange, though, when a box of .223 ammunition was found in a bureau drawer.

"M-16 ammunition," a policeman observed.

"But Steven didn't like guns," his colleague said.

"'Least he said he didn't like them. Come to think of it, he never joined us in any gun-control activity."

The policeman shrugged.

An hour later, the policeman had vanished.

Jimmy Deluce, a crop-duster from the Cajun country of Louisiana, and a dozen of his friends did not report for work. No one seemed to know where they went.

Nora Rodelo and two of her girl friends were last seen shopping together in Dodge City, Kansas. They dropped out of sight.

Anne Flood, a college senior in New Mexico, and a half-dozen of her friends, male and female, got in their cars and vans and drove away. A neighbor told his wife to come quick, look at that. Those kids are carryin' guns, Mother. Look like machine guns. Don't that beat all?

James Riverson, a huge, six-foot, six-inch truck driver from the boot heel of Missouri, and his wife, Belle, were last seen getting into James' rig and heading west.

A neighbor had called to him, "What're you haulin' this trip, James?"

James had smiled, answering, "A load of M-16s and ammo."

His neighbor had laughed. "M-16s! James, son, you are a card."

Linda Jennings, a reporter for a small-town Nebraska weekly, did not show up for work. No one had seen her since the day before. She had received a phone call and immediately begun packing.

"Young people!" her boss had snorted.

Al Holloway, a musician in a country and western band, did not make rehearsal. A friend said he saw him getting into his car and heading out. Said it looked like he was carrying a submachine gun.

Jane Dolbeau, a French Canadian living and working in New York, was seen leaving her apartment. A young man she had dated had waved at her, but Jane had not acknowledged the greeting. He said she seemed pre-occupied.

Ken Amato and his wife and daughter locked up their house in Skokie, outside of Chicago, and drove away.

Ben Raines sat in his den, listening to classical music and getting drunk. He had no idea that the gods of fate were laughing wildly, shaping his destiny.

SIX

"General Travee? There is a man on the phone claiming to be Col. Bull Dean. He says he wants to speak to Crazy Horse Travee. Begging your pardon, sir."

Travee laughed. "So the ornery ol' Bull is alive." He jerked up the phone. "Speak, you snake-eater!"

Bull laughed. "It was Adams, sir. Not me. The rebels are out of it. I can't tell you everything Adams did, 'cause I don't know it all. But I'll tell you what I do know."

"Give it to me fast, Bull. I don't think we have much time."

Travee listened for several minutes, nodding and grunting every now and then. Finally, he said, "What are you going to do, Bull?"

"I'm going to sit right here on my front porch and watch the ICBMs come in and go out. Fort Drum will surely take one nose-on, so I'll just sit here quietly until my time comes. I can't think of a better way for a worn-out old soldier to go out. Give 'em hell, Crazy Horse." He hung up.

Travee stood for a precious moment, his thoughts flung back over the years, his memories of a wild young Ranger named the Bull—the most decorated man in the history of America.

"It sounded to me, General," Logan said, "as though

you were genuinely glad to speak with that traitor."

Travee glared at him. "Shut your goddamned liberal mouth, you prick! Bull Dean is ten times the man you'll ever be. Now sit down, shut up, and stay out of the way, or I'll tear your head off and hand it to you."

Logan sat down in a corner, crossed his legs primly, and closed his mouth.

"VP Mills' wife is dead," General Hyde said, walking into the room. "California Highway Patrol just found her body."

"How did she die?" Rees asked. "And why? Killing Ruth was an unnecessary act of violence."

"She was shot in the head." General Hyde shrugged. "As to who killed her, we'll probably never know. We don't have that much time left us."

"Sir." An aide spoke to President Rees, his face white with strain and exhaustion. "The Russians have just formally broken off diplomatic relationships with the United States. Their embassy is closed and they are boarding planes to go home."

"Their UN ambassador?"

"He is airborne. Most of the ambassadors from the Soviet bloc countries are gone as well."

"Do we have contact with our embassy in Moscow?"

"No, sir. Everything is being jammed by the Russians."

"Damn," Rees cursed. "Have you spoken with the Chinese?"

"Yes, sir. The Chinese were unusually blunt. They said to pick a side and do it quickly."

"Did you give them our reply?"

"Yes, sir. They seemed pleased."

Brady limped into the room. "We have reports of

massive riots in Turkey, India, Iran, a dozen other countries. Three embassies have been burned to the ground, our ambassadors killed."

"My men?" General Dowling asked.

"All dead, sir. This time they died fighting."

"Good," Dowling said, clenching his fists. He and General Travee locked eyes for a few seconds. "It's time, C.H.," the Marine Corps commandant said. Travee nodded. Dowling turned to an aide. "Tim, order all marines on full alert. Battle gear. Tell them to stand by. I'll be goddamned if I'm going out with my thumb stuck up my ass."

Each man of the Joint Chiefs followed suit with his branch. Rees was not consulted, and his face mirrored his immense relief. Senator Logan jumped to his feet.

"None of you can give those orders without first consulting Congress." Hilton Logan was scared. The military scared him. Guns frightened him. Violence made him nauseous.

He was ignored.

General Travee spoke to his president. "Sir, I am declaring a national state of emergency—martial law. The Constitution of the United States is hereby suspended. I am assuming full control."

PART TWO

PART TWO

War is a contagion.
——Franklin Roosevelt.

Midnight—twelve hours before launch

Shooting, faint and far away, drifted to the men sitting on the park bench in New York's Central Park. A hard burst of gunfire followed, from automatic weapons. There were cars and trucks backed up for miles on the expressways around the city: a mass exodus.

"It's no longer safe in the city." The Albanian grinned, and the Chinese laughed at him.

"How many warheads and what kind?" the Chinese asked. "Not that it will do my country any good. I can't get through to them."

"Too many warheads. The gas is a form of Tabun, highly refined now, in a mist form. A half-drop on bare skin, or inhalation of the mist causes death within seconds."

"Tabun. Another of Hitler's brainchildren."

"That is correct."

"Do the Americans know of this Tabun form?"

"A few of them."

"How long have they known?"

"Years. Their nerve gas is similar."

The Chinese chuckled without mirth. "They must know, then, that Russia is saving most of her missiles for us."

"That is correct; but they know that Russia has a dozen Tabun-armed ICBMs pointed at America. No telling how many other types of missiles."

"It is my understanding that America has chosen a side in the upcoming confrontation."

"All of their missiles—so I have heard—will be directed at Russia and the eastern-bloc nations."

The Chinese stood up. Just before he walked away, he said, "Good luck to you."

Miami—eleven hours before launch

"A meeting in the open is dangerous," the Russian said to the Cuban.

The Cuban shrugged. "So is crossing the street—even in normal times. The Chinese know of your Tabun."

"So they will have a few days to perspire heavily from fear."

The Cuban looked out over the waters. So pretty and calm. His thoughts were of his family in Cuba. Those he would never see again. "How much of the world will survive?"

"What difference does it make?" the Russian said, rising to his feet. "We won't be here to see it."

"I do not share your tolerant view of death . . . comrade. I also do not understand why, since the KGB has known of this coup attempt for months, and also of the American double cross—if that's what it is—all parties involved do not just sit down and put a stop to it.

Before the world explodes."

The Russian laughed. "Because it is time, that's why. When the missiles fly, Saul, just close your eyes and pray to whatever god you believe in. You will have approximately eighteen minutes to tremble and wet your drawers."

The Cuban looked up at the Russian, contempt in his eyes. "At least I have a god, Peter."

"Better not let Castro hear you say that," he replied with a chuckle. He walked away.

Saul lit a cigar with hands that trembled. He watched the retreating back of the Russian. Everything was set . . . in motion. He could not stop it.

No one could.

The men in the sub waited. They had no fear of being detected, for they knew, as the Russian in Miami did, that it really made no difference who fired the first missile. It was time for a war. They knew, from monitoring Russian broadcasts, that the Red Bear was aware they were going to fire the Thunder-strikes. Had been for months; certain leaders had known of the coup attempt for almost a year, but had remained quiet. Communism was not working in Russia; more and more of its citizens were discontent, rumbling. They knew there would be an attempted revolt inside the mother country, had known of the plans for months.

General Malelov had said it was time for war.

General Travee knew it was time for war.

Premier Su knew it was time for war.

So let it begin.

Brady sat with the Joint Chiefs, having a last cup of

coffee, smoking, talking. Time was running out; down to hours, minutes. They talked of the panic in America, and in the world, and of the inevitability of armed conflict. They spoke of the burning, the looting, the savagery.

"We're going to have ICBMs coming at us from all directions," Travee said, glancing at his watch. "Very soon." He lit a cigarette and the men looked at him in surprise.

Brady said, "I thought you quit smoking years ago?"

"I did," Travee said, smiling, sucking satisfying smoke deep into his lungs. "But what the hell difference does it make now?" He laughed.

The men chuckled with him, watching him smoke and sigh with obvious satisfaction. "Well, boys," he said, "what about it?"

"I'm leaving for Gitmo in about an hour," General Dowling said. "I'm going to take my marines and fulfill a twenty-five-year-old dream. I'm going into Cuba proper, find Castro, and kick the balls off him." He looked at Admiral Divico. "You, Ed?"

Navy smiled, then sighed. "I've said good-by to my wife. She understood why I have to do what I'm doing. She's military as much as I am. I'm flying out of Edwards in just a few moments. I'll be on a flagship. You know what, though? God, would I love to have my shoes planted on the deck of the old *Missouri* when the ball starts rolling." He looked at Air Force. "You, Paul?"

General Hyde spat on the ground. "I'm leaving in just a second or two. I'll be in the left seat of one of our lumbering, antiquated old B-52s, trying to penetrate Russian air space, hoping a goddamned wing doesn't fall off from old age." He glanced at Travee. "Well, old warrior, looks like that leaves the country in your hands."

"Thank you all very, very much," Travee said dryly. "Since the flying White House was sabotaged, I'll be in Weather Mountain, directing our attack." He coughed. "Brady will be with me." He coughed again. "Goddamned cigarettes are gonna kill me!"

The men laughed, rose to shake hands, then parted, each going his own way to meet the enemy. They did not say another word. There was nothing left to say.

With less than ten hours before launch, the world went into a blind panic. In America, there weren't enough police and soldiers to control the frightened mobs trying to flee. Wild reports that hundreds of thousands of enemy troops were on the way split the airwaves. Troops were moving, but they were Russian and Chinese troops moving toward each other, not toward the U.S.

Rioting and looting in American cities began slowly, then picked up in intensity and savagery as night darkened the streets. Subways were jammed with frightened people running blindly, clutching a few possessions.

Freeways and expressways clogged, slowed, then became hopelessly snarled as cars and trucks broke down and were abandoned. For the most part, efforts to try to clear the interstates failed because civilians refused to obey military orders.

Civil defense and evacuation plans in America were a joke. Leaderless, the people were left to their own panic-stricken imaginations, and they ran wild.

The military had declared martial law, but the news of that only served to frighten the people more. The American people reasoned that if the military had declared martial law, then we must be under attack—

from somebody.

Because of jammed highways, the military had had to airlift troops in, and at night, troops in battle dress all look alike. Who could tell?

Automobiles became useless; death became indiscriminate. The elderly became the first casualties—most had no place to go, and others could not get where they wanted to go. The old could not move swiftly enough, so they were trampled upon and left to be robbed, assaulted, and killed. Children became separated from their parents. They sat on the curbs and howled their fright and were knocked out of the way by panicked adults. Some ran into the streets and were crushed by speeding automobiles. Others were left to wander the streets in total mindless terror and confusion. Older children found rocks and sticks with which they broke windows, then stole candy and food. The girls, those old enough—in most cases—were dragged into alleys and, at the very least, raped.

It is a fact that in times of great crisis, human animals prowl the streets in far greater numbers than normal. Weaponless, most people had no means with which to defend themselves. But criminals never register guns; and never seem to have any problem getting them. Shots were fired, fires were started, the flames and the gunfire and the screaming heightening an already near-impossible situation.

And the worst was yet to come.

A wire service reported that America was under attack from foreign countries. Flash. DJs hit the air with the news. More panic.

And, just as America has agents in every country around the globe, gathering intelligence and waiting to strike in case of open hostilities, most other countries have agents in America, waiting to do the same. They all have their orders: in case of attack, knock out communications and create panic and confusion. And that they did. They could not reach their home countries, and most of their embassies were closed, so they followed the earlier orders. The U.S. had begun jamming frequencies—as many as they could, and that created even more problems and confusion.

The Emergency Action Notification System—ENS—was ordered activated. It is an expensive and bothersome mess that has never worked, and many (if not most) DJs did not have the vaguest idea of what to do when the bells started clanging and the buzzers began buzzing and the tones began howling and whistling.

More panic.

Then the first missile was fired. It was not clear (and never would be) just who started the dance with whom, or why, but India and Pakistan exploded, and that part of the world began burning.

South America had erupted in warfare, as had the Mideast, and Africa. The world had, for years, balanced on the edge of insanity. The slender tightrope had snapped, and the world went berserk.

General Travee was attempting to talk reason with acting Premier Malelov, actually a general, of Russia. In that country, as in America, the military had been forced to take control. Prime Minister Larousse of Canada was listening in. The satellite hotline was humming—for the last time.

"Missiles have been fired, Travee," Malelov said, "from your sub. At us." His voice sounded tired, strained. "China has invaded our borders, the little yellow bastards pouring across like ants toward honey. Sadly enough—or is the word ironic?—it seems that many of my own countrymen have decided to forgo communism in favor of your form of government. We have a small revolt on our hands. What an inopportune time for that to occur, since it appears democracy is not working in either of your countries, *da?* Ah, well,"—he sighed, the sigh very audible over the miles—"perhaps it is time. Yes, I believe it is, and I think you do, too, Travee."

"Time for what?" Travee asked, knowing full well what the Russian general meant.

Malelov laughed. "Time to knock down all the pretty buildings and toy soldiers and many-worded diplomats and all forms of government—none of which appear to be working."

"Then what do we do?" Larousse asked.

"*We* won't do anything, Canadian. *We* shall be dead." Malelov chuckled. "But . . . perhaps out of the ashes, eh?"

"Fatalistic son of a bitch!" Larousse cursed him. "You could, we could, stop all this before it starts."

"That's what the English just told me moments ago." Malelov laughed, his dark humor tumbling through the miles of cold space. "I told them to pour a spot of vodka in their tea."

"We are not invading your borders," Travee reminded the Russian.

"Oh, hell, Travee!" Malelov replied impatiently. "Don't be so naïve. You know perfectly well—as I do— it's time. We've been rattling sabers and growling at one another for more than forty years. Isn't that right, Crazy Horse?" He chuckled. "I do so envy you Americans your nicknames. We Russians have to be so damned formal. I used to be known as the Wolf, but the central committee frowned on that nickname."

"Liked the ladies, eh?" Travee said.

"Oh, yes, Crazy Horse. But, like you, I'm getting old. Content with just one woman, even if she does look like a baked potato."

Travee had to laugh at the man. "Just enough time for some chitchat, eh, Malelov?"

"Just about, Travee," the Russian replied. "Yes, I think that is aptly put. No more time for serious talk . . . well, maybe a bit of talk before we enter that long sleep. Larousse, you silly Frenchman—I have some firecrackers for you. Coming your way very soon, now. What do you think about that, you who are—or were—always so afraid of helping your southernmost neighbor in her times of stress. Cowardly Canadians."

A moment of silence and outrage, then the PM spoke. "*Bâtard!*" He spat the word with all the venom he could muster.

Malelov laughed, the sounds of his howling echoing through the miles. "So I am a bastard, eh? Well, that would come as a considerable shock to my poor mother." The Russian then said something neither American nor Canadian could understand. Then, "I am glad my mother is in her grave, so she does not have to witness Russian fighting Russian."

Travee felt, after the Russian had spoken in his native tongue, that Malelov was up to something, buying time while he got the jump on the American missiles. The soldier in him surfaced. "Are we going to have war or a debating society?"

"Ah, American," Malelov spoke softly. "Can we not

85

have a few moments of camaraderie before we explode the world? Are you that anxious to die—I am not."

"No." Travee's voice was emotion-charged as he thought of his wife of thirty-five years, and of his sons and daughters and his grandchildren. He had sent them all to his birthplace—where he owned land—up in the far north of Wisconsin. Perhaps they would be safe there, but he doubted it. "No, I'm not that anxious to die. Malelov, you seem to be overcome with philosophical meanderings. . . . Perhaps you can tell us what brought the world to this point?"

"But of course," Malelov said. "General Travee . . . oh, excuse me, you are President Travee now, aren't you?" He laughed. "As I am now premier. As to the cause of this . . . misfortune we are about to bring to the world—or did *we* bring it? Oh . . . anger, frustration, helplessness, greed. No one cause. It was our country meddling in your business; your country meddling in everybody's business. And . . . perhaps it was the fact that both of our governments neglected a middle ground: something between the extremes. Not communism or socialism or democracy—but, well, I don't know. I will admit, now, that I am having serious doubts about my own political philosophies. One can only enslave a people for so long, be it physically, mentally, socially, or economically; then they revolt." He chuckled. "Is that not correct, Mr. President-General?"

"That is correct," Travee said.

"Your constitution is a most interesting document," the Russian said. "I have read it many times. Interesting, but vague. And totally unworkable to the satisfaction of all the people it must encompass. I believe, Travee, that from out of the ashes both of us will produce with our

86

missiles, there will arise a great number of small nations—including many within the United States. That is what I believe. Nations, small ones, that will serve their own people—those being willing to live under the particular laws of that nation. All, in the main, answering to some degree to one central flag, but not in the whole. Yes, that is what I believe. Have you ever given that any thought, Travee?"

"Yes," Travee admitted. "I have. But it won't work, Malelov."

"How do we know?" the Russian challenged. "Have either of our countries ever tried it?"

"Could we try it now?" Prime Minister Larousse suggested hopefully.

"No!" Malelov said, flatly and quickly. "It is too late. Too late for us. Ah! Enough small talk."

Travee was in constant communication with his northernmost tracking stations. No blips had yet appeared.

"No," Malelov said, his voice holding sadness. "It is too late. Crazy Horse knows. We are both soldiers. We know what we must do. Our generation, in both our countries, brought all this on: your country, Travee, with its maze of conflicting laws and rules; mine with its repression—I will admit it. So, our world is closing around us. However,"—he sighed—"from out of the ashes . . . and all that nonsense."

The men were silent for a time, their breathing heavy over the miles.

Suddenly, Malelov laughed. A great, booming laugh. "All right, you silly Frenchman. I have a present coming your way. Not many, but enough."

The PM cursed the Russian general.

"And you, President-General of the United States. Good joke, eh? *United* States? With your little secret army of rebels. Well, are you afraid, Travee? Are you holding your water well? Are you trembling with fear?"

"I'm not afraid of anything!" Travee thundered, the soldier in him rearing up.

"Good, good!" the Russian said. "We shall all be brave men to the end, *da?*" He laughed, but it was a sad laugh. "Well, American, Canadian—there seems to be nothing left to say . . . except, and as odd as it seems, I mean this: good luck, Crazy Horse."

"Good luck, Wolf."

The connection was broken.

"May God smile on our countries," Larousse said, then hung up.

Travee very gently set the hotline receiver into its cradle. He turned to a colonel standing nearby. "Codes activated?"

"Yes, sir. Tapes running, all systems go. Missiles ready for launch."

"Patch me through to General Hyde."

After a few seconds, the scratchy voice of Paul Hyde popped into the room. "We made it, C.H. The old bird held together and we're through Russian air defenses. I'm going to shove this payload right down their throats."

"Luck to you, Paul."

"Thanks, Charlie." The speaker went dead.

Blips appeared all over the Alaskan screen. "Russia has pushed the button, General. We're going to take a few. Eighteen minutes to impact on American soil. God! China is really getting creamed."

Travee nodded. "First launch intercept. Now! Now!"

The men were deep in the bowels of Weather Mountain, not too many miles outside of Washington, D.C.

Travee said, "Condition Red—strike. No turning back. No verbal orders to be obeyed past this point. Get me Admiral Divico."

Divico's voice rang through the room, clear and loud from his flagship. "It's still a beautiful sight, Charlie—launching these jets. Last time I'll get to see it, that's for sure."

"How's it look, Max?"

"Awesome." He was very calm.

"General Malelov was very philosophical about the situation," Travee said.

"He should be standing where I'm standing," Divico said. "He might change his tune. Well, Charlie, here they come, dead at me. I—"

The speaker screamed an electronic outrage. Travee knew the flagship had taken a hit.

"Sir?" an aide said. "Word from Cuba is General Dowling's marines are really raising hell on the island. Kicking ass all over the place."

Travee grinned. "With Dowling personally leading a charge, I'm sure."

"MIGs dogfighting with our people over the Keys, sir."

Travee nodded. "Order those designated subs to hit the bottom and stay there. Roll their DD tapes and be quiet. Order those designated silos to roll doomsday tapes and sit it out." He looked at the aide. "May God forgive me for what I'm about to do. Launch missiles! Fire! Fire! Fire!"

TWO

Ben awoke a few minutes before noon, his mouth cotton-dry. He stumbled into the kitchen, drank a glass of water, and took two aspirin. He looked out the window and grinned.

"World's still in one piece," he muttered. "Guess it was a false alarm." He opened the back door and stepped out on the porch, letting the screen door bang behind him. An angry buzzing followed the slamming of the screen door.

Ben looked around just in time to see a dozen or more yellowjackets charging out of the nest—at him. He threw up his hand and one stung him in the center of the palm. Wincing from the sudden pain, Ben struggled with the door. It had a habit of sticking, and chose this time to become obstinate. Several more of the wasps hit him, on the neck and face. Another stung him just below the left eye. His world began to spin. Just as he got the door open, a wasp buried its stinger behind Ben's right ear and Ben slumped to the kitchen floor, his feet hanging outside, holding the door open.

Yellowjackets swarmed him, stinging him on the arms, face, and neck. Using the last of his fading strength, Ben pulled his feet inside and the door closed. He slapped at his face, knocking several wasps spinning. He crawled

90

into the den and there, fell to the tile, unconscious. His face was swelling rapidly. He shuddered as the venom raced through his system; his breathing became shallow and his skin was clammy.

Ben slipped deeper into unconsciousness.

The United States fared well in the nuclear aspect of missiles landing on her soil. Most of the enemy missiles did not make it through our penetration screens. But several did. Washington D.C. took the first hit, turning the residents into dust. Several more cities met the same fate.

Nuclear warfare had progressed considerably during the decade just past. Almost all the missiles, of the nuclear type, that landed in America were of the so-called "clean" type. That is to say there was not much deadly fallout associated with them. But most of the missiles landing on American soil carried bacterial-type warheads that killed everything within a certain number of miles— depending on the prevailing winds. This was accomplished in a short time, then the deadly bacteria died.

Los Angeles, San Francisco, Seattle, Chicago, Detroit, Miami, Omaha, Boston, Philadephia, Memphis, and some fifty other cities went under during the strike. The first strike. Some of them were reduced to smoking dangerous ash, most to the state in which their citizens staggered about, dying on their feet of the plague or of Tabun-produced death. New York City no longer existed. The famous lady with her welcoming torch of freedom was now and would forever be only a memory.

The island of Cuba still floated, but most of her people, including the naval contingent and marines at Gitmo, were reduced to very small piles of dust.

Montreal, Toronto, Ottawa—gone.

Subs roamed the oceans of the world: Chinese, Russian, American, Australian, English—to name a few. Now, with the war plug pulled, and none of them knowing if there was to be a home base for their return, they all did their thing in proper style, thank you.

Melbourne, Sidney, and Brisbane were gone. Mexico City exploded and died in a raging hail of nuclear fire. Lisbon, Rome, and the monuments to justice and truth and philosophy in Athens were no more. Also destroyed were Karachi, Bombay, Madras, Calcutta, Rangoon, Bangkok, Hanoi, and Uncle Ho's city, better known as Saigon. No real reason for those cities to explode, but what good are spoils if there is no victor?

Europe blew apart: London, Dublin, Paris, Berlin, Warsaw, Brussels, and more. The major cities of Russia erupted under the impact of Chinese and American missiles. Troops clashed and fought and died because it is the nature of troops to do just that. To follow orders.

Montevideo, Buenos Aires, Rio, Santiago, the Canal Zone. Why not? The pilots and the skippers who ordered the pushing of buttons had no place to return.

There were many cities around the globe who came through unscathed—this time around. The first wave of missiles killed only about three-quarters of a billion people.

But governments—all governments—no matter how noble they might proclaim themselves to be, are vindictive.

And the doomsday tapes were silently rolling.

Ben did not know how long he was out; how long he

had been lying on the floor of his den, but it was full dark when he awoke. He looked at his hands: they were swollen grotesquely. He could not open one eye, and putting his hands to his face, he felt a mass of welts and swollen flesh. He tried to crawl to the bathroom where he kept his Benadryl—he was allergic to any kind of wasp or bee sting—but strength left him and he collapsed back to the floor.

In his dreams, his nightmares, he thought he was back in Nam. And as the sweat rolled from his body, he refought every battle a dozen times, screaming out occasionally.

It was dawn when he awakened, pulled himself to his feet, and staggered into the bathroom. There, he took several Benadryl tablets and thought of driving into town to the hospital. But he knew he'd never make it.

The phone. He stumbled to the phone to call his doctor. In the semidarkness of the den, his foot caught in a rocker and he fell to the floor, banging his head. Spinning colors became blackness as he fell tumbling into the darkness of unconsciousness.

The Air Force had lost nearly seventy-five percent of its planes and more than half its men. The Marine Corps was almost totally wiped out. The Army was reduced by more than sixty percent, and the Navy cut by more than fifty percent, with almost no ships or planes left.

The government of the United States, for all practical purposes, had ceased to exist. Weather Mountain had taken a hit dead on. Travee was dead.

Twenty-four hours after the first wave of bombings, many citizens of America still did not really know what had happened to them. They did not know what to do or where to go. They wandered about in a daze. This was America, they thought, and things like this just don't happen in America. Do they? Didn't Big Brother promise to take care of us? What happened?

There were those who lived on the fringe areas of the hot blasts; they were horribly burned, waiting to die—wanting to die. There were those close to the blasts who had instinctively turned their heads to look at the brilliant flashes and had felt their eyeballs turn to liquid and roll down their cheeks, leaving only empty sockets and unbelievable pain. Those people died; they were killed by others who panicked and trampled them wantonly.

Women of all ages were raped, tortured, and left to suffer and die in empty houses or barns or alleys or gutters. Children, raped, molested, hurt, wandered about, screaming their misery, alone and frightened; many of them were finally brought down by roaming packs of dogs.

In the prisons and jails, men and women, locked in their cells, were forgotten, left to die from exposure and starvation. Those roaming the walkways and runarounds would commit unspeakable acts on their fellow prisoners and then, in one final moment of desperation, they would hang themselves, hack open their wrists, or beat their brains out against steel bars or cell walls.

In the nursing homes and mental institutions, the insane and the old died without knowing why or how this was happening to them, left alone when the first panic struck the nation; actually, for many this was the second time they had been abandoned, the first having been when their children decided they didn't want old people around, messing up their social lives.

The old people and the insane soiled themselves, vomited on themselves, and then died as horribly as they had been forced to live.

Two days after the world exploded in nuclear and bacteriological madness, it began again as the doomsday tapes cued out and began the overkill. From deep in underground silos, the missiles roared toward their preset targets. Subs from Russia, China, and America, and a dozen other countries surfaced and hurled their payloads. The overkill began.

When there were no more cities or military bases to strike, or they were out of range, the captains of the subs fired their last missiles and let them fall where they may. It was a seemingly brutal, senseless act that most civilians would not understand. But military men and women who had served their respective countries lifelong understood it all too well.

Death was everywhere. Chaos and panic ran rampant world-wide. Live now! Who knows if there will be a dawn tomorrow. Surely there is no God, for He would not have permitted this. Rape, steal, kill—there is no promised land. This is all there is or ever will be.

After exhausting their payloads, the subs surfaced and raised the flags of their countries. The captains stood calmly and stoically on their conning towers and saluted the pilots who blew them into history. Many of the American pilots, out of fuel, with carriers and bases gone or out of range, cursed the enemy and rammed their jets into its subs, going down with their foes.

The former world, in which people were capable of producing constructive results, no longer existed.

THREE

He remembered getting up from the cold floor and slipping in his own blood. His head was a huge mass of pain. He stumbled into the bathroom and, using his one good eye, washed the cut and put antiseptic on the gash. Just that much effort exhausted him. He stretched out on the couch and went to sleep. Sometime during the night—what night, he wasn't certain—Ben rose stiffly and painfully from the couch to fix a bowl of soup. He kept it down for about five minutes before staggering to the bathroom and vomiting. Then it was back to the couch and a deep, almost comalike sleep.

On yet another morning, Ben managed to keep some soup and milk down and to take a shower before his weakness drove him to bed. He had glanced out the window and viewed a perfectly lovely day. He thought he had heard horns honking frantically sometime during the previous night, but he wasn't sure.

His face was still swollen and he was feverish, able to see out of just one eye, but he felt a little bit better. He knew he'd been very, very lucky, for he had counted as many of the wasp stings as he could see or feel, and reckoned he had been stung more than thirty times—maybe as many as fifty. As allergic as he was to stings, that many should have killed him.

He stumbled back to bed and pulled the covers over his head.

He opened his eyes and knew, on this day, finally, that he was going to be all right.

Well, Ben thought, I probably should have died. I'm a lucky man. Lord, have I been sick.

He rolled over in bed and stared at the red numbers on his digital clock radio. The numbers stared back. Almost, he thought, with a mixture of mute arrogance and accusation. The numbers seemed to be saying: Get up! Get up! You're not sick. You feel fine. So get up and get to work.

He pushed back the covers and slowly swung his feet to the carpet. He was just a little light-headed and shaky, but his forehead felt cool to the touch and the swelling was gone from his face and hands. He could see out of both eyes. And he was hungry—ravenous. Ben smiled. He doubted a dying man would get out of bed to get something to eat.

The numbers on the clock read five thirty-three. He wondered what day it was. He picked up his watch from the nightstand and looked at the day and date.

He couldn't believe it. "Damn!" he said softly. "I've been sick for ten days!"

It didn't seem possible.

Ben felt there was some significance to this date, but he couldn't place the importance of it.

Well, he thought, it'll come to me, I suppose.

He walked slowly into the kitchen, put some water on to boil, then went to the bathroom for a long, hot shower, the steaming water helping to revive him. He shaved, dressed, then had a cup of coffee while he fixed breakfast:

scrambled eggs and bacon. He ate that, then fixed a bowl of hot cereal. Finally, after two more eggs on toast, his hunger was appeased.

He looked out the kitchen window and again thought how lucky he'd been to come through alive. The day was bright and beautiful. He thought back, pushing his memory through the feverish haze of the past ten days. He remembered drinking lots of water, for the fever was dehydrating. He recalled eating several bowls of soup, some crackers, and drinking some milk. One time, he recalled, he'd fixed a bowl of cereal. That, he thought, was all the nourishment he'd had in ten days.

He shook his head. Well, that was all behind him. He would, by God, get several more of those cans of wasp spray, the kind that shot a stream for about twenty feet, and clear out the little bastards from around his house. But for now, it was time to get to work.

Monday through Saturday, Ben usually rose at five-thirty. On Sundays he tried to sleep late. But unless he had been up late, which was unusual for him, his eyes almost always popped open at five-thirty, with or without the clock radio.

Ben made himself a second cup of coffee, fixed a glass of ice water, then went into his small office and took the cover off his typewriter.

Sunday was another workday for him. Another day to face the typewriter and hope the muses were flowing. He belonged to no church—no organized religion. He had attended church as a child, and as a young man, but early in his adult life a discontent with religion had grown in him. Mass hypocrisy turned him off.

Ben had a slight headache, so he took two aspirins and then wound a fresh piece of paper into the typewriter.

Yeah, he remembered, he was to start a new book. He always, despite the number of books he had published, under a variety of names, viewed this moment with some anticipation and just a bit of fear. The beginnings of a new novel. Would it work? Would it jell?

Who the hell knew?

His agent said he liked everything Ben did, but agents are supposed to say things like that. What else? "Ben, you're a lousy writer. Why don't you give it up and become a plumber?"

Probably make just as much money. Ben smiled.

He glanced at his just-completed novel, all wrapped up for mailing. Do that in the morning, Ben thought. His books usually brought him a $3,500–$4,000 advance, a few thousand in royalties, maybe some overseas sales in the future . . . and that was that. Once in a blue moon, maybe a movie deal. Gravy.

He was a paperback writer; had long since given up writing for the hardcovers. He knocked out a book every four to six weeks. He would tackle anything from action books to love stories; had a pretty good men's adventure series going for him, and was building a good reputation among the publishing companies as a steady, producing kind of writer—nothing fantastic, nothing earthshaking. The type of writer whose books sold in grocery stores, variety stores, drug stores, and other paperback outlets. Ben would never win the Nobel for fiction, for Ben did not write to change the world's evil(?) ways. He wrote to entertain.

The world, Ben once told his agent, is someone else's bailiwick, not mine. Just like law enforcement, people get what they want, whether they'll admit it, or not. Same with government. Me? He laughed at his agent's expression. I'm just a country boy trying to make a living.

That memory amused him. He leaned back in his chair and smiled.

Country boy. Yeah, he nodded his head in agreement, I'm a country boy. Maybe with a better than average degree of urbanity about me than most country boys, but nonetheless, still . . . just a country boy. He liked black-eyed peas and beans and corn bread and fried okra and salt-meat sandwiches. But he also liked the good wines and fine cuisine found in the fancy restaurants of the world.

And he knew he was a snob when it came to music, having sampled it all and found it lacking . . . except for classical.

But he loved the South—especially Louisiana, with its rich heritage and diversity of people. There wasn't much in the way of culture where Ben lived. As a matter of fact, he often told his eastern friends, there really wasn't any culture where he lived: no little theater, no concerts, no ballet. Ben had once mentioned Zubin Mehta to a friend and the man had thought he was talking about a new brand of chewing tobacco.

But Ben liked the people in the Delta—for the most part. He had friends here, good friends. There were some real shit-heads on both sides of the color line, but there had never been any real trouble in this part of the state.

And damned little mixing, he reminded himself.

You stay on your side of town, and I'll stay on mine. I don't like you much, and I know you don't like me, but the government says we have to get along, so let's just make the best of it.

So far, so good.

Like that black city-council member once said, "It's better here than in a lot of places. 'Least we haven't started killin' one another—yet."

Wise disclaimer on his part, Ben thought.

Ben believed it was probably coming to the race-war point—someday. Probably soon. And he wasn't alone in that view.

Never married, Ben had experienced several intense love affairs that had ultimately soured, leaving him with a jaundiced eye toward everlasting love. He really didn't trust women; and his being a hopeless romantic didn't help matters. His books almost never had happy endings (something his agent used to bitch about). But the N.Y.C. man finally accepted that as part of Ben's style, and assumed that Ben was not going to change.

He pulled his attention back to the typewriter and the blank paper staring at him. But nothing flowed. He turned off the typewriter, then turned it back on, listened to it hum.

Mother's milk causes writer's block, he recalled reading one time. Or the lack of it.

I damned sure was sick from those wasp stings.

"Come on, Ben!" he scolded himself. "Get with it." He sighed, typed a few words, tore the paper from the machine, and wound in a fresh sheet.

That scene was repeated several times that morning, until finally Ben hit his stride, as he knew he would. He did not work from an outline, never knew where the manuscript was going, and let his characters develop themselves.

Ben settled down to write.

All the muses seemed to be working and the words were flowing well; no strain. He wrote for three hours, was satisfied with the start of his novel, and then, with a coffee taste in his mouth and a slight headache (he assumed that was from chain-smoking a pack of cigarettes), he shut it down for the morning.

Every Sunday morning Ben drove into town at about eleven o'clock to visit a friend of his who ran a service station. Every Sunday morning. Routine—almost never varied. Ben would visit for an hour, pick up the Sunday papers (three of them), and drive back home, where he would read himself to sleep, then work for several more hours in the afternoon.

Ben slipped his feet into cowboy boots, put on a long-sleeved shirt, for the day was unusually cool, and once more glanced at the calendar. The meaning of the date finally hit him.

"Well, I'll be damned!" He smiled. "It's my birthday. I'm forty-four years old." He laughed, happy to be feeling good after his bout with the wasps. "Happy birthday, Ben Raines—many, many more, partner."

Then he wondered why his parents hadn't called. They *always* called early.

He glanced around his empty, silent house, the joy of the moment becoming sullied just a bit because he had no one with whom to share his one day of celebration.

He shrugged it off and locked up the house.

The term "country boy" once more entered his mind as he walked across the yard to his pickup. He hummed an old country song as he walked, one of the few country songs he liked: "A Country Boy Will Survive."

Ben thought that ironic, since he was beginning a novel of disaster—Armageddon. The end of the world.

Getting into his pickup, he remembered both his

mother and father kidding him about his return to trucks; his father saying, "Boy, you started out in trucks when you was just fourteen. Held that damned old rattletrap together with spit, prayer, and baling wire. Hell, son—you remember. It didn't have any doors! You had the first seat belts in Illinois. You had to tie yourself in with rope to keep from falling out going around curves. Now that you're goin' to be a big-time writer, damned if you haven't gone back to trucks. You're just a farm boy at heart, Ben. Can't ever take the country out of the boy, eh, Ben?"

And his dad would laugh in that big hearty way of his. Good, solid country people.

Ben missed his parents, knew he would have to take some time off and visit them—soon. They were both getting up there in years. Both in good health . . . but, one never knew when the hands of time would grow too heavy and lose their grip.

Ben didn't like to think about that.

As he drove, Ben looked at the countryside, and at the houses he passed. Something seemed . . . well, odd about them. They looked . . . deserted, if that was the right choice of words. He shook his head. "My imagination," he said.

Ben wasn't a rich man—far from it. But he made enough from his efforts to live in comfort. His home was paid for, he had nice furniture, deep, rich carpet, and all the other accouterments that made life a bit more than merely an existence.

Ben Raines also drank himself into a quiet stupor every night of the week. Including Sundays.

But he was one of those rare people who never suffered a hangover. He could not remember ever having one.

And he hedged whenever he would question himself about why he drank so much. He never would admit his was a lonely life.

Writers drink, he would say.

Bullshit, his mind would reply.

It was never a very stimulating or productive self-conversation.

Sunday morning radio programing in most parts of the rural South is, at best, dismal—alternating (depending upon the stations one chose) between hillbillies yodeling praise to the Lord, black gospel groups shouting and stomping praise to the Lord, and nasal preachers hem-hawing and gulping praise to, or from, the Lord. Some of them speaking in tongues.

Ben never turned on his radio on Sunday mornings. And TV was just as bad. It was one of his great gripes that public broadcasting, in radio form, did not get into the area in which he lived.

Ben lived out in the country, literally. About ten miles outside of Morriston, a small town located at the bottom of the Delta of Louisiana. The town had a population of eight thousand: fifty percent black, fifty percent white. No industry. Lots of bars, black and white; never the twain shall meet. Music in the bars was soul or country. That was it. So, Pavarotti, do not waste your time coming to the Delta, unless you first appear on "Barbed-Wire Hoedown," yodeling; or on "Boogie Funky Wagon," beating on a drum and shaking your tushie.

It was gracious Southern living at its best and worst. Half-million-dollar homes and two-hundred-dollar shacks. Cadillacs and food stamps. Cotton, rice, soybeans, and wheat.

And football.

Ben cut his eyes to the ditch by the side of the road and his thoughts were abruptly returned to the present. He jammed on the brakes, sliding to a halt.

That was a body in the ditch.

He got out of his truck and, stepping over the water (when had it rained?), walked to the ditch and knelt by the man. The man had been dead at least a week; his corpse was blackened and stinking.

He walked back to his truck and flipped on the CB radio. "Give me a Montgomery Parish Deputy or a state trooper."

Nothing.

He repeated his call and received the same scratchy emptiness from the speaker.

His CB was a good one and he had had it on . . . a couple of days before the wasps hit him.

"Break-one-nine for a radio check," he said.

Nothing.

He monitored all channels and received the same on all of them. Nothing.

He sat in his truck for a moment, reviewing what he could remember of the past week, before he was stung. He had been shopping, was it Wednesday or Thursday? Had he listened to a radio or TV since. No, not since the night he had gotten drunk listening to the TV newspeople flap their gums about nuclear war.

Ben looked around him, at the clear day, sunny and bright. Obviously, no nuclear war had occurred. He suddenly felt uneasy. Or, had it? When had he heard those horns honking so frantically? He shook his head. Kids, probably, cutting up.

He glanced at the body in the ditch and then at his watch. Almost noon. "Well, this is silly!" he said. "There

105

is something wrong with my radio, that's all."

Then he thought about the radio in his truck. He turned it on, tuning in to the local station first. Nothing.

He punched all the preset buttons. Nothing. He spun the dial left to right, then went slowly back.

Nothing.

A finger of something very close to fear touched him. He shook it off. But something deep within him, some . . . sense of warning prompted him to punch open the glove compartment and take out the .38 special he always carried. Ben had blatantly ignored the government order to turn in all handguns, as, he suspected, had several million others. Ben despised Sen. Hilton Logan and everything he stood for. Logan was a dove—Ben was a hawk. Logan was a liberal—Ben was a conservative. A conservative in most of his thinking.

He checked the cylinder of the .38. All full. He shoved the pistol behind his belt and put the truck in gear. He had not recognized the dead man.

A mile further and he turned onto the road that was just inside the city limits. A half-mile further, on the edge of town, in an open field, Ben slowed to watch several large birds, vultures, rise from the ground at the sound of his truck. They flapped ponderously away. Full and heavy. Ben had only to glance quickly to see what they had been feeding upon: bodies.

This time it was fear that touched him—open, naked fear. "Did the balloon go up?" he asked aloud. "If so, why was I spared?"

He could not answer his question.

He drove on until he could drive no further. Two cars were blocking the street. Ben did not have to get out of his truck to see that the occupants' bodies were blackened and decomposing in death.

He backed up, turned around, and drove down a side street until he came to a residential area. He saw no signs of human life, but neither did he see any bodies. He wound his way to the service station and pulled into the drive. There, Ben sat in numb silence, staring at the windows of the Exxon station. The windows were smashed, broken; glass littered the drive. The body of his friend lay sprawled half in, half out of the door.

Ben got out of his truck slowly, not really believing all this was happening—had happened. He corrected his thinking. He knelt down beside the man. Mr. Harnack was stiff and black and stinking. Dogs had gnawed on him.

Ben stepped over the body and walked to the phone. He punched out the numbers of the police department, letting the phone ring twenty times. No answer. He called the sheriff's department. Same results.

Ben felt the butt of the .38, and the touch of the wood was reassuring.

He stood in the doorway and listened intently. He could not hear one human sound coming from the town.

He walked to the desk and turned on the small TV. He got the same results from every channel. And this was cable, coming from Chicago and Atlanta. Nothing from Chicago. Blank screen. The others had the civil defense emblem on the screen, but nothing to explain why.

Bold Strike. The words returned to him. Hunt a hole, partner. "I'm dreaming," Ben said, his voice sounding strange amid the silence and the death. "What the hell happened? It has to be a dream."

But he knew he was not dreaming.

He thought, this is nationwide—world-wide. Those

thoughts chilled him, bringing beads of sweat to his forehead. "Jesus, am I the last man on earth?"

Then the words of that grizzled sergeant drifted back to Ben as he stood in the doorway, looking out at the mute gas pumps. "Survive is the name of this game, men. Fuck a bunch of candy-assed civilians. When the balloon goes up—and it will go up, believe that—most civilians won't make it, 'cause they don't know their ass from peanut butter about stayin' alive. And what is so sickenin' is, they don't wanna know. They're content. They've got their pretty little houses, two cars in the garage, membership in the country club, and they think being tough means playing football. As far as they're concerned, everything is aces up. But they don't know the meaning of tough. They'll be the victims in any holocaust. But I'm gonna teach you men what tough is—mentally and physically. And when I'm through with you, you'll survive. If you men make it through the first wave, if you don't take one nose-on, most of you will survive."

Ben nodded his head and instinctively moved from the door into the darkness of the station's work area. He squatted down, all his training returning to him.

The sergeant had said, "Maybe most of you won't make the military your life's work; sure, most of you will pull your hitch and get out. But that's no matter, 'cause what you learn here in this school, and the other schools you go to; well,"—he smiled—"it'll stay with you. You made it this far, and that proves to me you want to learn the meaning of survival. So even if you get out, you'll push all this training way in the back of your minds—some of you will even try to forget it, 'cause it's nasty and dirty and dehumanizing. But you won't forget it, and if you ever need it, it'll be right there. Now, get on your goddamned feet and get ready to find out what you're really made of."

Ben squatted in the shade of the garage area until his legs began to protest from the strain. When he rose, walking a bit to relieve the kinks in his leg muscles, he had reviewed what he had been taught . . . years back.

And he knew one thing for certain: he was going to survive.

FOUR

He pulled his truck up to the pumps and filled his tanks, topping off his reserve tank. He found four five-gallon gas cans and filled them, placing them in the bed of his truck. He looked back at Mr. Harnack, nodded his head, and drove off, heading for the police station, only a few blocks away.

The dispatcher was dead, not a mark on him. On the note pad on the table was scribbled: "I'm the last one alive. Getting weak. No help. Atomic bombs hit some cities. Some type of germ stuff got the rest of us. God have—"

He never got to finish the sentence.

"Atomic bombs?" Ben said aloud, his voice hollow and echoing in the room. "Germs?"

It really happened! he thought. I slept through a goddamned war!

"Maybe I'm lucky I did," he muttered.

He started to pick up the mike to see if anyone would answer his call, then pulled his hand back.

"Yeah—somebody might answer it. But it might be somebody I don't want to see."

He knew only too well that many times human scum survived when others more deserving did not. Ben looked around the small station house (why do they always smell like piss?), could find nothing he felt he could use, then drove to the sheriff's office.

It was a repeat of the police station. All dead. The office was a mess: gas masks scattered about; books on deadly gases and parish evacuation plans tossed on the floor. The bodies were stiff and blackened. And smelly.

Ben opened the windows and then prowled the office until he found what he was searching for: the gun room. He selected two .45-caliber pistols, checked them carefully, then found leather for them and extra clips. He calmly filled two extra clips for each pistol. He smashed the glass of a locked gun cabinet and picked up an old Thompson submachine gun. It was in almost mint condition; he had heard the sheriff was, or had been, a gun collector. He checked the SMG, found it in bad need of oiling, then prowled around until he found a can of oil. The bolt worked effortlessly when he had finished and the wood gleamed. He found a drum for the weapon and three clips, boxes of .45 ammunition, and a canvas clip pouch.

There was nothing he could do for the dead men, so Ben carried the gear outside to the fresh air, and sat on the steps. He filled the drum, then filled the clips, inserting a clip into the belly of the old 1921 Chicago piano, as the Thompson used to be called. This one was a modern-day version of the old weapon, but still more than thirty years old. It was a heavy weapon, and its effectiveness was limited. But up to one hundred yards, its knockdown power was awesome.

Ben walked to his truck and stuck the .38 back in the glove compartment. He belted one .45 around his waist. Again, he turned on the radio, slowly working the dial back and forth. Nothing. He drove to a sporting goods store.

A man and woman lay among the wreckage, dead. The

store had been looted, but it had been done in haste, without much thought for real survival.

Ben spent an hour in the store, picking through the rubble, selecting what he felt he would need: all the forty-five ammunition he could find, which wasn't much, a portable stove, lantern, a sleeping bag, an ax, a good knife, a tent, a tarp, rope, two dozen other items. Then he drove to a local supermarket and set about picking up more items. The supermarket, like the sporting goods store, had been looted, but there, too, without much thought.

If everybody is dead, Ben thought, as he walked down the aisles, feeling just a bit foolish pushing a shopping cart, where are all the bodies? And if everybody is dead, who did the looting?

From the supermarket, he drove to a drug store. It had also been looted, but nothing of any real value taken. Drugs to make you high; drugs to make you low. False happy-time. Ben chose the healing drugs, then picked up bandages, iodine, tape.

Passing the cosmetic counter (he was amused to see it, too, had been looted), Ben paused as his reflection stared at him from a vanity mirror. He had never thought of himself as handsome, even as a teen-ager, his face had been more trustworthy than handsome. His hair was dark brown, peppered now with gray. His eyes were blue. He was just a shade over six-one—180 pounds. Even though he drank much more than he should, he was in good shape, exercising daily. He turned from his reflection.

He drove past several liquor stores and laughed at their condition: they were the worst looted of the stores. "Party time," he said with no mirth in his voice. "Eat, drink, and be merry. For tomorrow we may die."

He drove back to his house and unloaded his gear. I'm a looter, he thought. He built a small fire; then fixed a drink. He kept his mind clear of what he had seen that day, wisely not dwelling on it. Let the shock come gradually. At full dark, when he knew the big 50,000 watters kicked on, Ben spent an hour carefully searching the bands. Nothing. Tomorrow, he thought, I'll go back to town and find one of those world-wide radios. Somebody is out there.

And I've got to search the town for survivors.

He limited himself to only a few drinks, and fixed a good dinner. At nine, the strain of the day taking its toll, he went to bed. He was asleep in three minutes.

He had forgotten the phone!

Ben sat up in bed, cursing his stupidity. He glanced at the clock: seven-thirty. He looked at his wristwatch. Seven-thirty. Yesterday must have had more of an impact on him than he realized. Shock, maybe.

So the electricity was working, at least for a time. So, too, he reasoned, would be the phone system. For a while longer, at least.

He showered, shaved carefully, dressed, and fixed breakfast. He took his coffee outside and stood for a time, viewing the almost silent scene. Birds still sang, and that puzzled him. Somewhere a dog barked, and that puzzled him. Why a gas that would kill humans but not animals?

He looked back through the open front door. He was hesitant to begin the phoning, but it was something he knew he had to do.

He had to try to contact his parents, his brothers, his sisters. He walked back into the house. With a fresh cup of coffee in his hand, he began punching out the numbers

113

for long distance. He called his parents first, then his oldest brother, up in Chicago, letting the phone ring twenty times at each number. No answer. Really, he wasn't expecting any. He went down the line, all the way to his youngest sister, in Cairo, Illinois. Nothing.

With a sigh, he replaced the phone in its cradle. He picked up his weapons and drove into town.

He went first to the local Radio Shack (it had not been looted), and picked out a huge world-wide receiver. He sat outside the store, on the curb, reading the material on the receiver; then turned on the big radio. It didn't work—no batteries.

"Wonderful, Ben," he muttered. "Marvelous presence of mind."

He found batteries for the radio and turned it on, spinning the dial slowly, working first one band, then another. Sweat broke out on his face as he heard a voice spring from the speakers.

The voice spoke in French for a time, then switched to German, finally to English. "We pieced together the whole story." The voice spoke slowly. "Finally. Russian pilot told us this is what happened—from his side of the pond, that is. They—the Russians—had developed some sort of virus that would kill humans, but not harm animals or plant life or water. Did this about three years ago. Were going to use it against us this fall. Easy to figure why. Then they learned of the double cross. The Stealth-equipped sub. That shot their plans of an easy takeover all to hell. Everything became all confused. If we had tried to talk to them, or they with us, or the Chinese, maybe all this could have been prevented. Maybe not. Too late now. Some survivors world-wide. Have talked with some of them. Millions dead. Don't

114

know how many. Over a billion, probably. Maybe more. Ham operators working. It's bad. God in heaven—it's bad."

The message was repeated, over and over, in four languages.

"Goddamned tape recording!" Ben cursed. But he felt a little better. At least he knew what had happened. Sort of. But some of the message confused him: that part about "easy to figure why."

A snarling brought him to his feet, the .45 in his hand. A pack of dogs stood a few yards from him, and they were not at all friendly.

Ben leaped for the hood of his truck just as a large German shepherd lunged for him, fangs bared. He scrambled for the roof of the cab as the dog leaped onto the hood. Ben shot it in the head, the force of the heavy slug slamming the animal backward.

The dogs remembered gunfire. They ran down the street, stopped on the corner, and turned around, snarling and barking at the man atop the cab of his truck. Ben emptied the .45 into the pack, knocking several of them spinning. The rest ran away. Ben slapped a fresh clip in the .45 and climbed down. Shaken, he stood for a moment waiting for the trembles to leave him. He looked around him, carefully.

"From now on, Ben," he said aloud. "That Thompson becomes a part of you. Just like your arm."

He picked up the radio and got in his truck. "All I need is rabies," he said. "I live through a world-wide catastrophe and a fucking dog does me in."

He held out his hands; they were calm. He knew he must search for survivors in the town, and he was not looking forward to that.

He began driving the streets of town, discovering the bodies. A great number of people had gathered at friends' homes; many houses contained fifteen or more dead. He went to his closest friend's house, steeling himself as he drove. His friend was dead, as were his wife and kids. It appeared Ben was alone in the town.

He drove back to the sheriff's office and picked up a gas mask. The day was warming, and he figured the smell could only worsen.

At a paper-vending machine, Ben picked up a paper, smiling as he automatically inserted the money into the machine. The paper was ten days old, about the time he had been stung. He stood for a time reading, then remembered the packs of dogs and walked quickly back to his truck.

There had been a news blackout, and the paper didn't tell him much. War was imminent; that was about it. He did not know how many cities were destroyed, or whether it had been done by nuclear warheads or germs. He tossed the paper into the littered street, then instinctively looked around to see if a cop had seen him do it.

He shook his head sadly and started the truck. He touched the Thompson on the seat beside him. He would search every street in Morriston, then head out into the parish. Someone was alive . . . somewhere, and Ben intended to find that person.

But he could find no one alive in the town. And the dogs were getting vicious and much braver.

"A virus that kills humans, but not animals," Ben mused. He hit the steering wheel with the palm of his hand. "Sure!" he said, ashamed of himself for his stupidity. The tape had said, "Easy to figure why." And it was. Just walk right in and take over the country, void of humans, but with the livestock fat, healthy, and happy, munching away. An instant food source for the conquering army. But that army would have to move fast. . . .

Ben smiled grimly as his writer's mind began humming.

Not if they moved from within.

He wondered how long the plan had been in the works? How many people—if his theory was correct, and he would probably never know—in this country had been recruited. Hundreds, at least—perhaps thousands. Paratroopers would be standing by, ready to go in, crush any pockets of resistance. With a crash course in agronomy, they could keep the livestock and the land in good shape until the farmers arrived. Which would not have taken long.

Instant victory with a minimum of bloodshed. For them.

But it backfired. Ben wondered how many double crosses were involved. He wondered if he would ever know, and decided he would not.

His mind began racing—what a tale this would have made.

"Bastards!" he said.

Then he saw her.

He braked the truck, stopped, and cursed.

Of all the people in the world the good Lord chose to save . . . why this bitch?

And he was not in the least ashamed of his thoughts.

Ben got out of the truck and gave her a mock bow, clicking his heels together, Prussian-style. "Why, good morning, Mrs. Piper," he said acidly. "What a surprise

117

seeing you. Not a pleasure, but a surprise, and I mean that sincerely."

Even under the present circumstances, the look he received was one of intense dislike.

"Mr. Raines," she said, with as much acid in her voice as there had been in his. "You're armed! I was under the assumption pistols had been outlawed some time ago."

Fran Piper looked as though she had just that moment stepped from the pages of a fashion magazine: every dark hair in place, fashion jeans snugly outlining her charms—which were many. Fashion shirt—cowgirl, uptown-neat, all the snaps snapped.

"Yes, ma'am. Pistols were outlawed some years ago—three, I believe. Thanks to Hilton Logan and his bunch of misguided liberals. But be that as it may, ma'am. Here I am, Ben Raines, at your service. That trashy Yankee writer of all those filthy violent fuck books, come to save your aristocratic ass from gettin' pronged by all the slobbering rednecks that must surely be prowlin' around the parish, just a-lustin' for a crack at you. Ma'am."

"Raines," she said, her eyes flashing, "you just *have* to be the most despicable human being I have *ever* had the misfortune to encounter. And if that was supposed to be Rhett Butler, you certainly missed the boat."

"Paddle-wheel, I'm sure." He smiled.

"Huh?"

"Never mind. Actually . . ." Ben looked around him. No dogs in sight. "That was Claude Raines. He was my uncle."

She patted her perfect hair. "Claude Raines, the actor, was your uncle? Why, you never told us. . . ." Then she saw his smile and knew he was kidding her. "You bastard!"

Their mutual hatred went back more than a decade.

Midwesterners are difficult people to impress, and so inherited money does not impress most rural midwesterners—not those with any sense. Fran Lantier Piper had piles of money stacked all around her . . . from both sides of her family, and the family she had married into, but in the past hundred years neither she nor any one related to her had worked for a penny of it.

Ben's fifth novel—and he had received a little movie money from that one—had been about spoiled southern brats and inherited money and arrogance. Fran had told him—at a chance meeting at the public library (it came as a shock to Ben to discover she even knew how to read)— that she thought he should be run out of town for writing such nasty filthy lies about good decent gentle people.

Ben had laughed at her.

Furious, she had raced home and told her big brother, Lance, a local football hero, all about her encounter with that Yankee ruffian, embellishing the story substantially, with much batting of eyes and no small amount of tears and posturing. Lance had telephoned Ben, telling him he should be prepared to fight.

Ben had broken up with laughter. "You're really going to defend her honor?"

"I'm a-goin' to stomp you," Lance had drawled.

When Lance got out of the hospital, after a short stay in ICU, the Lantier family had tried—in the best southern tradition—to have Ben run out of town. Ben had weathered the short but furious storm of emotions and the situation had cooled over the years. But bad blood remained.

"You look puurrfectly chaarrmin' today, Miss Fran." Ben laid on enough syrup to drown a cat. He leaned against his truck. "Out for a little stroll among the bodies?"

"Your humor is gruesome, Raines."

"Well,"—Ben opened the door to the truck—"I guess I'll be seeing you, baby."

"Wait!" she screamed at him. "You can't leave me out here."

Ben looked at her. "Why the hell not? You don't care for my company and I sure as hell don't want to listen to you bitch all day."

"Because . . . because . . ." She looked at him, sensing he meant every word she had just heard. And he certainly did. "What kind of man are you?"

"The kind of man who doesn't like spoiled brats who run home and tell lies about people. Does that ring a bell, Fran?"

"Well . . . you beat him up, didn't you? Probably fought dirty, though."

"Fran?"

"What?"

"Fuck you!"

Tears began rolling down her cheeks. Whether they were real or staged for his benefit, Ben wasn't sure. But he closed the door to the pickup and waited, figuring the next few moments should be interesting . . . at least. He glanced around for dogs. None in sight.

"My husband is dead, in that house," she pointed to a mansion across the road. Ben reminded her that just down the road two elderly people had died when they could not afford to pay their electric bill and the power company had cut off their electricity. They had died of exposure.

She shook her head. "I had nothing to do with that."

"They also had nothing to eat in the house, Fran. They were your neighbors."

120

"*Those* people? *My* neighbors?"

"Skip it, Fran. People like you never understand."

"Why didn't you help them if you're such a charitable person?"

"I didn't know anything about their condition."

Again, she shook her head. "I don't know if my sister is alive, or not. She went to New Orleans the day . . . whatever happened happened. My mother and father are dead. I don't know where Lance is—"

"And I don't give a shit where he is," Ben told her, and meant it.

". . . And you're not making this easy for me!" she screamed at him.

"Why should I?" Ben looked at her. "I just don't like people of your ilk. But I'll be damned if I'm going to stand out in the middle of a road and discuss it with you."

She stamped her foot. "Well . . . at least take me into Natchez. I have friends there. I'm . . . well . . . I'm afraid to go alone, Ben."

"Take you into Natchez?" Ben fell against the truck and laughed. "Are you serious, Fran?"

"Perfectly." Her chin came up haughtily.

"Fran, don't you know what has happened?"

"No. There is nothing on the television or radio. But it was something of a disaster, I should imagine."

"And it's all going to get better in a little while?"

"Certainly. The government will come in and straighten everything out."

Big Brother will take care of me. "Fran, instead of Natchez, would you like me to take you to Tara?"

"There you go again, being flip."

She really doesn't know, Ben thought, looking at her. She *is* a beautiful woman, though. Poor little insulated

121

rich girl doesn't have an inkling of what happened. He reached into the truck and took out the world-band radio.

"Fran, listen to this. Try to understand what has happened." He turned on the radio, preset on the distant ham band, and he watched her face as the tape changed to English.

"I . . . I don't understand," she finally said, her face white with shock.

"It means, Fran, that civilization, as we know it, is probably over for a time. Millions, a couple of billion, dead. As for Natchez, forget it. Forget it all, honey." His voice took on a harsher tone. "It's over. If there are only two people left alive in this parish—using that as a comparison—two out of fifteen thousand. That's . . ." He did some quick mental math. "Say, 125 people out of every million left alive in the world. Now the figure is probably higher than that, alive, I mean, but that's still pretty grim statistics." And, he thought, what if this stuff has affected the minds of some—and, perhaps, their bodies? Mutants? Possible. Greatest story I could ever write and no one around to read it.

Shit!

"You're serious, Ben?" Big eyes wide. Pretty eyes.

"I consider death to be very serious, Fran."

"Well . . . exactly, what does this mean?"

"It means," Ben said slowly, "that you're stuck with me, and I suppose I'm stuck with you."

"Oh, Lord!" she said, then rolled her eyes and fainted.

Ben caught her just before she cracked her head on the blacktop.

"What a marvelous way to start a relationship," he muttered.

FIVE

She opened her blue eyes and looked at him as they rolled along the parish road. "Where are you taking me?"

"Where would you like to go, Miss Fran?"

She closed her eyes. "I don't know."

"Then shut up and help me look until you decide. And open your eyes. Look for people—alive. There's got to be some in this parish."

"All the wrong sort, I'm sure."

You may be correct there, Ben thought. "Just look, baby, and keep your social comments to yourself."

"What is that big ugly thing?"

Ben looked down to see if his fly was open.

"This!" She touched the Thompson.

"It's a submachine gun."

She looked at Ben, looked at the SMG, rolled her eyes, then looked out the window, her side of the truck. She shook her head.

"It's real, Fran. I assure you of that."

"I'm beginning to believe, Ben. Look. There's smoke coming from that house over there." She pointed, saying it with about as much interest as if she were discussing the price of kumquats in the supermarket.

The day was cool, temperature in the low sixties. But

not cool enough for a fire, Ben reckoned. He pulled into the drive and looked for dogs. None. "Stay in the truck," he told Fran.

"I most certainly will not! And don't you dare order me about, Ben Raines."

Ben nodded, wondering when she was going into shock. Probably, he guessed, when we drive through town and she sees all the bodies . . . with the birds and the dogs and the hogs eating on them.

"Then come with me," he said. "No play on words intended."

She opened the door.

"There might be fifteen guys in there, all ready to rape you."

She closed the door and locked it.

Ben checked to see if he'd taken the keys out of the ignition. He had. It would be just like Fran to drive off and leave him.

He walked up the stone walkway and tapped on the door. He held the Thompson in his right hand. The door swung slowly open. Ben did not know the man, but had seen him in town a number of times. In his early sixties, the man appeared to be in good health.

"Afternoon," Ben said, speaking through the screen door. "I'm Ben Raines."

"The Lord giveth and the Lord taketh away," the man replied.

"I beg your pardon?"

"Armageddon. The battle has been fought. So sayeth the Lord."

Although not a student of the Bible, Ben had read it. He asked, "Who won—Good or Evil?"

The question seemed to confuse the man. He

stammered for a few seconds, then closed his mouth and shook his head.

"Do you realize what has happened?" Ben asked.

"Armageddon."

Ben sighed and looked past the man into the living room of the home. A fire was raging in the fireplace and a woman was sitting in a chair. She was dead. Ben could smell her from the porch.

"Do you want to come with us?" Ben asked. "Can we help in any way?"

The man shut the door in Ben's face.

He walked back to the truck and unlocked the door. As they were driving away, Fran asked, "Who was that man?"

"I don't know." Then he told her what he had seen.

"That's awful. What are you going to do about it?"

"Nothing." Ben shook his head. "Nothing I can do. I'm not a psychiatrist. But I'd say the man has stepped over the line. Pushed over it by what happened. He may come back around; he may not."

"That's a pretty cold-blooded attitude, Ben. That poor old man."

"Those poor old people who died from exposure," Ben countered.

She glared at him while Ben wondered if this was another side of her, or if she was merely acting for his benefit. "You keep harping on that, Ben Raines. What would you have had me do about them? —Not that it matters at this date."

"Help them." His reply was terse.

"I see," she said. "Well . . . I would have thought—from reading your books—not that I've read many of them, you understand—that you would be the last

125

person in the world to advocate wealth redistribution. I thought you were a conservative."

"I am a Conservative, Fran, in most of my thinking. But I just do not like to see innocent people suffer needlessly. Not when enormous wealth is—was—piled all around them. As for wealth redistribution . . . it was coming, Fran. It would have been a reality before the end of the century."

"My daddy said that was communism."

"While he sat sipping his hundred-year-old cognac, admiring his antiques, in a house valued at about a million dollars—none of those things did he, personally, lift a finger to earn. I don't buy it, Fran. But it's all moot now, isn't it? We're all equal."

She shuddered at the thought of being equal with everybody. How . . . unfair!

They drove for another few hours, but saw no signs of life in the parish. Ben pointed the nose of the truck toward Fran's mansion. She was unusually silent.

"I'm going to take you back to your home, Fran—you can pick up some clothes. Then we'll go to my place. Don't worry, you'll be safe."

"All right," she whispered.

Ben waited in the huge den of the home while Fran filled several suitcases. Ben had never seen such wealth in all his life. He chuckled, thinking, Hell of a lot of good it did them in the long run.

I guess, he mused, if I had all this, I'd fight to keep it, too. Or would I? he questioned. I've never even dreamed of living like this.

He had never dreamed that grandly. He had not been raised to dream of wallowing in great luxury.

126

He helped Fran with her luggage, then, back on the blacktop, she said, "What are we going to do, Ben?"

"First off, don't look at the bodies in that field just up ahead. There aren't as many as I thought, but enough."

Naturally, she looked, and promptly got sick.

Ben stopped the truck and let her out to barf by the side of the road. He stood outside the truck, Thompson at the ready, on the lookout for dogs.

"I *hate* to be sick!" she said, wiping her mouth with the handkerchief Ben had offered.

"You'll get used to the bodies," he said. "I remember in training, the first time I ever ate dog meat. I—"

She doubled over and began up-chucking again. She straightened up, wiped her mouth, tossed the handkerchief in the ditch, and said, *"Goddamn you!"*

"Sorry," Ben said, motioning her back in the truck. "And I mean that, Fran. Fran?" She looked at him. "You've got urp on your sleeve."

She nodded, brushed at the urp, then waved her hand forward, like a scout with a wagon train.

"Head 'em up and move 'em out," Ben muttered.

"I beg your pardon?"

"How old are you, Fran?"

"Twenty-eight."

"You probably wouldn't remember that TV show, then."

"I'm sure it was violent and ugly."

Ben sighed.

She was silent until they had driven through the small town with the odor of death hanging over it. Then she said, "Let's be honest with each other, Ben. I don't like you, and I probably will never like you very much."

"Agreed."

"But we're stuck with each other."

"How true."

"All right, then. For however long we are forced to keep company with each other—and I assure you, it will not be long—let's try to be civil, if not friends."

Ben grinned. "O.K., Fran."

"I don't like to cook; won't cook. I hate any type of housework, refuse to pick up after myself, and I whine when I don't get my way."

Ben laughed at her honesty. "Do you do windows?"

She laughed for the first time that day. "No! But"— she looked at him, appraising him through frankly sexual eyes—"I don't like to sleep alone."

"That's a fair trade-off, I suppose," Ben said.

Fran didn't drink; gave her hives, she said. So Ben stayed sober that night. The first time in years, other than when he was sick or visiting his parents, he went to bed completely sober, and was glad he did.

Fran came to him, in his bed, smelling of subtle perfume and naked, her dark hair fanning the pillow beside him. As his hands found her, stroking her, and his lips worked at her breasts, she moaned and found him, working his penis into hardness. She straddled him, guiding him into her wetness, taking him with one hard, hunching motion. And from that moment on, for a half-hour, Fran had been, as one good ol' boy had described his events of the night before to a group of buddies, "a frantic fuck." She might not be worth a damn for anything else, Ben reflected, but she knew what she wanted when it came to sex; how she wanted it, and how to get the most out of what was stuck in her.

Ben left her sleeping to stand by the window in the den,

gazing out at the darkness. He knew the full impact of what had happened had not yet come home to him—not in its awful entirety . . . its horrible finality.

Certainly, it had not struck home with Fran. Out of one hundred percent total, she maybe, at the most, was admitting to herself ten percent of the appalling facts surrounding her.

Ben suddenly made up his mind: there was no point in staying here. He wanted to see what had happened around the nation. He wanted to . . . bury (the word had finally become acceptable in his mind) his parents, brothers, and sisters. If he could find them.

And, as a writer, he was a naturally curious sort of person. He wished he could see years into the future, see just what would be built out of all this tragedy. Out of the ashes.

Something far better than what we had just destroyed, he hoped.

He went back into the bedroom and slipped quietly into bed. Fran snuggled close to him, murmuring softly, something inaudible.

Despite his feeling toward her, Ben felt a soft prodding of sorrow for the young woman. Her type of person had always bought her way through the world. Now . . . what would happen to people like that? Ben knew most of them were not survivors.

He took her into his arms, her nakedness warm against him, and despite the excitement building in him as he awaited the dawning, finally drifted off into sleep.

"I still don't understand why we have to leave." Fran pouted, looking back at Ben's house as they pulled out.

"Aren't you curious, Fran? Aren't you the least bit

129

curious to see what has happened?"

"I just wish everything would go back to what it used to be. The way it was."

The rich getting richer and the poor contemplating armed revolution, Ben thought. "It might be that way again, Fran. But it's going to take years."

"I don't want to talk about it," she said.

"I'll think about that tomorrow." Ben grinned.

She turned her head away and looked out the window.

Ben drove back into town and stopped at the sheriff's office, picking up another gas mask. He had a hunch they would need masks along the way.

They drove over the Mississippi River bridge at Natchez, with Ben having to stop three times to move vehicles. It was then the gas mask came in handy, for the occupants of the stalled cars and trucks were in bad shape, having been sealed up inside the vehicles, practically airtight. He made up his mind that when he got into Natchez, he would change vehicles, get one with a winch on the front and heavy-duty springs, for there was some other gear he wanted to pick up along the way.

At a dealership, Ben walked around the trucks, finally selecting a demonstrator that had all the equipment he needed, including a CB radio.

"I still don't see why we can't pick up a Cadillac or Lincoln," Fran bitched, as she helped transfer the gear. "Then we could travel in some degree of comfort instead of bouncing along in a stupid pickup truck like a couple of gypsies."

Ben realized there was no point in trying to explain, so he kept his mouth shut.

The stench in Natchez was horrendous, and Ben, fearing disease, made Fran put on her gas mask. He drove quickly through the small city, heading east, where he would intersect with Interstate 55.

"This mask is hot!" Fran griped, her voice muffled.

Ben said nothing, but when she attempted to remove the mask before they were through the city, he let her. She quickly put it back on, her face pale as the odor hit her nostrils.

They saw no humans alive on the sixty-mile run to the interstate, just west of Brookhaven, but the carrion and dogs were having a feast.

"Just keep your eyes straight ahead," Ben told her. That, he did not have to repeat twice. She closed her eyes and kept them closed.

Common sense told Ben to skirt Jackson, but his natural curiosity overwhelmed caution and he exited off the interstate and drove into downtown Jackson.

"Oh, God!" Fran cried, as she looked at the bodies littering the streets. "Ben, let's get *out* of here."

"Wouldn't you like to drive up to the Metrocenter and do a little shopping, honey? Just think of all the nice items you could pick up—literally."

Her glance told him what he could do with his suggestion.

As they were turning around, a bullet slammed through the top of the windshield and Fran screamed.

Man is not that far from the caves, not that far from fighting over turf, food, women, survival. And if that man has been a part of any rough branch of service, if he took his training seriously, and if he has the slightest hint of pugnacity in him, that man will quickly revert back to barbarism.

Over Fran's screaming as Ben shoved her to the floorboard, he spun the wheel hard and slid behind an overturned garbage truck, effectively hiding the pickup and giving them cover.

"Stay down!" he told her.

This time she gave no static. She nodded her head, her eyes wide.

It all returned to Ben, everything piled on him in a rush of brutal memories: the dehumanizing training in the jungles, the mountains, the deserts, the deep timber. The months in Nam. The quick, white-hot fire fights. Survive.

"Hey!" Ben yelled across the littered street. "We don't mean you any harm. What's the idea of shooting at us?" But in his mind his thoughts were not peaceful. Just expose yourself, you son of a bitch. Just give me something to shoot at.

"Tell the cunt to get out of the truck!" a voice yelled at him. "Give us the woman and you can carry your ass on outta here."

The voice came from above, the second story of the building opposite the truck. Don't get yourself sand-bagged in here, Ben thought. There's probably more than one of them.

He slipped from behind his pickup and eased his way along the overturned garbage truck. The words of his combat-wise instructor came to him: "Don't ever look over an object—look around it, from either end, carefully."

Ben slowly pushed his head forward until he could see through the gap between end-loader and truck bed. He saw them, two of them, looking out of windows from the second floor of the building. White men wearing ornate cowboy hats, with feathers and ornaments. Urban cowboys. About sixty yards maximum, Ben calculated.

Slowly, with no sudden movement, Ben pushed the muzzle of the SMG between the space and sighted them in. Bracing himself for the slam and rise of the muzzle, knowing the weapon would climb from left to right, Ben started from the left window, low, and pulled the trigger, holding it back, fighting the jump of the powerful weapon.

Thirty rounds of .45-caliber ammunition chipped stone from the building and smashed windows, the sound echoing through the concrete canyon. One man was flung out the window. He bounced on the sidewalk and lay still. Ben could hear the other man moaning and crying. He tried to call out; his words were mushy, not comprehensible. Ben knew then he had hit him in the face and jaw.

"Start the truck," Ben called to Fran. "Pull it up here. You're going to have to drive. I'll ride shotgun until we get back to the highway."

"That man's hurt, Ben," she said.

"Fuck him! He opened this dance, not me." He slipped around the truck and got in. "Let's go. Head for the interstate, north. When you get to that shopping center on the right, pull off on the frontage road and stop at the first phone booth."

"You want to call somebody?"

"No. I want to find the nearest armory. Preferably an infantry unit."

"It's a little late to enlist, isn't it?" She surprised him with humor.

Gutsy girl, he thought. "No. I want to prowl through their supplies."

"Why?"

"Drive, Fran. Just drive."

At the armory, Ben was relieved to find that while the unit had been called out, a lot of their equipment was still in place. A lot of men had either been too sick to report, or had said to hell with it and not reported in. Probably a combination of both, Ben thought.

Ben plugged the small bullet hole at the top of the windshield and then began prowling the armory. He found the weapons room, but the steel vault was locked, and impressive-looking. He told Fran to keep an eye open for people, then went in search of a sledge hammer. He went to work on the outside wall of the concrete block building. When he had hammered a respectable hole in the blocks, Ben pulled a deuce-and-a-half truck up to the wall, hooked a steel cable to the blocks, and pulled the wall apart. He hammered at the steel inner wall until he had worked a hole in it, then hooked a double cable to it and pulled the vault open enough to slip inside.

"You sure you weren't a safe-cracker before becoming a writer?" Fran asked. When he did not reply, she asked, "What in the world are you looking for, Ben?"

"Hah!" Ben yelled. "Found it!" He had discovered the M-16s, but Ben—like many vets—disliked the weapon with an emotion bordering on hatred. He would have loved to have found an old BAR, but those were getting rare. He handed Fran a box, then another box. He stacked several more boxes outside, then climbed out to join her.

"Ben—what is this junk?"

"Grenade launcher, 40-mm high-explosive cartridges, and three boxes of hand grenades, mixed. White phosphorous, HE, and smoke."

"Thank you," she said dryly. "I don't ever remember being so impressed with a reply. What in the crap are you going to do with this . . . shit!"

"Survive. I wish they had some Claymores in there."

She sighed. "Ben, I don't even want to know what that is."

"It's a mine. Hell! They don't even have any det cord. What kind of an outfit was this?"

"I never knew you were like this, Ben. I thought writers were sensitive people." She looked at him. "Well . . . with you, I should have known."

He tapped the case containing the grenade launcher. "I wish I could find a fact sheet on this thing. Fran? Go rummage through the files and see if you can locate a fact sheet on the M203 grenade launcher."

"Ben, you're impossible!"

He took her by the shoulders and rudely shook her. It startled her. When he spoke, his words were hard and his voice was rough. "Fran? Let me tell you the way it is, baby." She gazed up at him, taking in the seriousness in his eyes. "Now, you heard that redneck call you a cunt back there, didn't you?"

She nodded.

"Women, Fran, of any kind or color, young or old, are going to be at a premium, I think. And a good-looking woman is going to be a real prize, worth killing for and more. And you are a good-looking woman. You've got the disposition of a pit viper and you're stubborn as a mule, but you're a beautiful woman. Now, listen to me. There is no law and order. None! You can't call a cop, now, Fran. What has happened is a total, complete, one hundred percent breakdown of law and order and civilization and rules and ethics and decency. We're back to the jungles and the caves, honey. Dog eat dog and the strongest man wins the woman. That's the way it's going to be for a while. Believe it. You're not a stupid woman, Fran, so I

135

don't have to tell you what a gang-bang is, do I?"

She shook her head.

"You ever been pronged up the ass, Fran?"

"Certainly not!"

"Yeah? Well, don't give up hope, baby, 'cause lots of guys like it that way—good and tight. And without me, and all the firepower I can muster, you're fair game. And you've got a pretty ass, Fran."

"That's disgusting, Ben Raines. You're . . . you're just telling me all this to scare me; make me dependent on you so you'll have someone to sleep with, that's all. Isn't it, Ben?"

"Honey," Ben said patiently, "if, or when, I find a community or a gathering of decent, civilized people, I'll dump you on them faster than I'd turn loose a polecat. Because I've got things to do, places to go, and events to record. I hope we'll find that in Memphis—I thought perhaps Jackson. I believe there are people here, good people, but they're hiding, afraid, and they have good reason to be. So if not here, then Memphis. If not there, some other place where you'll be safe, and I will find you a safe place. But until then, we're stuck with each other, and I don't know why, but I feel an obligation to take care of you. So you do what I tell you to do, Fran—when I tell you to do it—and I'll keep you alive. But for now, you carry your butt into that office and find me that fact sheet."

She stared at him for a long half-minute, both of them silent. Her expression a mixture of fear and respect for the man standing in front of her. "All right," she said. "You're quite a man, Ben Raines."

"I'm a survivor."

"I'm . . . I'm glad it was you who found me."

He nodded his head slowly. He felt that was as close as he would get to hearing a thank you or a compliment from her lips.

"I'll get you that sheet," she said.

They spent the first night on the road in a home just off the interstate, a few miles south of Winona, Mississippi. The home was pleasant, well cared for, and devoid of bodies. Fran picked a few late-blooming flowers to decorate the dinner table while Ben made dinner.

"I wonder what happened to the people?" she asked.

"Probably, no one will ever know. Maybe they were visiting friends when . . . it happened. Maybe they panicked and ran away."

She watched Ben, watched him as she had never watched anyone before in her life. He was never without a gun, and his walk had become that of a stalking great cat. His face and eyes had changed, becoming hard and cold. And she thought she would not like this man for an enemy, for he was unlike the other men she had known in her life. She wondered about his military life, for she had known many men who had served, but none like this one. Ben Raines was . . . a predator type. And she admitted— to herself—she was a bit afraid of him. She also knew she was lucky it had been Ben that found her.

At night, he ordered the lights out. "The two-legged animals will be on the prowl," he told her. "Safer this way." He had then pulled down the garage door and locked it.

"When we get close to Memphis tomorrow," he said, as she lay in his arms, the sweat of love-making cooling and drying on them, "we'll start monitoring the CB much more closely. All channels. We'll find us a place to hole up and keep our eyes and ears open—we'll see who comes to us. Maybe you'll get lucky and some decent people will have banded together."

"You really want to be rid of me, don't you, Ben?"

"No," he replied honestly, and his answer surprised him. "Well," he added, "yes. In a way."

"That is a confusing reply, darling."

"You're a survivor, Fran—but not the same type as I am. But"—he chuckled—"I have grown quite fond of you. In a way."

"Yes," she said, a wry quality to her voice. "We have gotten close, haven't we? Go ahead, Ben. Drop the other shoe."

"I want to see this nation, honey—as much as I can. From the Atlantic to the Pacific, from border to border. I want to see what was destroyed, and how. I am going to chronicle this happening, this event, and it's going to take me a couple of years to do that—maybe more. I'm going to find a good tape recorder and about a million miles of tape and talk to people. Then I'm going to find a beat-up old portable typewriter, put the tapes in some form of order, and hole up in the mountains or by the sea for a couple of years, work ten hours a day, every day of the week, and write it, just the way it happened."

"Ben? Who, may I ask, is going to be around to read the damned old thing?"

He laughed and cupped a warm round breast, rubbing the nipple against his palm. She stirred against him, her hand seeking and finding his maleness, fingers encircling it, feeling it start the process of thickening. She masturbated him slowly as her breathing became shallow, then a hot pant.

"We will have a civilization again, Fran," he said,

138

slipping his hand down the softness of her belly, to touch the dampness of pubic hair. His fingers found her and parted her, working in and out, his thumb on her erect clit. "A civilization . . . someday. And people will want to know exactly what happened. And they will read my work."

Ben knew she was not a student of history or even much of a reader when she asked, "But you'll be long dead by then, baby—so, who cares? So what?"

He kissed her and parted her lovely legs, slipping between them, positioning himself. He knew he was going to miss her after they parted.

"Ben?" she said, grasping his penis and inserting the head inside her.

"Yes, Fran?"

"Fuck me, Ben!"

Just outside of Memphis, south of the airport, Ben found a house that was free of bodies and was set back from the street, amid a large number of trees. He and Fran settled in. Once they saw a car drive slowly past, and another time a pickup truck, but he made no attempt to hail them, for they were full of hard-looking men, heavily armed, and they did not look like church-going types.

When the wind was right, the stench from the city was horrible.

By monitoring the CB, Ben learned there were people alive in Memphis, several thousand by the way one group talked, and it was that one group that interested Ben.

It appeared they were occupying about a ten-square-block area and clearing about a block a day, also sending out scouts to search for survivors. Their conversation on the CBs was intelligent, and they, of all the groups Ben monitored, did not use profanity. The base station used channel twenty-five and the call sign of Genesis. Ben decided to take a chance.

On the morning of their third day in Memphis, Ben used the CB in his truck to call them. "Break-two-five for Genesis," he called.

"This is Genesis. Who are you?"

"I'm friendly," Ben said. "But I have definitely seen some unfriendly types."

Genesis chuckled. "Yes, we do seem to have a few of those still roaming the city."

"I'm from Louisiana and I have a woman with me. I need to leave her in a safe place. I . . . may not be back."

"We're Christians, friend. She'll be safe with us. You don't seem to be too far away, but getting to us may prove dangerous. We're cleaning out the criminal element and the looters daily, but they still far outnumber us. We're just better armed and have some military people with us. Also U.S. Senator Hilton Logan is here. This is sort of a command post, you might say."

"Logan," Ben muttered, the mike off. "Of all the people to spare, you have to spare that bastard."

"That's sacrilege, Ben," Fran said.

"No, that's just common sense, Fran." He picked up the mike. "I'm driving a dark blue pickup truck. I'll be there shortly."

"We'll intercept and cover for you. Good luck."

Ben turned to Fran. "I think they're good people, Fran. Despite the fact that they took in Hilton Logan. You'll be safe. If I don't think you will be, I won't leave you with them."

She smiled. "Hilton Logan was going to be the next President," she said. "He's been a bachelor all his life.

140

Maybe it's time to change all that."

Ben laughed at her and knew then that Fran was a survivor.

"Aren't you terribly nervous with all these big bad guns all over the place?" Ben needled Logan. "How many times have you pissed your pants since you've been here, just thinking about all these pistols?"

The men stood alone. Fran had immediately been taken in by the women.

"I gather, Mr. Raines, you don't approve of my gun-control bill."

"I believe my first words when I'd learned it had passed were 'that goddamned do-gooder motherfucker.' I was, of course, referring to you, Logan."

The senator flushed. "How did an attractive, lovely woman like Mrs. Piper come to find herself in the company of one such as you?"

"Just lucky, I guess." Ben smiled at him. "Been swimming lately, Senator?"

The blood rushed to Logan's face.

Logan had been swimming off the coast of Florida when he had suddenly begun screaming that he was under attack by sharks, and one had just bitten him on the leg. When he had recovered from his swoon and had been pulled ashore, it was discovered he had some old fishing line wrapped around his ankle and thigh. Hilton Logan was not famous for his grace under pressure.

"You are despicable, Raines!" He spat the words.

"And you're a coward." Ben walked away, deliberately turning his back to the man.

That was the beginning of the hate between the two men. It would intensify in the years ahead.

Ben left an hour after dropping Fran off. The people begged him to stay, warning him of the horrors they had heard about, telling him of the dangers. But Ben was firm in his commitment.

"I'm a writer," he told a U.S. Army colonel. "Maybe not a very good one, but I wonder how many of us survived the . . . holocaust. What if I'm the only one left? And please don't think me pretentious for saying that. Someone has to travel this nation, record all that's happened, and I'm going to do it."

The colonel shook his hand. "Eight cities went under with nukes. Detroit, Washington, New York, Miami, Omaha, Houston, all the western part of Missouri, Baltimore, and San Francisco. That's the report I have so far. I suspect there are many more. The east coast from New Jersey all the way up to the Maine border is gone, so I'm told. The rest of the cities took germ-type warheads."

Ben told him of the tape-recorded message and where to find it on the band. The colonel shook his head. "I'll just be goddamned. I knew about the double double cross. Looks like now we have a triple cross." He told Ben all he knew about the events leading up to the war, then clasped him on the shoulder. "Luck to you, Mr. Raines."

"It's you who needs the luck, Colonel," Ben said. "If you're planning on staying around that bastard Logan."

"I heard that. Talk is the military—what's left of us— is going to install him as acting president."

"Good God!"

"My words exactly when I heard it. Look, Mr. Raines . . ." The colonel's words were spoken low so only Ben could hear. "What are you going to do with your Rebels?"

"My what?" Ben was taken aback.

"Your Rebels, sir. General Travee told General MacPeters that Col. Bull Dean called his Rebel commanders just at the last minute and put you in charge of them. 'Bout five thousand of them. Said he told Travee 'that ought to sober up the drunken son of a bitch.' Begging your pardon, sir."

"It's news to me, Colonel."

"Well, it's true, sir. The Rebels probably came out of this better than anybody—they knew what was coming down; had preset places to hide, with food and water and bottled air and protective gear."

"Where are they, now?"

The colonel shrugged. "I have no idea, sir."

Fran came to him and kissed him lightly and in a very ladylike way on the cheek, while Hilton Logan stood back and scowled at Ben. Being the best-looking woman in the area—that Ben had seen—the two were drawn like a magnet. The senator being somewhat of a ladies' man.

If, Ben thought, the ladies had a taste for shit.

"Ah do thank y'all so much, Mr. Raines." She gushed sorghum molasses all over him, for Logan's benefit.

Ben smiled. "Ah, too, have enjoyed yore company, ma'am." He returned a measure of ribbon cane syrup. "You have been like a light in the wilderness to me."

She leaned close, her body hiding the movement of her right hand as it gently squeezed Ben's crotch. "Don't lay it on too thick, you damned Yankee—he'll think we're both nuts!"

SIX

So now Ben was alone. He felt her absence more than he would have ever thought although he knew eventually they would have devoured each other with their conflicting personalities. But he missed her, nonetheless.

Steady pussy; he smiled as he drove. But he knew it was more than that.

He made it through Memphis without incident and headed north, on the interstate, toward Cairo. He spent the night in New Madrid, Missouri, a small boot-heel town. And as the night spread its blanket of darkness around him, it was then that Ben missed Fran the most.

The next morning, in Sikeston, Missouri, a few miles north of New Madrid, Ben pulled into a shopping center and found a good cassette recorder and several good quality cassettes. He also picked up a small portable typewriter. Turning at a slight noise, Ben saw a small boy, no more than nine or ten, racing out of the store. He called to him, but the boy refused to stop. Ben thought about chasing him, then gave it up. There were hundreds, thousands of places to hide. He only hoped the boy was not on his own, for Sikeston's streets and, he was sure, its homes, were littered with the dead, stiff and stinking.

He drove around the town, and saw a few more live people, none of whom would answer his call. He said to hell with it and pulled back on the interstate, heading north.

As he drove, he experimented with the recorder, making the first of what would eventually be thousands of vocal notes and observations and comments.

He thought about what the colonel had said to him and shook his head in disbelief. "Commander of a Rebel army!" He laughed. "Shit!"

And as he drove, he found the memory of Fran already fading as the excitement of what lay before him intensified and spread itself out in his mind, exposing to his mental light all the ramifications and historical aspects of his one-man Odyssean undertaking.

"Maybe a hundred years from now I'll be famous." Ben grinned, speaking aloud.

He would be, but it would be for something other than his writings.

As he crossed the river into Cairo, Ben slowed and became more alert, scanning the channels of his CB for any chatter—good or bad.

A voice leaped out at him. "Truck jist crossed the bridge."

Ben turned on the recorder, the volume up high to catch all the words.

"How many?" another voice asked.

"Jist the one dude."

"No pussy with him?"

"Naw."

"Damn! I don't think they's a goddamned cunt left in this town. How old is this dude? If he's a kid and he's pretty, we can take turns cornholin' him."

"Cain't tell. He's gittin' out of my sight, turnin' off on 51."

"We'll foller him, laid back, sort of. You listenin', Ralphie?"

"Yeah," Ralphie answered.

"You and Tarver take your pickup and block this side of 51, over there by that old beer joint we used to hang out at—you 'member it?"

"Yeah. Will do. If he's too ugly to cornhole, we'll have us some fun with him 'fore we kill him."

Ben's smile was savage, a pulling back of the lips into a snarl. "Sorry to spoil your fun, boys," he muttered. "But I'm going to see if I can't rid the world of some human scum."

Why is it, he thought, the scum always seem to survive any tragedy?

He shrugged away the age-old question and smiled grimly. What those scumballs didn't know was that Ben knew Cairo probably better than they knew it. He'd had his first woman—a whore—in Cairo, back when strippers were still bumping and grinding in various clubs.

Ben turned down a side street, jumped out of the truck, and walked to the rear. He quickly assembled the antitank weapon. It was a one-shot, one-time affair, and Ben had never understood why the Army had replaced the bazooka with it, as the bazooka could be used over and over. But, he didn't recall the Army ever asking for his opinion. He readied the LAW and laid it in the bed of the truck; then clicked his Thompson off safety.

Soon, he heard the sounds of a car approaching, and smiled when he saw the vehicle: a new Cadillac. Then he knew the mentality of the men after him: "white trash," folks in the south called them, and they were correct in that name. He listened to the CB in his truck to be certain he was about to zap the right men. The speaker rattled as

146

the volume grew louder with the approach of the Caddy. Ben waited until all transmissions were concluded, then stepped out of the alley and gave the men a full dose of .45-caliber medicine. Thirty rounds.

The Cadillac slewed to one side, the windshield a maze of pocked spiderwebs. It rolled up on the curb, banged into a storefront, then died in a gush of steam from the ruptured radiator.

Ben looked inside to see if they were both dead—they were—and walked slowly back to his truck, inserting a fresh clip from habit. There was little emotion in him as he pulled out into the street. He did not feel himself an avenging angel; did not feel that he, and he alone, had been appointed to rid the land of vermin. He did not even feel much satisfaction. (Is one supposed to feel satisfaction after stepping on a roach?) But he did feel that this scene would, in all probability, be repeated, if he lived, many more times on his journey.

Ben drove out of the city proper and headed north on 51. He stopped before he reached a bend in the road and slipped up behind a house, carrying the lightweight LAW. He had chosen the LAW over the grenade launcher because he felt it more accurate. He had taken five of them from the armory—all they had.

He looked around the corner of the house. The truck, with two men sitting in the cab, was parked about seventy-five meters away. He opened the LAW to its extended position, lifted front and rear sights, armed it, then dropped to one knee and sighted into the truck, making several adjustments before being satisfied. He fired the 66-mm rocket and it was dead-on accurate.

After the roaring concussion, when the glass and metal had ceased its hot raining, the area was quiet. Ben tossed the LAW aside and walked back to his truck. He suddenly felt eyes on him. He spun, the pistol jumping into his hand.

Several older men and women stood by the side of the road. One of the men held up his hand in a gesture of submission. "Peace, friend," he said. "We mean you no harm. You've rid this town of filth, and we thank you for it. We were listening to those heathen talk on our CBs."

The men were dressed in dark clothing, flat-brimmed hats; the women in long dark dresses, bonnets.

"Why didn't you men arm yourselves and do it?" Ben asked. "Why wait and let someone else risk his life?"

"Our religion forbids the taking of human life," the older man replied.

"Then you're fools!" Ben said. He had no patience with a people who would not defend themselves or their country.

"The Lord provided you," the man said, not taking exception at Ben's hot remark.

"This time," Ben countered. "The next time might turn out much differently."

The man shrugged. "The Lord will provide."

"Wonderful," Ben said, his voice loaded with sarcasm. He opened the door to his truck. "I have to go find my sister and her family." The tape recorder was running, recording it all. "I want them to have a Christian burial, if possible."

"We have been doing that," the spokesman said. "Street by street. For health reasons as well as decency. Where did your sister live?"

Ben told him.

The man consulted a notepad. "We have seen to that."

"Thanks."

"It is we who owe you, brother."

"Do you know what happened?" Ben asked. "Any idea what brought all this on?"

The man again shrugged. "The Lord's will."

"Yeah," Ben said dryly. "Right. As good an answer as any, I suppose."

The man smiled.

Ben got into his truck and drove away, up 51, heading toward the junction with highway 37. The darkly dressed people stood out in his mirrors, fading quickly. They looked so vulnerable standing there.

But, Ben thought—they had survived.

At a farmhouse just a few miles south of Marion, Ben pulled into the drive and looked for a long time at the place of his birth and his youth and his growing up—the good years, including the lickings he had received and so richly deserved, every one of them. He really did not want to go inside that old two-story home. But he felt he had to do it. Reluctantly, he drove up to the house and got out.

He stood for a time, looking around him, all the memories rushing back, clouding his mind and filling his eyes. He took in the land he had helped his father farm. Fighting back tears, he climbed the steps and opened the front door.

His parents were sitting on the couch, an open Bible on the coffee table in front of them. Ben's dad had his arm around his wife of so many years, comforting her even in death.

They had been dead for some time and were not a pretty sight for Ben to witness.

Ben walked through the house, touching a picture of the family taken years before, when life had been simpler. Suddenly, he whirled away from the scene and walked from the house, leaving his parents as he had found them. He carefully locked the front door and stood for a time, looking through the window at his parents. Through the dusty window, it appeared that his mother and father were sitting on the couch, discussing some point in the Bible. Ben preferred that scene. He walked from the porch, got into his truck, and drove away. He did not look back.

He spent the night on the outskirts of Mt. Vernon, fighting back depression that threatened to grow dark within him. Then, just before sleep took him, he felt a strong new resolve build within him. . . . What he was doing, this journey of his, was right and just; it had to be done. Ben wanted to discover why he was spared when so many others had died. Did the wasp stings have anything to do with it, or everything? Why had the deadly gases that had swept over the land killed some and not others? And he was right and correct in killing those who would prey on others less able to defend themselves.

Ben felt he was not alone in his one-man style of justice. He felt there were others like him throughout the country—the world. They, too, felt an outrage when witnessing the scum and slime who traveled the land, raping and killing and torturing at their leisure. Perhaps many who felt that outrage did not have automatic weapons and what was left of modern technology at their disposal; perhaps they were using clubs and stone axes, but they were his counterparts, nonetheless.

He stirred on the bed, shaking away his meandering philosophizing. Finally, he slept, dreaming of his parents and of an army of Rebels with no commander, no leader, no direction. He woke up tired.

His brother's home in Mt. Vernon was burned to the foundation. He had no idea where else to look, so he drove away, his CB on. There were people alive in the town, but they ran away when Ben approached them.

He angled to the northwest until he picked up highway 127, staying with it, passing through a half-dozen small towns, stopping in each to look around, to make recorded notes. There were people alive in each place, but they appeared to be in some sort of shock, not knowing what to do. It appeared to Ben they seemed to be waiting for someone to *tell* them what to do. The smell of rotting human flesh was almost overpowering.

"Why don't you clean up these dead bodies?" Ben asked them. "What are you going to do, just leave them to rot?"

"What business is it of yours?" he was asked.

Ben shrugged and drove away. "The hell with you," he muttered.

He saw, he guessed, about a hundred people alive in Springfield, but they were not receptive to Ben's questions. Most ran away when he approached them. He found one group that seemed to have some direction about them. They were not overly friendly, but neither were they openly hostile. Nine whites and three blacks; two women, ten men. He asked them a few questions, but the answers he received were of the monosyllable type.

"What are you people going to do?" he asked one of the women. She appeared to be the leader of the group.

She looked at him and walked away without replying.

End of interview.

Ben got the strong impression they all wished he would just leave.

Ben buried his second brother and his family in a common, shallow grave. Then, after working all afternoon, he realized how pointless it all was.

Millions, billions of people were dead all over the world, with no dignity in their dying. (Is there ever any dignity in dying?) Why should his family be any different? What the hell was the purpose of it all?

Ben threw the shovel on the grass and walked away as the cool fall winds blew across the yard. And that raised another issue in Ben's mind: he did not want to be caught in the North during winter; winter was rough in Illinois even under the best of conditions. No, he would drive on to Normal, see about his sister, then on to the suburbs of Chicago to see about his brother, and then he would head for the deep South or the deserts of the West.

No—he shook his head—let's take it, if we're going to do it, all the way: over to the east as far as possible, then work down the east coast, all the way down to Florida. Slowly work your way back up during the last of the winter weeks, then head west. Let's do it right, or not at all.

He found his sister—or what was left of her—in the back yard of her home in Normal. Dogs, or some kind of animal, had been feeding. Despite his earlier feelings, Ben could not leave her like that. He scraped a narrow grave in the back yard and then, gagging, moved his sister into the trench and covered that with earth and stones and concrete blocks.

Her husband he left in the house. In bed. Son of a bitch

had probably been taking a nap while his wife mowed the yard. Ben wouldn't have buried him even if he had been outside. Her husband was (or had been) a college professor at a local institution; a left-leaning type who got his nuts off just thinking about people like Hilton Logan, who wept every time a mass murderer was taken to the gas chamber or the barbecue chair. Ben despised him and the feeling was shared.

Ben drove on to the suburbs of Chicago, being very careful, all his senses working, for the chatter on the CB—on almost every channel—was picking up, and a lot of it was unfriendly. The hatred that Ben had sensed between the races had leaped to the surface after the catastrophe.

He heard a lot of "motherfuckers" and "honkies" on the CB, and a lot of what Ben called jive-talk. He also heard a lot of "nigger bastards, coons, shines, and porch monkeys."

The hate had erupted.

Ben had no intention of driving into downtown Chicago.

There was very little actual fear behind that decision, but a great deal of common sense. Ben was not a racist, but he did not believe in giveaway programs that merely squandered money without solving any social ills. He was an advocate of forcing people to work, but only as a last resort. He had always felt that hard work, some conformity, and some bending was needed from both sides of the color line.

Of course, he thought, all that is moot, now.

He adjusted the volume of his recorder to catch all the hatred that sprang from the speaker of his CB.

He gathered that a race war was building between the

153

blacks in the city and the whites in the suburbs. And he guessed, from listening to the chatter, that there must be fifteen or twenty thousand people alive in and around the city. So it was shaping up to be a hell of a battle.

What stupidity, Ben thought. We should all be working to build a wonderful new world from out of the ashes, all this misery. We should be putting past hates and distrust behind us, but instead, here we go again; nothing has changed.

Fools!

"The hell with you all!" Ben muttered. "Go ahead—kill each other. But you are going to regret you stayed in the city come this December, when the cold and snow hits."

He encountered no trouble until he reached the town where his brother lived. The roads were blocked and armed white men patrolled the area. Ben had to smile at the sight. A sad smile. Back to the jungles, he thought.

"I'm trying to reach my brother, if he's still alive," Ben told a group of men. "Carl Raines."

"I know him. He's alive. What do you want with him?"

"Well, goddamn it!" Ben almost shouted the words. "He's my brother. What the hell do you think I want with him?"

"Relax, mister," the man said, softening his words with a faint smile. "Sure, you can go see him, but you're not leaving once you get in."

"What?"

"We need every gun and every white man we can get in this fight. We're gonna wipe those damned niggers out once and for all. Then we can rebuild a decent society."

I don't believe I'm hearing this, Ben thought. He

stared at the man.

"Let him go in, see his brother." The voice spoke from behind Ben.

Ben turned to face an older, neatly dressed man. In his late fifties or early sixties, Ben guessed. "I thank you, mister," Ben said.

"We're all a little bit tense here, I'm afraid." The man offered an apology along with an explanation. "We're outnumbered, you see. I'll wait for you here; see you get back out. We have no right to detain you. This isn't your fight."

Ben nodded his thanks and drove to his brother's house through what appeared to be an armed camp. His brother was waiting for him in the front yard, a walkie-talkie on his belt. He had been alerted to Ben's arrival.

It had been eight years since the brothers had seen one another; the moment was awkward after they shook hands.

Ben opened the conversation. "Get Mary and the kids, Carl . . . let's get the hell out of here."

His brother shook his head. "No. Mary's still alive—thank God. Alice, she's the oldest, you know . . . she made it O.K. All the rest are dead, near as we can tell. Isn't safe to go into the city. Can't search for them. I hope they're dead. Be better than gettin' raped by them coons."

"I'm sorry, Carl. I saw to our brothers and sisters. Mom and Dad. All dead."

The older man nodded. "Figured they was. Lot of others in the same boat. Terrible thing. No, I'm not leaving, Ben. I'm staying here and protecting my home against looters. The niggers are tearing up the city—rapin' and killin'."

"Protect your home! Hell, Carl, there must be ten million homes standing empty across this country. Take your choice—live in the governor's mansion if you like."

"Be niggers in there, eatin' fried chicken and smackin' those five-pound lips. Doin' the jumpin' funky-humpy in the governor's office."

Ben stared at him for a moment, then shook his head. "What's changed you, Carl? You never used to feel this way. We came from conservative stock, yes, but you were not brought up to be a racist."

His brother's look was just short of being unfriendly. "You changed into a nigger-lover now, Ben? All them words you been writin' done this?"

"I won't even dignify that with a reply, Carl."

His brother refused to let go. "You didn't used to be a nigger-lover, Ben."

"Carl, I believe some of the things wrong with this nation—back when we had a nation, that is—could, and probably should be placed on the blacks' doorstep; probably *will* be placed there by historians. Me, for one. The give-me, give-me-more programs. But you can't, in all honesty, blame the black race for this"—he waved his hand—"horror."

"I'm not sayin' that, Ben. I'm sayin' now is the time to either get rid of them or put them back in their place."

"Get rid of an entire race! Ben, that's genocide. You can't be serious. Their place? Where the hell is that, Carl?"

"It damned sure ain't alongside me, Brother. Ben, I'm not gonna stand here and argue race with you; you always was too good with words. I'm just a workin' man. Besides, what we're doin' here . . . well, it's the principle of it."

"The principle of it!" The words rolled from Ben's mouth. He laughed in his brother's face. "How about the black children, Carl—you going to kill them, too?"

His brother shrugged. "Little niggers grow up to be big niggers, Ben. They're all taught from birth to lie and steal and lust after white women."

Ben was shocked and his face was tight with anger. "Carl . . . you don't mean that. Now, I'll admit I don't have many black friends." He grimaced. "Matter of fact, I don't have any. But you can't believe *all* black people are the way you describe them." He looked at his brother. "Carl," he asked slowly, "do you have any Jews in this . . . gathering of yours?"

His brother shook his head. "No. All they are is a bunch of nigger-lovers. Just like the goddamn ACLU. Hell, the Jews and the niggers support it. You're the one who has changed, Ben—not me. So maybe you'd just better carry your ass on out of here. You don't fit in with us."

"I sure as hell don't, Carl. That's one thing we agree on. Carl? How are you going to survive this winter? There's no electricity. Do you have a fireplace? How about food?"

"We'll get by with heating oil—lots of that in storage. We'll get the food from stores and warehouses."

Ben smiled. "By looting it, Carl? Isn't that what the blacks are doing in the city?"

"Why don't you just carry your Jew-lovin', nigger-lovin' ass on out of here?" The voice ripped at him from behind.

Ben turned, his eyes widening in disbelief. The small, wiry-looking man was dressed in a Nazi storm trooper's uniform. A swastika on his sleeve.

157

Ben looked around him: a crowd had gathered, and their faces were hostile. This was solid middle-class America glaring at him. Ben turned his gaze at his brother.

"Aw . . . no, Carl—not this. You're a vet. You fought against what this"—he waved his hand at the Nazi—"turd represents."

"Maybe, baby Brother," Carl said, "we were wrong back in '44. George, there, he's convinced me that back then our forces should have let Hitler go on and wipe out the Jews. Then we should have linked up with him and gone into Africa and cleaned up on the jungle-bunnies. I'm glad I was too young for the second world war, Ben. I think I'd have been ashamed to admit I was a part of it. Jews and niggers, Ben—they're just alike. And we're gonna do what should have been done a long time ago."

Ben stood for only a few seconds, looking at his brother. "I don't know you anymore, Carl."

"Get out, Ben. Right now. 'Fore some of my friends take it upon themselves to whip your nigger-lovin' ass."

"My pleasure to leave, Carl. I'm just glad Mamma and Dad don't have to see this."

The brothers did not shake hands. Ben brushed past him and the Nazi-lover, fighting back a very strong urge to knock the storm trooper on his butt.

SEVEN

Ben drove fast and he drove with anger eating at him. He just could not believe his brother had changed so, and he wondered just how many men and women this George commanded. Too many, he was certain. One would have been too many.

He drove first to the south, out of the suburbs, and then cut east, crossing over into Indiana. Just before dark, he pulled into a motel off Interstate 65. Thompson in hand, Ben prowled the motel. In one wing he found the rooms had been occupied and they held stinking, stiffening dead. But the entire east wing was clean and free of bodies. Ben chose a room, found the laundry room, and picked up sheets, pillowcases, and blankets. He was walking back to his room when he saw the dark shapes standing in the parking area.

About a half-dozen black men and women. No, he looked closer, one of the women was white—he thought.

Ben made no move to lift the SMG, but the click of his putting it off safety was very audible in the stillness.

"Deserting your friends in the suburbs?" a tall black man asked. Ben could detect no hostility in his voice.

"I might ask the same of you," Ben said.

The man laughed. "A point well taken. So . . . it appears we have both chosen this motel to spend the night. But . . . we were here first—quite some time. We were watching you. So . . . which one of us leaves?"

"None of us," Ben said. "If you don't trust me, lock your doors."

The man once again laughed. "My name is Cecil Jeffreys."

"Ben Raines."

"Ben Raines? Where have I heard that name? The writer?"

"Ah . . . what price fame?" Ben smiled. "Yes. Sorry, I didn't mean to be flip."

"I didn't take it that way. We're in the same wing, just above you. My wife is preparing dinner now—in the motel kitchen. Would you like to join us?"

"Yes, very much so. I'm tired of my own cooking."

"Well, then . . . if you'll sling that Thompson, I'll help you with your linens."

Ben did not hesitate, for he felt the request and the offer a test. He put the SMG on safety and slung it, then handed the man his pillows. "You're familiar with the Thompson?"

"Oh, yes. Carried one in Vietnam. Green Beret. You?"

"Hell-Hound."

"Ah! The real bad boys. Colonel Dean's bunch. You fellows were headhunters."

"We took a few ears."

They walked shoulder to shoulder down the walkway, Cecil's friends coming up in the rear. Ben resisted a very strong impulse to look behind him.

Cecil smiled. "If it will make you feel better, go ahead and look around."

"You a mind reader?" Ben laughed.

"No, just knowledgeable of whites, that's all."

"As you see us," Ben countered.

"Good point. We'll have a good time debating; I see that."

They came to Ben's room.

"We'll see you in the dining room, Ben Raines. I have to warn you though . . ."

Ben tensed; he was boxed in, no way to make a move.

". . . The water is ice-cold. Bathe very quickly."

Ben, like many, if not most, whites, had never socialized with blacks, never sat down at a table with a black person to have dinner—except for his time in the service, and there had been few blacks in his outfit. In truth, Ben did not really know or trust black people. He didn't know why he didn't trust them. He just didn't.

Ben despised the KKK, the Nazi Party—groups of that ilk—and he would never, ever, hurt a black person, unless that person was trying to hurt him; but, he admitted, as he bathed—very quickly—in the cold water . . . I guess I really don't like black people.

But why? he asked himself. Have you ever tried to know or like a black person?

No, he concluded.

Well, you're about to do just that.

He walked to the dining room through a very light mist. The smell of death hung in the damp air, but it was an odor that Ben scarcely noticed anymore.

"Mr. Raines," Cecil greeted him in the candlelit dining area. "How about a martini? No ice, of course, but I make a wicked martini."

"That would be great." A martini-drinking black? He

had thought most blacks drank Ripple and Thunderbird.

Come on, Raines! You're thinking like an ignorant bigot.

He sat down at the table. Moment of truth. He smiled a secret smile.

"Something funny, Mr. Raines?" a slender man seated to his right asked.

"Not really. Sad, more than anything else, I suppose."

"Ever sat down and had dinner with blacks?" a woman inquired. Her tone was neither friendly nor hostile . . . just curious.

Hell, Ben thought—they're as curious about me as I am about them. "Not really. Only in the service."

"Well, I can promise you we won't have ham hocks or grits," she said with a smile.

"To tell the truth,"—Ben looked at her—"I like them both."

A few laughed aloud; the rest smiled. An uncomfortable silence fell around them; it was punctuated by shifting of feet, clearing of throats, much looking at the table, the walls. It seemed that no one had anything to say, or, as was probably the case, knew how to say it.

"May I help anyone do anything?" Ben asked. "With dinner," he added.

"We thought we'd serve it buffet-style," Cecil said. "Easier that way. Pardon my curiosity, Mr. Raines—"

"Ben. Just call me Ben."

"Ben. Good. I'm Cecil. But I believe I read somewhere that you lived in Louisiana."

"That's correct."

"You're a long way from home."

"Burying my family: brothers, sisters, parents. Cairo, Mt. Vernon, Springfield, Normal, then into the suburbs of Chicago."

The woman Ben had thought white—he still wasn't sure what she was—asked, "They're all dead?"

"All but the brother in Chicago." He looked at her. She was very good-looking. No negroid features about her; but Ben sensed she was black, at least to some degree. "Your family?" he asked her.

"All dead. Cecil and his wife found me wandering . . . walking out of Chicago . . . getting out while I could. They took me in."

Cecil's wife entered the room and announced that dinner was ready. Ben was introduced to her. Lila. She was friendly and spoke as though she was highly educated. Cecil told him she had been a college professor. The news was not surprising.

The meal was deliciously prepared, and all ate slowly, enjoying the luxury of good food and good conversation. No one mentioned the slight odor that hung about them.

"Have any of you heard about radiation levels in and around the cities that took nuclear hits?" Ben asked.

"The upper east coast is the worst," Cecil said. "Those cities took a concentration of bombs, most of them nuclear. San Francisco took a low-level hit. What is it called . . . ? I don't remember. Kills the people but leaves the buildings intact. The United States was lucky in that respect. I've heard Russia and China really are gone."

"How about winds that carry the radiation?"

Cecil shrugged. "There again, nuclear warfare had progressed considerably . . . in our favor. I have heard there is no danger from that. But . . . who knows. I'm not a scientist."

Ben began putting faces and names together. The woman who had asked about his family was Salina.

Salina Franklin. There were Jake and Nora, a Clint and Jane Helms, and Anwar Ali Kasim.

Ben took an immediate dislike to Kasim, and felt equally bad vibes coming from him. Kasim confirmed his feelings when he spoke.

"How come you didn't stay with your brother and his buddies and help kill all the niggers in the city?" Kasim asked, his eyes alive with hate.

Salina rolled her eyes and shook her head in disgust. Lila sighed and looked at her husband. Cecil said, "Kasim, you're a jerk!"

"And he's white!" Kasim spat his hate at Ben.

"Does that automatically make me bad?" Ben asked.

"As far as I'm concerned, yes," Kasim said. "And I don't trust you."

"Maybe," Salina said, her words quiet, "he's just a man who sat down to have a quiet dinner. He hasn't bothered a soul—brother." She smiled at her humor.

Kasim didn't share her humor. "I see," he said, the words softly spoken but tinged with hate. "Well, now . . . Zebra got herself a yearning for some white cock?"

She slapped him hard, hitting him in the mouth with the back of her hand, bloodying his lips.

Kasim drew back his hand to hit her and found himself looking down the barrel of a .44 magnum. Cecil jacked back the hammer and calmly said, "I would hate to ruin this fine dinner, Kasim, since raw brains have never been a favorite of mine. But if you hit her, I'll blow your fucking head off!"

Kasim looked at the man in disbelief. He nodded his head when he saw the look in Cecil's eyes. "You'd kill me . . . for him?" He jerked his head toward Ben.

164

"You're twisting words out of context, Kasim," Cecil said, the muzzle of the .44 never wavering. "But you're good at that."

Kasim put both hands on the table, one on each side of his plate. "You know what those white bastards did to my sister."

"I know. But Ben Raines didn't do it."

"He's still white!"

Ben rose from the table. "I'd better leave, I suppose."

"Yes." Cecil surprised him. "I think it would be best. And I'm sorry for having to say that. I was looking forward to some intelligent conversation later on."

"Perhaps we'll meet again," Ben suggested.

"You put your white ass in New Africa, motherfucker," Kasim said, "and it'll be buried there."

"I will make every effort to avoid New Africa," Ben promised. "Wherever that might be."

"Mississippi, Alabama, and Louisiana," Kasim said. "A black nation. All black."

Ben smiled. "My home's in Louisiana, Kasim, or whatever your goddamned name is. And I'll give you a bit of advice. I'm going back to my room and go to sleep. I'll pull out just after dawn tomorrow. There will be no trouble in this motel—that I start, that is. But if I ever see you again . . . I'll kill you!"

"Words." Kasim sneered at him. "Big words. How about trying it now? Just you and me?"

"Drag your ass out of the chair, hotshot." Ben smiled.

"Cool it, Kasim," Cecil warned him. "You're outclassed with Ben. Let it lie."

Kasim met Ben's eyes for a long moment, then dropped his gaze. Ben walked away, toward the door. He paused, turned around. "It was a delicious meal, Mrs. Jeffreys. I thank you."

She smiled and nodded.

Ben's eyes touched Salina's. She smiled at him.

He walked out into the rainy night, leaving, he hoped, the hate behind him.

He was loading his gear into the truck at dawn, tying down the tarp when he heard footsteps. He turned, right hand on the butt of the .45 belted at his waist.

Salina.

"We all feel very badly about last night, Mr. Raines. All except Willie Washington, that is."

"Who?"

She smiled in the misty dawn. A beautiful woman. "Kasim. We grew up together . . . same block in Chicago. He'll always be Willie to me."

In the dim light he could see her skin was fawn-colored. "Does he really hate whites as much as it seems? All whites?"

"Does the KKK hate blacks?"

"They say they don't."

"Right. And pigs fly." They shared a quiet laugh in the damp dawn. "Kasim's sister was . . . used pretty badly, when he was young. Raped, buggered. He was beaten and forced to watch. The men were never caught. You know the story; it happens on both sides of the color line. He's about half nuts, Ben."

"I gathered that."

"There are a lot of differences between the races, Ben. Cultural differences, emotional differences. The bridge is wide."

"I do not agree with what my brother and his friends are doing, Salina. I want you to know that."

"I knew that last night, Ben. I think . . . we need more

men like you and Cecil; less of Jeb Fargo and your brother."

"Who in the hell is Jeb Fargo?"

"His name is really George, but he likes to be called Jeb. He came up to Chicago about five years ago—from Georgia, I think. Head of the Nazi Party."

"Yeah . . . I met him. I didn't like him. I agree with you, Salina. I hope his . . . mentality doesn't take root."

"It will," she predicted flatly. "What are your plans, Ben?"

He told her, standing in the cool mist of the morning. He told her all his plans, his schedule he had worked out in his mind while waiting for sleep to take him the night before. He told her of his home in Morriston, and how he had literally slept through the horror after being stung.

"That probably saved your life."

"What are your plans, Salina?"

She lifted her slender shoulders. "I'm with Cecil and Lila. Where they go, I guess I go."

"Last night, in the dining room, Kasim called you a zebra. What does that mean?"

She laughed, but it was a rueful laugh. "I'm half white, half black. My mother was a light-skinned woman, good-looking. My father was a handsome man. Yes, they were married."

"I didn't think you were—"

"Pure coon," she cut in, but she was smiling.

"That was not my choice of words, Salina."

She looked up at him, then abruptly put her hands on his shoulders and kissed him on the mouth. She turned and walked away.

Ben watched her leave; watched all of her leave, from her ankles up. She was very shapely. He touched his lips with his fingertips, then called after her, "Remember, my home is Morriston."

Her reply was a wave; then she rounded the corner of the motel. Ben sensed eyes on him. He looked around him, then glanced up. The face of Kasim, pure animal hate in his eyes, was staring at him from the second floor of the motel. His mouth was swollen from Salina's backhand slap.

"Goddamned, no good, honky motherfucker!" he hissed.

"I thought Muslims weren't supposed to use bad language," Ben said.

"I'll kill you someday," Kasim promised.

"I doubt it," Ben said. He got into his truck, cranked it, and drove away.

He could still feel the warmth of Salina's lips on his and Kasim's wild hatred.

It was disconcerting.

Ben headed south, driving until he came to highway 14, knowing it would take him through only a few towns, and eventually lead to Fort Wayne. He stopped at each small town, finding two or three alive in each. In almost every case, there was no direction to them, no leader; they were accomplishing nothing: not burying the dead, not cleaning the litter—nothing. Just waiting. For what, Ben didn't know, so he asked.

"Help," a man said.

"From whom?" Ben asked.

"The government, who else?"

"Man . . . there *is no* government. I doubt there is a stable government anywhere in the world. Don't you understand what has happened?"

168

The man looked at him and walked away. He called over his shoulder, "The government'll help us. You're wrong, mister. If the government wasn't gonna help us, they wouldn't have made ever'body so dependent on them. You're wrong."

"And you're a fool," Ben muttered. He drove on.

He found a dozen people alive in Rochester, all in their mid-to-late thirties; a few kids. They seemed genuinely excited to see him, asking where he'd been, what he'd seen, what he was doing. And, where was government help? Here, the women outnumbered the men, two to one; one woman made it very plain she would go with Ben; he had only to ask.

He did not ask, although she was a good-looking woman and Ben was beginning to feel sexual urges rise in him. He told them to be careful, told them what was happening in Chicago; then, after asking a few questions as to why they thought they had survived when others hadn't (none of them had any idea), he pulled out.

In one small town, he found three men alive. They were having a party. A long one. Drunk, and they had been that way for days. No, they weren't from town; come up from Marion, just wandering. Had Ben seen any broads?

He sent them to Rochester.

Ben cut off 14 for a time, then took a county road east to US 24, approaching Fort Wayne from the southeast. On the edge of that city, a billboard brought him up short, brakes smoking.

BEN RAINES—IF YOU'RE ALIVE AND READING THIS, OR IF ANYBODY KNOWS THE WHEREABOUTS OF BEN RAINES, HAVE HIM CONTACT US ON MILITARY 39.2. KEEP TRYING;

"Orders?" Ben said. "What fucking orders? From me?" Then it hit him: the Rebels. The colonel hadn't been kidding; the Bull had really done it.

"Well . . ." Ben muttered. "I'm not your commanding officer. Good luck, boys."

On the outskirts of Fort Wayne, he tucked his truck behind a motel and stayed the night, his sleep punctuated by sporadic gunfire.

He decided to leave Fort Wayne to whomever held the most firepower.

At dawn, after a cold breakfast, and feeling just a bit depressed, Ben gassed up his tanks. He had long since ceased trying to use the pumps; electricity was gone at nearly ever place he stopped, and the pumps were useless. But gasoline tankers were in abundant supply and bulk plants were full. Eventually fire or the elements or crazies might destroy the storage areas, but now he wasn't worried about fuel.

Until things began to settle down, and he felt they would in time, and until people accepted what had happened and tried to rebuild, Ben decided to skip the cities. But he would get as close as possible—within CB range, if he could—attempting to keep a pulse on what was happening.

The weather was raw when he pulled out, crossing into Ohio and picking up highway 24. Before he had left Louisiana (it now seemed so long ago), Ben had anticipated highways and interstates clogged with stalled vehicles, but that had not been the case, and as he drove, he saw why. On the interstates, exits and on-ramps were hopelessly snarled; traffic was backed up, in many cases, for a mile or more. It was hard work getting off and on the interstate system, and Ben knew that soon he would have to find a four-wheel drive with one hell of a good PTO winch on the front.

He stopped at an Ohio State Police building and prowled around until he found a Geiger counter; he wasn't that far from the area that had taken the most nukes and he wanted something to test with.

He did not want to get too close to Toledo for fear the bridges would be blocked and he might get himself into a bad situation. He crossed the Maumee River and took the river road on the east side up to Perrysburg. That was as close as he wanted to get to Toledo. And that almost proved too close.

Engrossed in CB chatter, he did not notice the motorcycles until it was almost too late. He was gassing up, the motor still on. He took an almost perverse pleasure (childlike, he realized) in wasting gas, since it no longer cost an arm and a leg to buy a gallon. He hoped the Arabs, who had gouged the world for years, were all rotting in their oil-rich beds, their imported French water growing bugs in it. It was American know-how that had brought in their fucking oil in the first place.

Ben pulled out onto the highway just as he heard the roar coming at him. A pistol barked and a slug spider-webbed the windshield. He squalled onto Ohio 199 just as another slug slammed through the rear window. Ben glanced at his side mirror; the motorcyclists were gaining on him, waving guns and shouting.

Two were tailgating him. Ben smiled grimly and jammed on his brakes. He felt a jarring impact as the bikers ass-ended the pickup; one was thrown over the cab to land on his head in the center of the road. Ben spun the wheel, corrected his slide, and stopped in the center of the highway. He grabbed his Thompson, opened the door, and cleared the highway of two-wheel vermin.

Those that were left wanted no more of Ben Raines. Whooping and hollering and shouting curses at him, they tucked their tails and split, man, leaving their wounded behind. Ben ignored the pleas for help from the riders sprawled in bleeding pain on the concrete. He didn't think they would have helped him had the situation been reversed.

Ben inspected his truck for damage. The rear was caved in, but the wheels would roll without scraping metal. A spring had popped, and one side stuck up in the air. But the motor was still running.

The truck limped along the highway for miles, while Ben looked for a national guard or reserve armory. He finally found one and pulled in. He selected a heavy-duty three-quarter-ton truck with only a few thousand miles on it and began transferring his gear, installing his CB. The truck had a military radio in it, so Ben set that for 39.2. He changed the oil and filters in the truck, tossed two spare tires in the back, then went prowling through the armory to see what he could find.

He picked up a few cases of C-ration and some dehydrated rations. That was about all he could find that he felt he could use.

He secured the place for the night, fixed some supper, and turned in.

"Lucky again, Ben," he muttered, just as sleep took him.

EIGHT

By the middle of October, Ben had traveled as far to the east as he dared go. Transmissions on the CB had dwindled to practically nothing, and lately he had been seeing some fresh bodies, all with signs of radiation sickness marking them. He knew they had died hard.

He cut south, and as he drove, he felt a sudden craving hit him. He chuckled as he recorded the craving for fresh sweet milk. He began looking for cattle, flexing his fingers as he drove. Been a long time since he'd milked a cow—years. Way back when he'd helped his dad on the farm. Those cows that had needed milking when the bombs struck; those cows that had been hooked up to milking machines. Agony, slow agony dying.

Then another thought struck him, driving out the craving for milk; the jails and prisons; the institutions that house the old, the sick, the insane.

Oh, my God!

Had anyone thought to check on them?

Why didn't I? he asked silently.

He headed the nose of the truck southwest, through Pennsylvania. He would skirt the cities and check the small towns, the jails and hospitals, work his way southwest, through West Virginia, then cut into Virginia, giving the hot areas of Washington and

173

Baltimore lots of room.

He finally gave up on the jails, the hospitals, the institutions: they were stinking pestholes, rotting bodies, and many of them had died in the most horrible manner. He drove on. Then, just a few miles north of Charlottesville, he saw a figure trudging along the road.

The figure whirled around at the sound of the truck, then jumped for the ditch, trying for the woods. But the jump was short, and the boy fell hard, grabbing at his ankle. By this time, Ben was on the scene. He stepped out onto the shoulder and turned, finding himself looking down the barrel of a small automatic pistol, held by a very pretty young lady.

"I don't mean you any harm, miss." Ben tried to calm her.

"Yeah? That's what the last bunch of guys said, while they were trying to tear my clothes off me."

"How'd you get away?"

"I kicked one of them in the nuts and split, man!"

"You want me to take a look at that ankle?"

"Not particularly. Why don't you just head on out? I'll be all right."

"I don't mean you any harm, miss. Please believe me. What's your name?"

"None of your damned business."

"O.K., None-of-Your-Damned-Business, my name is Ben Raines."

"Big deal. Who cares? Ben Raines. That sounds kinda familiar."

"I'm a writer. What are you, seventeen?"

"I'm nineteen, if that's any of your business—which it isn't." She fixed her dark blue eyes on him. "O.K., you

174

can look at my ankle if it means that much to you, but I'm gonna keep this gun on you all the time. One funny move and I'll shoot you."

"All right, that's a deal." Ben didn't have the heart to tell her that with an automatic of that type, one first had to cock it before it would fire. She had not cocked it.

Ben knelt down beside her and looked at her ankle. It was swelling badly. Sprained, he hoped, and not broken. She was wearing tennis shoes. Exactly what she should not have been wearing on a hike; no support to the ankles.

"It's sprained, None-of-Your-Damned-Business. We've got to find a creek with cool water and have you soak that for an hour or so."

"My name is Jerre. J-e-r-r-e." She spelled it out slowly. "Jerre Hunter." She looked down at her ankle. "It looks gross."

"Yes, it does, and it will probably get worse before it gets better. Come on, Jerre, put your arm around my shoulders and keep your weight off that ankle."

She gazed at him for a moment, then shrugged. "What the hell? You might rape me, but that's not gonna hurt as bad as my ankle hurts."

Ben laughed at her. "You can put that pistol away, too, Jerre. It's not going to fire unless you cock it first."

She laughed with him. "Doesn't have any bullets in it, anyway. Least I think it doesn't. I don't know how to load it." She tossed the pistol into the ditch.

The automatic bounced off a large rock, fired, and blew a chunk of wood out of a tree.

Ben looked at her and slowly shook his head.

Ben found a little fast-rushing creek with water cold

175

enough to turn one's finger blue just from testing it, and for an hour the two of them sat on the bank talking, while she soaked her ankle and bitched about the temperature of the water and how she probably would catch pneumonia, or how her foot would probably rot off from radiation.

She told him she had just started her second year of college in Maryland when the war talk started. Then the panic hit. She had been sick for a week or so while others around her had been dying.

Gross, she called the experience. The absolute pits, man.

"You want to know something else, Ben? I mean, on top of all this stupid war stuff, there is no music."

"By music, I assume you mean rock and roll?"

"Is there any other kind of music?"

"I wasn't aware rock and roll was music."

She cocked her head, blond hair falling over one eye, and stared at him for a time. "I think, Ben Raines, if we're going to be friends, we'd better not discuss our tastes in music."

"At least until you grow up." He smiled at her.

"Whatever."

When Ben asked why she was walking and not driving, she shrugged her shoulders and said she felt like walking, that's why. Plenty of cars and plenty of time should she decide to drive.

Ben knew better than to question the logic of the young (do the young have logic?), so he let that slide.

"How come, Ben," she asked, "we're not all falling over dead from radiation sickness? I mean, I thought great clouds of that stuff would be floating around."

"Clean bombs," he replied.

"Clean bombs?" She looked at him. "What kind of silliness is that? Sounds like a contradiction to me."

"It is, after a fashion." Then he told her of the tape he'd heard, and of the Rebels and of the triple cross.

"All that is so confusing to me. Coups. Takeover. Rebels. You're really a commander of a Rebel army, Ben Raines?"

"I guess so." He chuckled.

"Where are they?"

"I have no idea, Jerre. It wasn't my idea."

"I heard rumors of the Rebels. Just a little bit. Are they radical people?"

"I don't believe so. Law-and-order types, I'm sure. But Bull Dean was no radical."

"But he advocated the overthrow of the government, Ben. That's pretty radical, don't you think?"

Ben slowly nodded his head. "Yes . . . yes, that's true. But one would have to know the Bull, what made him tick. He would not have assumed power for any length of time. What Bull wanted was a return to law and order and morals and discipline. He wasn't a Castro or some two-bit dictator; just a man who believed very strongly in a government of the people, for the people, and more importantly, *by* the people."

"I don't believe we've had that type of government in a long time, Ben. Do you?"

"No," he said quickly and flatly. "Government got too big—too powerful. Agencies like the IRS had entirely too much power. Same with most government agencies. Well, it's all moot, now."

"But . . . what's that line, Ben, about ashes?"

"Tabb. 'Out of the dead, cold ashes, life again.' "

"Snap judgment time, Ben Raines." She looked at

him, her gaze serious. "I think you're a pretty good man—decent guy. I think you'll probably link up with those Rebels."

"No way, Jerre."

"Yeah, I think you will, Ben. You'll have to get your shit together first. But after that . . . yeah, you will. I've read some of your stuff. You're a dreamer and a romanticist and you'd like to go back about a hundred years—have those kinds of laws. Hell, Ben, maybe you're right. Maybe that's what the country needs. No harm in trying, is there?" She winked at him. "General."

"You're a nut." He smiled at her.

"But I'm pretty."

"Yeah," he said softly. "Yeah, you sure are."

"Gonna be dark soon, Ben."

"Yes." He looked at her ankle. Some of the swelling was gone. "We'll find a place to sleep down the road. You'll be all right—safe."

"I know it." She spoke the words as though she trusted him. "But the dark scares me," she admitted. "It didn't used to scare me until . . ." She let her sentence trail off to an awkward end. She sat staring into the rushing waters.

"Your parents?"

"It . . . it was dark when I got back home. Back to Cumberland. I found them in the back yard. All swelled up and gross-looking. I just sat in the den and bawled and hollered. I never felt so alone in my life. Then the guy who lived next door—he made it through, never got sick, or anything—he came over. He lost his whole family and it didn't seem, at first, to bother him. He said he was going to take care of me, just like I was his daughter. I believed him, so I went with him." She kicked dirt into the creek.

"He tried to get me drunk later on that night; said it would make me feel better. Then I knew what he was all about. Guys think they're so smooth, but given a little time, most girls can see through them. If the girl's got any sense. So I knew what was coming.

"Later on—I thought he'd gone to bed—I tried to slip out of his house, but he was watching for me. We had quite a tussle there on the floor; I marked him pretty good." She put those startlingly Prussian blue eyes on Ben. Honest eyes. "I'm not a virgin, Ben Raines, but I don't give it away wholesale, either. And that bastard really pissed me off. I think, had he played it right, I probably would have gone to bed with him. He was a handsome man, and I'd always thought him a nice person. Not that I cared anything about him, but . . . it would have been . . . well, someone to hold you—you know. I mean, everything was all screwed up. I don't know how to explain it."

Ben knew, but he remained silent, letting Jerre tell it all, her way.

"Finally, he hit me. Boy, did he pop me! When I came out of it, he was ripping my panties off me and talking really wild stuff. Said I was gonna be his private pussy. All kinds of stuff. I got really scared then. Not only because he was trying to rape me, but because I knew then he was really bonkers.

"We were by the fireplace, on the carpet, and when he stood up to take off his pants, I rolled away and grabbed a poker." Again, she gazed at him. "I think I killed him, Ben. Something popped when I hit him. I don't think he was breathing. But I wasn't about to stick around to do any nursing; I'll tell you that for a fact! I just took off.

Got in my dad's car and left.

"And do you know where I went? Where the damned car quit on me? Smart me! To Wheeling. Talk about a case of the dumb-ass. There was a mob of thugs roaming around. And you know they spotted me. You ever seen one little blond-headed girl trying to break the four-minute mile while being chased by fifty guys, all with their peckers out?"

Despite the gut-wrenching fear Ben knew she must have experienced, the panic within her at the time, he had to laugh at the way she told her story.

"And one of those guys was *huge,* man! What is it with men, Ben Raines? I mean, sex is good—terrific, when everything is right—but I don't go around thinking about it all the time. Men do, though, don't they? Sure they do."

"I don't know that we think about it all the time," Ben said slowly. "But a man is damned sure ready at a second's notice." He felt a little ashamed of himself, for he had already mentally undressed Jerre. He rose from the bank and held out his hand. She took it, her small hand soft in his. He pulled her to her feet.

"We'd better get on the road, Jerre. Find us a place to spend the night. Fix us some dinner."

"All right," she said quietly, her eyes studying him.

Ben had fixed a tub of water in which she could soak her ankle, and then had set about cooking dinner. She had eaten as if she had not had a morsel of food in days. Ben then shooed her off to bed.

He lay in his bed that night, and had to smile at all that Jerre had said that afternoon and evening. She was, Ben concluded, a teen-age character. Purely one of a kind, with the open honesty that Ben liked in people. He remembered how she had looked at his weapons, then at him.

"You really know how to shoot all these things?" she had asked.

Ben admitted that he not only did, but had done so, and he told her of the things that had happened to him since leaving Louisiana.

She shuddered as Ben told her of the men in Cairo and what they had planned for him. "That's gross, Ben!"

He recounted his search for his family, described the men and women in Cairo who would not fight for their lives or property, and his experience with his brother in Chicago, and what he and his friends were planning to do.

She had replied, "It wasn't just blacks chasing me in Wheeling; some of those guys were pretty decent-looking men. But I think I can understand how your brother and his friends feel."

"Oh?"

"Sure. That doesn't mean I agree with them—I don't; I think they're wrong. But I don't believe blacks and whites will ever get along. I mean, it's too late, now. But that's the way I feel."

Ben thought of Kasim, and agreed with her. Then he thought of Cecil and Lila and Salina, and silently disagreed with her.

"Why do you think that, Jerre?"

"That we won't get along? Because we're two different peoples, that's why. That's the main reason. Hey! I'm not a bigot, Ben Raines. Don't think that, because you'd be wrong. Let me tell you this, Ben. In high school, my best friend, and I mean my very best friend, was a Chinese girl named Sue Ling. From grade school up, all the way to

181

graduation, we were inseparable. Then we went to different schools, but we kept in touch. I tried to find her after . . . after it happened. But I couldn't.

"Then in college I had friends of different nationalities, lots of them: East Indian, Thai, Vietnamese, Arabs, American Indians . . . oh, you know what I mean . . . lots of different people."

Ben waited for her to drop the other shoe.

"But I never had a black friend. Do you know why that is, Ben Raines, big-time-author-of-some-importance? And a general, to boot."

He laughed. "You tell me, Jerre Hunter, girl-who-broke-the-four- minute- mile-while-being-chased-by-fifty-guys-with-their-peckers-out."

She giggled, then laughed, then put her hand on his forearm. She sobered. "I'm leveling with you, Ben—I don't know. Lots of reasons, I think. One: I don't like to walk down the halls of my school and have half a dozen black guys say, 'Hey, baby! You wanna fuck?' And that's happened, Ben. All over this country. But the news-people, oh, they wouldn't report anything like that. Or maybe it's because when one of us is asked out by a black guy and we say no, we're automatically accused of being a racist. Well, a little of that goes a long way. Does it ever occur to people that the choice of dating is up to the person being asked? That chemistry has a lot to do with it? But Ben, I've seen black guys I'd go out with—but *they* never asked me. It's like the one bad apple, I guess. I don't think you're a racist, but what I've said sure makes me seem like one, and I'm not. I guess . . . I don't like to be pushed. I choose my friends—they don't choose me." She shook her head. "I'm not saying this right."

"No, Jerre, I don't believe you're a racist. You're not

the type." Is there a *type?* he silently questioned.

"My daddy wasn't a racist; neither was my mother. They both worked with black people and the word 'nigger' was not in their vocabulary. I said it once and got slapped for saying it. So it wasn't my home life that made me feel . . . however I feel."

"Tell me about your friends of other nationalities, Jerre. You don't mind if I record this? Good."

"Well . . . Sue was just like me—like you—in the way we think. That's not right. In the way we *act.* So was Rajah, and Mark Little Bear. They were . . . were . . ." She looked at Ben.

"Western?"

"Yeah! That's it—kind of, but not quite. They acted . . ." She again looked at Ben.

"Like us?"

"In a way. They still had their identities, but they didn't try to shove their culture down my throat. What am I trying to say, General?"

"Probably that they conformed to our level of acceptance, but still maintained their own culture. We think alike, Jerre."

She gazed at him, her eyes serious. "But is our thinking right, Ben? Correct?"

"I don't know, babe."

"I think we were a nation of bigots, Ben."

Ben thought of his brother in Chicago, and of the hate of Kasim. "Still are," he said. "On both sides."

He opened his eyes at the sound of her footfall, and looked at her as she stood in the open doorway to the bedroom.

"You're not like any man I've ever met, Generalauthor Ben Raines. I think you're a tough man, and I think you're also a sensitive man. Funny combination. You're a warrior, I guess. But a good one. That woman, back at the motel—the one who kissed you. She was black, wasn't she?"

"Half and half." Ben spoke from the bed. "Kasim called her a zebra."

"Hell with Kasim." She had not moved from the doorway. "I liked the way you described Cecil and his wife. Lila. They sound like nice people and I believe you liked them. I think I would, too. But just as our race has rednecks and trash, so do the blacks. So that makes Kasim a nigger. But not Cecil and his wife and that other woman. That's what I was trying to say this afternoon, Ben. No matter what race a person might belong to, there are classes of people. Good people and bad people. I just don't believe everybody is equal, Ben. I think people—all people—need education. I think education is the key to solving almost every problem."

"So do I, Jerre."

She moved closer to the bed. Ben could smell the clean, fresh soap scent of her.

"I'm confused, Ben. If the war hadn't happened, would the race problem ever have been solved?"

"Not in our lifetime."

"You sound so certain." She limped to the bed and sat down.

"I guess I do."

"I said education is the key to solving problems, Ben. But . . . I don't believe you can have one set of rules for some people and another set for other people."

"Like I said, Jerre, we think alike."

"But how do you *make* someone learn?"

184

"Not constitutionally, I can assure you of that. But short of separate nations . . . well, let me ask you this: if a baby won't eat, and will starve unless something is done, what does a doctor do?"

"Well . . . I guess . . . hell, he force-feeds it. But, Ben, no one can *force* a person to learn if that person doesn't want to learn."

"You can if you have access to the home."

"Is that what you want to see happen, Ben?"

"No. That would be the ultimate totalitarian society."

She put her hand on his chest and felt his heart beat against her palm. "I sure would like to sleep with you, Ben. But I sure don't want to get pregnant."

"I will sure do my best to see that doesn't happen, Jerre."

So she came to him, all soft and young and full of fire and excitement and very little experience with sex.

Ben opened the shirt she wore to sleep in and kissed her breasts, his tongue tautening the nipples while his hand stroked her belly and slipped downward to the center of her. His fingers found her wet and ready to receive him.

Young slender arms around his neck, she cried out as he entered her, and she met his thrusts with powerful upward lunges as the tight heat of her encircled his swollen maleness. She yelled as her first climax shook her and then they settled into the ageless rhythm of the game with only victors to signify the coming of Omega.

And while the world tumbled in chaos about them, two were not alone.

NINE

They spent two days in the house, allowing Jerre's ankle to heal and talking of many things; learning of each other. They played little sex games that enabled Ben to learn when she was ready to receive him: the half-closing of her eyes, grown cloudy with passion; the shallow breathing that turned into hot huffs of anticipation.

"You're really a hot little number," Ben kidded her. "Must have had a repressive childhood."

"Either that, or I just like to screw." She smiled. "You dirty old man."

When they pulled away from the house by the side of the road, Jerre said she wanted to see Chesapeake Bay. So Ben cut east to Tappahannock and then to Reedville. Then, like a couple of kids (one was), they walked the beaches, pounded by wind and sea, holding hands and playing. They built a sand castle (not a very good one, for the wind blew it apart), and spent the night on the beach, in a large double sleeping bag, huddled in each other's arms. Just before dawn, a hard rain drove them into a Bayside cabin.

In that cabin, for the next three days, they forgot the world existed (not much of it did). Jerre complimented Ben, his chest swelling with pride when she told him he was amply endowed in the male department—she'd

186

never seen one so big. Then, giggling, she told him she'd only seen two before his and he chased her out of the cabin onto the beach. When he had caught her, and they had made love, Jerre allowed as to how if he had any more in that . . . certain department, she probably wouldn't be able to take it all.

Then she told him she lied a lot and raced him back to the cabin.

The winds turned cold and Ben cast a thoughtful eye at their surroundings. "This cabin's not made for winter occupation, honey. I think we'd best be moving on."

"Haulin' ass," she said with a smile.

And it was with sadness that they left. Kind of like a travelogue, Ben thought. And so, friends, it is with a sad heart filled with fond memories that we now leave the quaint village on the tropical isle of Bonda-Bonda.

Ben remembered those travelogues from Saturday afternoon matinees. Jerre hadn't even been born when those were discontinued.

Ben sighed, feeling his age.

By now, much of the stench of death had left the land. More than a month had passed, and the rains and the winds and the passing of time had softened the odor. But a faint sickly sweet smell still clung to the earth.

Packs of dogs roamed the countryside, quickly turning wild, reverting to the survival instinct, never quite fully bred out of them: the German shepherd, the Doberman, the husky, the malamute, the pit bull, the boxer, the chow.

Lesser, smaller breeds died for the most part: the little poodles, the Chihuahuas, certain breeds of collie—

almost all toy breeds were no more. Working breeds lived.

"Be careful and don't get too far away from me or the truck," Ben cautioned Jerre. "Dog packs are running wild."

"What else can they do?" she typically asked.

"Nothing. They have to survive. And they will survive. I just don't want them surviving on *us*."

She was thoughtful for a moment, her eyes looking at but not seeing the passing landscape as they drove away from the bay, heading inland. The land had a sameness, an emptiness.

"Will you shoot every dog you see with your guns?" she asked, jaw set, ready for an argument.

"No, Jerre—of course not. But I will shoot any rabid animal we see, and I'll shoot to survive." He told her of the incident in Morriston. "In a few months, rabies will be a problem, I think. Then I should imagine it will taper off, more or less back to normal, like most animal diseases."

"I'd like to see your home in Louisiana, Ben Raines. But I don't think I will—at least not this time around."

He looked at her, more than a glance, for he had not tired of seeing her: the shape of her face, the smoothness of her skin, the wild tangle of her blond hair.

"When I feel I'm getting too attached to you, Ben, I'll leave. Walk away, and not look back, even though I'll want to look back—not go. I'll survive, General—'cause you'll teach me that. If I had any sense, I'd stay with you, despite the difference in our ages. But right now, I'm cute to you. I don't talk like you and I'm young and kind of have a bad mouth. Cute. But that cute would get frayed around the edges pretty quick, I'm thinking."

Smart kid, he thought.

"So what I want you to do, General, is teach me to survive. 'Cause . . . well, I have some things to do after a while. We won't talk about them now. For now, we'll stop along the way and you pick me out a gun, teach me how to shoot it; teach me how to spot those who are going to hurt me—if you can, and I think you have that instinct built in. Then . . . when the time comes, I'll cut out. I'll tell you about it, Ben—when the time is right."

Ben wondered what she had up her sleeve; he had felt all along she was holding something from him.

"All right, Jerre. I'll teach you what I can, in the time left us. But I'll be honest. I'm going to miss you when you decide to leave."

She nodded. "I'll miss you, too, General. Believe that." She touched his arm. "You were dreaming last night, Ben—have for several nights. What were your dreams?"

"Strange dreams, babe. You'll probably think me an idiot."

"No, Ben. I'd never think you that. But I do think you have a destiny."

Worry clouded his features for a few seconds. He sighed. "Funny you should say that. That's what the dreams are all about. I've been dreaming of a land that has mountains and valleys and beautiful plains; of cattle and crops and a people living free, under simple laws, a government formed—really formed—of the people and run by the people. The dreams have bothered me."

"You're going to do something fine and good, Ben. I really believe that."

He smiled.

"What you thinking about?"

"Stopping this truck and the two of us going over to that picnic table and making out."

"Then what the hell are you waitin' on, General?"

At a sporting goods store outside of Richmond, Ben found a cache of illegal pistols, just as he had in every sporting goods store at which he'd stopped. Obviously, as could have been predicted (and was) not too many people really paid much attention to the gun-control act of Hilton Logan.

He picked out a nine-shot .22 magnum revolver and a belt and holster for her, then handed her the gear. "Get the feel of this. Point it, cock it, dry-fire it, and go boom-boom. If you can point your finger, you can fire a pistol. I'm going to put together a pack for you: ground sheet, light tent, sleeping bag. I'll fix you a stash of dehyd food later on . . . when I sense you're ready to pull out."

He left her going "boom-boom," and prowled the store. He took all the .45-caliber ammunition (which wasn't much), then opened a compartment in the gun vault, stepped back, and smiled at his discovery.

"Well, now," he muttered. "Just look at that. I'll just bet that old boy wasn't supposed to have those."

A pair of Ingram submachine guns, M-10s, 9-mm. There were extra clips for both of them, thirty-two-round clips. Ben looked around the store and smiled gleefully when he found, hidden under a counter, two cases of 9-mm ammo. He picked up, from the same compartment in the safe, two Browning 9-mm automatic pistols, and the leather to go with them. Saying nothing to Jerre, he took the gear to the truck and stowed it. Back in the store, he chose a 7-mm bolt-action rifle that had been drilled for scope, a good scope, and went looking for ammunition.

"You planning on starting a war, Ben Raines?" Jerre asked him.

"No." He laughed at the seriousness on her face. "But a thought just occurred to me: when is the last time you had a fresh steak?"

She smiled and licked her lips. "Not since all the trouble began."

"We will tonight," he promised her.

They skirted Richmond, searching the bands on the CB for chatter. The talk was rough: Killin' niggers and killin' honkies and lookin' for pussy.

"That is so sad," Jerre commented. "The whole world is in a state of chaos; no telling how many millions of people are dead. We don't have a government—nothing, and all those . . . fools can think of is old hatreds and prejudices and raping and looting."

"Those are the bad people, Jerre; they've been here all along. They always surface after or during a tragedy. There are, I believe, lots of good people left alive."

"Then where are they?"

"Staying low, keeping out of sight, waiting for the trash and the scum to kill each other off."

"I hope they do!" she said, with more heat in her voice than Ben had ever heard.

"They won't," he replied. "Hell, they never have."

"You're sure you want to watch this?" Ben asked her. They stood in a pasture between Hopewell and Richmond. A pasture filled with lowing cattle.

"Yes," she said. "If I'm to learn how to survive, I've got to know it all. The days of me going into Safeway and

191

getting a ribeye are over. And they won't be back for a long time, will they, General?"

Maybe never, he thought. "No, they won't." He looked over the herd. "Pick your dinner, Jerre."

She pointed.

"No, that's a bull. Let's leave him to do his thing."

A cow came up to them, lowing softly, looking at them through soft liquid eyes.

"Oh, Jesus Christ, Ben! I can't watch this."

Ben cocked his .45 and shot the animal. The cow's legs buckled and she fell to the ground, quivering and dying.

"You son of a bitch!" Jerre cursed him.

When Ben replied, his voice was bland. "Welcome to the Safeway, dear."

She stood glaring at him, rage in her eyes.

"Can you drive a tractor?" Ben asked.

No reply.

"All right, then stay here. I've got to crank one of those tractors in the shed."

"Why?" she asked, her voice shaky.

"To drag the cow over there," he pointed. "We've got to hoist it up, cut its throat, bleed it, then butcher it."

"Gross," she said. "The absolute, bottomless pits, man!"

The gross, absolute, bottomless pits left Jerre that evening, while Ben was grilling the thick steaks.

"Make mine rare, Ben," she said. "And I mean, really rare. That smells so good!" Then, at his smile, she laughed. "O.K., Ben, so I got my first lesson in what's in store for me. But, Ben—I'd never seen anything like that before. Lord, I'd sure never seen the *inside* of a cow."

They were grilling the steaks in the back yard of a

farmhouse. Here, as in so many homes Ben had stayed in, from Louisiana to Chicago, to the east, then down through the country to Virginia, there were no bodies, no signs of any trouble.

"Most people haven't," he told her. "You'd be surprised at the number of people—grown men and women—who don't have the vaguest idea how to even cut up a chicken for frying."

"I used to love fried chicken and mashed potatoes and gravy. Mamma used to . . ." She looked away from Ben, sudden tears in her young eyes.

Eyes that would, Ben felt, grow much older, very quickly, if she was to survive on the road. "You believe in God, Jerre?"

She wiped her eyes and nodded. "Yes, sure. But after all this"—she waved a hand—"it makes a person wonder."

"Maybe He decided to give a few of us a second chance."

"I don't understand, Ben. If that's the case, why did He let so many bad people live?"

"I can't answer that, babe. I was simply putting forth a theory, that's all. No proof to back it—none at all."

"How will people like me survive, Ben? I mean, you told me you haven't hunted for sport in years . . . yet, all this seems as natural to you as breathing. All that training you had in the service, I guess. But . . . people like me, who have never fired a gun, never butchered an animal, how will we make it in a world that has come down to this: dog eat dog and the strongest survive? I'm lucky, and I know it more and more each day. I found you and you're going to teach me as much as you can. But the others—what about them?"

"People are tougher than even they suspect," Ben

said. "I think we all have a . . . hidden reserve in us; a well of strength that only surfaces in some sort of catastrophe. I also believe that in the long run, good will defeat evil."

She thought about that for a time. "You mean, even if we have to return to the caves for a time?"

"You could say that. Sure. That's what we've done, in fact, in essence." He grinned to soften the seriousness of her mood. "Dad raised us to be resourceful, but to be kind to those less fortunate, not to be mean to others." He thought of his brother in Chicago. "Maybe Carl forgot what Dad taught us."

He turned the steaks and was lost in his own thoughts. As always, the recorder was on. At first it had spooked Jerre, her every word being recorded. But she had quickly grown accustomed to it. She had said, "I guess all writers are kind of nuts."

She brought him back to the present. "Maybe your brother did, Ben. Forget, I mean. But you're only looking at the bad he is doing, or contemplating doing. I don't agree with what he's doing, but every coin has two sides. Look at the other side.

"Maybe your brother got tired of not being able to walk down the street at night without fear of being mugged, or his wife and daughter being raped. Maybe he got tired of seeing criminals and thugs and street punks being treated like they were something special instead of what they are: just sorry bastards. Maybe he got tired of seeing his taxes go to support criminals instead of their victims. It's a long list, Ben, and you know it as well as I. Criminals being provided extensive law libraries so they can look for a loophole to get out of prison. I think that's wrong. I'm no screaming liberal, Ben. I think if you do the crime,

194

you've got to be prepared to do the time.

"We had a professor at school who used to rap with us a lot. He was a history professor, and he really had his shit all together. I hadn't thought about him until you told me your political philosophy a couple of days ago. You know, when I asked if you were a Democrat or a Republican. You said you were forty percent conservative, thirty percent liberal, ten percent evolutionary anarchist, and twenty percent revolutionary anarchist. That's just about what Professor Hawkins used to say.

"He said that someday, in the near future, he believed, if the courts didn't stop pampering criminals, and return to the public their right to defend themselves, the citizens were going to take matters into their own hands and start dealing with punks in a very swift and hard fashion, and to hell with the judicial system. He said it started back in the late seventies with neighborhood watch programs and citizens' patrols and what have you. And he said it was a disgrace the courts had let the law-abiding, tax-paying citizens down so rudely, and, he said, so arrogantly.

"I asked him what he meant by arrogantly, and he said, 'by putting the rights of criminals ahead of the rights of the law-abiding citizens.'

"He said a lot more, but I've never been able to forget that part."

Wise beyond her years, Ben thought.

"Oh," she said, "one more thing: he said rich or poor, for our judicial to work, the laws have to be the same. And he said it would probably take a revolution to accomplish that. And he said we had too many laws on the books and too many loopholes."

"You agree with that, Jerre?"

"Yes. I didn't agree wholeheartedly at the time, but I do now."

"I think you'll make it, Jerre."

She looked at him in the light from the lantern, then touched his arm. "Yeah, so do I, Ben."

Jerre rose to walk into the kitchen, where she was baking potatoes in the butane stove. Ben watched her go, thinking: not long, now. A few more days, maybe a week, and she'll be gone. We'll find a group of young people and there will be some handsome young fellow, and she'll go with him.

And will you be jealous? he asked himself, a half-smile on his lips.

"Yes," he spoke softly to the night. "Yes, I will."

The first time Ben allowed Jerre to fire the .22 mag, he had stepped off twenty-five feet from a huge cardboard box and told her to blast away at it. She missed the box with all nine rounds.

"It might help," Ben said dryly, "if you would open your eyes."

"This thing is so loud!"

"Reload it," was his command.

She dropped the pistol three times during the reloading process. Ben said nothing; he let her find her own way. She could do nothing but improve—damned sure couldn't get any worse. Each time she dropped the weapon Ben picked it up, checking for barrel blockage. What he did not need was a young lady with some fingers blown off. Or a hand.

Jerre practiced for an hour the first day. By the end of that time, she could hit the box five out of nine times.

"It's hopeless," she said, disappointment on her face.

"I think you did very well. You'll get better."

They drove through the outskirts of Petersburg. And it was there Ben found the first organization geared toward rebuilding. But neither Ben nor Jerre wanted any part of this group. The leader was a Fundamentalist preacher (Ben didn't ask of what) who reminded Ben of a certain member of the old Moral Majority (title self-proclaimed). This one was too slick, too glib, too quick with a smile—an answer for everything.

"That guy makes my skin crawl," Jerre observed. "Let's get the hell out of here."

Although many members of the group had heard of Ben, and some actually had begged him to stay, the preacher's protestations over Ben's leaving were weak, spoken without much sincerity. Ben pegged him as a man who would be king, and wanted no interference from the outside.

"He was afraid of you, Ben," Jerre said.

"He won't last long," Ben predicted. They were heading southeast on U.S. Route 460, toward Norfolk—or what was left of it. Saboteurs had just about destroyed the city. "There will be a few dimwits who'll follow him to the end, but most of those people back there are too intelligent to listen to his line of bullshit for very long."

"He sounds stupid," Jerre said with the blunt honesty of the young. "And I don't think he's very sincere. To tell you the truth, I think he's an asshole."

Ben laughed at her.

They drove as close to the Norfolk/Portsmouth/Virginia Beach area as Ben felt was safe. Smoke still clung over the area, smarting their eyes. They pulled back a few more miles and spent the night in a motel.

"Why is it," Jerre asked, "that most of the bad people seem to be located . . . concentrated, I guess, in the cities, the larger places?"

Interesting question, Ben thought. But he hedged it, saying only, "Remember that when you strike out on your own."

"Don't worry." She smiled at him over their dinner of C-ration. "I have vivid memories of Wheeling."

"And the four-minute mile."

"And fifty peckers," she capped it.

They made love slowly that night, very gently, both of them sensing their time together was growing short. Ben was steeling himself for the time Jerre would leave him. He had grown more than fond of Jerre, and though he tried to keep that from her, he sensed she knew.

They backtracked to Suffolk and then headed south, taking highway 32 to Edenton. Ben stopped at every town along the way, looking for survivors . . . but he was stalling and knew it. And worse, he felt Jerre knew it.

During those last days, she sat very close to him most of the time, her left hand resting on his thigh. She spoke very little as they traveled through North Carolina, through the dead and silently littered towns. They watched the packs of dogs slink and snarl at their arrival and departure. They drove over to the coast and down to Nags Head.

Ben had picked up a Polaroid and had made a hundred pictures of her, and she of him. They walked the beach and picked up bits of driftwood and shell. Ben sensed she had something to tell him, but he did not push her. She would tell him in her own time.

They spent a week on the beach, Ben teaching her what he could of survival. She became a fair shot with the pistol, could pitch a tent and properly ditch it, build a fire and cook over it. But Ben did not have the time to teach her, to instill in her, the sixth sense of knowing when danger approached, and who to trust. And how could he teach her, in so short a time, to shoot first and ask questions later? That took learning the hard way. Ben hoped she would make it.

One morning Ben awoke to find her gone from his side. He called for her, and she quickly stepped back into the cottage. She looked at him, her eyes serious.

"Let's pack it up, Ben. Head west. O.K.?"

"O.K., babe. How far west and any particular reason for that direction?"

She nodded. "Time to level with you, General." She tried a smile that didn't make it. "I heard on the road that kids were going to gather at the university at Chapel Hill the first and second weeks of November. The word was passed up and down the line. The reason . . . ? Ben, I don't want to hurt your feelings, and please don't take this the wrong way, but—"

"But the adults screwed up the world and maybe you young people can do better this time around," Ben finished it for her.

"You're a wise man, Ben Raines."

"I'm a survivor, Jerre."

"Am I, Ben?"

"I think you'll make it, babe."

Ben skirted Raleigh and they spent their last night together at Pittsboro, a few miles south of Chapel Hill. They made love slowly and then she cried herself to sleep, lying in his arms.

In the early morning hours, just before dawn, Ben felt her slip from his side and dress quietly in the darkened house. She left a note on her pillow and softly kissed him on the cheek. He pretended to be asleep. Jerre opened the door and looked back at him; then she stepped quietly out of his life, closing the door behind her. He listened to the sound of her footsteps fade.

Ben rose from his blankets to stand by the window. He looked out into the dim light and watched her walk up the highway, toward the gathering of hopeful young people. As they had approached the small town, Ben had seen more and more young people, all heading for Chapel Hill.

They had smiled and waved at Jerre. They had flatly ignored Ben.

When Jerre was gone from his sight, Ben turned on the battery-operated lantern and picked up the note she had left.

Dear Ben,

I'll make this short, 'cause if I try to write too much I'll just tear it up and stay with you, and I think that would be bad for both of us—at this time. Maybe what I'm doing is foolish. I don't know. But I feel it's something I have to do. The world is in such a mess, I have to try to do something to help fix it. Maybe the young can. I don't know. In my heart I kind of doubt it, but we have to try— right?

The mood I get from the kids I've talked with is they blame the adults for the mess we're in. I don't think that is entirely fair, personally. You're a good man, and there must be others like you. But give us a chance, huh?

I don't know what my feelings are toward you, Ben. I

like you a whole lot and I think I probably love you a little bit. That's a joke—I think I probably love you a whole lot. That's one of the reasons I've got to split. There are other reasons, of course, but my feelings toward you are right up there at the top.

You've got places to go and things to do before you find yourself—your goal, preset, I believe—and start to do great things. And you will, Ben. You will.

I hope I see you again, General.

Jerre

Ben carefully folded the note and put it in a waterproof pouch where he carried other precious, silent memories: a picture of his mother and father, his brothers and sisters, a girl he had once loved. And now, Jerre. He put in the pictures of Jerre with her note and closed the flap, securing it.

He sat on the edge of the bed for a time, the scent of her still in the air, on the pillowcase, the sheets.

"Good-by, Jerre," Ben said aloud.

He packed his gear and pulled out. Had he turned north, instead of south, he would have found her sitting at the side of the road, crying, looking down the empty road. Looking south.

TEN

Ben was maudlin for a time, his thoughts moody, filled with regret and self-pity. But as he drove, his mood began to lift as he realized Jerre had been right in her young wisdom: she needed to be with her own kind, her own age—at least for a time. He wished the young people well, but did not believe they would accomplish a thing. Except to get themselves killed. Back in 1960, when Ben was sixteen years old, he had believed in Camelot. But the years of combat and of seeing the mute silence of the dead and the screaming of the wounded and the starvation of the peoples in parts of Africa had convinced him that only the toughest survive—there is not, there was not such a place as Camelot.

But, he thought, forcing a grin, let the young people try; maybe they can build a better world from out of the ashes. God knows the last two generations sure fucked this one up.

He drove down to Sanford and angled over until he linked up with the interstate. The on-ramp was blocked, so Ben dropped the truck into four-wheel drive and drove until he found a place where he believed he could get on the highway. He drove down to Dillon and there he spent the rest of the day practicing with the M-10 and getting the feel of the 9-mm pistol. Ben concluded the little SMG

202

did not have the knockdown power of the heavy old Thompson, or the range, but it was lighter and easier to handle. He elected to stay with it.

The barrel extension/silencer increased the range a few yards—about sixty-five yards max—and made the weapon easier to control, for the padded extension/silencer served much as a rifle fore-end. Without it, the Ingram made a hell of a racket. Even with it, it sounded like a fast-quacking duck with a speech impediment.

Ben fixed his dinner and turned in. His dreams were intense, waking him several times. They were mixed—about his parents, his brothers and sisters, Fran, and always, Jerre. And the dream of a free land, run by the people, always intermingled with the others. The Rebels, leaderless . . . waiting.

At first light, he drove over to Shaw Air Force Base, thinking surely, of all places, there would be life here; a military organized disciplined order to things.

No one challenged him at the main gate. The door to the sentry hut banged and slammed in the wind; the lock was broken.

The base was eerily silent, but there were no bodies to be seen. Ben drove around the huge complex, stopping at random to check buildings and barracks. Nothing. Finally, in a service club, Ben found four men playing cards. A general, a captain, and two sergeants. They did not seem at all surprised to see him. They tossed the deck of cards on the table, shook hands and introduced themselves, and invited Ben to sit down, have a drink. Booze was free.

Drink in front of him, with the first ice Ben had seen since leaving Louisiana, he asked, "Is this it?"

"Meaning all the life on this base?" the general asked.

"Yep. What you see is what you get."

Ben told him what he was doing, attempting to do.

"Very admirable of you," the captain said. "But who in the hell is going to read it?"

"There are a number of people still alive," Ben told him. "Probably a lot more than we realize."

"Oh, sure," the general said. "I figure maybe . . . oh . . . twenty to thirty million here in the States. Hell, me and Jake here"—he jerked his thumb toward the captain—"have flown all over the States during the past six weeks or so—been in voice contact with hundreds of people. You know the Rebels are looking for you?"

Ben nodded. "So I've heard."

"Don't want to be their commander, huh?"

Ben hesitated. "I . . . don't know."

"You must be something special for the Bull to put you in charge of the whole shebang." Ben said nothing. The general grunted. "You know, probably, that when the military gets it all together—take another ninety to one hundred twenty days—that craphead Logan will be named president."

"So I heard. I can't think of anything more appalling for the country."

"I agree."

"Then . . . ?" Ben looked at the general.

"Why Logan? Hell, it's a joke, Raines. An ugly, profane joke. He's the only one left, we think. He ran like a scared rabbit and ducked into a hole. The others went up with Washington and the suburbs. I flew over what's left of our great boondoggle. It's awesome, boy, awesome."

"Oh, come on, General! There has to be another senator or representative around . . . somewhere!"

204

"Oh, sure. Of course. Let's see." He smiled, beginning a count on his fingers. "We've got that young fellow from Iowa—"

"Senator Billing," Ben said. "First-termer. O.K., General, I get the point. Logan is senior."

"That's it. All the secretaries are gone. Every last one of them."

"Supreme Court?" Ben asked.

"All gone . . . as far as we know. They can't be found."

"General,"—Ben leaned forward—"one of you people take over; don't give it to Logan."

The general shook his head. "No way, Raines. No way. And we talked it over. There's . . . twenty six generals and four admirals who came out of it alive—all branches of the service. And that includes *retirees*. Hell, we've got one so old he really thinks he's on Corregidor, waiting for MacArthur to return. No one has the heart to tell him that was almost fifty years ago. I was two years old! No way, Raines." The general smiled. "Besides, way I heard it, Logan has a plan for the U.S. to come out on top after this tragedy."

"Let me guess, General." Ben's tone was icy.

"I figured you'd want a shot at it, boy."

Ben resisted an urge to tell the general he was no "boy." The general, at most, was about six years older than Ben. But rank has a way of doing that to some men.

"It wasn't a double or even a triple cross Adams was pulling off—it was more than that."

"Keep talking."

"I always figured Logan was hiding something. I never did like or trust that man. He's a pseudoliberal, isn't he?"

The general smiled.

"The Bull won after all."

205

"No, Adams won," the general said. "The Bull killed him, somewhere up in New York State, way I heard it. Logan was the mastermind behind the whole caper. The hitch came when the Rebels found out about Logan and Logan found out the Rebs were gonna shoot him if they ever got their hands on him. He is not a well-liked man among conservatives, son."

"Now, wait just a minute." Ben held up his hand. "This is getting a little complicated. The Rebels didn't know Logan was really behind it all?"

"That's the way I hear it. Neither did Colonel Dean . . . until the very last, oh, eight or ten days before the balloon went up."

"But . . . why would Logan hide his true feelings all these years? For what purpose?"

"To be the most popular liberal in the world, Raines. Hell, the minorities loved him. He was a shoo-in for the White House. He only had the Rebels as a backup in case he lost. But everything went haywire: coups all over the world; a minor revolt in Russia; the Thunder-strikes; the Rebs in the sub."

"I see," Ben said slowly. "He . . . once he got into the White House, then he could show his true colors. and with the military behind him—and something tells me they would back him—he would be more than president, wouldn't he, General?"

"He'd be king."

"Logan is going in to help all the poor third-world nations after he gets you people organized, isn't he, General."

"It'll take . . . oh . . . four to six years. Maybe eight."

"To colonize."

"Ugly word, Raines."

206

"The truth sometimes is, *boy*."

The general chuckled.

"Adams couldn't convince his people that Logan was really a good guy. His people wouldn't buy it," Ben conjectured. "And once Adams leveled with them about Logan, they refused to back Adams and Logan."

The general nodded his head, only once.

"You were part of it, weren't you, General?"

Again, the nod.

"But . . . why?"

"Oh, hell, Raines. Nobody really *likes* niggers or Jews or greasers. They're all fuck-ups. They're not equals. We'll use them to serve us, work for us, but not side by side. And that isn't my plan—that's Logan's plan."

"Separate but not quite equal, eh?"

"More or less."

"It'll never work, General."

The general's face brightened. "Sure it will, boy. You don't know the American people like I know them. Deep down, boy, we're the master race. Besides, we've got the guns—most of them. And the military will be revered in our society—not like it used to be. Logan plans to resettle the people, reeducate them, kind of reprogram them, so to speak. All at the same time he's offering the hand of good fellowship to the jungle-bunnies in Africa."

"Changing the subject momentarily, General—you don't mind if I stall for a bit more time?"

"Not at all, since you're not leaving this club alive." The general's eyes were hard.

Ben had figured that out all by himself. Under the table, he slipped the M-10 off safety, speaking just a bit louder to cover the metallic click. "How come, General, we survived, and so many others didn't?"

The cassette recorder was rolling, taping it all.

"Good question, Raines. I've given it a lot of thought, and reached this conclusion: beats the shit outta me."

"For a fact, General, the truth: Russia and China?"

"Gone. Hell, boy—you don't think we actually destroyed all those nukes, do you, back when the final SALT was signed? No way. There is nothing left, sonny. Human, that is."

"Fallout?"

"We'll be getting some—but don't worry, you won't be taking any of it. We won't be taking much. Too many clean bombs used."

"You men in on the general's plan to be part of the master race?" Ben asked the trio.

"All the way, partner," the captain said. The sergeants nodded.

Ben pulled the trigger of the M-10, working the weapon from left to right, clearing the room of all living things in front of its stuttering muzzle.

He rose from his half-crouch to look at the carnage he had wrought. They were all dead. He got into his truck and drove to the communications center of the base. He stood for a moment looking at the maze of electronic equipment. None of it looked familiar. He finally managed to turn on what he hoped was a radio transmitter and set the dial to 39.2. He keyed the mike and watched the VU meter jump with needle action.

"Here goes nothing," he muttered, then took a deep breath. "This is Ben Raines," he spoke slowly. "I hear you people have been looking for me."

"How do we know you're Ben Raines?" a voice jumped back at him. "We've had two dozen crank callers."

"How do I know you're who you claim to be?" Ben challenged.

"The Bull told us about the last time you two saw each other. He shouted something to you as he stood in the door. We know what he said. And if you're Ben Raines, so will you. Do you remember those two words?"

"Bold Strike," Ben said.

"Sorry, General Raines, sir. But we had to be certain. Lot of snooping going on."

"General!" Ben blurted. "Man, I'm not a general."

"Yes, you are, sir. Begging your pardon."

"I'd like to know just who in the hell told you that!"

"Colonel Dean, sir."

"A colonel can't make anybody a general."

"The Bull can—and did, General."

Ben released the mike button. "Shit!" he said. "Now what?" He pushed the mike button. "How . . . ah . . . do I scramble this thing?"

"On which end, sir?"

"Both ends!"

"What is the number on the transmitter facing?"

Ben looked, found about forty-eight different numbers. He settled on the largest number that seemed permanent.

"Look to your left, sir," the voice told him. "A switch with the word 'scramble' just above it. Flip the switch."

Ben looked. There it was. He felt like an idiot. "Some general I am," he muttered. Keying the mike, he said, "Am I scrambled?"

"Repeat, sir."

Ben repeated.

"Scrambled now, sir."

Ben informed the voice of what had just transpired in the service club.

"Yes, sir. We know Logan is planning world-wide power play under the guise of a good-neighbor policy. But our immediate concern is: what do we do?"

"Are you people nationwide?"

"Yes, sir."

"Can you handle explosives?"

"We can do anything with explosives, General."

"I am *not* your general!"

"Yes, sir."

Ben sighed. He waited.

"General Raines? Are you still there?"

"Oh, for Christ's sake!" Ben punched the mike button. "You wanna know what you can do? I'll tell you: you can order your people to slip onto every military base in this nation and destroy every goddamned plane they find."

"Yes, sir, very good, sir. That will prevent Logan from getting the jump on us. We have men among us who can fly those planes, sir. Shall we take some for our use?"

"What use!" Ben yelled.

"For the defense of our nation, sir."

"What fucking nation!" Ben screamed.

"The one the Bull told us you had planned. The one you used to talk about in 'Nam."

Ben's sigh was long and frustrated. "By all means . . . ah . . . to whom am I speaking?"

"Lieutenant Conger, sir."

"Fine. All right, Conger. If you people have places in . . . ah . . . ." He closed the mike switch and thought for a few seconds, then said, "Idaho or Montana, take them there. Pick up anything you feel you might need along the way. Do you understand?"

"Yes, sir!"

With the mike closed, Ben said, "Goddamned yo-yo. That ought to keep them busy."

"General Raines?" The voice popped and snapped.

"What!"

"Where are you, sir? I need your location so I can send some personnel to guard you until you link up with us."

"Guard me? Goddamn it, I don't need anyone to guard me!"

The voice was silent for a few seconds and Ben was sure he had broken off transmission. "Yes, sir. You said General Ruther, sir? That'd be Shaw AFB. We'll have our South Carolina contingent pick you up as soon as possible. I—"

Ben began shouting into the mike, not knowing whether the man called Conger was off the air listening or still jabbering his nonsense. "Now, you listen to me!" Ben roared. "I am *not*—repeat—*NOT* your commander. I hereby appoint you, Conger, as commanding officer of the army of the Rebels, or whatever in the hell you're called. Do you understand that?"

"Affirmative, sir. But you can't make me commander."

"Why the hell not?"

"Because Bull Dean was my uncle. He gave his life for this country, and he said you were to command after his death. And, sir, that is that."

Ben knew when he was whipped. "Fine, Lieutenant, dandy. You have my orders. Carry them out. I'll be in contact . . . sometime."

He cut off the transmitter before Conger had the time to object. He looked at the radio and said, "I am not your commanding officer, son. Period. Good-by. Good luck."

211

Ben prowled the base until he found the ordnance hut. He broke open the building and began picking through the explosives. He was too rusty to trust himself if he used any type of timer, so he chose several crates of incendiary grenades and began the job of filling five-gallon cans full of high-octane jet fuel and pouring some around the line of jets on the tarmac. He then began the job of destroying the aircraft.

When he had finished, he was covered with soot and hard of hearing from the booming explosions. This was one runway that would be a long time getting cleared and repaired.

He then drove around the base, tossing grenades into every other building, and setting the base ablaze. He drove out the main gate, smiling. He said, "Fuck you, Logan."

Ben took highway 601 down to Orangeburg, then picked up highway 21. He spent the night in a home by the side of Interstate 95, about fifty miles north of Savannah. In the morning he would drive close enough to listen to CB chatter, then decide if he was going into the city.

The next morning, after reviewing the talk on the CB, he decided he most definitely was not going into the city.

He skirted the city, between Savannah and Fort Stewart, on Interstate 95. South of the city, he picked up highway 82 and once more began checking towns along the way, making notes into his recorder, and letting Conger and his band of reactionaries slip from his mind.

Just a few miles outside of Jessup, at a roadside picnic area where he had stopped to eat a can of C-ration, Ben heard a growling. He turned slowly, picking up the M-10 with his right hand.

At first he thought it was a wolf sitting in the bed of the truck, on a tarp-covered crate, and peering over the side at him. Ben took a closer look and could see its upturned tail. This was not a husky, he concluded, but a malamute, the largest of the breed. The dog looked to be about thirty-two inches high, about eighty to ninety pounds. Big. It was wolf-gray with a black mask area around its almond-shaped eyes.

The animal yawned, exposing teeth that could tear a man to painful chunks of meat very quickly Then the malamute closed his mouth and looked at Ben. It was neither friendly nor hostile, just curious. Ben dumped what was left of his C-ration into a piece of paper and placed it on the ground beside him.

"Come on," he said.

The dog jumped from the truck and walked to the food, eating it in two bites. He looked up at Ben, as if asking, but not begging, for more. Ben opened another can and dumped that on the paper. The animal ate, then walked to the ditch beside the small park and enjoyed a noisy drink of water. His thirst quenched, he walked back to the truck, jumped up into the bed, and lay down, closing his eyes as if he had been doing that, on this truck, all his life.

Probably belonged to someone who rode it around in a pickup truck, Ben thought.

"Well," Ben said, "if you want to ride, you can damned well ride. I'm not going to tell you to move."

The dog opened its eyes, looked at Ben, then went back to sleep.

Ben policed the area, dumped his trash into a container, and got into the truck. He opened the sliding glass of the rear window, cranked up, and pulled out. After a few miles, the animal stuck his head through the window, looked at Ben, who was holding his breath; then licked Ben on the cheek. Ben rubbed the animal's head and the dog barked happily, then settled back on the canvas.

"Looks like I found a friend." Ben grinned.

So Ben and his new friend, whose name, Ben discovered, when he checked the tags on the collar, was Juno (probably, Ben thought, a shortened version of Juneau, Alaska), spent the day and the evening getting acquainted. And Ben and the dog took to each other. He had not had a pet since his boyhood days in Illinois and, after spending a little time with Juno, he wondered why he had not. He found Juno to be alert, probably no more than three years old, and seemingly intelligent.

Ben's sleep that night was deep and secure, for the animal was attuned to the night's every noise. During the night, Juno had snuggled up to Ben's sleeping bag, the closeness and warmth comforting to both man and beast.

Lost a girl friend and found a dog. Ben smiled as he drifted off.

The next morning, however, Ben discovered he was crawling with fleas.

Juno met his new master's reproachful scratching with a look of doggie disgust, as if saying, "What the hell? Lay down with dogs, what do you expect?"

At the first town they came to that morning, Ben picked up a supply of flea powder and spray, and several flea collars. Then he bathed both Juno and himself and that solved the problem of fleas.

Ben headed southeast out of Callahan, having no desire to travel through Jacksonville. He had seen a few people. They were, for the most part, silent and withdrawn, but some were openly hostile. He picked up talk on his CB, but none of it was friendly. He had stopped along the highway several times to look at bodies. They were all no more than two or three days old and they had been shot.

A few miles down the highway, Ben found a body hanging from a tree alongside the road. A crudely lettered sign hung around the neck read: NIGGER.

Further on, he found the body of a white man hanging from a tree. The sign around his neck read: JUSTICE WILL PREVAIL.

"Wonderful," Ben remarked. "I am so happy to find our judicial system—inadequate as it was—is still flourishing."

He drove quickly out of that part of the state. Even Juno seemed relieved to be on the move.

At Raiford, Ben followed the signs to the big prison, but long before he saw the wire and the walls he smelled it and turned around, heading back. A huge flock of buzzards circled in the sky.

He wandered the northern part of the state, all the way over to Hampton Springs, seeing a few people, some friendly, some hostile. He saw signs of looting and violence everywhere he went.

Then, while turning the dial on his portable radio, he heard the music. He was so startled he pulled off the road and turned up the radio. The music faded and a voice sprang out.

"Yes, sir, folks, it's a bright, beautiful day here in the city with the titties. Temperature in the mid-seventies and you're listening to the SEAL with the feel, Ike McGowen, watchin' the records go 'round. Are you listening, world? If so, and you're the friendly type, just head on down to the coast to Yankeetown and be received. But if you're hostile, just carry your ass on, brother."

Ben laughed and wondered if SEAL meant Navy SEAL—sea, air, and land—or was just a nickname. He decided to find out. As he drove, he kept looking for a radio tower. He didn't spot it until he got to the water's edge, and it was the crudest looking tower he had ever seen, leaning precariously to one side, looking as if it might topple over at any moment. Ben pulled into the drive of the large, oceanside house and got out.

A gaggle of bikini-clad young ladies, bouncing and jiggling, came racing out to meet him. They were all armed with automatic weapons. Kind of took away from the beauty of their bare skins. A man with a CAR-15 walked behind them.

"I'm peaceful," Ben called. "I really can't speak for the dog—only known him for a few days, but I think he's friendly."

"What's your name, friend?" the man called.

"Ben Raines."

"I'm Ike McGowen. What's the dog's name?"

"Juno."

"Well, Ben and Juno, come on into radio station KUNT and set for a time."

Ben laughed at the old joke of call letters. "KUNT?"

Ike returned the laugh. "Yeah—it's a little fuzzy around the edges but mighty fine, man. Mighty fine."

In the sprawling house, Ike introduced Ben. "This one here is Tatter, and that's June-Bug, and that one there is Space-Baby, and that one is Angel-Face. The blond is Honey-Poo. That dark one all sprawled out on the floor, too goddamned lazy to get up is Bell-Ringer. She claims to

216

be a black person of the Negroid persuasion, but I think she's just been out in the sun too long." Bell-Ringer smiled and gave him the middle finger. She smiled at Ben, then went back to reading her book. Ike said, "We got all the conveniences, friend. Generator for electricity which gives up light, music, and hot water. So fix yourself a drink and let's talk. Then we'll vote."

"Vote? Vote on what?"

Ike grinned. "To see if you'll stay with us for a time—or leave."

"Well, I wasn't planning on staying, but I'll take your offer of a drink."

"Aw." Ike waved off Ben's idea of leaving. "You look like an O.K. sort of guy. Hell, hang around awhile. Tell us your story and we'll vote."

Over his bourbon and water, Ben told them what he was doing—and had done. He told them about the general at Shaw AFB, about Logan, the Rebels.

"I wondered if you were the writer. Yeah, I've heard about the Rebels; talked to them a couple of times on 39.2. I don't know much about them—what they're all about—but they sound pretty straight. Hell, Ben, we can't throw a general out of here."

Ben grimaced and they all laughed.

"You don't strike me as the DJ type," Ben said to Ike.

Ike grinned, his boyishness coming through. "I'm not, really. But I always wanted to be. No," he said, sighing, "I'm—was—in the Navy. SEAL. We were doing some training at Fort Walton Beach when the balloon went up. Talk about confusion, man. Jesus! Nobody knew their ass from peanut butter. I got sick as a dog." He looked at Juno. "No offense, pooch. And wandered around in a daze for about a week. Ran into Bell-Ringer; she was in the process of gettin' raped by a bunch of rednecks—so I sorta jumped in and did my survival bit on her behalf, since her below was all filled up, so to speak."

Bell-Ringer shot him the bird.

"You killed them." It was a statement on Ben's part, not a question.

"I damned shore did." Ike grinned. "Me and my little ol' CAR-15. Then, the next day, we ran into Tatter and June-Bug and we all sorta migrated down here. The others just wandered in when I got the station on the air." He looked at the ladies. "Let's vote. All in favor of Gen. Ben Raines stayin', raise your hand, or your foot, or lift a tit—do somethin'."

All hands went up.

Ike's grin widened. "You're home, General. Let's get you unloaded."

Juno was cuddled up to June-Bug. He had already made up his mind to stay.

Ben couldn't blame him for that.

ELEVEN

"Have there been many visitors around?" Ben asked. It was dusk on the coast and the gulf was as beautiful as the Prussian blue eyes of Jerre; it gleamed softly, bathing the sand with a peaceful glow. For a moment Ben thought of Jerre and he was saddened.

Honey-Poo picked up on the gentleness in his voice and stirred. Ben was conscious of the vibes from her, and she of the vibes from him.

Ike looked at both of them and grinned knowingly. "Yeah, several have tried to come in here and take over; throwin' their weight around, runnin' off at the mouth. But I've taught all these gals about weapons, and they won't hesitate to blow the ass off a troublemaker. Those guys didn't last long. We buried 'em right over there." He pointed. "The other side of that house way down yonder. I guess the word spread after the last shoot-out; hasn't been any more rednecks or trash comin' around. But we hear it's really tough up in the north part of the state, and really bad down in Jax and Tampa. Some of the other cities, too."

Ben spoke of the bodies he'd seen hanging by the side of the road and he elaborated on what was about to happen—if it hadn't already occurred—in Chicago and some of the other cities around the nation.

"Right and wrong on both sides," Bell-Ringer said; then rose from her chair and went inside.

Ike followed her.

"They got a thing for each other," Honey-Poo said. "I think they're gonna get married here pretty soon."

Suddenly, without any warning, Ben thought of Salina. "She's a beautiful woman." And she was.

"Smart, too. Was going to college in Gainesville, working on her Ph.D. in something or the other. Doesn't talk much about it, though. Guy she was going with—not steady or heavy—was killed two or three days after the war, or whatever the hell it was that happened."

Ben told her of the tape recording he'd heard, sitting in front of the Radio Shack in Morriston—a thousand years ago, it seemed.

"Yeah, Ike heard that same tape."

"Bell-Ringer's boyfriend, or just friend, whatever—how did he get killed?"

"She doesn't say much about it, but I gather he was kind of a militant. Didn't have much education, but was trying to do the right thing—her words—in his own way. I don't know who started the shooting the day he was killed—she kind of thinks he did—but anyway, he got dead and she just wandered for a day or so until those 'necks caught up with her and were taking turns raping her. That's about all I know about her."

"You?" Ben looked at her. About twenty-five, in the prime of mature beauty. High full breasts, long sleek legs, long thick hair.

"I worked in a bank down in St. Pete."

"No boyfriends?"

"Just on a social basis, nothing heavy. You know what I mean?"

Ben nodded. "Yes."

"Tatter was a schoolteacher." She laughed. "Really! June-Bug was a college girl. Space-Baby worked for the government down at the cape. And Angel-Face was a housewife. Woke up one morning and her husband was lying dead, next to her. She said it was awful. Kind of freaked her out for a time." She looked up at him from the pallet on the darkening sun porch. "You're really going to travel around the country, seeing what happened and talking to people?"

"Yes, I am."

"But, really, Ben, we did hear you are the commander of that Rebel army. Really!"

"You heard wrong. I am the commander of no army. I'm a writer. That's it."

"Ummm," she said. "Well, how long do you figure this project will take you?"

"Several years, probably." If I don't get sidetracked. Damn you, Bull!

She sighed. "That'd be fun, I guess. Kind of adventuresome. Like the pioneers, in a way." She shook her head. "But I'm not very adventuresome. I'm a chicken."

"Well, I'm going to winter around here, I think. For a couple of months, anyway. Maybe three. I think I'll take a run down the coast tomorrow and find a place to stay."

"Want some company?" she asked softly. Her voice was like an invitation to dine—on her.

"Sure. I think we're compatible."

She grinned up at him. "I imagine we are. You like to fuck, don't you?"

Ben and Honey-Poo were more than compatible; she

told him on that first night at Ike's place that she liked to be around a man, didn't like to sleep alone, liked to do for a man. But . . .

"Don't trust me too much, Ben. I mean, I'll be true-blue as a puppy for a time, then I'll get itchy feet and hungry eyes. I won't mean to hurt you, but I will leave when I feel like it. So don't fall for me, O.K.?"

"I'll do my best," Ben said, running his hand over her belly, then down to the tangle of pubic hair. She moved under his strokings, sighing as his finger found and entered her wetness. "What's your real name, Honey-Poo?"

She hissed her pleasure and arched her hips upward, meeting his thrusting finger. Her hand found his stiffness and slowly began working him. "Prudence."

"I'll stick with Honey-Poo."

"Stick it in me first, Ben."

Christmas

It was raw for this stretch of Florida, the temperature hovering around the forty-degree mark and the winds cool enough to bring out sweaters and jackets and to warrant a big roaring fire in Ike's den.

It was a wedding day.

Ike sat with Ben in the den; Bell-Ringer was in the bedroom with the girls, getting ready. For once (the only time since Ben had arrived), Ike was in a semiserious mood.

"Go ahead and ask it, Ben," he prompted. "I know it's on your mind. So get it over with."

Ben drained his coffee cup. Since he was to act as the "minister," he felt it only proper he should be sober. For a fact, no one else was.

"You're sure about this, Ike? Sure you're doing the right thing?"

"Flat-out certain."

"What are the odds of you two making it, Ike?"

"We've already made it, Ben. Lots of times." Ike grinned at him.

"Get serious, Ike!"

"O.K." He sobered. "I figure we got maybe a ninety to ninety-five percent chance of coming out with the roses. And I think that's a hell of a lot better odds than most marriages. Even when times were normal, quote/unquote."

Ben had to agree with that. He glanced at his watch. A half-hour until post time. "Where are you from, Ike?"

Ike flashed that boyish grin. "North Mississippi."

"Are you kidding me?"

"I'm serious, Ben. So yeah, I kinda think I know what I'm doing." He popped the tab on another beer. "My daddy was a member of the Klan, so I grew up hatin' niggers. Well, I still don't like niggers, Ben Raines, any more than I like white trash, or sorry Mexicans, or bad Norwegians. Come to think of it, Ben, there is, was, just a whole hell of a lot of folks from Texas I never did cotton to, but that don't mean there wasn't a whole lot of real good folks in that state. You see what I'm sayin'? I figured you did. Bell-Ringer isn't a nigger. She's a real nice person that has a pretty good tan, that's all."

"But she's still a black."

"Shore. So what?"

"I had to be sure you understood that, Ike. I have to know her real name, Ike."

"Megan Ann Green. And my name is Ignatius Victor

223

McGowen. And if you call me Ignatius during the ceremony, I'm gonna bust you right in the mouth."

Ben laughed out loud. "I'll stay with Ike."

"My daddy was a banker," Ike said softly. "Good one, too, I guess. Made a lot of money in his time. But he had dreams of the old South: cotton fields white in the fall, plantations, mint juleps—he wanted to see the day when blacks would once again be slaves. He really did, talked about it. He hated blacks. He tried to teach me to hate them, but it never took—not really. I always felt kind of guilty about it. Well,"—he sighed—"we had a big fight my senior year. That was '70."

Ben gave him a startled look. "You don't look that old, Ike. That would make you . . . in your mid-thirties."

"I owe it all to my clean living." Ike smiled. "Anyway, I left home the day, or the night, I graduated high school. Joined the Navy, went into UDT, then the SEALs. Been with 'em ever since."

"You ever been back home?"

"Oh, sure. I went back a bunch of times. Dad and I made up, in our own peculiar way. Dad died in . . . let's see . . . '80. Mom joined him in '81. Hell, Ben, I'm a rich man; all that property Dad left me. I just didn't want to leave the Navy."

A warning bell began dinging in Ben's brain. "What are you going to do, Ike? After the wedding, I mean."

Ike smiled. "I'm goin' on back to north Mississippi, Ben. Farm my land."

"That's spite, buddy—and you know it. You're asking for a lot of trouble, Ike. Not just for you, but a lot of grief for Megan."

Ike shook his head. "I think, Ben, once the initial wave of hatred subsides—if it does"—he put a disclaimer on it—"you'll see a lot of changes in the way people think. That was my original thought. But with Logan going in as the next president, and all you've told me about him . . . I don't know. I've been thinking a lot about that, and also one of those books you wrote: that one about a nation within a nation, a government really for the people and by the people. And I've been thinkin' about your Rebels, too."

"They are *not* my Rebels, Ike."

"Yeah, I think they are, Ben." Once again, that smile. "You see . . . I'm one of them."

Ben looked at him, then slowly nodded his head. "O.K., that fits. Conger got in touch with you, didn't he?"

"Yep."

"Now what?"

Ike shrugged. "Now . . . nothing. Hell, General, I'm not going to push you. Go on for a time, see the country, write your journal. Your duty will come to you after a time."

"My . . . duty?"

"That's right, Ben. Duty. The old Bull picked you to lead his children, so to speak. Conger told me about you telling him to destroy all the planes they could, and so forth. Good idea. But what's that about Idaho and Montana?"

Ben told him of his dreams, of a land with mountains and valleys and cattle and crops and contented people, all living under laws they had all agreed to live under and with.

"Your nation in the book, Ben?" Ike asked softly.

Ben sighed and shook his head. "I don't know, friend. I guess so. I've got to think about it for a while, though."

"You do that, buddy. We have time. You know, Ben . . . know what Big-Brother's problem was?"

"No," Ben said, not understanding where Ike was going.

"Well . . . Big Brother said—told us—we had to like everybody we met. Right off the bat, that was some kind of stupid. Ever since the beginnings of time, all the way to the caves, Ben, I'll bet you there has been some kind of caste system and there will *always* be some sort of caste system. No government can order a person to like another person; hell, the personal chemistry between the two might be all wrong. . . ."

Jerre's words, Ben thought.

". . . It just won't work. There was a philosopher, Frenchman, I think, can't remember his name, but I read something by him that has always stuck in my mind. A fellow was askin' this man his likes and dislikes: do you like Germans? No. Do you like Italians? No. Do you like Jews? No. Do you like Negroes? No. Do you like Catholics? No. Protestants? No. Finally, the man got exasperated and asked him just who he did like? The philosopher looked at him and said, 'I like my friends.'"

Ike grinned as he popped open another can of beer. "That's the way it's got to be, Ben Raines. You think about it. We'll keep in touch."

"You're quite a philosopher yourself, Ignatius Victor McGowen," Ben said.

Ike poured a can of beer over Ben's head.

A few weeks after the wedding, the radio station went off the air (the tower fell down one night), and the party broke up, each going his or her own way. Tatter and June-Bug went to Mississippi with Ike and Megan; Space-Baby

226

and Angel-Face slipped out one night without even saying good-by.

"They kinda have this thing for each other," explained Honey-Poo.

"How about you?" Ben asked.

"Well, Ben Raines,"—she smiled—"I been thinking about hittin' the road. There was a ham operator on the other night talkin' about this big party that's goin' on over at St. Augustine. I 'magine that's where Space-Baby and Angel-Face went, or will eventually land."

"When were you thinking about pulling out?"

"Oh . . . I was kinda thinkin' about pullin' out today. I'm packed. I think you and me have about run our course, don't you, Ben?"

Ben allowed he believed they had. She was about to screw him to death.

"You got things to write about, Ben. And me? Well . . . I guess I'll go party until the day I die. I wish you lots of luck, Ben Raines."

"Same to you, Prudence."

She kissed him on the cheek, patted Juno on the head, and went bouncing out the door, in search of a perpetual good time in what was left of a world's madness. She waved good-by as she bounced off in a Jeep that had been painted pink.

And Ben was alone once more. Juno stuck his muzzle into Ben's hand and whined softly.

Well, not quite alone.

Ben pulled out his portable typewriter and began writing the first of his journal; it was, he knew, a mammoth undertaking. And he wondered if he could, or would, ever finish it; for always in the back of his mind were the Rebels and his dream of a free land of good laws and good government. He could not shake them away.

In March, with the weather warm, the sun bright, and the gulf sea blue-green, a period of restlessness hit him. He drove into Tampa, knowing it was a foolish thing to do.

The city was a littered, pockmarked battleground. Fires, still smoking, scarred its former beauty. Ben made one quick pass on Interstate 75, turned east on Interstate 4, then went up to the University of South Florida. It was as if he had stepped from one world to another. The campus was peaceful, almost serene. He parked his truck, locked it, and walked the campus. It had a deserted feel, but for the most part, had not been disturbed by looters.

Naturally, Ben thought; ignorant people don't loot books. He rounded a curve in the sidewalk and came to an abrupt halt. An elderly gentleman sat on a bench, reading a book and eating a sandwich. The man was dressed in a dark suit, white shirt, and dark tie. His shoes were polished, and he was clean-shaven. He looked up.

"Ah! I do so hate to be the bearer of bad news, young man, but we are not holding classes. I really can't say when this institution will reopen its door to welcome the young seekers of knowledge."

"We come in idealistically and leave with money our only goal."

"Precisely."

"It will reopen someday," Ben said. "Hopefully," he added.

"Glad you added that disclaimer," the man said. "I wish I shared your optimism." His eyes drifted to Ben's M-10 and the canvas pouch of clips; the 9-mm belted around his waist; the knife hanging on his left side. He

228

looked at Juno, looking at him.

"Handsome animal. Is he friendly?"

"He has been so far, sir."

"Please." The man gestured toward the empty bench beside him. "Come—sit down. Despite your rather rugged appearance and your formidable display of arms, you behave as though you might have more than a modicum of intelligence. Join me in some conversation."

"Watch Juno," Ben cautioned the man. "He swipes food." He sat down, looking at the book the man had been reading: *Selected Works of Wadsworth*. "Interesting reading, but shouldn't you be reading something on survival?"

The man chuckled and patted Juno's big head. Juno grabbed his sandwich and ate it in two gulps.

"See what I mean?" Ben said.

"There is ample food to be had, son. For as long as I shall live—which, hopefully, won't be much longer."

"Why would you hope that?"

"This"—the man waved his hand—"is—was—my entire life. I taught here since its opening day. Before that I was at the University of Florida—Gainesville. I have been a professor for all of my adult life. I know nothing else. And I am seventy-five years old. What else is there for me?"

"Life."

"But a life without flavor. What is your name, young man?"

Ben told him.

"And you did what before everybody went away?"

Went away? Ben glanced at him. "I was a writer. But I doubt you ever read any of my books."

"I fear you are correct, Mr. Raines. But I am so glad

you came along. Tell me about yourself, what you plan on doing. Enlighten me."

Ben felt the elderly gentleman did not have both oars in the water; probably the tragedy had been too much for him to cope with and he slipped just a bit. But Ben told him in detail, if only to have someone to talk with for a time.

The professor clapped his hands and giggled. "Oh, wonderful!" he cried. "Now I can go without feeling guilty about leaving her."

"Go?" Ben queried. "Go, where? Leave her? Her who?"

"Whom, son."

"Are you sure?"

"I'm a professor, young man."

"Yes, sir."

"To join my friends in that great classroom in the sky. Where the debates are endless and the merits of Wadsworth and Tennyson and all the greats are discussed with the respect and admiration due them. And Kipling can take Gunga Din and both of them can squat on the coals until their nuts roast."

Now Ben was certain the man's bread was not fully baked.

"I like Kipling," Ben said.

"I shall ignore that outrage. Look, look!" The man pointed. "See that building over there? See it, see it?" Ben said he did.

"That's where I live. With April."

"April is your wife?"

"Good heavens, no! My wife has been dead for . . . umm . . . well, a long time, I suppose—haven't seen her around. No, you see, April was a student of mine—last year. She survived the . . . ah, what did happen, son?"

Ben told him what he knew and what he surmised.

"Is that right? Umm? Well, I've often wondered about it."

"There wasn't anyone you could ask? No one came around here?"

"Only those rather large, boorish types. Very hostile. But you've informed me, so I won't worry about it any further." He peered at Ben through his thick glasses. "What were we talking about?"

"April."

"April? It's not yet April, is it?"

"No, sir," Ben replied patiently. "It's March. April was a student of yours."

"Oh, yes! Now I remember. Yes, well . . . April took it upon herself to look after me. Not that I need any looking after, mind you. And she is beginning to annoy me with all her fussing about. She's not my type of woman at all. Not at all. She is . . . rather . . . a clinging-vine type. Not that there is anything wrong with that—not at all. She just doesn't have big titties. I like women with big titties. My wife—God rest her soul, wherever she is—had big titties. I used to love to play with her big titties. Don't you like big titties?"

Ben nodded his head in agreement. Even Juno was looking at the man rather strangely.

"Well . . ." The professor selected a pill from a tiny pillbox. A white pill. He swallowed it. "Now that April is going to be all right, I can go without guilt."

"What did you teach, Professor?"

"Chemistry."

"And what was that you just took?"

"KCN."

231

"And that is?"

"Potassium cyanide."

The man stood up, smiled, waved bye-bye to Ben and Juno; then grabbed at his chest and fell to the ground in convulsions. A moment later, he was dead.

"Shit!" Ben said.

He walked over to the dorm the man had pointed out and entered the cool hall. "April," he called. "April! Are you here?"

"No! Go away."

"April, I'm Ben Raines. I had the . . . ah . . . misfortune to encounter your friend, the professor. He told me about you and then the old fool took cyanide. He's dead."

Footsteps on the stairs and a heart-shaped face peered around the corner. A very pretty face with large dark eyes. Huge glasses in front of the eyes. "He's really dead?"

"Yes. I'm sorry."

"Yeah, me, too." She stepped from around the corner of the stairwell. "But that son of a bitch was about to worry me to death. Always complaining about my titties."

She came a bit closer. She was dressed in jeans and denim shirt. Maybe her titties weren't large enough to suit the professor, but the pert little lady was unmistakably female and well enough endowed to suit Ben.

"He said you were a student of his—last year."

She laughed. "Yeah, he would. Hell, mister, he wasn't a professor. That was just his nickname. He was a dealer."

"I beg your pardon?"

"A dealer, man. Like in dope. Hell, every kid on this campus knew the old 'Professor.'"

Ben shook his head. "Well, every man is entitled to make a fool of himself once in a while. He sure had me fooled."

"Oh, he was well-educated, for a fact. And he *used* to be a professor. But that was a long time ago. He kept messin' with the female students. No telling how many he got pregnant. He finally was barred from teaching in this state."

Ben stepped closer. She did not seem afraid of him. "He did seem genuinely concerned about you."

"I think he was, in his own strange way. He was all right until about two months ago. That's when his wife died."

"He told me his wife had been dead a long time!"

"Yeah? Well, he lied a lot. His wife's upstairs in a box."

"Jesus!"

"Yeah, you can say that again. That's when he started slippin' downhill. Quickly. Called me his daughter at one point and then wanted me to give him a hand job with the next breath. As if he could get it up."

Ben could but shake his head.

Her eyes went from Ben to Juno. "That's a pretty dog. Does he bite?"

"I guess he would if you made him angry. April what?"

"Simpson. I guess the professor told you to take care of me, right?"

"He mentioned something to that effect, yes."

"Well . . . you don't look too old. Can you get it up?"

"I beg your pardon?"

"Keep a hard-on. Man, I'm horny!"

"I'll do my best," Ben said dryly.

"I'll get my things. What are you going to do with

233

the professor?"

"What do you want done with him?"

She shrugged. "He loved the campus. I'd leave him where he is."

"All right."

"Ben Raines, right?"

"Yes."

"So I'll be with you in a shake, Ben Raines."

And Ben had found yet another survivor.

TWELVE

Heading back to his house just a mile south of Ike's place, now deserted, Ben answered the girl's seemingly endless chain of questions and asked a few of his own.

"Why didn't you leave campus, April? If the professor was giving you such a bad time?"

"Where would I go? Where could I go? And do what?" She put her dark eyes on him. "I went home once, right after . . . it happened, after I got well from being so sick. Back to Orlando. Found my parents. Dead. I didn't know what to do so I just went back to what I'd grown accustomed to: the campus. I'd been there four years; all my friends were there. Or had been, that is. I tell you one thing, though. The professor might not have had all his beans baked, but he knew people, and he saw something in you he could trust. Lots of guys had been there before you came—all looking for women. But he never said anything about me."

"How often did you leave the campus?"

"Only once after I got back from Orlando. That was when Penny had joined us in the dorm. Penny Butler, from Miami. Seventeen years old. Things had sort of calmed down, and we went for a walk, just to look around, you know? Some guys started chasing us—all of them drunk and mean-looking. They caught Penny. I can still

235

hear her screaming while they were dragging her into a department store. I hid in a grocery store right next to the department store. I was afraid to move; so scared I thought I'd die. I didn't know what to do. I found a pistol under the cash register, but I didn't know what to do with it. It was kind of like the one you have on your belt. How do you work the damned thing? I've never fired a pistol in my life—any kind of gun, for that matter.

"They took turns raping her; and it wasn't just rape. They did . . . ugly things to her. I could hear them through the walls, laughing and shouting. They . . . buggered her, you know? Then they beat her when she wouldn't . . . suck them off. I guess she agreed to do anything they wanted, 'cause the beating stopped. I heard them talking about her taking three guys at once. You know, one in the mouth, one up the ass, and one the . . . normal way. One of them must have been real big, 'cause Penny kept screaming in pain and then they'd beat her again."

She sighed. "I . . . guess they beat her too much. All of a sudden it got real quiet. She wasn't screaming. The guys laughed some more, then walked out of the building, up and street. I slipped out the back door of one building and in through the back door of the department store. She was just lying there on the floor, naked, her eyes open, but she was dead. Her neck was at a funny angle. I guess it was broken. I checked her pulse, wrist and neck, but she was dead. Ben?"

"Uh-huh?"

"How come there's so many shitty people in the world? How come they lived and the good people died?"

Jerre had asked pretty much the same question. All Ben could do was shake his head.

* * *

April kept pretty much to herself in the big house by the beach. She was impressed by Ben's determination to write a chronicle of the disaster, and she helped whenever she could. But when it got down to the actual writing of the journal, Ben told her to take a hike; he worked alone.

She did not take offense, seemed to understand. So she walked the lonely beaches, picking up driftwood and sand dollars and shells.

Ben had sensed their time together would not be long, for in their conversations, April had let it be known, loud, clear, and proud, that she was a liberal; she opposed capital punishment, believed in gun control, loved the ACLU, was thrilled with Hilton Logan, hated the military, et cetera.

Ben had listened to her blather and babble and then had told her that if she so much as mentioned Hilton Logan or the ACLU to him again, she would find herself back on the road—alone.

She got the message.

On the first day of April, 1989, Ben told her to get her gear together, they were pulling out.

She asked no questions.

They drove up to Perry, then took highway 221 to Georgia. They saw no one along the way, but Ben felt certain someone had seen them. His senses were working overtime, and he could not shake the feeling of being watched . . . tracked.

April surprised him by saying, "I think we're being followed, Ben."

"When did you pick up on it?"

"When we crossed into Georgia."

A few miles south of Moultrie, Ben pulled off the road and tucked the pickup behind a service station. He checked the M-10 and his 9-mm pistol, then he hooked a couple of grenades into his belt.

"Stay back here and keep quiet," he told April. "Keep Juno with you."

He was getting some very bad vibes concerning just who was following them—or what. Then he heard the sound of motors coming up the road from the south. The engines were running ragged, as if they had seen hard use and had not been serviced properly. Or at all.

Two military trucks came into view, camouflage paint jobs. Two men in each truck. That he could see, that is. Ben felt there were probably men in the back of each truck. He clicked the M-10 off safety and stood by the side of the station. He pulled the pin from a grenade and held the spoon down with his left hand.

The trucks slowed as the drivers spotted him. The trucks pulled into the parking area and stopped, their engines cut. The morning was very quiet. When the men got out of the cabs, Ben fought to keep from laughing.

They were dressed in a mishmash of military and Georgia Highway Patrol uniforms and were a living caricature of the Hell's Angels. But Ben could sense a real danger all around him.

"We are a part of the Georgia Militia," a pus-gutted, unshaven man said. "It is our duty to see to it that no riffraff enter this state."

"Then what are you doing here?"

"Huh?"

Ben said nothing, just looked at the men.

"Are you friendly?"

"To my friends."

"That's not much of an answer, mister."

"Wasn't much of a question."

"Who do you have traveling with you?" The man licked thick wet lips. That he was asking about women was obvious.

"I don't figure that's any of your goddamned business," Ben told him bluntly. The M-10 was off safety, on full auto.

"I don't care for your attitude, mister."

"One of life's little tragedies, I'm sure."

"I don't much care for you, either."

"Where's your sheet and burning cross, redneck?"

"Well now." The man smiled. "We got us a nigger-lover here. 'At's allraht though. I ain't had me no smoked meat in some time. Got you a nigger gal travelin' with you, huh? Stand aside."

"Fuck you!" Ben lifted the M-10 and shot the man in his pus gut; at the same time he tossed the grenade at the others. Ben dived for the protection of an abandoned car.

The fragmentation grenade blew, and left one dead and two badly wounded on the ground. Before the rocking sounds had abated, Ben lobbed another grenade into the rear of the first truck and hit the ground. The frag grenade blew, sending one man through the ribs of the canvas mount and over the side of the truck. Someone screamed in the back of the truck.

Ben rose to one knee and sprayed the back of the second truck, changed clips, and waited. A man lunged out of the truck and tried to run. Ben put a short burst into his back, knocking him face-down on the concrete.

It was over. It was silent. The smell of gunpowder was thick, mixing with the heavy blood odor. Ben's legs were shaky and his hands trembled. But he and April were alive. Juno was at his side, the hairs on his back and neck raised, his fangs bared. April came around the corner of the building and put one hand to her mouth as she saw the carnage and smelled the shit and the piss from relaxed bladders and bowels. She was sick for a moment, wretching onto the gravel. Ben changed clips in the M-10 and slung it over his shoulder. He pulled out his pistol and walked to the bed of a truck. All dead. He stepped to the other truck and looked inside.

One man was alive, but just barely.

"Help me," the man pleaded.

"All right," Ben said, then raised the 9-mm and shot the man between the eyes. He walked back to April. Her face was pale, lips bloodless.

"I can't believe you did that, Ben."

Ben turned his back to her and walked away.

In Moultrie, Ben found quite a group of people, more than a hundred, he guessed, gathered at a local church. He had to struggle to hide his amusement. It had taken a world-wide catastrophe to bring blacks and whites together—at least here in Moultrie.

He told the crowd what had happened down the road. They seemed to sigh as one in relief.

"There is no Georgia Militia, Mr. Raines," a man said. "That was Luther Pitrie and his pack of filth. We're Christian people here, or try to be; no way would we tolerate that kind of man among us."

"He tried to make trouble for you?"

"About three months back. He had gathered around him some thirty or forty of the worst types of trash you could imagine. Convicts, ne'er-do-wells, degenerates.

240

They strutted in here just as we were picking up our lives and trying to restore some reason for being. He killed one man. I guess rage overcame us; we buried eleven of those who came with him. The rest have not been back."

"Good for you," Ben said, conscious of April's look of horror.

"Please stay and have supper with us, Mr. Raines. Spend the night. I know what happened today was a terrible experience; doubly so for Miss Simpson. Rest awhile, you'll be safe and you certainly are welcome."

Good people, Ben thought. I hope there are a great many more pockets of people such as these.

"You've heard what's happened in Chicago?" the leader of the small band in Moultrie asked.

Ben shook his head. "No, I haven't." But he had a quick flash of *déjà vu*.

Carl.

"Well, communications are, at best, spotty—we rely mostly on ham operators for news, and we don't get that very often." The man paused to butter a slice of home-baked bread. Real homemade country butter.

Ben said, "I was in Chicago last fall—couple of weeks after the war. The suburbs, actually. I didn't like what I saw brewing."

"The brew exploded, I'm afraid. Some sort of movement started there. Neo-Nazi, fascist—something of that type."

"Don't forget the Klan," a woman said, bitterness in her voice. "My brother is part of that mess in Chicago. Went up there when he heard what they were doing. Couldn't wait to get right in the middle of it."

"So is my brother," Ben said quietly.

The clicking of knives and forks ceased; conversation was momentarily halted.

"I'm sorry to hear that, Mr. Raines. Yes,"—the man shook his head—"a Raines was mentioned in one broadcast we monitored. A Carl Raines is one of the leaders."

"The damned fool!" Ben muttered.

"I said the same thing, Mr. Raines," a black woman said. "My first cousin was on the other side of what took place up there."

Ben looked at her. "What *did* take place?"

"There was spotty violence all winter. The whites controlled the suburbs, the blacks controlled the city. The whites cordoned off the city, wouldn't let the blacks out. And last winter was a particularly brutal one. Many died from exposure. Expressways were blocked and guarded, same with bridges and avenues. The white group raided national guard and reserve armories, got mortars and cannons, began shelling the city. It was a regular war. Then, a couple of months ago, a full-scale military invasion took place. Not the regular military, but the whites. There were no prisoners taken . . . on either side. From what we've heard, it was senseless and brutal."

"Who won?" Ben asked, a sour taste in his mouth. He thought of Cecil and Lila. And of Salina.

"Well," a local minister said, "if it can be called a victory, the whites did. Then they turned on the Jews, the Latins, the Orientals. Everyone not . . . what's the old term? WASP?"

"Yes," Ben said. "It had to come. Sooner or later. I wrote it was coming."

"I read that book of yours, Mr. Raines," a black

woman in her mid-thirties said. She sat across the table from Ben. "I didn't like it when I read it—I thought you surely had to be a racist. Then I reread it and changed my opinion of you. You're a complex man, Mr. Raines, but I think you mean well . . . for those who, in your view, deserve the well-meaning."

"Thank you." Ben acknowledged the decidedly left-handed compliment.

The minister said, "The party seems to have grown in strength over the months. So far it is still mostly centered in the Chicago and central Illinois area, but it is fanning out. And"—the man tapped his finger on the table—"it is not comprised only of filth like that dogfighting Pitrie and his ilk. From what we can gather by listening to the broadcasts, some rather . . . at one time anyway . . . level-headed men and women are joining. That's the . . . ones I don't understand."

"I do," Ben said. "And I can tell you who they are: businessmen and -women who lost their businesses through boycott or riots; men who had wives or daughters mugged or assaulted or raped by Latins or blacks and then had to watch while our courts turned them loose—if they ever even came to trial—because of the pleadings of some liberal bastard lawyer whining about past wrongs, that had absolutely nothing to do with the crime; store owners who were repeatedly robbed and were unable to do anything about it or who watched criminals turned loose because of some legal technicalities; people who lost their jobs because of hiring practices. It's a long list, with right and wrong on both sides. But the hate finally exploded into violence—the hate directed toward the minorities. Many of us, of all colors, wrote of its coming. No one paid any attention to us. Well . . . now it's here."

"That's the part of your book I didn't like," the black woman said.

"Two wrongs don't make a right." Ben defended what he had written, so many years before. "But don't misunderstand me. I am totally, irrevocably opposed to what is happening in Chicago. I just saw it coming, that's all."

"Be careful on the road, Mr. Raines," the minister cautioned him. "I'm afraid it's going to get much worse before it starts to get better."

The black lady looked at Ben. "I believe you wrote that, too, didn't you, Mr. Raines?"

"Ben, it's *stupid* going into Atlanta!" April told him. "The same thing might be going on there as happened in Chicago."

"We won't go into the city proper," he assured her. "But I want to get close enough to hear what's going on."

They were on Interstate 75, heading for Atlanta. An hour out of Moultrie.

A few miles further, Ben saw his first manned roadblock on an interstate.

"Oh, hell, Ben!" April said, her fingers digging into his leg.

"Relax." Ben patted her hand. "Let's just see what's happening. Hold the wheel for a minute." He took a grenade from the pouch at his feet on the floorboards and pulled the pin, holding the spoon down with his left hand, just as he had back at the station with the so-called Georgia Militia.

Ben rolled up and stopped, lowering his window, his

left hand out of sight. "Howdy, boys—what's the problem?"

"We just like to see who is comin' and goin' out of Cordele, mister. No real problem."

"Uh-huh," Ben said.

"I can see your right hand, buddy. But I can't see your left hand. You wouldn't have a gun pointed at me, would you? One word from me and that bunch over yonder," he jerked his head, "would shoot this truck full of holes."

"You like to shoot strangers who have done you no harm?"

The man's eyes narrowed. "That's kind of a dumb question, mister."

"Humor me," Ben said, but there was no humor in his voice.

The man spat a brown stream of chewing-tobacco juice on the highway. "You 'bout half smart-ass, ain't you?"

"Maybe. Maybe I just don't like to be stopped for no reason. Ever think about that?"

"Not often. Git outta the damned truck. Both of you."

Ben smiled and lifted his left hand. The man almost swallowed his chewing tobacco. "No. You get on the running board. My fingers are getting tired. I might just decide to drop this out the window."

"Man, you are nuts! That thing ain't got no pin in it! Jesus Christ!" he hollered. "Don't nobody shoot, or nuttin'. This crazy son of a bitch is holding a live grenade."

"Fragmentation type. Get it right."

"It's a frag type. Lordy, Lordy!"

When Ben spoke, his voice was loud enough for all to hear. "Now all you men listen to me. It is not my intention to bother a soul—unless that person first bothers me. And you people are bothering me. Now you get on the running board and tell your buddies to open that goddamned roadblock."

"I ain't botherin' you, mister. Lord, no—I ain't botherin' you. TEAR DOWN THAT FUCKIN' ROAD-BLOCK!" he screamed.

The blockade came down. The man stepped up on the running board. That put his face level with Juno's muzzle and bared teeth. "Oh, Lord!" the man hollered.

Ben stepped on the gas and drove up the interstate, out of rifle range, stopping in the middle of the highway. "Get off," he told the man.

The man did so, gladly. "Mister," he said to Ben, "you jist ain't pullin' a full load."

"Yeah? I heard that the first time I ate a snake during survival training."

The man paled.

"Now you listen to me," Ben told him. "I don't know what kind of trouble you people have had with thugs and punks, and you definitely have a right to keep those types of people out of your town. But you do *not* have a right to keep people from traveling on this interstate."

The man bobbed his head in agreement, watching with great relief as Ben inserted the pin back into the grenade. "Yes, sir."

"If I were you, I'd dismantle that blockade. Some-body's liable to come along and really take offense at being stopped and questioned."

"More than you did?"

"Hell, friend." Ben smiled at him. "I'm a saint compared to some folks roaming around out here." He put the truck in gear and rolled on, leaving the man standing in the middle of the interstate, shaking his head and mumbling.

"Ben?" April asked. "Why did that roadblock make you so angry?"

"I really don't know," he confessed. "I think maybe the arrogance of the people behind them—some of them—has always irritated me. And the structure itself somewhat. But the reasons have always been the real irritant with me: checking for a driver's license, to make certain it's the proper license for the state you're living in. What earthly difference does it make? If you can drive in California you can certainly drive in Utah. Or if you can drive in Hartford you can drive in Dallas. Country should have had one national driver's license and to hell with it." He smiled. "That's one of my very few pet gripes, April."

"The others?"

Ben grinned. "Those people who take it upon themselves to tell others what to read, what to watch on TV, or see in the movies. Or out of a township of one hundred people, fifty-one don't drink liquor, so they tell the remaining forty-nine they can't drink in their homes, or purchase a six-pack or a bottle in that township. What a person does in his or her own home is nobody else's business. But I'm death on drunk drivers, April. I have always believed that if a drunk driver kills someone, the charge should be murder—not manslaughter. And"—he grinned—"nobody on the face of this earth loves a drink of whiskey any more than yours truly. But I don't drive when I'm drunk, or even drinking very much for that matter. I used to, though. Until one night I almost ran over a kid on a bike. That was about ten years ago. That put a stop to it—for me. Don't get me started, April. My beliefs are intense."

"You're a complex man, Ben Raines."

"Maybe. And maybe I'm just a man who doesn't want to get too far away from the basic concepts of living."

"What if a drunk driver ran over and killed a loved one of yours, Ben—what would you do?"

"Now?"

"No. I mean, back when things were normal."

"My first inclination would be to kill him. But that would be wrong for several reasons. Our laws—back when things were normal, as you put it—were far too lenient on most criminals, especially the drunk driver involved in fatal accidents. So how can you blame the guy for drinking when the penalty for getting caught really, in many states, almost encouraged the drunk driver? No, education and stiff laws are the answer, and then gradually, over a period of years, as people become accustomed to those laws, and a generation grows with them, that's when you get tough with those who flaunt the law. Not abruptly. Not unless *everybody* in that state, and I don't mean fifty-one percent of the population, I mean about ninety percent of the population, agrees with those harsh laws. This fifty-one/forty-nine plurality is now and always has been, to my way of thinking, a crock of shit."

"How about those people, say, to use your figures, that ten percent—what happens to them? Those who disagree with it?"

"They can live with it, or leave."

"That's hard, Ben."

"Yes."

April was silent for several miles; miles that passed in silence, with only the humming of the tires on concrete

248

and the rush of wind.

"All this . . ." She waved her hand, indicating the emptiness of highway, the silence of the land all around them. "All this doesn't really bother you, does it? I get the impression you're looking forward to rebuilding."

Ben thought about that question. "I guess I am looking forward to the rebuilding, April. As to it bothering me? No, I guess it really doesn't. Not to the extent it should, I suppose."

"Why?" She glanced at him. "You don't believe all this is God's will, or something hokey like that, do you?"

"Hokey? Well, yes. I have to admit I've wondered about the hand of God in all this. Haven't you?"

"I don't believe in God," she said flatly. "I think it's a myth. I think when you're dead, you're dead. And that's it."

"That is certainly your right."

"Not going to give me a lecture about it?"

"Not me. Believe what you want to believe. That is your right."

"How about prayer in public school?"

He laughed out loud. "You're really hitting all bases, aren't you? All right, April. Fine, for those who want to pray. Those that don't could whistle 'Dixie' if they so desired."

"And take a lot of abuse and bullshit from the kids and the teachers, too, huh?"

"Root cause, honey."

"I beg your pardon?"

"Root cause. Ignorance, prejudice, thoughtlessness, all those things will never be stamped out unless and until we attack the root cause. And that's in the home."

"Total state control, Ben? That's just a bit Orwellian,

249

don't you think?"

"Yes, it is. But if our present method of education isn't, or wasn't, eradicating the inequities, what would you suggest as the course of action?"

"What inequities? Give me an example."

"One kid wants to play sports, another kid wants to study music: the piano, the violin. Each should be able to do as he or she wishes without being ridiculed for making a particular choice. But it didn't work that way. The kid who chooses to pursue a life of music is often—ninety-nine percent of the time—subjected to taunts and jeers and ridicule for his choice, while the kid who wants to play sports is adored and given honors. The sadness of it, April, is this: the kids who ridicule and jeer have to have learned it at home; their parents have to be condoning it. Perhaps not knowingly, but still condoning it. If they do no more than refuse to broaden intellectual horizons, they're condoning and passing their ignorance on to their kids."

"Ben . . . do you want a *perfect* society?"

"No," he said. "Just a fair one."

And he thought of the mountains. And of the Rebels. Waiting. Something stirred deep within him.

April looked at the man; took in his lean ruggedness. How fast he was, to react to a deadly situation. He had a . . . dangerous look about him. She said, "You look the type to spend Sunday afternoons in front of the TV, watching football."

"I did, for years," Ben admitted. "Still think it's a great sport. Played it in high school. But it's gotten—had—out of hand. I began to open my eyes and my mind and to look and listen to all that was happening around me; with my friends and others; what they were teaching

250

their children. I was at a friend's house one evening, watching Monday-night football. I heard my friend tell his boys that anyone who didn't play sports was a sissy and probably a queer. I thought, what a terrible thing to tell a child, and told my friend so—in front of his kids. That man hasn't spoken to me since."

"And never will again," April reminded him.

Ben glanced at her. "I don't consider his death any great loss to the world."

THIRTEEN

Ben had pulled off the interstate just a few miles south of Fort Valley and headed east. "Just wandering," he told April. "We're not on any timetable."

At a small town located on a state highway, Ben pulled over when he saw a group of elderly people gathered on and around the porch of a general store. When they saw the truck stop, they ran as if in a panic.

"Why are they afraid of us?" April asked.

"There is a certain type of filth in this world that preys on the old. I think these folks have been the victims of those types of slime. Let's see."

But when Ben opened the door to the truck, he found himself looking down the twin barrels of a shotgun. It was, he thought, like looking down a twin culvert. He lifted his eyes to meet those of the man standing on the porch, behind the shotgun.

"I didn't stop to harm anyone," Ben said. "I'm a writer, traveling the nation, attempting to chronicle all that has happened. If you people are in some sort of difficulty, perhaps I can help?"

"Lower the shotgun, Homer," a woman's voice said. "He speaks as though he has some degree of education."

The shotgun was lowered to Ben's legs. "One funny

move, sonny," Homer said, "and I'll shorten your reach considerable."

Ben forced a grin and told Juno to please stop growling. Juno licked him in the ear. "I can see where that 12-gauge would definitely do it, sir." He cut his eyes to the door of the general store. An elderly woman stood looking at him. Ben nodded. "Ma'am."

The woman asked, "Where did you attend school, young man?"

"The University of Illinois, ma'am. For about twenty minutes. I didn't like college."

She laughed. "What books have you written?"

Ben began reeling off titles and the various names he wrote under. She waved him silent.

"That's enough. Some of those books were pornography, Ben Raines. Filth. The sex acts were too descriptive. We're all adults; we know how the act is done."

Ben laughed. "But I'll bet you read every word, didn't you, ma'am?"

She grinned and moved out onto the porch. "I taught English for fifty-five years, Mr. Raines. You need to learn about the positioning of adverbs and the splitting of compound verbs."

"And don't forget who and whom and me and I."

"Yes," she said, sitting down in a chair. "That, too." She pointed to April, sitting in the truck. "Are you and that young lady married, Mr. Raines, or are you living in sin?"

"No, ma'am, we're not married. As for living in sin, I wouldn't know about that. She doesn't believe in God."

"I'm Nola Browning, young man. *Ms.* Nola Browning,

253

thank you. We have all gathered here from several small communities in this area. I'll introduce you around a bit later. Given a little age, your young lady will come to her senses concerning God and what is His. If not," —she shrugged—"her loss, not His. As to our troubles . . . well . . . it seems we have a gang of hooligans and roughnecks roaming the countryside, preying on the elderly . . . those who survived God's will, that is."

"They have been here?" Ben questioned. "Bothering you folks?"

Ms. Browning laughed without mirth. "Bothering us, sir? Oh yes, I would say so. They came up on us . . . what, Mr. Jacobs? Three months ago? Yes, something like that. They roughed up the men— humiliated them, I won't go into details—then they left. We hoped they would not return. But of course, they did.

"The second time they took all the weapons in the town. Mr. Jacobs hid his shotgun in a ditch; they missed that. Then they disabled all our vehicles. Left us stranded here. They've been back a number of times since then. The last time just the past week. Mrs. Ida Sikes is the youngest of us all: she's sixty-two. They took turns raping her. Then they pulled Mrs. Johnson out of her house and raped her the next time. A woman a trip. Mrs. Carson is next. She's sixty-five, but still a very attractive woman. The things they said they were going to do to her . . . well, they were rather perverted, to say the least. So can you help, Mr. Raines? Yes, very probably. But there is only one of you, fifteen of them, at least. What can you do?"

Ben smiled, and Ms. Browning noted that his smile was that of a man-eating tiger who had just that moment spotted dinner. "Oh, I imagine I can think of something suitable for them, Ms. Browning. I used to write a lot of action books."

"Yes," the schoolteacher replied. "And correct me if I'm wrong, sir, but didn't I read in some column that you had been a mercenary at one time?"

"I prefer 'soldier of fortune,' ma'am."

"Of course you do. As for your books . . . I so enjoyed your action stories, especially when your hero rid the world of thugs."

"Well, we'll see if I can't make one of my heroes come to life and lend a hand here."

"I imagine you can, Mr. Raines. And will. You don't look at all milksoppish to me."

"Ben?" April asked.

"Umm?"

They lay in bed, waiting for sleep to take them.

"What type of . . . slime would do something like what's been happening to these people here. I mean . . . I just don't understand."

Ben chuckled quietly. "What's the matter, little liberal? You finding that the real world is a little tough? I bet when you were in college you supported all the correct causes, liberal, of course, didn't you?" She stiffened beside him. "I bet you leaped to the defense of every lousy punk and shithead the state brought up for burning in the chair—or whatever they do—did—in Florida."

"You going to rub it in?"

"No, I just wanted to bring it up, that's all. See if I was right in my assessment. I was. Well, Ms. Browning—and that's a tough old lady—said she thought they'd be back tomorrow. Then you can see what kind of slime would do such a thing. After I kill them."

"Ben Raines, the one-man hand of retribution, huh?"

"Just doing what the courts should have done a long time ago. We should have never stopped public hangings."

She shivered beside him. "You scare me when you talk like this, Ben. You sound as if you're going to enjoy . . . doing it."

"I am."

Ben put away the light M-10 and carefully loaded his Thompson with a full drum. He hid that, along with a pouchful of clips and several grenades, behind sacks of feed he had stacked in an alley between the general store and a deserted shop. He buckled on both .45s, jacked a round in each chamber, and kept both of them on half-cock. Then, with a grenade in his hand, he sat down on the porch of the store and waited.

Homer Jacobs was guarding the women in the basement of the local Baptist Church. Ben had given him an automatic shotgun he had picked up at a police station in Florida: a riot gun, sawed-off barrel, eight rounds of three-inch magnums in the slot.

He heard them long before he saw them. They came in fancy vans, their loud mufflers roaring. Rock and roll music was pushed through straining speakers; it offended the quiet and the beauty of early spring.

But, Ben reckoned, anything these punks did would probably be offensive.

Everything fit according to what Homer and Nola and the others had told him, right down the mag wheels on the vans. Ben rose from the porch and stepped out into the street. He wanted them to come to him, even though he knew he was taking one large risk. If it had been only three or four of them he would have taken the 7-mm rifle and picked them off one by one. But with this many he couldn't take a chance of even one getting away, for that one would probably gather more scum and return, and the revenge on the elderly would be terrible.

No, he had to kill all the punks.

The lead van roared to a stop amid squalling tires. Four vans in all.

Ben did not know that Ms. Browning had slipped away from the church and made her way up the alley and into the general store. She sat behind the front counter, watching Ben. She was a good Christian lady, believing strongly in helping those who could not help themselves. She had never mistreated a human being or an animal in her life, and would rather bite her tongue than be rude to a civilized person.

When integration had come to her school, back in the sixties, she had not retired, as had so many of her friends. Instead, Nola had gone right on teaching—in the public schools. She had been raised, from a child, to hold "Nigras" just a cut beneath her (or a full one hundred eighty degrees, as the case may be), and while she did find many of their ways alien to her own way of life, she also found many exceptional Negro children with a genuine desire to learn and advance. Ms. Nola Browning concluded (and it was a horrendous decision for a Southern lady and a member of the D.A.R. and the Daughters of the Confederacy to make) that we are all God's children and to hell with the KKK and George Wallace. She had been booted out of the Daughters of the Confederacy, but that was all right with Nola; they had to live their lives and she hers.

But on this day, Ms. Nola Browning wished and hoped and prayed with all her might this young man (anyone under sixty was young to her), who had more guts than sense, would kill every one of those trashy bastards who had terrorized her town.

She hoped God would forgive her dark thoughts and slight profanity.

She felt He would.

"What's on your mind, hotshot?" The punk on the passenger side sneered at Ben.

Ben knew the only thing a person outnumbered can do is attack. And that's what he did. At the sound of the roaring mufflers, Ben had pulled the pin of the fragmentation grenade and held the spoon down. He smiled at the punk.

"You know anything about Constitutional rights?" Ben asked.

"Yeah, pops—we all got 'em."

"Wrong," Ben said, releasing the spoon. It pinged to the ground. "You just lost yours."

He tossed the grenade inside the van.

He was leaping for the protection of the stacked feed bags before the punks could get the first scream of fright past their lips.

The grenade mushroomed the van, and Ben knew that was four shitheads out of it permanently. As he leaped for the protection of the feed bags, he rolled another grenade under the front of the third van: a high-explosive grenade. The grenade lifted the van off its front tires, setting the punk-wagon on fire.

On his belly, looking out the side of the stacks, Ben leveled the Thompson and pulled the trigger, holding it back, fighting the rise of the powerful SMG. He sprayed the remaining two vans.

If nothing else, Nola thought, he's stopped that damnable music.

Ben emptied the sixty-round drum into the vans, then pulled out both .45s, hauling them back to full cock. He waited, crouched on one knee.

"Oh, Jesus God!" The cry came from the rear van. "There's blood and shit ever'where. Ever'one's dead. God, don't shoot no more—please!"

Ben waited.

"We's a-comin' out. Don't shoot no more."

"We's," Ben muttered. More than one.

We's! Nola thought, a grimace on her face. Illiterate redneck trash. Forgive me, Lord, but a rose by any other name is still a rose. Thank you, William and Gertrude.

"Hands high in the air!" Ben shouted. "If I see anything except skin in your hands, you're dead, bastards!"

He could have phrased that a bit more eloquently, Nola thought. But it was firmly spoken with a great deal of conviction.

Two young men, apparently unhurt, slowly got out of the van. Their faces were pale with shock and disbelief. Only two minutes before they had been riding high— king of the territory. Now their kingdom was in smoking ruins. And worse, they had peed their jeans.

"You." Ben spoke to a punk with a pimply face and what Ben assumed was a mustache under his nose. "Face-down in the street and don't even think about moving." The punk obeyed instantly. The dark stain on the front of the other's jeans appeared darker.

The elderly of the town appeared, walking slowly up the street. Homer with the riot gun in his hands; another

259

man with a rope. He was fashioning a noose.

The punk on his feet fainted. The would-be tough on his belly started blubbering and hollering.

"Y'all cain't do this to me! I got rights, man."

Ben smiled, a grim warrior's baring of the teeth. "So do other people, punk. Violate theirs, and you lose yours." He turned to face the man with the rope. A noose was made. "Do with them as you see fit."

They did. And that problem was solved permanently.

The people of the town cried when Ben and April pulled out. They were tears not only of sadness, but of relief and gratitude, for Ben had removed a horror from their lives. Before leaving, Ben had driven into a nearby town, prowled the stores and homes, and taken a small arsenal back with him: rifles, pistol, shotguns, and plenty of ammunition.

"You're off the beaten path here," Ben told them. "You shouldn't be bothered too much. But the next time a gang like that comes through—and there will be a next time, bet on it—don't let them get the upper hand on you. One or two of you go out into the street. The rest of you get behind cover and poke your weapons out the windows; let the bastards know you're armed and ready to shoot. And don't hesitate to fire. Your lives are on the line.

"I've brought you CBs and two base stations; I've set them up for you. You've got a long-range radio to monitor news. I don't know of anything else I can do. I've gotten you several new cars and a van; all the medicine you asked for. I guess that's about it."

All of the elderly wanted to scream out to him: you could stay with us.

But none of them would do that. They knew he had done enough—more than most would have done.

Ben shook the men's hands and kissed the ladies on the cheeks. Then he drove away. He did not look back.

When the tiny town was no longer in sight, April asked, "What will happen to them, Ben?"

"Some of them will die this summer from heart attacks, trying to put in gardens. Some will probably die this winter from the cold, or from fire. Medicines will run out. And if they're really unlucky, punks and crap-heads and other assorted scum will find them."

"You're such a cheerful bastard, Ben Raines. You could have told me everything would be all right."

"I would have been lying."

"Nobody ever seems to care about the old people. Not their kids, not the state, especially the federal government—when we had one, that is."

"Of course not, little liberal. The kids take off because they don't want to fool with the old folks. What was good for their daddy isn't good enough for the modern-day youth. The state can't provide because they're too busy spending money keeping up with government rules and dictates—most of which are no business of the federal government. Our central government was far too busy handing out billions of dollars each year protecting the rights of punks, funding programs that never should have been started in the first place. They were too busy seeing to it that rapists, muggers, murderers, child molesters, armed robbers, and others of their dubious ilk were not overcrowded in jails and prisons; that they received free legal assistance—at taxpayers' expense, I might add. That a committee was always present in Europe to speak out on the standardization of the screwhead—and that is no joke; and all sorts of other worthwhile tasks. Hell, they didn't have time to worry about a bunch of goddamned old people. What the hell, little liberal . . . priorities, you know."

Ben felt her hot eyes on him. "You conservatives really piss me off, you know that? It's so easy for you people to find fault with social programs, isn't it?"

"I thought helping the elderly was a social program, April. I'm all in favor of that. Or have you forgotten what we were discussing?"

She folded her arms across her chest and refused to look at him. "I was going to ask what you would have done, Ben—but I think I know. Able-bodied welfare recipients would have been forced to work, wouldn't they, Ben?"

He looked straight ahead, up the highway. Let her get it all out of her system, he thought.

"Women who birthed more than two illegitimate children would have been sterilized, right? The death penalty would be the law of the land. Chain gangs and work farms and convict labor. You people are sick!"

How to tell her she was right to a degree but way off base in the main? Ben kept his mouth shut.

"Damn it, Ben, talk to me! It's all moot now, anyway, isn't it?"

He sighed. "No, April, it isn't moot. Not at all. Someday . . . some way, we'll pull out of this morass and start to rebuild. That's the way people—especially Americans—are. And we'll do it. I just don't want us to make the same mistakes all over again."

"But you want tough, hard laws, don't you?"

"Yes, I do."

"Don't you think criminals have any rights, Ben?"

262

"Damned few. They sure as hell don't show their victims any rights, do they?"

"I will never, ever, forget the way those boys cried back there, Ben. And you helped *hang them!*"

"They were not boys, April. They were men. You think I would have hanged a thirteen- or fourteen-year-old? What kind of monster do you think I am?"

Miles rolled past before she spoke. "How far is Macon, Ben?"

"Twenty-five or thirty miles west of us."

"There is a college there."

"Wesleyan. I would imagine there might be some people there. Would you like me to drop you off, April?"

"Yes," she said softly. "I would, Ben."

Actually, there was quite a gathering of professors and young people at the school. And actually, Ben was more than a little relieved to be free of April.

Jerre, he figured, had more sense in her big toe than April had gleaned from her years at college.

Which is very often the case.

Ben headed up the interstate, toward Atlanta. The truck was running rough, black smoke beginning to pour from the tailpipe. But Ben whistled as he drove. Somewhere around Atlanta, he thought, I'll prowl the dealerships and get me a truck that's got a tape deck in it, get me a bunch of symphonies, and keep on trucking. Literally.

Juno and me. See the country. His thoughts drifted to Jerre, as they often did since the day he had left her. He wondered how she was faring; had she found herself a nice young man? He hoped he would see her again. And he felt he would. With that thought, his mood lifted and

263

he clicked on the cassette recorder and began taping. Suddenly, with an unexpected and unexplained warmness, he thought of Salina.

He cut off long before he reached Atlanta and using state and county roads, he took a winding route around the city. But he saw no one as he drove. No signs of life for more than sixty miles of traveling through the Georgia countryside. That puzzled him.

South of Atlanta, there had been hundreds of survivors, but the closer he drew to the city, the more it appeared that no one had survived. His curiosity finally got the better of him and at Lawrenceville he cut toward the interstate and headed into the city.

He stopped at two dealerships before, at the third dealership, he found the truck he wanted. This one had been ordered for a local sheriff's department and had all the equipment Ben felt he would need. He walked through the parts department, found a cassette player, and installed it.

He installed a new battery, changed the oil, and patted the accelerator. The pickup fired at first crank. "American workmanship isn't dead," Ben muttered. "Just most Americans."

He transferred his gear and drove to a bulk plant where he filled up the main and reserve tanks; then he rolled on into the city. A dead city. Ben began to see huge billboards. One read: REPENT, THE END IS NEAR. PREPARE TO MEET YOUR MAKER.

There were dozens more like it, and one that read: BEN RAINES—CONTACT US.

He knew who had put that one up, and he ignored it.

He checked his map and drove out to Dobbins AFB. He

smiled ruefully when he saw that the aircraft had been destroyed. He prowled the base, trying to ignore the skeletons, clad only in rotting rags and bits of stubborn flesh, that dotted the streets.

Depression hit him, the worst he had felt since Jerre's leaving. Why no survivors here? An entire city . . . wiped out. Why? He was speaking into his mike, recording his depression, his sense of loss and bafflement. Juno whined through the open rear glass, reminding the man he was not entirely alone.

Ben clicked off the recorder, patted Juno's great head, put the truck in gear, and headed for the front gate. Something nagged at him, some suspicion about this city. He could not pin it down.

As Ben drove out of the base, he passed the headquarters building. A few red, white, and blue rags fluttered in the breeze atop the flag pole.

Ben stopped and with all the dignity he could muster, he brought down the flag.

FOURTEEN

The first of May found Ben in the middle of the Great Smoky Mountains, sitting in a motel room in a deserted town, eating a cold lunch.

These mountain people, he concluded, were weird! He couldn't get close enough to any of them to say a word. At a little town just south of Bryson City, one of them had made the mistake of taking a shot at Ben. Ben had reacted instinctively and had spent the next few, long hours watching the man die from a stomach wound.

"Why did you shoot at me?" Ben had asked. "I wasn't doing a thing."

"Outsider," the man had gasped. "Got no business here. We'll get you."

"Why do you want to 'get me'?"

But the man had lost consciousness and Ben had never learned the answer to his question—at least not from the man he had shot.

Sitting in the motel room, Ben was filled with doubts and questions. Where had all the people in this area gone; the people of Atlanta? What was the use of spending years writing something . . . ?

His head jerked up as Juno growled softly, rising to his feet, muzzle toward the door.

"We don't mean you no harm, mister," a boy's voice

266

said. "But if that big dog jumps at me, I'm gonna shoot it."

Ben put a hand on Juno's head and told him to relax. He clicked on the recorder. "So come on in and sit," he said.

A boy and a girl, in their mid-teens, appeared in the door. They looked to be brother and sister. Ben pointed to a couple of chairs.

The boy shook his head. "We'll stand. Thank you, though."

"What can I do for you?" Ben asked.

"It ain't whut you can do for us," the girl said. "It's whut we can do fer you."

"All right."

"Git your kit together and git on outta here," the boy said. "They's comin' to git you tonight."

"Who is coming to get me—and why?"

"Our people," the girl said. She was a very pretty girl, but already the signs of ignorance and poverty were taking their toll.

The poverty and ignorance of her parents, Ben thought.

Root cause—in the home, passed from parents to children.

When will we ever learn?

"I've done nothing to your . . . people."

"You kilt our uncle," the boy replied. "Ain't that doing something?"

"Your uncle shot at me for no reason. All I was doing was standing by the side of a stream, trying to fly-fish for my supper."

"Our roads, our mountains, our fish," the girl said.

"I see," Ben said, his words spoken softly. "And you

267

don't want any outsiders here."

"That's it, mister."

"If you feel that strongly, why are you warning me?"

The question seemed to confuse the boy and girl. The boy shook his head. "'Cause we don't want no more killin' 'round here. And if you'll leave, there won't be no more."

"Do you agree with your people's way of life?"

"It ain't up to us to agree er disagree," the boy said. "The word's done been passed down from Corning. And if you stay here, mister, you gonna die."

"Who, or what, is a Corning?"

"The leader."

"Ah, yes." Ben smiled, but was careful not to offend the young people, or rib their way of talking or thinking. "Let me guess; this Corning is the biggest and the strongest among you. He is a religious man—or so he says—and he has a great, powerful voice and spouts the Bible a lot. Am I right?"

"Mister,"—the girl's voice was soft with awe— "how'd you know all that?"

Ben looked at her. She was shapely and ripe for picking. "And I'll bet this Corning . . . I'll bet he likes you a lot, right?"

"He's taken a shine to me, yeah."

"No doubt." Ben's reply was dry. How quickly some of us revert, he thought. Tribal chieftain. He stood up and the kids quickly backed away, toward the open door. "Take it easy. I won't hurt you. Are you going to get into trouble for coming here, warning me?"

The girl shook her head. "We come the back trails. We know where the lookouts is." She met his gaze. "You leavin'?"

"Yes. I'll be gone in half an hour. And I thank you for warning me."

She stood gazing up at him. "We're not bad people, mister. We jist don't want no more of your world, that's all. Why cain't ever'body just live the way they want to live, and then ever'body would git along?"

Why indeed? Ben thought, and once again, the Rebels entered his mind. He felt compelled to say something profound to the girl. Instead, he said simply, "Because, dear, then we wouldn't have a nation, would we?"

She blinked. "But we ain't got one now, have we?" Then they were gone.

And fifteen minutes later, so was Ben.

He drove up to Knoxville, where he found a large group of people, perhaps five hundred or more.

"Is this all?" he asked over a cup of coffee at a Red Cross building.

"No," a man told him. "I would imagine there's probably . . . oh . . . four or five thousand alive in the city . . . taking in all the suburbs. But the rest of the people are just existing. They seem to be waiting around for the government to move them."

"For the government to do *what?* Forgive me; I didn't know we had a government."

The man laughed. "Yeah? Well, it's kind of sketchy, I grant you, but it's real, and moving, getting bigger every day, so I'm told. You haven't heard about the government's plan?"

Ben shook his head.

"They want to pull all the people together in several centralized areas, each area to be three or four states, maybe less than that: agriculture, industry, business.

269

Then, after a time, just like it was two hundred years ago, move people out to homestead. Really!" He laughed, noting the look of incredulity on Ben's face. "And you know what? People are following orders; they really are, just like cattle. The government's moving the people in the cities first. Everyone from Atlanta—so I'm told— was shifted to someplace—Columbia, I think—in South Carolina. Just happened a few weeks ago."

One question that had been in Ben's mind was now answered.

"They want to settle the east coast first, the heavy industry areas, then the midwest—the breadbasket, so to speak; Texas and Louisiana for the gas and oil, and the far West—California, Oregon, Washington."

"And the people are really allowing themselves to be herded like cattle? Told where to live?"

"Sure. That shouldn't surprise you. Big Brother's been doing it to us for years. Most folks don't even question the orders to move."

"Do we have a president? Or king, or whatever?"

"Yes." The man scratched his head. "But durned if I can tell you his name right off. We're really out of touch here. It's . . . like that hotel chain."

"Hilton Logan."

"Yeah. That's it. Strange, though. I seem to recall he never was too thrilled with the military, yet they installed him as president. I can't figure that one out."

Ben let that slide. "You don't seem to be following orders here too well. Don't feel like moving?"

"Well . . . to tell you the truth, until things calm down a bit, I think I'll just keep me and mine right here. I've heard it's going to get tough in the deep South."

"Let me guess. New Africa."

270

"That's what I hear from people passing through. Some of those people are militant. But I don't really blame them. We—all of us—have shit on the blacks for years. Hurts my mouth to say that, but it's true. Then I guess we overcompensated for two or three decades. You heard what happened in Chicago?"

"I heard."

"Are we *ever* going to get along, Mr. Raines?"

Ben shrugged. "I hope so. Tell me; since Washington is gone, where is the seat of government?"

"Richmond, Virginia."

Ben drove nonstop to Chapel Hill, North Carolina. But the young people were long gone.

"You don't know where they went?" Ben asked a scholarly looking gentleman.

"No, sir, I don't. I'm sorry. They scattered in all directions. Several thousand of them. Going to solve the world's problems, so I understand." His smile was sad. Sad and knowing. "I fear they will soon learn the truth about the world. Some of them already have, so I hear."

"What do you mean?"

"Dead. Quite a number of them. That is what I have heard. No proof. Do you have a daughter or son with the young people?"

"No. Just a young friend."

"Name?"

"Jerre Hunter."

The man's face sobered. "I'm very sorry. . . ."

And the words hit Ben hard, leaving him almost physically ill.

". . . but I'm not familiar with that name. As I said, there were several thousand of them."

Ben headed north. At the Virginia line, he carefully hid his automatic weapons, keeping only a rifle and one pistol visible. If the government was rolling—even in a minuscule fashion—law and order was going to be the first business to be settled. And lawmen might take umbrage at the sight of submachine guns.

Besides, Ben had a hunch Hilton Logan was not just coming out of the closet with his true feelings. Ben thought, and had for some years, that the man was just a little insane.

He was stopped three times before he got thirty miles inside Virginia. The last time he allowed his anger to push past his control.

"What in the hell is going on?" Ben demanded. "Why am I being treated like a criminal?"

The Virginia trooper wore no expression on his face. Neutral. Impassive. A tree. A big fucking oak tree. "Where is the registration for this truck?"

But Ben had him on that. Before leaving the dealership he had carefully filled out a bill of sale and all other necessary papers. He had notarized them himself, signing the notary's name with his left hand and putting plates on the truck from another truck parked in the shop. It had been a spur-of-the-moment act. Now Ben was glad he'd done it.

"Cute," the trooper said, not believing a word he had just read. He returned the papers to Ben. "But I won't argue with you. What's your business in Richmond?"

"The first lady—and I use that term loosely, assuming Logan has married or is shacked up with Fran Piper—and I are from the same town in Louisiana. I thought I'd just drop in for a little chat."

"President Logan married a lady named Fran, yeah."

The trooper looked at Ben, then shook his head. "Raines, what do you think this is, some sort of joke?"

"The . . . ah . . . first lady is. I wasn't kidding about that."

"You really know her?"

"Unfortunately. I fucked her for about a week—last year. Right after the war."

"No kidding! Hey, she's a looker. Was it good?"

"You ever had any bad?"

Both men laughed at the old joke. The ice was broken, the tension gone. Big buddies now; talk about pussy. They introduced themselves. Shook hands. Formal ceremony. Ben and Mitch, standing chatting in the middle of silent devastation. Not two hundred yards away, the bones of an entire family lay rotting in a house.

Ben leveled with the trooper, taking it from the beginning. He condensed it considerably, but hit the high points.

Mitch whistled. "You really carrying all that armament?"

Ben showed him.

"Shit!" the trooper said.

"You would suggest I not go to Richmond?"

"Not unless you want to spend the rest of your life in the pokey. That is, providing the soldiers guarding President Logan didn't shoot you right off."

"Martial law?"

"Tight as a virgin's cunt."

Ben nodded. "Tell me, since it appears unlikely I'll be heading into Richmond, what, exactly, has Logan done?"

"Well." The trooper sighed, removing his Smoky-the-Bear hat. "He's pissed off a bunch of people—of all colors, I might add. Seems Logan wasn't so much in love with the minorities as people thought."

273

"What do you mean?"

"Word is he's gonna send troops into this New Africa place, down in Mississippi and Louisiana."

"When?"

"Don't know that. But I do know the niggers down there are gonna fight the order, so it promises to get bloody. And he's got his own private little army, down in Georgia, headed up by an ex-mercenary."

"What's the merc's name?"

"Only thing I've heard is Parr."

"Kenny Parr. I know him; soldiered with him in Africa. He's no good. Fight for any flag."

"Yeah. That's what I heard. Logan's shuffling the remaining citizens around. And he's collecting all the guns; .22 rifles and 410 shotguns is all he's letting the people keep."

"Son of a bitch!" Ben swore.

"Yeah," Mitch agreed. "I never was in favor of gun control. But I guess I'm lucky to have a job doing what I've been doing for ten years. Although I wouldn't want it to get out that I've been talking with the leader of the Rebel army. Logan's put a bounty on their heads." He spoke the last softly.

"And mine?"

"No." The trooper shook his head. "He hasn't."

"You knew who I was all along?"

"Yeah."

"Why didn't you . . . arrest me, or whatever?"

"To tell you the truth, Mr. Raines, in my way of thinking, the Rebs haven't done anything to warrant arrest or killing. There's been a lot of accusations thrown at them, but no proof to back it up. And . . . well . . ." He trailed it off into silence.

"You're not real sure you approve of all Logan's

doing?" Ben finished it.

"Yeah," he said heavily. "I guess that's it. It worries me more than a little. I'm afraid he might—will—go too far with this thing. I . . . just don't believe he has the right to tell people where to live, what to do. But . . . until the people start bristling up and snarling about it, I guess I'll go along with it."

"And when they do that?"

The big trooper met Ben's eyes. "I know where a contingent of Rebs is hiding."

Ben didn't press that. "What are we using for currency now?"

"Plain old greenbacks. The storage area where the emergency currency was held took a direct hit—or one of them did, at least. Be a lot of millionaires around for a time, but new emergency currency will be printed as soon as a new mint is established and plates are made."

An idea, actually several ideas at once, all jumbled, popped into Ben's head. "Want to do me a favor, Mitch?"

"Probably. Name it."

"Pass the word down the law-enforcement line that I'm dead."

A thin smile passed briefly over the trooper's tanned face. "You got it . . . General."

He turned and walked away.

"I'll get new ID," Ben called after him.

"Be a good idea. You're gonna be a wanted man pretty damned quick, I'm thinking." He paused at his car and stood looking at Ben.

"How do you figure that?"

"I read that book of yours, Mr. Raines—the one that caused all the controversy. I liked it. And I'm thinking you're gonna pull something pretty quick. I might decide to join you. See ya 'round."

*   *   *

Ben drove to the top of a high mountain and turned
on his military radio, preset to 39.2. He tried for several
minutes to raise someone, but received no reply. He
drove into the nearest town and began driving up and
down the street to look for a ham operator's antenna. On
his final pass through the town, he found one. He
prowled several stores before finding a big enough
portable gasoline generator to drive the equipment. It
was after ten o'clock before he finally got the equipment
hooked up and humming. It was another half-hour before
he managed to locate a Rebel unit. During that time he
had spoken to people in Nigeria, Burma, Australia, and to
some ships at sea.

"I won't ask you where you are," Ben said. "Just listen
to me. How many people and how much equipment have
been moved west?"

"Quite a lot, sir. But we don't know what the hell we're
doing it for."

"Just continue with the movement. Now then; I want
you and all your people to begin searching the towns and
cities. Pick up every ounce of gold and silver you can
find. Also all the precious stones. Move it west to the
holding areas. Be careful, there are bounties on your
heads."

"Yes, sir, we know. Sir? A new land, sir? That what
you're planning?"

"Maybe. I don't like what Logan is doing."

"Neither do we, sir. When will you be in touch again?"

"I . . . don't know. I don't think I will until we can set
up a different frequency. Just carry on."

"Yes, sir."

Ben holed up for a few days, trying to straighten out

276

his thoughts, telling himself if he was going to lead the Rebels, then goddamn it, he should do it, and quit assing around about it. But he couldn't convince himself to stop his journal and do it. There was time, he finally concluded. He had time.

But deep down, he doubted that.

He finally pulled out, angling gently southward, recording all that the Virginia trooper had told him, including the trooper's own doubts, but leaving out the trooper's name. He also recorded all he knew about the first lady (which was plenty), but discreetly left out the fact that during their nights together she had licked his pecker like it had been made of peppermint candy.

Some things are personal. Ben grinned.

He turned west, picking up Interstate 40. At Crossville, he began seeing vehicles pass him, on the other side of the median, all heading east. And he picked up some interesting CB chatter.

"Wonder who that ol' boy is, headin' west?" The question popped out of the speaker.

"Don't know. But he better be careful if he's headin' into Nashville. Logan's people will sure turn him around and point him in the right direction."

"Yeah," a female voice said. "After they take all his guns and shake him down like he was a criminal. At first those guys came around asking nice-like. Then they started getting hard-nosed about it. Oh well,"—she waxed philosophical—"South Carolina is probably nice. It's just I don't like being forced to do something I don't want to do."

"How many times have you said—back when the nation was whole—that people out of work should be forced to work?" The voice of the questioner was unmistakably black.

"Maybe I was wrong in saying that," she admitted. "The shoe sure is on the other foot now, isn't it?"

"But we're all in the same boat," the black man said. "And I don't like it either."

Ben pulled off the interstate at the first open exit and headed south. Forcing people out of their homes, he thought. The son of a bitch is really forcing people to relocate and retrain, against their will.

But it always looked good on paper, he reminded himself. Also reminding himself that he had written it . . . several times.

"Logan," he said aloud, "I just flat out don't like you."

Ben kept to the little-traveled county roads, being very careful as he went under the overpasses of the interstates. He spent the night just inside the Alabama line and was up and moving at first light, heading back to Louisiana, but planning several stops along the way.

He found a group of men working on farm equipment outside of Cullman. They were shocked at what Ben told them.

"Forcing people to resettle?" a black man said. "But that's not constitutional."

"I don't think we have a constitution," Ben replied. "I'll wager, with the coming of martial law, it's been suspended. The government can do anything it wants to do with the muscle it has."

"We've been out of touch for months," a man admitted. "Busy working, trying to restore a way of life."

"You haven't heard about the trouble in Chicago between the races?"

No one had.

Ben told them what he knew and also about the plans

for a New Africa and what the government planned to do with that idea.

The black man was very explicit with his views. "Fuck a New Africa. I'm not an African; I'm an American. This is my home—our home." He waved at the group, a mixture of blacks and whites. "We're all friends, working together—root hog, or die. And no son of a bitch is going to run me off what is mine."

All agreed with him.

Another area where the problems between races had been solved.

At least temporarily; Ben added a disclaimer. But it was a start.

"You'd better get some radios and start keeping in touch with what's happening. I think it's going to get nasty."

Ben pulled out, heading to where Ike said he'd be, making the run in only a few hours. For a time, it was old home week; then Ike got serious.

"I think, Ben, things are gonna turn to shit, real quick. You know about the bounties on the Rebs' heads?"

Ben nodded.

"Word is being passed up and down the line about your death. I told Conger and Voltan and some of the others to hang loose, I didn't believe it."

"I thought it best."

Ike agreed. "Good idea. Well,"—he sighed—"we been tryin' to get this land in shape—do some truck farmin'. People gotta eat. But . . . Logan's gonna move in here sooner or later. I don't know what to do."

"Where are Tatter and June-Bug?"

"Oh,"—Ike's face brightened, losing its tension—"they found themselves a couple of ol' boys and got married. Whatever me and Megan decide to do . . .

they're with us."

Ben looked at Megan. "You haven't had any trouble with the rednecks?"

She shook her head. "Only one incident."

"Trashy bastard came around here," Ike said. "Runnin' off at his mouth. I remembered him from high school. Son of a bitch didn't get out of the ninth grade— so stupid he quit—and he's talkin' about me marryin' a low-down nigger."

"What happened?" Ben asked, although he hardly had to ask, knowing Ike's volatile temper.

"I killed him," the ex-SEAL said calmly. "Took his body into town and dumped it on the courthouse square. Folks been right friendly since then."

Despite the awfulness of the statement, Ben had to smile. "If you can't educate them to mind their own business, kill them—right?"

Ike shrugged. "I don't have the time or the inclination to educate folks, ol' buddy. Way I figure it, we're back to the days of the old West. You do your thing and I'll do mine. Think whatever in the hell you wanna think—I got no right to restrict you there—but don't insult me or mine; don't steal from me or mine; don't try to hurt me or mine; and don't manhandle me or mine. Just live and let live. You get in trouble, I'll help you, but by God, if I get in trouble, you'd better help me."

"Ike, what do you think about the West? Where I've sent some of the Rebels."

"Idaho and Montana?"

"Yes."

"Wild and beautiful. Everything a man could ask for. Grow good crops and raise fat cattle. Cold as a witch's tit in the winter."

"Beats being told where to live."

"And being told what kind of job to do and what time to get up and go to sleep and all that happy crap. Yeah, it sure does beat it." He rose from Megan's side. "I'll be right back, Ben. Hang on."

Megan looked at Ben. "We're going to have a lot of trouble with Logan, aren't we, Ben?"

"Yes. And when it comes, it's going to come very quickly."

"Logan scares me. I didn't trust him fully; a lot of my people didn't. What is that line about the 'man who would be king'?"

"Yes. That's the way I see it. I think he's unbalanced."

Ike returned with a large suitcase-looking container, metal, with electronic inputs on the front and a collapsible antenna on the side. "This is a very high-frequency radio, Ben. I borrowed a couple of them from Keesler on the way up. Built in scrambler, the whole bit. This thing will transmit three thousand miles and receive world-wide." He showed Ben how to adjust the band. "This is if you wanna contact the Rebs. This one is for me."

"If I decide to head west, Ike—"

"Hell, you've already made up your mind to go. I know you well enough to see that."

". . . Lots of high mountains out there."

"So get on top of one of the mothers, General."

"Ike? You be careful—you hear me?"

The stocky Navy man laughed. "Lord, General, you worry more than an old mother hen. Come on, let's get something to eat. We got a lot of jawin' to do before you pull out."

FIFTEEN

Ben changed his mind about going to Louisiana, knowing the only reason for the visit was to see Salina. So he crossed the river at Helena, south of Memphis, and headed across Arkansas, making good time, staying on the secondary roads. He skirted Little Rock, not daring to go any further north. For from Fort Smith in Arkansas all the way up to just a few miles south of Kansas City, everything was gone; that area had taken both types of warheads. He spent a night by a lake in the mountains, fishing in the late afternoon sunlight. He caught more fish than he could possibly eat and was cleaning them, preparing to fry them on his portable Coleman stove when Juno growled low in his chest.

"We're friendly." The voice came out of the brush. "I have some children with me."

"Come on in," Ben said, keeping one hand on the butt of his pistol.

A black man and woman, with several kids in tow walked up to the cabin porch. The man stuck out his hand. "Pal Elliot." He smiled his introduction. "This is Valerie. And these," he said, pointing to the children, "in order, starting with the oldest, are Bruce, Linda, Sue, and Paul."

Two blacks, one Oriental, one Indian.

Ben shook the offered hands and smiled at the kids. "Ben Raines," he said. He sat down on the porch and motioned for the others to do the same. "You folks live around here?"

Pal smiled. "No, just passing through. Like a lot of other people. I was an airline pilot, based in L.A. Valerie was a model in New York City. We met about seven months ago, I think it was."

"Six months ago," she corrected him with a smile. "We picked up the kids along the way. Found them wandering."

"No children of your own?" Ben asked.

"No. But he did." She looked at Pal. "Lost his whole family. You?"

Ben shook his head. "I was—am—a bachelor. Lost my brothers and sisters and parents." He grimaced in the fading light.

"Memories still painful?" Pal asked.

"No, not really. One brother made it out—up in Chicago. Suburbs, actually. We met . . . had a falling out."

"Carl Raines?" Pal asked.

"That's the man."

"We passed through that area," Valerie said. "Very quickly. It was . . . unpleasant."

"Well, folks . . ." Ben stood up, rubbing his hands together. "How about staying for dinner? I have plenty of fish."

"We'd like that," they said.

"I knew I'd heard that name somewhere," Pal said. It was evening in the mountains. The air was soft with warmth, the lake shimmering silver in the moonlight.

283

The children played Rook in the den of the cabin; the adults sat on the porch, smoking and talking and drinking beer. "'Way you write, hard law and order, I had to think you were a racist—at first. Then you did some other books that had me confused about your . . . reasoning. What is your political philosophy, Ben? If you don't mind my asking, that is."

"No, I don't mind. I . . . think I was rapidly becoming very apolitical, Pal; pretty damned fed up with the whole system. I did a couple of books about it. I was fed up with the goddamned unions asking for more money than they were worth—trying, in many instances, to dictate policy to the government. I was very weary of crime with no punishment, sick of the ACLU sticking their noses into everybody else's business. Oh . . . don't get me started, Pal. Besides, as a young lady once told me, not too long ago, it's all moot now, anyway."

"Is it, Ben?" Pal asked. "What about Logan?"

Ben chuckled. "Our president-we-didn't-elect? Yeah, I know. I gather you folks aren't responding to his orders to relocate?"

"Logan can take his orders and stick them up his nose," Valerie said. "I never did like that man; didn't trust him."

Megan's words.

"I shall live," she continued, "where I damned well choose to live."

Ben told them about Ike and Megan; of New Africa and what the government planned to do. And then he told them, just touching on it, of the idea that was in his mind—to get their reactions.

They both were excited. "Are you serious with this, Ben?" Pal inquired, leaning forward.

"Yes, I suppose I am. I know I am. I've been resisting it for months. I didn't believe Americans would follow Logan's orders, falling in line like lemmings on the way to the sea, blindly following orders. You two have witnessed it?"

Pal nodded. "Yes. Several times during the past few months. People are being forced to relocate, many of them against their will."

"You were going to tour the country, write about it?" Valerie asked.

"Was," he said. "You people?"

"The kids have to have schooling," Pal said. "And I'm told a man named Cecil Jeffrey and his wife, Lila, are really doing some fantastic things down in Louisiana."

"I just told you what Logan planned to do about New Africa," Ben reminded them.

"Maybe it won't happen."

"You can't believe that."

"No," Pal said quietly. "I suppose not. White people have always been fearful of an all-black nation, whether you will admit it, or not. But I suppose we have to try. I have a master's in science; Valerie, a master's in business. They are going to need teachers."

"But I just told you—"

"I know—I know." Pal waved him silent. "But after all that has happened . . . all the horror, I thought perhaps the government would . . . let us alone, let us rebuild."

"You know they won't."

Pal and Valerie said nothing in rebuttal.

Ben told them of Kasim, ending with, "I intend to kill that man if I ever see him again."

"Why, Ben?" Valerie asked. "You seem a fair man.

But even in you, there is hate. Why?"

"Because . . . he is not what you people need, any more than my people need the KKK. What we both need is understanding. Always have. I'd meet Kasim halfway, try to work it out, but he doesn't want that. With him, it's whole hog or nothing. If you go to New Africa, if Logan lets it exist—which he won't—you, both of you, will be attempting to teach truth and knowledge and fact, in a western manner. Kasim will be teaching hate without reason . . . in robe and turban. You'll be pulling against each other. It won't work. I'd like to see a nation—a state, if you will—where we teach truth, as supported by fact; the arts, the sciences, English, other languages, fine music—the whole bag. I have this theory—very controversial—that we are, should have to start from scratch. Gather up a group of people who are color-blind and as free of hates and prejudices as possible, and say 'All right, folks, here it is; we, all of us, are going to wash everything clean and begin anew. Here will be our laws, as we choose them. We will live by these laws, and they will be enforced *to the letter* . . . equally. Always. This is what we will teach in our schools—and *only* this. This is what will happen when a student gets out of line. Everything will be in plain, simple English, easy to understand and, I would hope, easy to follow.' The speech would have to end with this: 'Those of you who feel you can live in a society such as we advocate, please stay. Work with us in eradicating prejudices, hatred, hunger, bad housing, bad laws, crime, etc. But those of you who don't feel you could live under such a system of open fairness—then get the hell out!'"

Both Pal and Valerie were silent for a few seconds after Ben finished. Pal finally said, "That, my friend, would be some society, if it would work."

"It would work." Ben defended his theory. "If the government—the central government—would leave the people alone. It would work because everyone in the system would be working toward that goal. There would be no dissension."

"Don't you feel that concept rather idealistic?" Valerie asked.

"No, Valerie, I don't. But I will say it would take a lot of bending and adjusting for the people who chose to live in that type of society."

"Ben Raines?" Pal looked at him. "Let's keep in touch."

As he drove away the next morning, Ben thought: Now there are the types of people I'd like to have for neighbors, friends. Good people, educated people, knowledgeable people, with dreams and hopes and an eye toward the future.

He waved good-by as he headed for the highway that would take him into Oklahoma. On the second day, he headed for Oklahoma City. He had installed a scanner in the truck, depending on the people to warn him of any upcoming meeting with Logan's military or other unfriendly types.

He stopped often, talking with people. Yes, they had heard of the new president, and of his orders to relocate the people. But no, they didn't think they'd go along with that. This was their home, and here was where they intended to stay.

"What if he sends people in here to move you forcibly?" Ben asked.

They didn't know what they'd do.

At the University of Oklahoma, he met a group of young people and spent two nights there, talking with them.

"Some of us were in the original group from Chapel Hill," a young woman told him. "I don't believe there are many of us left."

"Run into trouble?" Ben asked.

The young woman patted Juno for a moment, rubbing his head for a time before answering. "We weren't ready for what came at us," she admitted. "We didn't—most of us—have guns. All in my group were city-born and -reared. I'd never fired a gun in my life. We thought people would want help in getting organized again. You know, planting gardens . . . all that. And we did find a few old people who really appreciated what we did. But all over the country, people are setting up their own little governments. . . ."

So his idea was not novel; he didn't expect it was.

". . . And man, some of those people didn't want us around—at all! We found religious nuts—and I mean *nuts*—Jonestown types, survivalists, kooks, crazies, drunks, maniacs. You name it, we found it.

"A lot of our people went into the cities." She shook her head. "They never came out. Then we started getting smart; rigged up our cars and Jeeps and pickups with CBs—and boy, did we get wary. We finally got it through our heads that if we were going to survive, we'd damned well better get with the program; get ourselves some guns and learn how to use them." She waved her hand. "You see those two hundred-odd kids here, Mr. Raines? This is it. With the exception of one small group, this is all that's left out of about thirty-five hundred young people who left Chapel Hill. This is it! I never knew what that expression about it being a jungle out there really meant . . . until we . . . went out to save the world." Her laugh was bitter, and not suited to the young woman.

Ben looked around him at the beaten-down, disillusioned young people. He thought: all your fancy cars and pretty clothes and gold throat jewelry and extravagant allowances from overindulgent parents didn't prepare you for this, did it, kids? All the fancy words from college professors didn't do a damned thing to help you cope with hard reality. But when he spoke it was, "So now what, kids? All of you just going to give up?"

Two dozen pairs of eyes shifted to him. Hostile, hurt eyes. Ben grinned, knowing he had hit a tender spot.

"What's it to you, man?" a boy asked.

Ben shrugged. "Maybe nothing. Maybe I should just move on. Losers never appealed to me."

"Hey!" The spokeswoman almost shouted the word at him. "What do you want from us, mister? Huh? We tried to do what we felt was right. So O.K. . . . maybe we blew it this time around; that doesn't mean we're not going to try again. So why don't you just get off our case, O.K.?"

"And what are you young people going to do when your favorite liberal hotshot-turned-two-bit-dictator sends his troops in here to move you out to a relocation center? Just be herded like stupid cattle?"

"We talked about him. O.K., so he wasn't what he appeared to be. But he was a damned sight better than Nixon, wasn't he?"

"No," Ben said. "He damned sure wasn't—isn't. And what the hell do you people know about President Nixon? You were babies when Watergate went down. All you know is what you've read, written by biased newspeople, and what you've been force-fed by feather-headed college professors who are so far out of touch with reality they should be forced to wear earphones, plugged into the vibrations of history." He sighed, grinned, and said, "I didn't mean to lecture you, kids."

"It's all right, Mr. Raines," a young man said, a grin on his face. "I kinda enjoyed it. Anyway . . . we don't know what we're going to do. You got a plan of some sort?"

"Yes. You might like it, you might not." He was thoughtful for a moment. Committing yourself, Ben? he asked himself. Maybe, came the reply. "But first let me ask you this: was there no group that fought back from the outset? Fought against the slime and the scum and the looters and such?" He had mentioned nothing of Jerre.

"There was one person," the young woman replied, choosing her words carefully. "She came into Chapel Hill with a pistol belted around her. She ignored the laughing from a lot of us—me included. She went around talking to bunches of people, like she was choosing her group very carefully. She picked about twenty-five–thirty people, then they split; didn't even stay for the speeches. Which were a bunch of shit," she said with a grimace. "I heard later the girl made all her group get guns and practice with them. She ran it like a military unit. She was the boss—no doubt about it. Blond girl, real pretty."

Ben smiled.

"Name was . . . Sarah . . . no! Jerre, that was it."

"Where did her group go?"

"West, I think. Yeah. Said she was going to Idaho or Montana, maybe Wyoming." She paused. "Why would anyone want to go there?"

"To be free," Ben said.

"Would you please explain that?"

He did.

And knew then he was committed.

"When will he be here, Jerre?" a young man asked her.

Jerre turned her eyes eastward. Her face was burned dark from the sun, as were her arms; her hair was sun-streaked and cut short.

She was not the leader of this group, which included Steven Miller, the college professor; Jimmy Deluce and his group from Louisiana, Nora Rodelo and her friends, Anne Flood and her group, James Riverson and Belle, Linda Jennings, Al Holloway, Jane Dolbeau, Ken Amato, and a few of the western-based Rebels. But she knew Ben Raines, and Bull Dean had put Raines in charge, so that made the girl somebody special.

"He'll be here," she said. "I don't know when, so don't ask me, but he'll be here."

"Equipment coming in," a Rebel called.

They all moved to the line of trucks rolling up the mountain road. The young man who had asked the question put his arm around Jerre's shoulders.

"Will you still be my girl when he gets here?" he asked.

"That depends."

"On what?"

"I'll know when he gets here. Then I'll tell you."

Ben left the young people arguing and debating the merits of his plan and quietly slipped away, Juno at his side. Just north of Chickasha, he connected with highway 81 and took that straight to Kansas. He began meeting

291

more and more people, spending a week in Kansas. He did not want to get too close to Nebraska, for that state had taken several hits and was considered "hot."

Obviously, Logan's plan to relocate people was not meeting with much success in Kansas. When he asked them about it, they looked at him as if they were conversing with a fool.

"This is the breadbasket, sonny," a farmer told him. "The government's gotta have grain, and we produce it. No . . . I think they'll let us alone. Besides, I said Logan was an idiot when he first started runnin' off his mouth twenty years ago. I still think he's not pullin' with both oars."

At Hays, Ben got on highway 40 and followed that all the way into Colorado. He saw the ruins of Denver and it made him almost sick. It had been one of his favorite cities.

"Damned shame, isn't it?" The voice came at him from his left.

Ben spun, the 9-mm in his hand. Juno had been off taking a pee.

"Whoa!" the man said, holding out his empty hands. "Son, you are quick with that thing. I'm friendly."

The man wore a pistol on his hip; but it was covered with the leather of a military-type holster. USN on the side of the flap.

Ben holstered his 9-mm. "Navy?"

"I was, for twenty-four years. Captain when the war broke out. Chase is my name. Lamar Chase."

"Ben Raines." They shook hands. "What happened to Denver?"

"It didn't take a hit, if that's what you're thinking. Enemy saboteurs hit the base, and hit it hard. For some reason, I don't know why, spite probably, they also placed fire-bombs in the city, in very strategic locations. Gas mains blew. The wind was right. And Denver is no more. I was on leave at the time. Took my wife up into the mountains and sat it out."

"I have some fond memories of this city. Or what is left of it. I took some training up at Camp Hale."

The Navy man smiled. "I thought you might be one of those boys. Hell-Hound?"

"That unit never existed, Captain—you know that."

"Shit!" the Navy man said.

Ben took a closer look at the initials on the leather flap. USNMC. "Doctor?"

"You got it. You look like the survivor type, son. Shoot first and ask questions later." He motioned to the curb. "Let's sit and talk. Where are you going?"

Ben sat with the doctor and talked.

"Ambitious project. Luck to you. What do you think about our president?"

"I used to fuck his wife."

Dr. Chase laughed so hard tears streamed from his eyes and he had to rise from the curb, holding his sides. He wiped his eyes and said, "Beautiful. I needed a good laugh. Come on, Ben—have supper with me and my wife. I've got something I'd like to discuss with you—if you're the Raines I think you are."

"I thought you might be the one I've been hearing about," the doctor said, patting his wife's hand. It had been a delicious dinner, the conversation sparkling. "So what do you think of my plan, Ben?"

"I'd say you've been sleeping in my mind for the past ten years."

293

"Yes," Chase agreed with a slight nod of his head. "I got part of it from a book of yours. Enjoyed it immensely. Didn't agree with everything you advocated—you got a bit Orwellian in parts—but I went along with about ninety percent of your thoughts."

"I don't know how much time we have." Ben toyed with his coffee cup.

"Months," the Navy man assured him. "I believe."

Ben glanced at him, questions in his eyes.

"You say you're committed now," Chase said. "All right, so let's get the ball rolling. I know, from listening to radio broadcasts, you've got about five thousand people working, moving gear, or ready to move gear, into those areas you chose. All right, let's do it.

"Logan? Well . . . he wants to be king," Chase explained. "He's lived for so long, hiding his true feelings, I think the man is a bit unbalanced. I really think Logan started out with good ideas; wanting to do good things for the people. He was an idealist, but so are you, to an extent. But yours is a pragmatic idealism, and I don't mean to sound paradoxical. You are a conservative with a slight liberal twist to the conservatism. Logan grew up hating guns—they frighten him. He hates the military; really hates cops, authority. But he will use them both to gain his own end. With Logan, any good thing he might accomplish will be done in accordance with *his* interpretation of the law of the land. Whatever it might be at the time. But you, Ben Raines, you've held our laws in contempt for years; you don't give a damn for the prevailing laws of the land. There is a hardness in you that will probably be your downfall—but we don't have to go into that. I can live with it; you're not inflexible.

"You and Logan—and this might surprise you—are

somewhat alike. But while he advocates a pulling together of the States, you advocate a dozen countries within one mother cocoon, each with their own system of justice; but answering, in part, to the mother. I agree with you. I think that is what would have become of our nation if the war hadn't struck the world.

"Logan has a hard pull ahead of him; splinters have begun forming. But they are not embedded firmly and Logan's people will pull them out—in time. That's why I believe we have time to set up and get ready." He sighed. "I think, Ben, your concept is a good one—and a fair one—and I'd like to be a part of it. I'll be here, doing my bit, gathering around me some people that will fit into your—our—type of society. I know more than a few."

"I wonder how many people would—could—live under the type of government we advocate?"

"More than you might think, Ben. But fear is the foundation of all governments. That's not an original quote. Adams, I believe made that statement. And your government will be based on the same, but with a type of fear that all involved will have accepted—willingly. It will work."

For a time, the doctor thought. Until Big Brother gains enough strength to crush it. Or tries to crush it. But how does one kill a dream, an idea, whose time has come?

By now, Ben had grown accustomed to the empty interstates and highways. Always a loner, he enjoyed the solitude of his wanderings. He listened to the winds sing through the open windows, a sighing, melodic accompaniment to his voice as he spoke into the mike, the tape hissing, recording his thoughts, his observations, his plans for the future—a verbal transcription of the worst tragedy to strike the earth since God sent the flood, and of the society that Ben wanted to build out of the ashes of war.

Did God do this?

That question was one that Ben often pondered as he lay in his blankets. But if He did—why? He certainly didn't spare just the so-called "good people." At least Ben had not seen any modern-day Noah.

When the weather was good and the skies, alive with sparkling diamonds in the darkness of space velvet were fair, Ben liked to spread his ground sheet in the open and sleep under the canopy of nature. He was not afraid of anything or anyone slipping up on him in the darkness, for Juno had proven, time and again, to be a marvelous watchdog. Ben never used a leash or line on him because although the malamute did roam, he seldom roamed out of earshot.

And Ben dreamed, his dreams a curious fusion of Jerre and Salina. In his dreams, he relived the nights of love-making with the blond Jerre, and fantasized of making love to the dusky Salina. His dreams left him restless upon waking, and sometimes irritable. And he knew he'd damned well better find him a woman pretty quick, or else take matters in hand. And that thought amused him. For while he knew the biggest liar in the world was a person who claimed never to have masturbated, and the second biggest the person who said he was going to quit, self-abuse was not Ben's forte.

At Craig, Colorado, Ben cut straight north on highway 13/789 and headed into Wyoming, wild and beautiful country. He drove over to Rock Springs, on up to the Grand Teton National Park, then headed into Idaho. He saw very few live people, and spent most of his time prowling through stores and banks, picking up diamonds and gold. When the load got to be too much, he cached it along the way, making very detailed maps as to the spot.

Spending time in the Grand Tetons, it was there Ben realized, with a pang of guilty conscience, that he had not used the radio Ike had given him. So on a cold, clear night, he cranked up the set.

"Son of a bitch!" Ike roared, back in Mississippi, his exasperated voice ringing from the earphones. "Where the goddamned hell have you been? We've been worried about you, walking the floor, you no-good prick! You—"

Megan took the mike, her voice calm. "How have you been, Ben?" she asked.

"Fine, Megan. Seeing the country, setting up little groups to go into . . . that area we discussed. What's the situation where you are? Besides Ike losing his temper, that is."

"Logan's people have been in here once, and we have rumors they are coming back. The next time to get a bit rough about us relocating."

"What'd they have to say about Ike's guns?"

"Said he'd have to give them up."

"No son of a bitch is takin' my guns!" Ike roared in the background.

"Be quiet, Ike," Megan said. "Ben? Word is Logan is preparing to move against those blacks who have settled in Louisiana and parts of south Mississippi. This fall is the deadline he's given them. Some mercenary is going to lead the push."

"Kenny Parr. I know him—he's no good. But New Africa never had a chance to begin with. I told them that."

Ike came on the air. "Do we prepare to move, General?"

"Yes," Ben said, taking the final step toward total commitment. "I'll see both of you in a week or so." Ben signed off.

Two days later he was speaking with Dr. Chase and his wife.

"Time to move?" the doctor asked.

Ben nodded his reply.

Chase smiled. "Give up your plans to write the history of the tragedy?"

"For the moment. Doctor, I know you have to be part of the Rebels, so get your people together and start moving toward Idaho." He unfolded a map. "Right there. Strip everything bare as you go. Take it all. I want everything you people think we can use. It's going to rust and rot if we—or somebody—doesn't take it. So let's us use it to rebuild."

"The finest medical facilities in the entire world." Chase smiled. "A dream come true."

"So let's do it."

"That sounds like an order, Mr. Raines."

"If that's the way you want to take it, Captain."

He grinned. "Yes, sir, General." He saluted.

Ben returned the smile. "That's the sloppiest salute I believe I've ever seen."

The doctor shrugged. "Hell, I was in the medical corps—not one of you crazy gun soldiers."

Americans will take only so much pushing before they begin shoving back. It takes a lot of shoving, but even mild-mannered people have a point one had best not step

298

past. After three decades of wasteful spending, high taxes, a terrible no-win war, political upheaval, race riots, several near-depressions, and, finally, a world war unequaled in history, many of those Americans left alive . . . got mad.

Now when Logan's agents moved into a community to shove the people out, they were met, in many instances, with violence.

Resistance groups were formed, hastily thrown together without much thought given as to the participants' qualifications as warriors. They were crushed, brutally, by the regular military, government agents, and Logan's own private army. Many military men quit, deserted, rather than act as Logan's bully boys.

The newly reorganized Joint Chiefs of Staff met, discussed the matter, and the head of the JCs asked for a meeting with President Logan. Admiral Stevens pointed a finger at his commander in chief, and fired off a salvo.

"Now you listen to me, Mr. President. You are *not* going to use American military men as our equivalent to the Irish Black-and-Tans of years ago."

"The what?" Logan asked. He had never been a student of history. The subject bored him.

Admiral Stevens sighed, kept his temper in check, and thought: you dumb son of a bitch. He said, "Bully boys."

"Oh."

"I'll agree, Mr. President, we have to keep this nation whole, but not by Americans knocking other Americans' heads. We will keep order, as set forth by the Constitution, but as far as I'm concerned, martial law is hereby lifted and the Constitution is restored."

"I will say when that happens, Admiral. Not you."

"Mr. President, your plan is a good one—as far as it

299

goes—if, and that is one hell of a big if, the American people want to go along with it. Obviously, a lot of them do not. So let them alone. We're all Americans; we've all shared the same horrible experience and somehow managed to survive. My people—the military—don't have the men or the time or the inclination to run around this wrecked country forcing people out of their homes. And they won't be a part of it. I've got ships with no one to captain or crew them; electronic equipment with no men to man it; bases that are virtually empty—same with all branches. And there is just a whole hell of a lot of bases that have been blown up, equipment and planes destroyed. And that is *since* the hostilities ceased."

"Those damned Rebels!"

The admiral shrugged. "Maybe—maybe not. Maybe they figure if you can form an army of mercenaries, they can, too."

"*I* happen to be the President of these United States, Admiral. I would like to have a group of fighting men who are loyal to me, something I sense you are not."

The admiral stiffened at the slight toward his allegiance. "Sir, I am loyal to this country—not toward any one man, but this nation as a whole. The military put your ass in that chair, we can damned well take it out."

Logan smiled. "No . . . I don't believe you've got the manpower to do that, Stevens."

"Is that the way the game is played, Logan?"

Logan giggled. "My ball, my bat—my rules."

The admiral nodded stiffly. "I get your point . . . sir."

"Dandy. You may be excused now."

After the admiral had walked out of the room, his back ramrod stiff, slamming the door on his way out, Logan picked up the phone.

"Yes, sir," an aide said.

"Get me that mercenary, Parr, down in Georgia."

Ben pulled into his driveway at five o'clock in the afternoon. Nothing had changed except the lawn had flowers where none had been before. There was a station wagon parked beside the house.

Since the outskirts of Shreveport, Ben had seen hundreds of blacks. No one had bothered him; they had all been friendly, waving to him and chatting with him when he stopped.

But the vague and somewhat amusing—to him—thought was: he knew how Dr. Livingstone must have felt.

Well, Ben thought, getting out of the truck. There is a lot of land to be had. I'm not going to spill any blood for an acre in Louisiana.

He left his M-10 on the seat and walked up the stone walkway to the front door. He felt kind of silly knocking on his own front door. But as he raised his hand to tap on the door, the door swung open.

"Come on in, Ben Raines," Salina said. "I've been waiting for you."

"Hello, Salina." Ben returned the smile. He revised his original appraisal of her: she was not just a good-looking woman. She was beautiful.

"I was about to invite you in, Ben, but that would be rather silly of me, wouldn't it? This is your house." Her eyes found Juno. "What a beautiful dog! What's his name?"

"Juno."

She squatted down and held out her hands. Juno shoved past Ben and came to her, almost knocking her

301

down with his eagerness to be petted. Ben stepped past them and into the house. Not much had changed; the house was a great deal neater and cleaner than when he'd left it. He said as much.

"You're a bachelor—a man." She smiled. "Most bachelors aren't much on housekeeping." A mischievous light crept into her eyes. "'Sides," she mush-mouthed, "us coons have been trained for centuries to take care of the master's house while he's away seein' to matters of great import."

"Knock it off, Salina," he said; then saw the twinkle in her eyes and realized she'd been ribbing him. He gave back as much as he got. "You're only half-coon. So the house should be only half-clean."

"O.K." She laughed. "Call this match a draw. You hungry, Ben? Dinner's going to be at seven. Guests coming over. We knew you were coming."

"How?"

"Tom-tom's!"

Ben grimaced at her laughter. "I'll be hungry by seven, I assure you."

The twinkle in her eyes became a flashing firestorm. "Well, got corn bread, fatback, and greens."

"Salina, you're impossible!"

She laughed. "You think I'm kidding?"

She wasn't.

Ben sat in the den with Cecil and Lila, Pal and Valerie. "I'm beginning to get the feeling I'm a lone moonbeam on a dark night," he said.

They did not take offense, as Ben knew they would not, but shared his laughter. It certainly was a dark night and the house was lit only by lamps and candles.

"Another month," Cecil said, "and we'll have full power restored. So the engineers tell me."

Pal laughed and leaned forward, looking at Ben. "The truth, Ben—what was the first thought that popped into your mind at Cecil's statement?"

"Nigger-riggin'," Ben said honestly.

"You're an honest man, Ben Raines," Lila said. "O.K.—how do we combat that type of thinking. Not that you meant it; I don't believe you did. But that . . . type of thinking is so ingrained in so many white minds, how do we overcome it?"

"By education and by trying harder. That's my opinion."

"Education . . . ?" Salina let the question remain open-ended.

"On both sides, of course."

"Let's be sociable this evening, people," Valerie said. "Let the poor man alone about race. We're just six people, all full after a good meal, so let's relax some, huh?"

"I don't mind, Valerie," Ben said. "Really, I don't. Had people in the country gotten together like this years ago—more than really did—so much could have been accomplished."

Ben was silent for a moment, then asked, "Kasim?"

"He's around," Cecil replied. "When he learned you were coming in he cursed and decided to skip Salina's invitation—which she felt forced to offer, I must add in her defense. Any other time he would have broken his neck getting over here. He has feelings for Salina that, unfortunately for Kasim, she does not share."

"And never will," Salina added. "He's a pig!"

"He is an uneducated man, Salina," Lila said softly.

303

"He's a prick!" Salina said flatly.

Cecil shook his head and said, "Are you planning on staying, Ben?"

"No, I'm not. I'm heading over to north Mississippi first, then pulling out to the northwest." He met Cecil's steady gaze. "Cecil, as long as you have Kasims in your society, it won't work."

The man shrugged. "I feel you are correct; he has too much hate in him. But what would you have me do, Ben? Kill him? Drive him out?"

"I know what I would do, Cecil, but I don't walk in your shoes. He's your problem. If he ever becomes mine, he won't be a problem long." Then he laid it out for the group, told them all he knew about the new government, what he had seen and heard. And it did not surprise Ben to learn they knew more about it than he.

"Yes," Pal said. "We monitor the broadcasts. But perhaps Logan will leave us alone long enough . . . well, until we are strong enough to resist his forces. All we want to do is live and let live."

Ike's words, Ben thought.

"You're welcome to spend the night with us, Ben," Lila said.

Ben smiled. "This is my house."

She cut her eyes to Salina. "Then perhaps you'd better come with us, Salina."

"I like it here," Salina said. Ben could feel her eyes on him in the dim light.

Cecil shook his head, a frown on his lips. "You're making a mistake, girl; it'll only cause hard feelings. You must know that."

"My decision."

"You're half-black, half-white," Lila said, a tinge of

anger in her voice. "Are you making your choice? Is that it?"

"You're the only one talking about color and choices. If Ben is color-blind, so am I."

Pal and Valerie sat quietly, saying nothing, staying out of the verbal confrontation, now exclusively between the two women.

"You know Kasim will fly into a rage when he hears you've . . . spent the night with Ben. And Ben,"—she cut her eyes to him—"there is nothing wrong with sex between two consenting adults. But there is much more than sex involved here. Try to see it from our point of view."

Ben shrugged.

"Let him fly into a rage," Salina said. "The stupid bastard's half-crazy anyway."

"Salina . . ." Lila leaned forward, taking her hands. "Think about it. Think. . . ."

Salina jerked her hands away. "I have thought about it!" she snapped. "All my damned life I've thought about it. Where *do* I belong? Believe me, I've been the one living with that question, not you. For twenty-five years I've lived with it. If I make a statement that is contradictory to the quote/unquote 'black' way of thinking, I get my white father tossed in my face. If I'm around a group of whites and make any statement defending something a black person has done, I get my nigger mamma tossed at me. And don't you think for one second I haven't thought about 'passing.' I have not only thought about it, I've done it, many times. Hey—I like the white world. It's free and a whole lot easier to move around in. So, by God"—she slammed a small fist on a coffee table—"don't any of you presume to tell me what I can or cannot do. *I will do* what I want to do, when *I* choose to do it. And with whomever *I* choose to do *it*." She jumped to her feet and ran from the room, crying.

Ben wisely kept his mouth shut about Salina's decision and poured another cup of coffee from the service on the coffee table. He said blandly, "More coffee, anyone?"

"Thank you, no," Cecil said, a slight smile working at the corners of his mouth. "Do you always stir up hornets' nests wherever you go?"

"That's not fair," Valerie said. "Ben hasn't done a thing except to come home. *His* home." Lila, her composure restored, laughed at her husband's pained expression and patted his leg. Valerie said, "There *will* be trouble over this, Ben. Kasim will indeed go berserk."

"Willie, you mean?" Ben said, the words popping from his mouth before he could bite them off. Valerie looked blank; she, of course, would know nothing of Kasim's Christian name.

"That annoys whites, doesn't it?" Cecil asked, stuffing his pipe. "The Muslim bit, I mean."

"Annoys?" Ben shook his head. "No . . . I don't believe annoys is the right choice of words. I think a lot of whites are amused by it. And perhaps frightened, if they would admit it."

"Umm. Frightened, yes. So are a number of blacks. But amused? Why?" Cecil asked.

"Because they don't believe the blacks are taking their religion seriously. They think that they're doing it solely to be different. Wearing turbans and robes."

Cecil smiled. "Would you find it terribly difficult to believe that I, too, am amused by it—in some blacks?"

"No, not at all. You're an educated man, and a fair-thinking man."

Juno rose from the floor, stretched, and went into the room after Salina.

Cecil said, "When both man and beast accept a woman, I guess that pretty well settles it." He lit his pipe. "Be careful, Ben Raines, many of the pressures in an interracial relationship come from within rather than from without."

"I am aware of that."

Cecil looked at him, his face a tanned study in the dim light. "So you believe education is the key to a black person's acceptance by the whites, eh?"

"Education on both sides, yes. And conformity on both sides, as well. Root cause."

"Yes, I read that in you. Have to get into the home before matters begin mellowing out, eh? Interesting. Rather Orwellian, though."

Dr. Chase's words.

". . . Don't know how you'd manage that," Cecil remarked. "I'm going to tell you something, Ben. Tell you something because we are here, now. I think you've stood on the sidelines and watched all the action between the races for too long, electing to remain neutral." He held up his hand as Ben opened his mouth to protest. "No—let me finish, Ben. Please. Let me assure you that black people know all the white arguments. All of them; know them by heart—hell, we've heard them all our lives.

"Ready? Good. In an election, blacks will vote color rather than intellectually, even though the black man may be less qualified than the white. Yes, that's true. At least in nearly every election I've ever seen. But, my God, Ben, how else could the black people get representation. I mean . . . after all, we're supposed to remain in our

307

place. Wherever in the hell that is.

"All niggers steal. Well, that's bullshit and we both know it. At least the connotation the whites attach to it is crap: that *all* blacks steal. I've never stolen a thing in my life. But because I am black I am tarred with the same brush as those blacks who do steal. It makes about as much sense as saying all Italians belong to the mafia.

"Niggers have no morals; all they want to do is drink and fuck. Did you patronize many redneck bars, Ben? Have you been in many conversations—and I use that word laughingly, taking into consideration the intellect of the average redneck—with 'necks? Need I say more?

"Nigger is lazy; won't work. Some black people *are* lazy; so are some whites. It's about even.

"Niggers are smart-alecks. Meaning: don't talk uppity to a white person. You ain't as good as me. Don't argue with a white man. Kowtow. Yes, sir—no, sir.

"Niggers are emotional. Yes, many of us are. There is a cultural as well as pigmentation difference between blacks and whites. But it amuses me, Ben, to hear some whites say that. Especially if one has ever witnessed the carrying-on in a white Pentecostal church, or other churches of that particular ilk.

"You know what I'm saying, Ben! I don't have to continue in this vein. The point is: how will you combat those myths and prejudices in your society? And yes, we know of your plans. We have fine electronic equipment located around the area. Our people have done some excellent nigger-riggin'." That was said with a smile and Ben had to laugh.

"Ben? I didn't ask for the job of leader down here. One day I looked up and it was being handed to me. No one asked if I wanted it. They just handed it to me. I don't need and don't want any New Africa. I have been accepted in 'your world' all my life. My father was a psychiatrist, my mother a college professor. I hold a Ph.D.—and not from one of your all-black southern colleges. I worked hard to gain my degrees. My father saw to that—no favors. I graduated with a 3.9 from one hell of a fine university. I have been married for ten years and I have never slept with another woman." He smiled. "But the temptation has sometimes been almost over-powering."

Lila stirred by his side. Smiling, she said, "Keep talkin', sucker."

"Logan?" Cecil spat the word. "He's a nigger-hater. Always has been. Those of us with any education saw past his rhetoric. And he—with the help of his mercenaries—is going to try to crush us down here. And probably will. But we have to try, Ben. Have to try—no!—we've *got* to show whitey we can have a Christian, decent, productive society without his help.

"Kasim? Piss on Kasim! His bread isn't baked. He was a street punk and that's all he'll ever be.

"You're going to look up one day, Ben—very soon, I believe—and the job of leader will be handed to you. Like me, you won't want it, but you'll take it because you believe in your dreams of a fair world, fair society. I read you like a good novel, Ben. You opened yourself up to viewing when you said you weren't staying; you were heading west. You're going for the states Logan is leaving alone for a time. And you're going to form your own little nation. Just like we're attempting to do here. Good luck to you—you're going to need it. I—we—may join you out there."

"You'd be welcome, Cecil. There are too few like you

309

and Lila and Pal and Valerie."

"And Salina," Lila added, her eyes twinkling.

Ben smiled.

"And you're right, Ben," Cecil said. "It's in the home. Root cause."

Ben's words.

"One of my earliest recollections is of Mozart and Brahms," Cecil reminisced. "But you think the average southern white would believe that? Not a chance. He'll put down black music—which I detest—while slugging the jukebox and punching out the howling and honking of country music.

"My father used to sit in his study, listening to fine music while going over his day's cases, a brandy at hand. My mother was having a sherry—not Ripple,"—he laughed—"going over her papers from the college. My home life was conducive to a moderate, intelligent way of life. My father told me, if I wanted it, to participate in sports, but to keep the game in perspective and always remember it is but a game. Nothing more. No, Ben, I didn't grow up as the average black kid. That's why *I* know what you say is true. Home. The root cause.

"I went to the opera, Ben. Really! How many violent-minded people attend operas? How many ignorant people attend plays and classical concerts? How many bigots— of all races—read Sartre, Shakespeare, Tennyson, Dante?" He shook his head.

"No, you find your bigots and violent-minded ignoramuses seeking other forms of base entertainment. And I'm not just speaking of music.

"Do you know why I joined the Green Berets, Ben?" Ben shook his head.

"So I could get to know violence firsthand. We didn't

have street gangs where I grew up. To try to understand violence." He laughed aloud, heartily, slapping his knee. "Well, I found out about it, all right; I got shot in the butt in Laos."

"Enough," Lila said. "Let's don't you two refight the war. I've heard all your stories. Tomorrow is a workday. Let's go home."

They all stood up, Cecil saying, "Both our peoples have a way to go, Ben."

"Think we'll make it?"

"I don't know. But I'll wager that with your ideas and my ideas we could give it a hell of a try. Think about that, Ben Raines."

After they had said their good nights and good-bys, for Ben was pulling out in the morning, Ben walked into the bedroom. "Are you all right, now?"

"Of course, I am," Salina said, her voice small in the darkness. "I always lie in the dark and bawl and snuffle."

"You heard everything that was said?"

"I'm not deaf, Ben."

"Well . . . you want to head out with me in the morning?"

"Maybe I like it here."

"Sure you do. Stay here, and if you're not killed by Parr's mercs, you can marry Kasim and live happily ever after."

"That is positively the most dreadful idea anyone could offer. Thank you, no."

"I repeat; would you like to head out with me?"

"Why should I?"

"You might see some sights you've never seen before."

"Ben, that is a stupid statement for a writer to make. If

I haven't seen the sights before, of course I'd be seeing them for the first time."

"What?"

"That isn't a good enough reason, Ben."

"Well . . . goddamn it! I like you and you like me."

"That's better. Sure you want to travel with a zebra?"

Ben suddenly thought of Megan. "I'll tell everyone you've been out in the sun too long. But let's get one thing settled; when I tell you to step-and-fetch-it, you'd better hump it, baby."

"Screw you, Ben Raines!" She giggled.

"I also have that in mind."

She threw back the covers and Ben could see she was naked. And beautiful. "So come on. I assure you, whitey, it doesn't rub off."

SIXTEEN

Ben, Salina, and Juno pulled out before dawn, heading east, to Mississippi. Salina thought it best she tell no one verbal good-bys, so she left a note. Both Ben and Salina thought it best. Juno offered no opinion; he just liked to travel.

"I thought I was opinionated," Ben said. Faint streaks of red mingled with gray in the eastern sky. "With some strong ideas. But Cecil lays it right on the line, doesn't he? I like him."

"You agree with him, Ben?"

"Yes, I do. We both agree that the root cause for most of this nation's inner problems lies in the home. But . . . my solution—as he said—was Orwellian. Other than that, I don't know how to correct it."

"You could start by killing all the rednecks," Salina suggested. Ben did not think she was joking.

He smiled, thinking: she may be half-white, and look almost pure white—with a dark tan—but she was raised among blacks. The next few months should be interesting. Or years; the thought came to him, and he was comfortable with it.

"Let me tell you something about rednecks, Salina," he said.

"I know all I need to know about them. I saw pictures

313

of them in Alabama and Mississippi during the civil-rights movement in the sixties. I saw them putting high-pressure water hoses on little children; saw them throwing rocks and bottles; saw the churches that were bombed and burned; and the bodies of black people who were killed. I've read many accounts of the KKK—night riders." She shuddered. "Thanks, Ben, but no thanks."

"If you'd have looked a bit more closely at those pictures, Salina, you'd have seen some fear as well as hate on those white faces."

She glanced at him. She waited.

"Don't you know that a lot of whites—many more than will admit it—are afraid of black people? The myth of the black man—subhuman species, only a few centuries away from being an ape."

A very small smile creased her lips. She fought it back. Ben did not ask why the smile. But he hoped she was thinking of Kasim.

"As for rednecks, Salina, allow me to play devil's advocate for a moment. Back when things were normal, if you'd had a flat on the highway—"

"Don't use me, Ben," she interrupted. "I don't look black."

"All right, then, two black, black women. Your slick dude in the three-hundred-dollar suit, driving the fancy car is not going to stop to help those ladies—not ninety-nine times out of a hundred. But some ol' boy wearing a cowboy hat or a ball cap and boots with mud on them, bouncing along in a pickup truck will stop. I've watched that scenario played out a hundred times over the years. And that ol' boy will work and sweat and bang his knuckles and cuss under his breath. But *he will* change that tire for those black women.

314

"Traditionally—and unfortunately, this is changing —your good ol' boys were the first to volunteer during a war. Call them rednecks if you will—I do—and many of them are. Point I'm making, babe, is this: you look closely at most people, you'll find *some* good in them. Maybe not much, but some. Unless he's a punk, pure, and then you can search forever and not find anything of redeeming value."

"Kluckers—KKKers—have redeeming values?"

"I feel certain many of them are good solid family men, hard workers in their churches and on their jobs. Aren't those redeeming values, Salina?"

She reluctantly agreed with a short bob of her head. "I read all your books while at your house, Ben. You never wrote much about the black experience."

"I don't *know* anything about the black experience— as you call it. How can I write anything about it?"

A smile crossed her mouth. "Oh . . . I wouldn't say that, Ben. I'd have to say you did a pretty good job of getting into the black experience last night."

Ben groaned. "Very funny, Salina. Yeah. Cute."

She laughed at his expression. "I think, Ben Raines, inside you, buried deeply, there is just a little bit of bigot."

"I'll certainly agree with that."

"Oh?"

"Sure. I'm prejudiced against anyone, of any color, who wants acceptance, but refuses to conform—even just a little bit—to gain it. Agreed, everyone has a right to dress the way he or she chooses, but if that style is blatantly against the norm, a shop owner has the right to say, 'No way am I going to hire you—you'd scare my customers to death.' Sorry, Salina, but that's the way I

315

feel about it. And before you jump down my throat, remember that Cecil—and Pal, too, I'm thinking—have *always* been accepted in my quote/unquote 'world.' Care to dwell on why that is?"

"Oh, Ben! I could tear that hypothesis to shreds. You don't know Cecil like I know him. I can't speak for Pal—not really—but Cecil is a snob, and damned if I don't think you are, too. In music, in taste of clothes, theater, literature; the whole bag."

"Well, then, three cheers for snobbery, if that's what it takes. Yes, I am somewhat of a snob, Salina. And I damned sure offer no apology for it."

"Go on, Ben," she urged. "Let's get it all said. Clear the air; plug up all the openings."

Ben glanced at her and grinned.

She grimaced. "Very funny, Ben. Yeah. Cute."

"There isn't that much to clear, babe. Education on both sides. Conformity—there again, on both sides . . ."

"Words, Ben—words. I've heard them all before. How do you plan to implement them into action?"

"I won't have to. Because the people we shall gather around us will accept them willingly. That's the simplistic beauty of the society I advocate."

"Correct me if I'm wrong, Ben. You will take the cream of all races and the rest can go to hell?"

"That's not . . . entirely the way I envision it."

"But close enough?"

"Ummm . . . O.K. Yeah."

"Seems like a man named Hitler had a plan something along those lines."

"Oh, come on, Salina! Goddamn. Don't compare me to that nitwit."

"Honey . . ." She put a hand on his arm. "Don't get

angry. I'm not comparing you to Hitler. What I'm saying is there are flaws in your logic. What you envision is grand—what I know of it. But what of the people of limited intelligence? Those of small imaginations? You've made no allowance for them."

"But I have, Salina: education."

"Forced education, Ben?" she asked softly.

"If I have to."

"Maybe it's time," was her reply. She picked up a map and looked first at it, then at the town they were passing through. "Ben, where are we?"

Ben looked around him and cussed. They had been talking and arguing so heatedly he had taken the wrong turn. They had to backtrack ten miles to get on the right road.

On the way through Mississippi, Ben told her of Ike and Megan. She simply refused to believe a man born and reared in Mississippi would marry a black woman.

"I'm telling you," Ben protested. "I married them— down in Florida."

"*You* married them? God, what a ceremony that must have been."

"I thought it was rather nice," Ben said. "Except for the beer running out of my ears."

"Someday," she said, her tone one of utter disbelief, "you will have to tell me about it." She patted his arm. "I'll let you know where and when." She glanced at his ears and muttered something under her breath.

"Well, I'll just be damned!" Ike said, grabbing Salina in a bear hug and kissing her on the mouth. "White boy from Louisiana done got hisself a half-breed coon. Will

317

wonders never cease?"

Ben had told Salina all about Ike's career as a SEAL. She struggled against his bear hug, then gave up. "Turn me loose, you . . . redneck aquatic freak!"

"Oh, I like her." Ike grinned, turning her loose. Megan took her in tow and told her to pay her husband no mind. The salt water had corroded what little brain he had.

Ben and Salina spent two days with Ike and Megan, talking over plans to move west. Ike assured Ben he would do his part; his people had been busy securing trucks, gathering up everything to rebuild. They were ready to roll.

"Logan's people been back?" Ben asked.

"Be back next month, so my people say."

"We'll be settling in by then."

"You and Salina taking the point?"

"Leaving in the morning."

"Radio back when you're ready for us."

On the way west, Ben and Salina spent their first night at a lake on the border between Louisiana and Texas. Salina had never fished in her life, and Ben had a good time teaching her the rudiments. She caught a white perch, was finned trying to get it off the hook, and cussed—very unladylike.

She held out her hand to Ben. "Make it all better," she said.

Ben poured iodine on the small cut. After she had finished her dance of pain, she shoved him in the lake and walked back up to the cabin, leaving him floundering and hollering.

Sitting on the dock, a blanket wrapped around him,

318

Ben fished and cussed, caught a mess of perch, then cleaned them for supper.

It was peaceful on the lake as the sun was setting, bathing the water, creating hues that bounced off the shoreline. Salina sat a few feet from him, in a chaise longue. She wore a bikini that could have been stuffed into a cigarette package that still had room for a few smokes.

Leaning back in his own lounge, Ben studied her profile (and her curves, which were many and provocative) in the glow of fading sun. She was not a tall woman: five-four, she had told him. Her facial features were soft, delicate, her skin a gentle fawn color.

"Why are you staring at me?" she asked, turning her head, meeting his eyes.

"Because I like to look at you. You're a beautiful woman; surely you must be used to men staring at you?"

"What were you thinking as you looked? Be honest."

Ben grinned.

"Sure," she said dryly. "That. Of course."

"Among other things," he added, which was true.

"And whitey says all niggers think about is sex. You people better get your act together. You're hypocrites."

"Well,"—Ben's grin broadened—"I've always heard that if a man just has to marry, marry a white woman. If he wants a good piece of ass, get him a black gal." He waited for the fire storm.

She rose slowly from the lounge and came to him, pulling him to his feet. "Old man,"—she smiled—"you are going to pay for that remark."

"I just repeated what 'they' say, that's all." Ben pulled her to him and they stood for a moment, mouths silent now, but their lips speaking silent messages.

"Uh-huh," she whispered.

They walked hand in hand into the cabin.

Juno sat looking up at the darkening sky. And if he had a thought that could be put into words, it would be: humans sure do act funny.

Waco appeared to have been hard hit. From what they could see, Ben calculated less than one percent of the population had survived. Baylor was almost deserted, only a handful of people on the campus.

"Why is it, Ben," Salina asked, as they walked the quiet corridors of a science building, "that in some towns a great many people survived, in others almost no one?"

He shook his head, unable to answer her question. He still did not know why he had survived when others had not.

Back in the bright sunlight, she asked, "Why do you always go to universities and colleges, Ben?"

"I'm looking for a . . . friend."

Salina picked up on the hesitation. "She?"

He told her about Jerre.

"Did you—do you—love her?"

"A little bit, yes. But I worry about her a lot more."

"Ummm," she replied.

They headed west. Occasionally, Ben would feel Salina's eyes studying him as he drove and he knew she had questions she would like to ask, about Jerre. Ben wondered how he would answer them when the time came. He thought he knew.

Less than a year after the world-wide war, the United States Government was off and running, with Hilton Logan at the reins. The east coast was being resettled, from the edge of the hot areas in the northeast, down to central Florida. Law and order was being reintroduced to the citizens. The regular military watched as Logan's army, under the command of Col. Kenny Parr knocked heads, confiscated weapons, shuffled people about, and listened grimly to the rumors of large bands of so-called Rebels moving west, stripping entire cities as they went. But the lawful military was very small, now, and they did little except maintain a presence and wonder what Logan would do next.

Logan chose as his vice president a man the regular military approved of; a man of good sense, who weighed the issues at hand and then acted, not out of emotion, but out of what he felt would be the best for the country. Aston Addison. Maybe, the military thought, there might be hope for the nation yet.

Mid-June found Ben and Salina in the state of Idaho, just on the southernmost fringe of the Great Primitive Area, on the south side of the Fork. Ben had spoken with Ike, and those who supported a free state were moving, from all over the nation, toward Idaho.

Ben cranked up his radio and called in. "How many do we have, Ike?"

"'Bout five thousand, I figure, not countin' the Rebs. How many folks alive where you are, Ben?"

"Damned few. It's wild and beautiful, Ike."

"Not too far from where you are, Ben, there's a platoon of Army Rangers from Fort Lewis . . . or what's left of Lewis, that is. They've split with Logan. Down a way from them, there's what's left of the west coast SEAL team. They don't like Logan either—but they like what you and I have planned and are ready to move to join us.

Rebuild. I talked with some folks from up Canada way; they were hard hit. They'd like to pitch their hats in the ring, too."

"O.K., Ike—let's get cracking."

"I'll see you in about a month, partner. Excuse me— General."

"What do you really know about Ben Raines?" President Logan asked his wife over dinner.

The question startled her, caught her off guard. She had not thought of Ben in months. Did not know if he was dead or alive. She pondered her husband's question for a moment.

"Well . . . he's a rude man, very arrogant, sarcastic. But he's also a very tough man—not just physically but mentally. I don't think he's afraid of anything. He's smart, too. Why do you ask?"

"He was put in charge of Bull Dean's Rebels."

"Are you serious?"

"Yes. But I don't know if he accepted that charge. At first, word was he did not. Then the word was passed that he was dead. But he was spotted out west just a couple of weeks ago. Rumors persist that he is forming some sort of . . . state . . . nation out there. Didn't he write about that one time? Some sort of free state?"

"Yes. Rather a trashy novel. Where out west?"

Logan shook his head. "I don't know. The military won't really cooperate with me; don't like me. Never have. But damn it, I'm only doing what I think is right and best for the country. And Colonel Parr is all tied up with minor revolts. He and his men put down one group, another pops up. My God, you'd think I was trying to deny them their sex lives instead of just taking their guns. What is this morbid fascination with guns, anyway? People are really *dying* fighting over a gun. It's stupid, Fran. Ignorant."

"Hilton?" Fran touched his hand. "Leave Ben Raines alone."

The word went out, all over the nation: head west. If you don't like the crap that is coming out of Richmond, head west. Get trucks and head west. Stop at every national guard and reserve armory and strip it bare. Same with every base. Search every deserted town for gold and silver and precious gems. Take every piece of medical equipment you can find; bring anything you think we might be able to use, from panty hose to bulldozers. But if you're lazy, gossipy, unethical; if you lie, cheat, or if you're ignorant, you'd better stay away. . . . Odds are you won't fit in with the crowd.

Tell lawyers to stay the hell out; we don't want them, don't need them. Our laws will be very simple and very few and enforced to the letter; no muddying the water. They will be enforced to the letter. No exceptions. No deals. No plea-bargaining. No twisting of words—truth. Our nation is going to be a bit different from that to which you've been accustomed. We're going to try something; see if it will work. So leave us alone.

The message went into every state and a lot of countries. A lot of people heard it, liked it, and packed up.

And a lot of people heard it and didn't like it.

"He's your brother, Carl," Jeb Fargo said. "What's he tryin' to pull?"

A large farm in Illinois; a cooperative venture that encompassed hundreds of thousands of acres. Run by a group of men and women who went by no official name, but whose members secretly embraced the teachings of Hitler and the goose-egg mentality of the Klan. To Logan, they were hard-working, God-fearing people who caused no trouble but just wanted to work the land and do what was best toward restoring this devastated nation to its former glory.

Logan loved them. Addison was suspicious of them. The military knew exactly what they were.

Lots of churches scattered throughout their lands. Funny thing though: wasn't a nigger or a dago or a chink or a greaser or a Jew in the bunch.

And their churches did not teach love—the ministers preached hate.

"I never was close to Ben," Carl replied. "Lot of difference in our ages."

"We'd best keep an eye on what he's doin'. Might even send some men out there next year. You'd be in charge. You know, Carl, I kinda had my eye on that land out there for us. Good cattle country and farmland. Word is, Carl, your brother's livin' with a nigger gal."

"Ben!"

"That's the word I get. Hell, messages we been interceptin' tell us they's all kinds of undesirables headin' out there: slants, Jews, burr-heads, greasers—all kinds of filth. We cain't have that, Carl. Cain't let them people get a toehold in some of the best land in the country. Brother or no brother, he's got to be stopped."

"When you want me to go, Jeb?" Carl said. "I'll go." The thought of his brother actually kissing a nigger made him sick at his stomach.

"I'll let you know, Major Raines," Jeb said.

*   *   *

All sorts of people were heading west, to join those already there.

There was a young man named Badger Harbin who had met Ben and Salina in Idaho. He just wandered up to them one day, introduced himself, and said he was there to stay.

Ben could not believe anyone would have the first name of Badger, but the young man assured Ben that, yes, that's what his daddy had named him.

Sid Cossman was a New Yorker who had once owned a radio station in upstate New York. He had lost it by refusing to bow to the often dictatorial whims of the Federal Communications Commission. Sid did not like Big Brother.

Lieutenant Conger was the platoon leader of a contingent of Rebels coming in from the East.

Bridge Oliver was with the SEAL team from southern California.

A man named Clint Voltan was a major in the Rebel army formed in the West.

And Sam Pyron was about to make his move toward freedom.

Sam, a West Virginia boy, sat by his grandfather's bed. He was watching the old man die.

The grandfather met the young man's eyes. "Git outta here, boy. There ain't nothin' you can do for me." He coughed up blood and pus.

"I'll stay with you, Granddad," Sam said.

"Just like your mother—hard-headed. Boy, listen to me. You gotta run!"

"I'm not leavin' you."

"You killed a Fed, Samuel."

"He started it. Tryin' to tell me I got to move. To hell

with him. That's probably where he went, too."

"I know, Sam—I know. It ain't right, but big government almost never is. I think you better link up with them survivalists that was livin' over 'crost the mountain and get gone from here."

"The Rebels?"

"Yeah."

"I thought you didn't agree with what they stood for, Granddad?"

"I don't agree with ever'thing they talked about—them I knowed in the bunch—but I do agree with most of it. 'Specially them wantin' to bring the law back to the common folk, back to some common sense." He coughed for a moment, then caught his breath, pain in his eyes.

"Maybe all this misery was due us, boy—I don't know. I cain't help but think the Lord had something to do with it. I figure He was gettin' awful tired of what was happenin' down here. And maybe it's a good thing, too. That Rebel that was by last week when I was so awful sick, he said they's a man settin' up out West. Said that feller was gonna have a land where a man can live free— all races. It's past time for that, too. Wasn't gonna be no damned lawyers screwin' up ever'thing with fancy words. That'd be the greatest thing since corn bread, Sam. I hate a damned lawyer. This man out West—accordin' to the Reb—is gonna make the law so plain, so simple, so easy to follow, that even a child can understand it. That's the way it oughta be. He said that so long as a person can mind his or her own business and follow jist a few simple rules, a man can live the way he sees fit.

"Our laws, Sam—back when we had a country—went from bad to worse to stupid. I seen all the trouble comin' years ago; 'fore even your mamma was born. Country

326

went bad; people quit wantin' to work for a livin', wanted the government to do for them. Damned unions got out of hand; kids got too big for their britches. Too many cops, too many lawyers, too many laws the common man couldn't understand. Judges sittin' on their brains, turnin' bad people loose without punishment. No morals nowhere. Government stickin' its nose in ever'body else's business when they couldn't even keep their own house clean. It had to come to an end." He coughed up blood and gasped for breath.

"Sam?" The old man's hand groped for his grandson as his eyes filmed over with near-death. He fought back the darkness.

"I'm here, Granddad." Sam took the old hand.

"I want you to remember what I'm about to say, Sam; carry it with you all your life. What's yours is yours, provided you worked for it, and you paid for it—or is payin' for it—and don't no man have no right to take it from you by stealin'. You got a right to protect what's yours by any means at hand. And don't never let no smart-mouthed lawyer tell you different.

"There ain't no human-person god, boy. 'At's something them hoo-hawin' TV preachers never learned. But they shore thought they was God, all the time a-tellin' ever'body else how to live, what to read in the books and papers, what to see on the TV and in the motion pitchers. I ain't sayin' they wasn't good folk in their hearts, just that they di'n' have no right tellin' other folk how to live. Them TV preachers had a God complex-thing 'bout 'em. But they was wrong, Sam.

"If a man is tryin' to do right by his family, by his job, or them that work for him, and be a good neighbor in time of need, then whatever else he does, Sam . . . ain't

327

nobody else's damned truck! Man's got to live by and with his conscience, boy. And if you was taught right in the home, then you'll do right outside it. Some of them fancy-talkin', fancy-dressin', high-up judges might ought to sweep off they own back doorstep 'fore they start tellin' others to clean they steps. Same thing with preachers and politicians. And that damned Logan is gonna be the ruination of ever'thing. He's two-faced, boy, and crazy as a road lizard!

"Sam, listen to me. There ain't but one set of rules a man's *got* to follow, and they come from God—written in stone and handed down. Man's rules come second—always. No badge, no man-made law, no government job or high uppity office ever made no man . . . God."

He was wracked by coughing. He vomited up pus and blood, then closed his eyes. A few hours later, he slipped behind the veil.

Sam Pyron buried his grandfather in the rocky soil of West Virginia. He had no other family left alive. Sam took his grandfather's old .30–.30 lever-action Winchester and struck out for the highway, down where old man Garland lived—or used to live. Garland had an old pickup truck that had been sitting idle since the war. Sam figured that with a fresh battery and some gas, he'd get that old truck running again.

Then he'd head west.

He was eighteen years old.

There was something in the way Sam walked the mountain road, with a rifle in his hand, a knife on his belt, and a small sack of food slung over his shoulder; some mannerism that might make a knowledgeable person recall the descriptions of other mountain men, free men, of another century. Men who fought and died for freedom, the right to live their own lives without fear of tyranny, from within or without the government; to live without fear of the lawless, or those who would impose their own selfish wills on others.

This young man was reminiscent of the men who called themselves Green River Boys, or Rough Riders; those who rode with Darby's Rangers, or Major Rogers, or who suffered in silence at Valley Forge; the men and women at Buchenwald or Dachau or the men who stormed the beaches on June 6, 1944; and the men who rode to make a stand at an old church in Texas—called the Alamo.

SEVENTEEN

President Logan called for his VP to have lunch with him. He came right to the point. "Aston, there is a bunch of people, four or five thousand, maybe more, all heading west. They are stealing everything that isn't nailed down. And sometimes that doesn't even stop them."

The VP looked up from his salad. "Why are they heading west?"

"To link up with Ben Raines, I suppose. They even stole a railroad."

"Hilton—that's impossible! You can't steal a railroad. That's stationary. They took the engines and cars, perhaps. But what do they want with it?"

"To transport all the things they're stealing! Aston, they've broken into military bases and armories and stolen God only knows how much heavy artillery and bombs and guns and anything else they could get their hands on. Radar is gone from many places. Highly sophisticated electronic gear, computers—you name it, those people took it. A bunch of those crazy navy porpoises stole an entire base. Everything! They even took the damned portable buildings!"

"Porpoises? SEALs?"

"Whatever. Yes, that's the bunch."

"An entire base? Hilton, no one can steal an entire base!"

"Well, they did. Probably had some damned Seabees with them, too. I made a speech on the Senate floor one time, I remember it well. I said that Green Berets and Rangers and SEALs and all those special units should be disbanded. They're all nuts! I said—"

"Just calm yourself, Hilton. These are breakaway units of the military?"

"Some of them, yes. I hate the military."

Hilton had once been forced to stand in front of his training platoon, back in '59, with his M-1 rifle in one hand and his pecker in the other hand, reciting, "This is my rifle, this is my gun. This is for shooting, this is for fun."

It had affected him. Deeply.

"Send the military to stop them," Aston suggested.

"The military couldn't stop a hamster—driving a red wagon. And until I can replace the top men, they refuse to even acknowledge I'm the president. They hate me. Colonel Parr is far too busy with the relocation efforts."

"Hilton, disband that bunch of mercenaries before they get out of hand—too powerful."

"No. They are loyal to me, and that's more than I can say about the regular military. I need Colonel Parr and his men."

"All right, then do this for me: break up that bunch of people in Illinois. You know what they are, Hilton."

Logan shook his head. "No. If we ever need someone to control any nigger uprising, they'll come in handy."

"The blacks helped put you in office years ago," Aston reminded the man.

The president ignored that.

Aston wanted to reach across the table and slap the man. But he knew he had to keep his head, keep his wits about him. He had suspected years before that Logan was using the minorities only as stepping stones; that he really, deep down, was a bigot. But someone with a calmer head had to be close to Logan and, he had told his wife, "Looks like I'm it."

"So what are you going to do about this Raines person?"

"Nothing. Nothing I can do. We're spread too thin as it is. We've lost too many agents in the mountains of West Virginia, Kentucky, Tennessee, and North Carolina trying to bring some law and order there. Damned hillbillies are shooting at anything that moves."

"We need them to work the mines."

"I know, I know. That's why I had to compromise with them." He shook his head. "I'm only doing what I feel—what I *know*—is best for the country."

Aston excused himself and left the table. His thoughts would have been grounds for treason.

By late August, everyone who was coming in . . . was in. The three-state area looked like the world's largest supply dump—and probably was. Entire towns had been stripped bare. Every ounce of precious metal and every chip of precious gem had been carefully searched for and taken. Billions of dollars of gold, silver, and precious stones were now under guard in Idaho, Wyoming, and Montana. With these Ben planned to back his new currency.

Many people, even after almost a year had passed, still did not fully understand what had happened. If there had been a war, they asked—who won?

How does one tell another that nobody won—everybody lost.

When the breakaway units of the military began

arriving, they were met by a few people who had survived, wary people.

"Is the military coming in?" a woman asked. "Dear God, we need help in the worst way."

"Sort of," a SEAL told her. "Don't worry—we'll help you."

"Looks like you're coming in to stay," she observed, taking in the growing mounds of equipment and supplies.

"Yes, ma'am. We sure are."

"Then you'd better know that a gang of outlaws and thugs say they control this area. They've been stealing and killing and raping for months. They took our weapons and disabled our vehicles."

"Where are they hiding, ma'am?"

"They aren't hiding. They took over the town of Challis."

"Holding any prisoners, ma'am? Any innocent folks?"

She shook her head.

The SEAL smiled.

He and his team were back the following afternoon. He told the lady, "You don't have to worry about them anymore, ma'am. They won't be back."

"Will they be tried?" she asked, looking around for prisoners. She saw none.

"They've been tried, ma'am."

The few survivors in each state were in almost total confusion due to lack of organization, something nearly all governments discourage. For local militias, except those under government control, cannot be established in the United States, not for over a hundred years. For, as had been pointed out, most governments, certainly including the government of the United States, are based on fear; fear of the central power, fear of the IRS, fear of the FCC, fear of the FBI, fear of the ICC, fear of the state police, fear of the local police, fear of everything. That is the only way a massive government can work. If the people were armed and organized, and of one mind, they just might start hanging rapists, murderers, armed robbers, burglars, and others of that slimy ilk—those they didn't shoot from the outset, that is.

And the people (who, so the myth reads, comprise the government, and are supposed to *tell* government what *they* want, and the government is then supposed to do it) would truly be in control. Government doesn't like to even think about that happening. Scary.

The young people from the colleges Ben had visited rolled in and looked around. They were wary, for they believed the adults had caused the original mess (which was true), and they weren't too certain this new state would be any better. But they decided to give it a try.

Jerre saw Ben, at first from a distance, and for a time kept her distance as she realized the woman with Ben was more than just a friend. Then she worked up enough courage to speak to him.

"Hi, Ben."

Ben turned from his work and let a smile play across his face. He was aware of Salina watching intently. He took Jerre's outstretched hand, held it for a moment, then released it.

"You're looking good, Jerre. I was worried about you, wondering if you made it."

She nodded, as emotions flooded her. She wondered if those same emotions were flooding Ben. They were, but not to the extent they filled her. "This is Matt." She introduced the beefy young man beside her.

Ben shook the offered hand. "I'm glad you two could join us up here. There's a lot of work to do. Going to live here in Idaho?"

Jerre shook her head. "No, Ben. We thought we'd try it over in Wyoming. Maybe go back to school in our spare time."

"That's a good idea. We'll have the colleges open in a few months."

There seemed to be nothing left for them to say; at least that they could say.

"See you, Ben." Jerre smiled.

Ben nodded, watching the young couple walk away. Matt hesitated, then put his arm around Jerre's shoulders in a protective way; a possessive way. Ben had to smile at the gesture.

"That your young friend, Ben?" Salina asked.

"That was her."

"Just friends, huh?"

"Sure—what else?"

"Uh-huh." She smiled.

Ike and Megan had brought about a thousand people with them, people the glib ex-SEAL had picked up along the way. "Just folks," he called them.

"What are you going to call your new state, Ben?" Megan asked.

"Mine?" Ben said, surprised. "This is not mine. Call it Montana, Idaho, and Wyoming. What else?"

"Who is the governor?" Tatter asked. "The leader— the man in charge?"

"There isn't any," Ben replied.

"Well, then, Ben Raines . . ." She smiled. "I guess we'll have to have us an election."

335

"Just don't nominate me. I'm a writer, got a lot to do. I'm not a politician."

And Ben could not understand why everyone smiled.

Winter comes early in that part of the nation, and there was still much to do in preparation. The few residents left in the three-state area, while certainly glad to see the newcomers, were still not quite certain what was going on around them. But it looked as though things were shaping up—in a hurry.

The trucks and trains and planes continued to roll and rumble and roar into the area, bringing in looted booty from all over the nation. And more people arrived, some of them the type that wanted something for nothing. They did not last long. The graveyards began receiving new additions to their silence. For this was frontier country, and while the East had been settled and under law (and lawyers) for three centuries, much of this part of the nation had been settled for only about seventy-five years. Justice here came down hard and swift, but as fair as Ben could make it, considering the conditions under which his people were working. Here, no one needed to steal, there was work for all, and everybody worked—or got out. Or died.

As Logan's laws became more tyrannical, more people fought back, and Logan could do less to stop Ben Raines and his people in their breakaway nation. But Logan could do something about those blacks who were bent on creating a New Africa.

"Logan's mercenaries have pushed the blacks out of south Louisiana," Cossman told Ben. "He's told them if they want to work the land and reopen the factories, to go ahead. But the oil and the gas belong to the government,

336

end quote."

Cossman had looked at the communications equipment and grinned, rubbing his hands together in glee. Now, under his direction, if it was broadcast from anywhere in the world—or space, for that matter—he could and would monitor it. In a very short time, the three states controlled by Ben's People, as Logan had begun saying, would have the finest communications network in the world, including public radio and TV, free from the constraints of the FCC and the mumblings and threats of pressure groups, who used to maintain (and would again) that they "only wanted what was best for the people."

"He won't stop there," Ben said. "He'll never permit a New Africa. Is Cecil Jeffreys in charge down there?"

"Right."

"Can you get him on the horn?"

"I can try."

It took twenty-four hours to reach Cecil.

"Ben!" His voice crackled through the speakers. "I hear you're doing great things up there. Congratulations."

"I hear things aren't going so well for you."

"There have been a few minor setbacks," Cecil admitted, caution in his reply. Both men knew Big Brother was listening, monitoring the conversation.

"Don't believe a word Logan says, Cecil."

"He said he'd let us reopen the factories and work the land, Ben."

"Perhaps for a time, buddy, but Logan is a liar, and you know it. He's power-mad and has been all his life. He'll do anything to gain that power. Look at the switch in philosophy he's made."

"We have to try, Ben. How is Salina?"

"Great. Fine."

"Ben? Word I get is that you're breaking away from the constitution. Dangerous, if true."

"It isn't true, Cecil. We're not breaking away from it; we're returning to it."

"We just got some people in from up North. They say there is a hit team coming after you. Can't pinpoint exactly when."

Salina's fingers dug into his arm. "Hit team?" Ben questioned over the miles. "Government?"

"No. Jeb Fargo."

"I know who he is: little Nazi prick."

"That's all I know, Ben. So you be careful; you've made more enemies than we have."

After the men said their good-bys and good luck, Salina said, "Logan is somehow tied in with Fargo. I never did trust that man."

"One day Cecil will look up, and there'll be troops standing on his front doorstep. You let just one white person report he or she's got trouble in New Africa; just let one of Cecil's blacks screw up one time and Logan will crush his dream."

"*Cecil's* blacks, Ben?"

"He's the leader, honey—so he'll get the blame for failure."

"And here, Ben?"

"I'll get the blame; it's my dream. But most people here are—for now—white."

"And that makes a difference?"

"You know it does, Salina."

"Everyone expects a nigger to screw up, right?"

"You said it, babe, not me."

It had been talked about for years: breaking the United

338

States up into several nations. But it had never been taken seriously. Until now.

Survivors were, or so it seemed, fleeing their devastated homelands, from all over the world, all of them heading for the land of opportunity: America. And Logan, with his small military, seemed unable to stem the tide or kill the dream.

And as is probably the case with many high-level decisions from heads of state, it was the wife of the king, the premier, the prime minister, the chief, or the president who made the final decision, or at least outlined the plan.

"People are unemployed, Hilton," Fran told him. "And just look at all these tacky people coming in from the islands and Europe and Lord only knows where else. Start the draft up. It will give people something to do. And just look at all the ex-soldiers coming in, too. Officers among them. They will be grateful to you for giving them work, and in return, you'll have loyalty from them."

"Marvelous idea, Hilton," Dallas Valentine, the secretary of state said. "And we can get rid of those officers who dislike us so."

Hilton agreed; then said, "But all these people setting up little kingdoms around the country?"

"Oh, big deal," Fran told him, a pout on her lips. "Let them have their two-bit little kingdoms—for as long as they last. Look what we control: the oil, the gas, all the ports that are usable, all the shipping, the bread-basket areas. We've got a lot more area than we have people to settle it. So let these people try—you know they're going to fail, ninety-nine percent of them. And when they do, they'll look to you for help, and you'll be a big man to them when you bring them back into the fold. Then, as we grow stronger, we can crush those who didn't fail."

"Marvelous idea, Hilton," Dallas said.

Logan smiled. He liked to have yes men around him. Made him feel good. He also liked that term: bring them back into the fold. It was kind of religious-sounding. He'd have to ask Rev. Palmer Falcreek over to the White House for lunch with him . . . soon. Tell him about it. Falcreek was such a good man. Already he was setting up a committee to boycott any film that came out of what was called the New Hollywood. Falcreek wanted only good, clean, wholesome entertainment. Dogs and horses and stuff like that. Cowboys with inexhaustible six-shooters. None of that wiggle-jiggle stuff.

"Of course, you're right, dear," Hilton said. "Why shed blood?"

"*Our* blood," she corrected. "You've got Colonel Parr and his men to do all that physical stuff. And Jeb Fargo and his bunch if you have to use them . . . for tacky little jobs."

"Jeb Fargo?" the president questioned. "What has he to do with this? His people are farmers, dear."

Yeah, Fran thought, with submachine guns and blazing crosses. "Oh, Hilton! I declare, sometimes you're so dense. Fargo is a Klucker from Georgia. They ran him out of Mississippi years ago." She didn't tell him Fargo was also a Nazi. It had not taken her long to learn what many people had learned years before: her husband was not always with it.

"Klucker?"

"KKK, dear."

"Oh. Well . . . I didn't know that. I know only that he is loyal and a good, decent, churchgoing man. Palmer Falcreek says he has the good of the country at heart."

Long as he could run around in a bedsheet burning crosses, Fran thought. "Of course, dear." She smiled at him.

Under the table, Fran slipped off her shoe and ran her little foot up the pants' leg of Dallas Valentine, almost causing him to drop part of a fricasseed chicken into his lap. She liked ol' Dallas—he was hung like that ol' boy used to fuck her in the barn when she was just a teenager. Had a cock about a foot and half long, just like Dallas. She felt sorry for Dallas. Had a wife that looked like a cross between a prune and a hockey puck. No angles, no curves, no planes. Just one great big round wrinkle.

"I think Fran has the right idea," Dallas said.

Bet your ass, I do, Fran thought. Just as soon as we can get alone and I can get my hands on that garden hose you call a pecker.

"I'll give it some thought," Hilton said.

But all knew the decision had been made.

So the president handed down the orders to the mercenaries under Kenny Parr's control: do not interfere with people attempting to set up so-called free states. Move only if people attempt to seize those areas already under U.S. control.

And the president ordered a complete census taken, and a draft order put into law.

Now it became a game of wait-and-see.

Spring

The harsh winter had passed, and the mountains and the valleys and the plains were blooming with the birth of the cycle. The roar of tractors was evident as the plows

341

cut into the earth, preparing the land for planting. Ben was on a tour of the three-state area now, in a Jeep with Maj. Clint Voltan.

"Home at last." Voltan smiled, topping a hill and stopping. "Never figured I'd see this land again—not as a free man, anyway. Sure is peaceful and pretty here."

"Why did you think you'd never see it again?" Ben asked.

"You don't know?" Voltan wore a surprised look. "No, I guess you don't." He smiled. "I'm a murderer, Mr. Raines. Oh, yeah. This"—he waved his hand at the expanse of land—"belonged—belongs—to me. My ranch. I was doing pretty good, me and my wife, until some modern-day rustlers started runnin' off my beef. My wife, she used to like to ride in the mornings, she come up on them. They raped her, left her after they used her—pretty badly. Well, I went on the prowl for them; thought I recognized the tire tracks. I was right; I did. There were three of them. I found 'em in a bar one night—called their hand. One of them was just drunk enough to admit what they'd done. They said—right out in public—that my wife had offered it to them. All three of them backed each other up. I knew they were lyin' for a number of reasons. Mainly 'cause my wife—and they didn't know this—had lost her mind. The doctors told me that most women can cope with the emotional stress of rape. Alice—that's my wife—couldn't. I gut-shot all three of them, right there in that bar; then stood there and listened to 'em squall and die." He laughed, but it was a rueful bark of no humor. "Good old straight Voltan, believing in the system. I'd never even had a traffic ticket before then. Sure . . . the law put murder warrants out on me. I ran for about a year, then joined up with the western-based Rebels. After the war, I went to the institution where my wife had been confined. Found her—dead of course. Buried her."

"Do you ever feel you were wrong?"

Voltan thought about that for a few seconds. "No, sir. I don't. I think rape should carry a stiff sentence. I think that if rape is proven, beyond any doubt—lie detectors, PSE machines, even hypnosis—I think the rapist should not only have to serve a tough sentence, but should be gelded like you would a bad stallion."

"I agree with you," Ben said.

"We gonna have soft laws in this area, Mr. Raines?"

"I hope not. Clint? Why is everybody asking me these questions? No one has elected me to anything."

The rancher-Rebel smiled. "Well, you have been, kind of, in a secret way."

"I beg your pardon?"

"You're it, Mr. Raines."

And the words of Cecil came to him. "You're going to look up one day, Ben, and the job of leader will be handed to you. Like me, you won't want it, but you'll take it."

"All right, Clint," he heard his voice say. "If I'm elected, I'll serve."

"You'll be elected, Mr. Raines."

"I'll be a tough law-and-order man." He looked at the rancher. "Better warn the people of that."

"'Bout time somebody got tough in this country."

"Two thirds of the world's population dead," Cossman said. "They think that's final. Here at home, over a hundred and fifty million, and still climbing." He and his crew had been monitoring government bands.

"What's the population of our three-state area?"

Ben asked.

"That, I can tell you precisely," an aide said to Ben.

Ben had been governor of the three-state area for almost six months, and he could not get accustomed to the title or the attention paid him.

"Sixty-seven thousand, four hundred and twenty-two people," the aide said. "Our final head count was completed yesterday afternoon."

"Umm," Ben said. "I thought the preliminary figures were somewhat higher?"

"They were. We lost twenty-seven thousand people in the first two months of . . . ah—"

"My taking office," Ben finished it.

"Win some, lose some, el Presidente," Ike said. Outwardly, the only thing Ike took seriously was Megan and his farm/ranch. But Ike took the new government of the three-state area very seriously. He desperately wanted it to work. And he believed it would—given time. Time.

"They just didn't believe they could conform or adapt to the tough law-and-order system we advocate," Dr. Chase said. "And they didn't like what we're setting up in our schools, either."

"But"—the aide spoke—"on the other hand, we've got almost ten thousand people on the outside who want to come in. And the number is growing by a hundred a day. A decision has to be made on that, sir. Quickly."

"How many can we screen a day?"

"If we really hump it . . . maybe fifty. And that is pushing it."

"I don't want the screening relaxed. Each new person must be given a lie-detector test/PSE test as to background, criminal record, conformity. And the

344

aptitude tests must still be given verbally, by race opposites. We've culled a lot of would-be troublemakers and bigots that way."

"Those lawyers with what's left of the ACLU are really raising hell about those tests, sir. And our laws." The aide looked uncomfortable, for he knew only too well how Ben felt about the ACLU.

Ben glared at him. "I thought I told you to get those bastards out of here."

The aide shuffled his feet. "Sir—they say we'll have to use force to get them out."

"Then use force. All that is necessary to remove them. They were not invited—are they ever? I don't want them in here." Ben softened his tone. "Look, boys, I know they mean well, and they have done some good—back when conditions were more or less normal. But we don't have time for hair-splitting legal technicalities. We're not going to have it when our laws and legal system are finally drawn up; and that is being done this very moment.

"You all know where we stand on issues. The people have voted on them, all over this three-state area. We've been holding town meetings since early last winter on the issues we'll live with. Now, ninety-one percent of the people agreed to our laws. The rest left. And that's the way it's going to be or you can take this governorship—that I didn't want in the first place—and I'll go back to writing my journal."

"Ben—" Dr. Chase said.

"No!" Ben stood firm. "I came into this office this morning and there was a damned paper on my desk asking me to reconsider the death penalty for that goddamned punk over in Missoula."

"He's sixteen years old, Governor," an aide said.

"That's his problem. His IQ is one twenty-eight. The shrink says he knows right from wrong and is healthy, mentally and physically. He is perfectly normal. He stole a car, got drunk, and drove a hundred fucking miles an hour down the main street. He ran over and killed two elderly people whose only crime was attempting to cross a street . . . in compliance with the existing traffic lights. He admitted what he did. He is not remorseful. I would reconsider if he was sorry for what he'd done. But he isn't. And tests bear that out. He has admitted his true feelings; said the old people didn't have much time left anyway, so what the hell was everybody getting so upset about? He's a punk. That's all he would ever be—if I let him live—which I have no intention of doing. If he puts so little emphasis on the lives of others, then he shouldn't mind terribly if I snuff out his.

"So, Mr. Garrett,"—he looked at a uniformed man standing quietly across the room—"at six o'clock day after tomorrow, dawn, you will personally escort young Mr. Randolph Green to the designated place of execution and you will see to it that he is hanged by the neck until he is dead. The day of the punk . . . is over."

"Yes, sir," Garrett said. "It's about time some backbone was shoved into the law." He left the room.

Ben looked around him. "Any further questions as to how the law is going to work?"

No one had anything further to say. Ben left the room to have lunch with Salina.

"He's a hard man," an aide said.

Ike stood up and stretched. "Hard times, brother."

EIGHTEEN

There were many who left the three-state area, but many more stayed and more wanted in. Some of those who came in also left after seeing what was happening, but most stayed. Life was not easy; rebuilding and conforming never is. Eighteen-hour days were not uncommon; there was a lot to do and everybody able was expected to work without whining about it.

There were those who could not, or would not, as the case may be, accept or adapt to the new laws being written by the people; and many of those laws were not easy to follow, for the people had reverted back to what used to be known as a code of conduct.

Violate that code, and one might find himself or herself in serious trouble. As one old-timer, long a resident of Idaho said, summing up the new system (actually an old system), "Man's got two ways of gettin' rid of leaves in his yard; smart man will rake them up, put them in bags, carry them to the dump where they'll be disposed of in a safe manner. Stupid man will set them on fire in his yard and not give a thought about the smoke blowing in his neighbor's window. Man does the latter now, he's liable to end up with a busted jaw. And there isn't a law on the books against it. Out there in the proper forty-seven, man don't have to think much about what he does. Here, you'd better damned well give it some thought—a lot of thought. I like it here. Peaceful. Once we got rid of the troublemakers. And it didn't take long."

Many roads leading into the three-state area were destroyed, deliberately, to prevent easy access. There were signs posted all along the borders, warning travelers that the laws in these states were very different from those to which they had grown accustomed, and justice came down very hard and very swiftly.

The world still tumbled about in disorder and confusion and almost total disorganization. There were millions of people out of work and they did not know how to catch a fish or skin a rabbit or plant a garden. Gangs of thugs and punks and hoodlums roamed the country, stealing and raping and killing. All across the nation, from border to border, sea to sea, various groups of different ideological persuasions were breaking away and setting up little communities, sure their way was the right way—the only way. True, caring Christians; semireligious, demented fanatics; cult worshipers; and left- and right-of-center organizations were establishing little governments. All would fail in only a few months as Logan's forces grew stronger; or they rotted from within. Only one would last for any length of time, and its concepts would never die.

How hated Ben's system of government was did not come home to the people of the three states until late fall of the first year. Ben had stepped outside of his home for a breath of the cold, clean air of night. Juno went with him, and together they walked from the house around to the front. When Juno growled, Ben went into a crouch, and that saved his life. Automatic-weapon fire spider-webbed the windshield of his truck, the slugs hitting and ricocheting off the metal, sparking the night. Ben jerked open the door of the pickup, punched open the glove compartment, and grabbed a pistol. He fired at a dark shape running across his yard, then at another. Both went down, screaming in pain.

A man stepped from the shadows of the house and opened fire just as Ben hit the ground. Lights were popping on all over the street, men with rifles in their hands appeared on the lawns.

Ben felt a slug slam into his hip, knocking him to one side, spinning him around, the lead traveling down his leg, exiting just above his knee. He pulled himself to one knee and leveled the 9-mm, pumping three shots into the dark form by the side of the house. The man went down, the rifle dropping from his hands.

Ben pulled himself up, his leg and hip throbbing from the shock of the wounds. He leaned against the truck just as help reached him.

"Get the medics!" a man shouted. "Governor's been shot."

"Help me over to that man," Ben said. "He looks familiar."

Standing over the fallen man, Ben could see where his shots had gone: two in the stomach, one in the chest. The man was splattered with blood and dying. He coughed and spat at Ben.

"Goddamned nigger-lovin' scum," he said. He closed his eyes, shivered in the convulsions of pain; then died.

Badger came panting up, a robe over his pajamas, house slippers flapping. "God, Governor! Who is he?"

Ben stood for a time, leaning against the side of the house. Salina came to him, putting her arms around him as the wailing of ambulances drew louder. "Do you know him, Ben?" she asked.

"I used to," Ben's reply was sad. "He was my brother."

PART THREE

THE SWIFT YEARS

The death of Carl Raines probably did more to ensure the immediate survival of the three states than any other single act. It shocked Logan when the news finally reached him, and Logan, like most people who heard the story, reasoned that if a man believed so strongly in an idea he would kill his brother . . . that man had best be left alone. And for almost five years, the Tri-states, as they were referred to, were left alone.

The world, and especially America, began to take shape and resume order, law, and some stability. In America, with the drafting of young men now in its fourth year, and the replacing of ranking officers with men who were loyal to Logan, the military was perhaps the strongest in the world. Acting under orders from Logan, the military, systematically, state by state, began crushing those people who had established their own forms of government. The nation was once more whole—almost—whether the people involved wanted it, or not.

East of the Mississippi River, the nation was as one—no pockets of resistance left. And there was no longer any area known as New Africa. Cecil, knowing there was no way he could win against division after division of military might, quietly pulled down the flag of New Africa and told his people the dream was dead.

Most of the blacks chose to remain where they were, farming the land, working the reopened factories. But the experience had been bitter for Cecil. Cecil and Lila, Pal and Valerie, and about a hundred more blacks left the South and headed west, to the Tri-states. Ben immediately named Cecil as his lieutenant governor and Pal the secretary of state.

"Won't that irritate a large number of people out here?" Cecil asked. "Naming blacks to high positions?"

Ben had smiled. "You don't know the caliber of people living in the Tri-states."

"You've been practicing selective population?" Pal asked.

"Yes," Ben answered. "Amazing how much trouble you can avoid by doing that."

"And amazing how illegal it is." Cecil's reply was dry.

"Maybe out there." Ben jerked his thumb, indicating the area outside Tri-states. "But not in here."

"Kasim has decided on guerrilla warfare," Pal said. "He's got several thousand men and women behind him, and there are lots more who quietly support what he's about to do. It's going to be bloody, Ben, for there is a lot of hate in that man."

"It's going to be bloody here, too," Ben said. "Someday."

Of the hundreds of towns and cities that once stood in the Tri-states, many were destroyed, having first been picked over; whatever could be used was labeled and stored. The area was returned to land. The residents, if any, were moved to newer, nicer homes and apartments and told to maintain them. There would be no slums in the Tri-states.

The people were pulled together for many reasons: to conserve energy, to stabilize government, for easier care, and to afford more land for the production of crops, as well as to afford better protection for the people in health care, police, fire, and social services.

The elderly, for the first time in their lives, were looked after with care and concern and respect. They were not grouped together and forgotten or ignored. Careful planning went into the population centers. Young, middle-aged, and elderly were carefully grouped together in housing and apartments. Those elderly who wanted to work, and could work, were encouraged to do so. They could work as long as they wished, or until they tired, and then could go home. The knowledge of older citizens is valuable and vast, and Ben knew it. Older citizens can teach so many things—if only the younger people would listen. In the Tri-states, they listened.

In order for this to work, the pace had to be slowed, the grind eased, the honor system restored; the work ethic, in both labor and management, renewed. It was.

Here, for the first time in decades, there was no welfare, no ADC, no WIC, no food stamps, no unemployment; but what there was was jobs for all, and all adults worked. Everyone. Those who would not, because they felt the job offered them was beneath their dignity, or because of laziness, apathy, and/or indifference, were escorted to the nearest border and booted out. They were told not to come back. If children were involved, they were taken from the people and immediately adopted.

It was harsh treatment, and by American standards, totally unconstitutional. But if Ben worried about the legality of it, the worry was not evident in his day-today living.

Ben took particular care in the defense of the Tristates. Heavy artillery was ready to roar; defensive and offensive were tatics worked down to a fine state of readiness. Bunkers and hidden positions were stocked and checked and maintained. Roads and bridges could be wired to detonate, if and when it became necessary, in only a few hours. Radar hummed twenty-four hours a day. Radio-controlled antipersonnel mines were ready to be placed. Tanks were in abundance, and their crews were highly trained. The armed forces of the Tri-states ranked among the best in the world, their training a combination of Special Forces, Ranger, SEAL, and gutter-fighting. Every resident of the Tri-states, male and female, between the ages of sixteen and sixty was a member of the armed forces. They met twice a month, after their initial thirty-week basic training, and were on active duty one month each year. And the training was a no-holds-barred type. Any interference with the day-to-day activities of the Tri-states would be met with brutal and savage retaliation and Hilton Logan knew it. Logan hated Ben Raines, but that hatred was tempered with fear.

"It would cost us much more than it's worth to take the Tri-states," the Joint Chiefs told Logan. "Raines has the equivalent of seven divisions—all combat-ready and prepared to fight to the death. His people are better trained than ours. Leave Raines alone, Mr. President. For if we didn't kill them all, every man, woman, and child, they'd group and fight as guerrillas, and we'd have another civil war on our hands. The only way we could possibly defeat Tri-states at this time is with the use of nuclear weapons, and that is totally out of the question.

Another two to three years . . . maybe. But not now. Not without it costing us dearly."

Tri-states was left alone.

The government in Richmond, the police, and federal agents watched all that was going on in Tri-states, watched it with awe and consternation, and to some degree, envy. Ben had gathered his people, of all backgrounds, all races, and molded them into a highly productive society, virtually free of prejudice, and totally devoid of crime. And what irritated Logan the most, was that Ben had the *best* people; the best doctors, the best scientists, the best computer programmers, the best farmers, financial planners, and so on down the line. And Ben's society was working. That irritated Logan constantly.

The central government knew the people of the Tri-states had aligned themselves with the Indians of the West, working closely with them, and if they moved against Ben and his people, dozens of Indian tribes would join with Ben in the fight, and the central government of Richmond just wasn't strong enough to fight that—not yet.

In the West, what the remaining tribes of Indians thought they needed in the way of supplies and equipment, they seized, just as Ben and his people had done. And now, with the help of personnel from the Tri-states, the Indian had what he had lacked for years: organization.

The Indians held meetings with other tribes to decide what first to do; and they worked together, putting aside centuries-old hatreds. Where there had once been a scarcity of water, it now moved freely. With the help of "borrowed" earth-moving equipment from deserted construction sites, and engineers from the Tri-states, the flow of water helped irrigate the crops and cool the thirst of a hundred and fifty years of wasted promises, broken treaties, and millions of words from Washington—all lies.

The Indians armed themselves with modern weapons, stockpiled millions of rounds of ammunition, canned goods, blankets, vehicles, spare parts, and all the other items they might need for war—when the white man came to reclaim land that was not his to begin with.

The Indians built new homes, with modern plumbing and running water. They laid down hundreds of miles of water pipe. They diverted the flow of electricity into their own communities and built clean, new modern schools and hospitals. Many reservations no longer resembled a nightmare from a hobo jungle. For now the Indians had had restored what the white man had taken from them: pride. Now they could live as decent, productive human beings—the only true Americans, really. They could have done all this decades back, had they been afforded the means, instead of being treated like animals.

Teams of doctors, engineers, medics, teachers, and construction workers from the Tri-states worked with the tribes and became friends, welcoming each other's advice, each promising, if possible, to help the other if and when things began to turn sour and raunchy, as they both knew they would, in time. Time—a very precious commodity.

No, the government in Richmond did not have the manpower just yet to stop the Indians or the Rebels in the Tri-states. Tri-states and the Indians would have to wait.

TWO

"I'm tired of waiting," Hilton Logan told VP Addison. "I know there is no easy answer, but we simply can't allow much more of this to continue. If those two groups ever get a really firm toehold—and our intelligence people say they are talking of a written alliance—it'll be the devil getting them back into the Union. Maybe impossible."

"The Union is still here, Hilton," Aston replied, listening more to the drumming of the rain on the window than to the president. The VP often had a full-time job just trying to soothe the ruffled feathers of President Logan. Didn't the man know his wife—the first lady—was screwing half the men in Richmond? Her secret service detachment spent more time covering her tracks than protecting her life. Aston sighed. "We have to walk lightly, Hilton; don't want to kick off a civil war."

"I don't put much faith in the military's warnings." The president looked at his friend. "They always overreact. Aston, I can't believe you think we should do nothing. Just let the Rebels and the Indians continue without federal guidance?"

The VP laughed at that. "I haven't heard them asking for our help—have you?"

The president shook his head, refusing to reply.

Instead, he let himself warm to his inner hatred of Ben Raines. He despised the man; refusing to admit even to himself that it was not just hatred, it was jealousy.

Aston rose from his chair and poured the coffee. "My God, Hilton . . . our *guidance* got us where we now are. Our *guidance* cost the U.S. many of our friends overseas. Our *guidance* bled the middle class dry with taxes. It was our constant interference in the private lives of citizens that attributed greatly to the downfall of this nation. Guidance, Hilton? Goddamn!"

"I don't happen to agree with you, Aston. People need a central point from which to seek advice and guidance." He thumped a fist on his desk. "Aston, we've *got* to break the backs of the Rebels. Maybe cordon them off, fence them in; then take the Indians out first. Yes," he mused. "Look, let's face facts. They've stolen three states, and they have no intention of returning them. Because of their resistance, many others in this nation have refused to hand over their guns, and many others are arming themselves with illegal weapons. We've got the makings of a damned gunpowder society in this country. When will people learn that when government passes laws, those laws are to be obeyed? It's for their own good! No, Aston, if we can hammer the Rebels into submission— for the good of the entire country—the rest of the nation will fall into line as well."

"Oh, yes," Aston replied, sarcasm thick in his voice. "That's very good. The world is still stumbling about, attempting to recover from a germ and nuclear war, and you want to start another war. For the good of the country, of course. Hilton, leave the people of the Tri-states alone."

Hilton Logan rubbed his temples; his headache had

returned. It always did whenever he discussed Ben Raines. He thought: God, how I hate that bastard. Even Rev. Falcreek hates him. And he loves everybody . . . even Jane Fonda, so he says.

"Aston," he said wearily, "they've hanged and shot people out there in . . . Tri-states." He spat the words from his mouth. "Capital punishment is the law of the land." It wasn't, and he knew it. "They've shut down the roads—or blown them up—turning the place into a damned fortress. Colonel Parr won't even go near the place; says Ben Raines is crazy in combat. A damned ex-mercenary is governor of three states. That is incredible. Aston, they refuse to allow my agents to even come into the place and look around. They threw an FCC inspector out—literally. Some nitwit named Cossman said if he came back he'd tar and feather him. Everybody carries a gun out there. My God, Aston—even the *ladies* carry guns. Those nuts are teaching war in the public school system. The entire country is an *army!* They—"

". . . Have no crime," Aston interrupted. "And zero unemployment. And fine medical care—for everybody—on an equal basis. And good schools, and the best race relations anywhere in the world. And do you know how they've accomplished all that in such a short time?"

"You're damned right, I do, Aston! By throwing out any person they consider an undesirable."

"That's only part of it, Hilton, and you know it. No—they've done it in part by education and partly because they've formed a government that is truly of and by the people. It might behoove us to take lessons from Ben Raines."

"Hell, no! Never!"

Aston tapped a thick letter on the president's desk.

"Here it is, Hilton. You read it. Ben Raines has made the first peace overture. He says they will pay a fair share of taxes to the government of the United States, to be decided upon; vote, live under the American flag, and fight for it, if need be. But they run their own schools, they have their own laws, their own way of doing things. Hilton, there doesn't have to be any more bloodshed. We could have a powerful ally in Ben Raines' Tri-states."

"Spitting in the face of the Constitution?"

Aston smiled grimly. "We did—years ago. What gave us the right and not them?"

"I don't agree with you about that, and you know it." The president swiveled in his chair to watch the rain splatter on the window. Damned demonstrators were still out there, protesting something or the other. He wished they'd all fall down and die from pneumonia. "The damned Indians are rebelling, too. Just taking things that don't belong to them."

"Just like our ancestors did to them, a couple of hundred years ago."

"And it's all Ben Raines's fault," Hilton said. "Everything is his fault. He . . . if he were only dead!"

And I've heard the same said about you, Aston thought. "Hilton, it's a brand-new world out there, and we're going to have to adapt to it. These are changing times, so let's change with them."

"I am the President of the United States. I give the orders. End of discussion."

"I don't like the sound of that! Hilton, something else: it's been almost five years since the military put us in office. Tell me; when will proper elections be held?"

Hilton Logan swiveled in his chair, glared at his VP, then turned to once more gaze at the rain. "When I say so."

Logan was right to a degree about the laws in the Tri-states. People *were* hanged and shot. More than a hundred the first years; fifty-odd the second year; ten the next year; and none since then. It is a myth to say that crime cannot be controlled, and the government of the Tri-states proved that by simply stating they would not tolerate it, and backing up their words with hard, swift justice. But capital punishment was not the law of the land. They had prisons, and they were as prisons should be: not very pleasant places to be, but with adequate rehabilitation facilities, the violent housed far from the nonviolent, and weekly visits from ladies so inclined toward that type of employment—which was legal in the Tri-states . . . and regulated . . . and taxed.

No one had to steal; there were jobs for anyone who wanted to work, but everyone who lived in the Tri-states and was able to work . . . worked.

During the first year in the Tri-states, there were marriages among the Rebels, as they began the job of settling in. Steven Miller and Linda Jennings; Al Holloway and Anne Flood; Ben and Salina.

"Yes, suh." Ike grinned. "Once that ol' boy got himself a taste of brown sugar, just couldn't stand it."

Megan shook her head and tried not to smile. "Ike—you're impossible!"

Bridge Oliver married a lady from Texas—Abby. Pal Elliot married Valerie. Sam Pyron married a girl from south Louisiana who kept the West Virginia mountain boy in a flat lope every waking hour.

Nora Rodelo married Maj. Clint Voltan and took in five homeless kids to raise.

Ken Amato became news director for the Tri-states' broadcast system.

Nora, along with Steven and Linda, took over the task of rebuilding the Tri-states' school system. At the end of three years, they had perhaps the finest school system operating anywhere in the world.

The school system, free of politics and top-heavy bureaucracy, concentrated on the needs of the children's minds, stressing hard discipline along with the basic educational needs of the child.

Steven Miller, believing that the child not only needs, but wants fair discipline, and that a child's mind is chaotic, at best, ran a tough but excellent school system. His teachers taught, or attempted to teach, how to make a living once the young person left school. They taught music (fine music), literature, and the three R's— beginning at an early age. And they taught courses that could not be offered in any other public school in America: respect and fairness toward one's fellow man . . . to a degree. They were taught that to work is the honorable path to take. And they openly discussed bigotry, the kids learning that only people with closed minds practiced it.

In the Tri-states, public schools operated ten months a year. Every student over the age of fifteen was given five hours of weapons training each week, forty weeks a year, and studied the fundamentals of guerrilla warfare. Military service was mandatory.

Physical education was rigid in the schools, from organized sports to PE. Everyone took part, including the teachers still young enough to take rough physical training. But it was done with an equality that is seldom seen in any other public or private schools.

For in sports, Ben stressed that games were just that— games, and no one should take them too seriously. They were not life-or-death matters, and in reality, accomplished very little. And anyone who would fight over the outcome of a game was tantamount to being a fool. He told the young people that games were meant to be fun, win or lose, and when, or if, he sensed games were becoming more important than scholastic efforts, he would put a stop to them, and the schools would have intramural activities only.

Although Ben had been a fine athlete in high school, he despised the jock mentality and would not tolerate it in the Tri-states. Coaches walked a narrow line in Tri-states' schools.

The young people needed someone to look up to, and they found that person in Ben and his philosophy. After the war, the young were confused as to what was right and wrong—and what had happened to cause such a tragedy.

Ben, sitting on a desk in the classroom where he was conducting an impromptu question-and-answer session, laughed. "That is probably the most difficult question you could ask me, but I'll try to give you an answer.

"Perspectives got all out of order, not only in America, but around the world. People demand freedom, and if they have to do it, they'll fight for freedom taken from them—real or imagined.

"Our country, I believe, began to parallel the Roman Empire in many ways. Historians saw it, warned of it, but too few listened—until it was too late.

"The Romans had great, unworkable, and expensive social programs. So did we. The Romans built super-highways. So did we. The Romans began to scoff at great teachers, philosophers. So did we. They had social unrest. So did we. They built great arenas so the citizens could go on weekends and watch sporting events. So did we. The Roman Government became top-heavy with bureaucracy. So did ours. The Roman Government became corrupt. So did ours. Right on down the line. And as theirs came to an end, so did ours.

"Here in the United States, such things as patriotism, love of God, duty, honor, became the objects of ridicule. A day's work for a fair day's pay was replaced by greed; and if the product was faulty, the worker didn't care. Strikes became the rule instead of the exception. Craftsmen became a thing of the past when the assembly line took over and goods were thrown together with no regard for the consumer. Those responsible forgot that we are all consumers.

"Morals sank to an all-time low. The sixties and seventies were times of great liberalism in America. It got out of hand and we went off the deep end, sinking more and more into debt. We came off the gold standard and began printing more money—without anything to back it. Just paper.

"We had great tax reforms in the Senate and House in the mid-eighties, greatly lessening the burden on the lower and middle classes. But most of them never got out of committee. Money backed many members of Congress, big business. When they spoke, Congress listened. So instead of the wealthy paying the brunt of the taxes, the lower and middle classes paid them. It was wrong, but Congress refused to correct it.

"On the world scene, the unions in Britain must share much of the blame for the country's downfall. Massive land reforms came much too late in Central and South America. Russia's economy finally collapsed. Guerrilla warfare spanned the globe.

"Here at home . . ." Ben sighed and thought for a

moment. "The central government became too powerful, moving into every facet of public and private lives. Big Brother came out of fiction to become reality. Our laws became so vague and so left-leaning, the average citizen did not even have the right to protect what was his or hers.

"Anytime a government takes away the basic liberties of its citizens, it will inevitably lead to war. And it did."

"Will we have to fight for what we have here, Governor?" a teen-age girl asked.

"Yes," Ben said. "And probably very soon."

"Why don't other people just leave us alone?" another asked. "What business is it of theirs, anyway?"

"Dear,"—Ben smiled sadly—"people have been asking that of government since the first government was formed. And government has yet to come up with a satisfactory reply."

Ben and Salina took two kids into their home, twins, a boy and a girl. They were handsome, well-mannered, and intelligent. Of course, all parents think that of their children.

Tina and Jack originally had come from Arizona. In hiding, they had watched their father shot to death by a gang of thugs and their mother raped repeatedly, then killed as she tried to run away, in the opposite direction from where her kids were hiding. But she bought them enough time to get away. Neither Jack nor Tina had any love or compassion for the lawless.

Their story was similar to that of almost every adopted child in the Tri-states. The young who lived through the holocaust, like their elders, needed very little prompting to demand harsh penalties for criminals. They had seen firsthand what permissiveness in a society can produce, and they wanted no part of it.

Jimmy Deluce, Jane Dolbeau, Jerre Hunter, and Badger Harbin remained single. Jimmy flew for the Tri-states' small air force; Jane and Jerre worked as nurses at one of the many free clinics in the Tri-states; and Badger became Ben's bodyguard.

That was not something Ben wanted, or really felt he needed, but after the assassination attempt, Badger announced his new job and moved in. He lived with the Raineses and became a constant shadow wherever Ben went.

Badger idolized the governor, as did most of the Rebels and residents of the Tri-states, and would have jumped through burning hoops had Ben suggested it. He was also devoted to Salina, but not in any overt sexual manner. That thought had occurred to him, but once he had become so preoccupied about it he had walked into a wall and broken his nose.

Salina noticed his attention, however, was amused by it, and finally mentioned it to Ben one night.

"Yes, honey," Ben said, laying aside the book he was reading, "I've noticed it a couple of times. But I don't know what to do about it. Has he made any advances?"

"Oh, Ben!" She laughed. "For heaven's sake—no. I just think he needs a girl, that's all."

Ben smiled.

"A wife, Ben." She returned his smile. "I'm talking about a nice girl for Badger to marry."

"Badger's shy, that's all. I know he . . . ah . . . visits a lady—or ladies—at the . . . ah . . . house just outside of town."

"Along with several hundred other men," Salina remarked dryly.

"But it's Jerre and Jane I can't figure out." Ben carried

368

on as if his wife had said nothing. The communities in the Tri-states were small, deliberately so, and everybody knew everybody else. "Both of them young, good-looking, smart. Yet, they both seem so detached from everybody. Neither of them date. I mentioned both of them to Badger the other day, and he looked at me as if I were an idiot. Is something going on I need to know about?"

Salina smiled at her husband. Years back Ben had told her about Jerre and the relationship they had had for a few weeks. But Ben believed all that was past. Salina knew better. What good would it do to tell him Jerre was hopelessly in love with him? And Jane had also developed an enormous crush on Ben. She wondered if they had discussed their feelings with each other? What good would it do to tell him the entire Tri-states knew about it? That both of them knew Salina knew? She shook her head.

"No, darling—nothing going on that I know of."

"Ummm." Ben picked up his book and resumed his reading. The subject was closed.

Salina laughed at the man she loved and rose to check on the twins. Tina had a friend over that night and they were in the bedroom, discussing, of all things, karate. Ben insisted that all Rebels and dependents become at least familiar with some form of self-defense—the killing kind, preferably—and Tina had taken to karate and the other forms of gutter-fighting that were taught to Tri-states' regular army. She had now advanced to the dangerous state, and the seventeen-year-old was considered by her instructors to be a rather mean and nasty fighter.

Jack, on the other hand, had two left feet when it came to weaponless, hand-to-hand fighting. He just could not master the quickness of unarmed combat. But he loved weapons, spending as much time as possible on the firing ranges. At seventeen, he was an expert with a dozen weapons, and a sniper in his unit of the reserves.

There had been much discussion, some of it heated, between Ben and Steven Miller as to the advisability of teaching war in public schools. In the end, however, the professor had acquiesced to Ben's demands, agreeing, not too reluctantly, that it was, for the time being, essential in the Tri-states' schools. The professor conceded that if the Rebel way of life was to flourish, the young had to be taught to defend it.

Jack was cleaning Ben's old Thompson SMG when Salina entered his room. The young man looked up and smiled. "Hi, Salina." He held up the Thompson. "Great, huh?"

Salina smiled, nodded at the weapon's "greatness."

"Yes, I know, Jack," she said, her voice soft.

"Yeah. I forget sometimes, Salina. You saw combat, didn't you?"

Her face changed expression, hardening. All the memories came rushing back to her, filling her brain with remembrances she had tried very hard to suppress: the horror of the killing and raping in Chicago; the running in pure terror for days afterward.

She blocked it out, sealing it away, shutting the memory door.

She looked at the young man she loved as her son. She looked at the gun in his hand. "Yes, Jack. I know what combat is." She closed the door and walked back into the den to be with her husband.

"Talk to me, Ben! Put down that damned book and *talk to me!*"

Her outburst startled him and he choked on the smoke

from his pipe. Ben was trying to give up cigarettes—they were very scarce and stale—and had turned to a pipe. That wasn't much better. He looked at his wife, hands on her hips, glaring at him. "What's going on, Salina?"

"Ben, is there going to be another war? Is everything we've worked so hard to build going to be destroyed?"

"What? Huh?" Ben looked confused, having gone from Tara in Georgia to his wife yelling at him in about one second. Quick trip. "You've lost me, honey."

She sat down on the hassock in front of his chair, taking his hands in hers. "Will there be more war? Are we going to have to defend what we have here? Is Logan going to send troops in here? And is it worth it, Ben?"

He leaned forward, putting his arms around her, loving the feel of her. Not an emotional man, Ben seldom told her he loved her. But he did love her, very much.

"Yes," he said softly. "Logan hates me—us—and he'll try to smash us. As for the worth; are you happy here?"

"You know I am," she murmured, face pressed into his shoulder. "Happier than I've ever been. But I do wonder about our life here, if what we're doing is the right thing for the young people. Tina is an expert in killing with her hands; Jack is playing with your old Thompson. It just upsets me. These kids have seen enough in their young lives. More war for them, Ben?"

"Honey, if it upsets you, I'll take that old Thompson away from Jack. I'll—"

She abruptly pushed away from him. "Damn it, Ben! You're missing the point." She stood up, pacing the den. "Is there no middle ground for us? Can't we compromise with Logan?"

"I've written to him, offering to meet and discuss a compromise. He didn't respond. You know that."

"Then war is inevitable?"

"That's the way I see it."

She lost her temper, pacing the den in a rage, pausing to pick up an ashtray to hurl it against a wall. She thought better of it.

"Shit!" she said; then put the ashtray back on the coffee table.

Ben, as millions of husbands before him, did not know what to do, or really, what he had done. "Honey," he said, preparing to put his foot in his mouth, "let me call the clinic and the doctor will send Jane or Jerre over with a sedative. Or maybe you two can just chat. That ought to—"

Salina suddenly became very calm. Icy. She spoke through clenched teeth. "Oh, my, yes. By all means, call Jane or Jerre. Maybe one of them understands you better than I." She whirled and marched to their bedroom, her back ramrod straight. She slammed the door so hard the center panel split down the middle.

Juno ran under a coffee table, overturning it, dumping ashtrays and bric-a-brac on the carpet.

The young people, who had gathered in the hall to listen to the adults argue, slipped back to their rooms and shut the doors . . . quietly and quickly.

Ben looked to his right and saw Badger standing in the foyer; the shouting had brought him out of his small apartment on the side of the house.

"What did I do?" the governor general of Tri-states asked his bodyguard. "What did I do?"

The young bodyguard shook his head. "Governor, with all due respect, sir; somebody ought to tell you the facts of life."

"*What the hell does that mean?*" Ben roared. "And who asked you in the first place?"

"Pitiful." Badger frowned. "Just plain pitiful." He turned and went back to his apartment.

Juno looked at him, showed Ben his teeth, then padded out of the room.

For several hours that night, Ben slept on the couch in the den. During the early morning hours, Salina slipped into the den to waken him. Together, they got into their own bed, Salina snuggling close to him.

"I'm sorry, Ben," she whispered.

"I would have been the first to apologize," he said, caressing her. "But I didn't know what I'd done. Still don't."

"I know, Ben." She moved under the stroking of his hands.

"I understand," he said. But of course, he didn't.

She smiled in the darkness as he touched a breast and she moved a slim hand down his belly.

At breakfast, Salina fixed Ben his favorite foods while he went into the yard to cut her a rose from the many flowering plants around the house. She did not mention to him that he whacked off half the bush to get one rose; merely laughed and thanked him, poured him more coffee, and wondered if she could graft the mangled part back on.

Jack, tactful for one so young, made no mention of his plans to visit the shooting range later that day, and Tina stayed home, helping her adopted mother around the house.

Juno viewed it all with an animal's patience.

Life in the Tri-states was really not that much different from that in other states or countries.

THREE

The communications people in the Tri-states had the finest electronic equipment in America—perhaps the world—for they had commandeered only the very best during their searches. From listening posts high in the mountains of the Tri-states, they monitored dozens of broadcasts daily, not only in America, but around the globe. They listened to military chatter, broke the codes, and knew what was going down, when, and where. They knew the government in Richmond was watching and listening to their every move, as they were listening and watching them.

Kenny Parr's mercenaries, fighting alongside the regular military had swept through Louisiana and Mississippi, crushing Kasim's small army of guerrillas. Kasim was dead, but he had killed the mercenary Parr before he'd died.

The nation was slowly, painfully, being pulled back together. The central government, under the direction of Hilton Logan and, Ben suspected, the military, was taking absolute control . . . again.

But they kept out of the Tri-states.

A small town stood almost directly in the center of Tri-states. Its name was changed to Vista, and that became the capital. Their flag was a solid, light blue banner with three stars in a circle. A constitution had been drawn up during the first year, much like the Constitution and Bill of Rights of the United States, but going into detail and spelling out exactly what the citizens of Tri-states could receive and expect if they lived under that document.

Early on, Tri-states was broken up into districts and elections were held to choose spokespersons from each district. At the end of the second year, Ben was elected governor for life, running with no opposition and no campaign. The laws of the Tri-states were set by balloting, and were firm against amending.

The first session of the legislature (to be held one time each year, no more than two weeks in length) was probably among the shortest on record, anywhere. Major Voltan, a spokesman from the second district, summed it up.

"Why are we meeting?" he asked. "Our laws are set, they can only be changed by a clear mandate from the people. No one in my district wants anything changed."

Nor in any of the other districts, it seemed.

"The constitution states we must meet once a year in session." Ben spoke.

"To do what?" a farmer spokesman inquired.

"To debate issues," Cecil said.

"What issues?"

There were none.

"Like the Congress of the United States?" a woman asked. "We're supposed to behave like they do?"

"More or less," Cecil said.

"God help us all."

Laughter echoed throughout the large room.

"I move we adjourn so we can all get back to work and

do something constructive," Voltan said.

"Second the motion."

"Session adjourned," Ben said.

Tri-states' laws, the liberal press said, and even after a nuclear war the press was still controlled by liberals, constituted a gunpowder society.

They were correct to a degree.

But those reporters with more respect for their readers and viewers—and they were outnumbered by their counterparts—looked at Tri-states a bit more closely and called it an experiment in living together, based as much on common sense as on written law. Most of those reporters concluded that yes, Tri-states could probably exist for a long, long time, and it was no threat to America. And, yes, its citizens seemed to be making the Tri-states' form of government work, for they were of a single mind, and not diversified philosophically.

But could this form of government work with millions of people? No, they concluded, it could not.

And they were correct in that assumption . . . to a degree.

But most people can govern themselves, once basic laws are agreed upon; *if* those people are very, very careful and work very, very hard at it.

That a people must be bogged down in bureaucracy; beset by thousands of sometimes oily, rude, arrogant, and frequently hostile local, state, and federal "civil servants"; licensed, taxed, and harassed; ruled by a close-knit clan of men and women whose mentality is not always what it should be and whose weapons are power; be dictated to by judges who are not always in tune with reality; and yammered at year after dreary year that a couple of senators and a handful of representatives have the power to decide the fate of millions . . . is a myth.

And Tri-states proved it.

There was not much pomp in Tri-states. Ben's governor's mansion was a split-level home on the outskirts of Vista. In good weather he rode to work in a Jeep.

Ben was on the road a lot, visiting the districts, listening to grievances, if any; and they were few. But of late, the one question asked, the one question paramount in the minds of Tri-states' residents was: what happens when we open our borders?

The residents had met in open town meetings (something that was required by law before any decision affecting the lives of the citizens was initiated) and finally had decided to open their borders to the public, if any persons wanted to visit. They had been wholly self-contained for almost six years. Maybe it was time.

But most viewed the border openings with highly mixed feelings.

The Tri-states' communications people contacted the major TV and radio networks, and the major papers, asking if they would like to cover the opening of Tri-states' borders.

All did.

"Now the shit really hits the fan," Ike projected.

The driver of the lead bus brought it to a hissing halt and motioned for the chief correspondent of CBN to come to the front. "Take a look at that, Mr. Charles." He pointed to a huge red-and-white sign that extended from one side of the road to the other, suspended twenty-five feet in the air. Other buses and vans stopped and discharged their passengers. Cameras focused on the sign and rolled, clicked, and whirred.

"It hasn't been up long," a reporter from Portland said. "I've been out here a half-dozen times during the past six months and this road has always been blocked. And no sign." He looked at the message.

WARNING—YOU ARE ENTERING THE TRI-STATES. YOU *MUST* STOP AT THE RECEPTION CENTER TO FAMILIARIZE YOURSELF WITH THE LAWS OF THIS STATE. DO NOT ENTER THIS AREA WITHOUT PERMISSION AND KNOWLEDGE OF THE LAWS. YOU MUST BE CLEARED AND HAVE ID. —WARNING

The internation symbol for "danger—keep out" was on either side of the huge sign.

"I think I want to go home." A young lady grinned. In truth, a mule team could not have dragged her from the area.

The knot of press people, sound people, and camerapersons laughed. Clayton Charles put his arm around the young woman's shoulders. "Come, now, Judith—where is your sense of journalistic inquisitiveness?"

"Well, the nuke and germ war came so fast no one had a chance to cover it. So, maybe this will do."

Larry Spain, reporter for another network, pointed to a steel tower, much like those used by the forest service, except that this one was lower. The tower sat inside the Tri-states line, across the bridge.

"Low for a fire observation tower," he said.

"Look again," a friend told him. "That one's got .50-caliber machine guns to put out the blaze. Jesus! These people aren't kidding."

They said nothing as they all looked at the tower. The muzzle of the heavy-caliber machine gun was plainly visible. Silently, the men and women climbed back aboard their vans and buses. A moment later they were the first outside reporters to visit the Tri-states (legally) since the states' inception. One reporter would later write: "The soldier in the tower never made a hostile move; never pointed the muzzle at us. But it was like looking at the Berlin wall for the first time."

The vehicles pulled off the road and onto a huge blacktop parking area. Set deep in the area was a long, low concrete building, painted white. On the front and both sides of the building, in block letters several feet tall, painted in flame red, were the words: ENTERING OR LEAVING—CHECKPOINT—ALL VEHICLES STOP.

"I think they mean it," someone said.

"Very definitely," another said.

"Unequivocally," Judith replied.

"Explicitly," another reporter concurred with a smile.

"Knock it off." Clayton Charles ended the bantering.

The bus driver turned to the press people before they could enter the building and spoke to the entire group. "I want to tell you people something," he said. "I have friends in the Tri-states; I've been checked and cleared and am moving in here next month. . . . So listen to me. It might save you a broken jaw or a busted mouth, or worse.

"Whatever impression you might have of the people who live in the Tri-states—put it out of your mind, for it's probably wrong. Even though they are doctors, dentists, farmers, shopkeepers, whatever, I'm betting you're thinking they are a pack of savages or crazy terrorists. If you do, you're wrong. They are just people who won't tolerate trouble—of any kind. You'd better remember that.

"Don't go sticking your nose in their business uninvited. The laws are different here; you're liable to get punched out. I hope all of you are going into this assignment with an open mind—I really do. 'Cause if you get cute with these folks, they'll hurt you. Even the kids are rough."

A lone male reporter stood in the back of the crowd and solemnly applauded the driver's speech. "How eloquently put," he said.

The driver looked at him; then slowly shook his head in disgust, as did many of the press people. Barney had the reputation of being rude, arrogant, obnoxious, and a double-dyed smart-ass.

"Barney," Judith said. "I know we work for the same network, and are supposed to be colleagues, and all that, but when we get inside, stay the hell away from me, O.K.?"

Barney smiled and bowed.

The reception center was large and cool and comfortable, furnished with a variety of chairs and couches. Racks of literature about Tri-states, its people, its economy, and its laws filled half of one wall. A table with doughnuts and two coffee urns sat in the center of the room; soft drinks were set to the right of the table. Between two closed doors was a four-foot-high desk, fifteen feet long, closed from floor to top. Behind the desk, two young women stood, one of them Tina Raines. The girls were dressed identically; jeans and light blue shirts.

"Good morning," Tina said to the crowd. "Welcome

380

o the Tri-states. My name is Tina, this is Judy. Help
yourself to coffee and doughnuts—they're free—or a
soft drink."

Barney leaned on the counter, his gaze on Tina's
breasts. She looked older than her seventeen years.
Barney smiled at her.

"Anything else free around here?" he asked, all his
famous obnoxiousness coming through.

The words had just left his mouth when the door to an
office whipped open and a uniformed army Rebel stepped
out, master sergeant stripes on the sleeves of his tiger-
stripes. He was short, muscular, hard-looking, and deeply
tanned. He wore a .45 automatic, holstered, on his right
side.

"Tina?" he said. "Who said that?"

Tina pointed to Barney. "That one."

"Oh, hell!" Judith whispered.

"Quite," Clayton concurred.

The Rebel walked up to Barney and stopped a foot from
him. Barney looked shaken, his color similar to old
whipped cream. The filming lights had been on, and no
one had noticed when a camera operator began rolling,
recording the event.

"I'm Sergeant Roisseau," the Rebel informed the
reporter. "It would behoove you, in the future, to keep
off-color remarks to yourself. You have been warned;
this is a one-mistake state, and you've made yours."

"I . . . ah . . . was only making a little joke," Barney
said. "I meant nothing by it." The blood rushed to his
face, betraying the truth.

"Your face says you're a liar," Roisseau said calmly.

"And you're armed!" Barney said, blinking. He was
indignant; the crowd he ran with did not behave in this

manner over a little joke. No matter how poor the taste.

Roisseau smiled and unbuckled his web belt, laying the pistol on the desk. "Now, fish or cut bait," he challenged him.

That really shook Barney. All the bets were down and the pot right. He shook his head. "No . . . I won't fight you."

"Not only do you have a greasy mouth," Roisseau said, "but you're a coward to boot."

Barney's eyes narrowed, but he wisely kept his mouth shut.

"All right," Roisseau said. "Then when you apologize to the young lady, we'll forget it."

"I'll be damned!" Barney said, looking around him for help. None came forward.

"Probably," Roisseau said. "But that is not the immediate issue." He looked at Tina and winked, humor in his dark eyes. "So, newsman, if you're too timid to fight me, perhaps you'd rather fight the young lady?"

"The kid?" Barney questioned, then laughed aloud. "What is this, some kind of joke?"

Judith walked to Barney's side. She remembered the bus driver's words and sensed there was very little humor involved in any of this, and if there was, the joke was going to be on Barney. And it wasn't going to be funny. "Barney, ease off. Apologize to her. You were out of line."

"No. I was only making a joke."

"Nobody laughed," she reminded him, and backed away, thinking: are the people in this state humorless? Or have they just returned to values my generation tossed aside?

"No way." Barney shook his head. "You people are nuts!"

The camera rolled, silently recording.

Roisseau smiled, then looked at Tina. "Miss Raines, the . . . gentleman is all yours. No killing blows, girl. Just teach him a hard lesson in manners."

Tina put her left hand on the top of the desk and, in one fluid motion, as graceful as a cat, vaulted the desk to land lightly on her tennis shoe-clad feet.

She stood quietly in front of the man who outweighed her by at least fifty pounds. She offered up a slight bow. Had Barney any knowledge of the martial arts, he would have fainted, thus saving himself some bruises.

Tina held her hands in front of her, palms facing Barney, then drew the left one back to her side, balling the fist. Her right foot was extended, unlike a boxer's stance. Her right hand open, palm out, knife edge to Barney. Her eyes were strangely empty of expression. Barney could not know she was psyching herself.

Barney did notice the light ridge of calluses that ran from the tips of her fingers to her wrist, and another light row of calluses on the edge of her hand, from the tip of her little finger down to the wrist. He backed away, instinctively.

Almost with the speed of a striking snake, Tina kicked high with her foot, catching Barney on the side of the face. He slammed backward against a wall, then recoiled forward, stunned at the suddenness of it all. With no change in her expression, Tina slashed out with the knife edge of her hand and slammed a blow just above his kidney, then slapped him on the face a stinging pop. Barney dropped to his knees, his back hurting, his face aching, blood dripping from a corner of his mouth. He rose slowly to his feet, his face a vicious mask of hate and rage and frustration and disbelief.

"You bitch!" he snarled. "You rotten little cunt."

Roisseau laughed. "Now, you are in trouble, hotshot."

Barney shuffled forward, in a boxer's stance, his chin tucked into his shoulder. He swung a wide looping fist at Tina. She smiled at his clumsiness and turned slightly, catching his right wrist. Using the forward motion of his swing against him, and her hips for leverage, she tossed the man over her side and bounced him off a wall. Quickly reaching down, her hands open, on either side of his head, Tina brought them in sharply, hard, slamming the open palms over his ears at precisely the same moment. Barney screamed in pain and rolled in agony on the floor, a small dribble of blood oozing from one damaged ear.

Tina smoothed her hair. She was not even breathing hard. She looked at Master Sergeant Roisseau. "Did I do all right, Sergeant?"

The reporters then noticed the flap of Roisseau's holster, lying on the desk, open, the butt of the .45 exposed. And all were glad no one had tried to interfere.

Then, from the floor of the reception center, came the battle cry of urbane, modern, twentieth-century man. Unable to cope with a situation, either mentally or physically, or because of laws that have been deballing the species for years, man bellows the words:

"I'll sue you!"

The room suddenly rocked with laughter. News commentators, reporters, camerapeople and soundpeople; people who, for years, had recorded the best and worst of humankind, all howled at the words from their colleague.

"Sue?" Clayton managed to gasp the word despite his laughter. "Sue? Sue a little teen-age girl who just whipped your big, manly butt. Really, Barney! I've

384

warned you for years your mouth would someday get you in trouble."

Roisseau spoke to the girl still behind the desk. "Judy, get on the horn and call the medics and tell them we have a hotshot with a pulled fuse." He faced the crowd of newspeople.

"You're all due at a press conference in two hours. Meanwhile, I'd suggest you all help yourselves to coffee and doughnuts and soft drinks and study the pamphlets we have for you." He glanced at Barney, sitting on the floor, moaning and holding his head in his hands. "As for you, I'd forget about suing anyone. Our form of government discourages lawsuits. You'd lose anyway."

"I'll take this to the Supreme Court!" Barney yelled.

"Fine. Governor Raines is someday going to appoint one for us. Next twenty or thirty years. We don't recognize yours."

"Well, who is the final authority on Tri-states law?" a woman asked.

Roisseau smiled. "Just about anyone in the area . . . over the age of ten. As you study the simplicity of our judicial system, you'll see what I mean. We don't use any Latin base or legal double-talk. It's all in very plain English. If you're asking who would make the final decision on an issue—if it ever got that far—Governor Raines and half a dozen people whose names were pulled out of a hat."

"Well, that's the damnedest form of law I ever heard of in my life!" Larry Spain said.

"I'm sure that's true," Roisseau said. "But what is important is that it works for us." He walked back into his office, closing the door.

Moments later, the medics came in and looked at

Barney. They said he had a split lip, several bruises, a slightly damaged eardrum—nothing serious—and a severely deflated ego. They sat him in a chair, told him to check into any clinic if he began experiencing dizzy spells, patted him on the head, told him to watch his mouth, and left, chuckling.

"Very simple society we have here," a reporter observed. "Live and let live, all the while respecting the rights of others who do the same. Very basic."

"And very unconstitutional," another remarked.

"I wonder," Judith mused aloud. "I just wonder if it is."

"Oh, come now, Judith," Clayton said, shaking his head. "The entire debate is superfluous. There is no government of Tri-states. It doesn't exist. The government of the United States doesn't recognize it. It just doesn't exist."

Several Jeeps pulled into the parking area. The reporters watched a half-dozen Rebel soldiers—male and female, all in tiger-stripe—step out of the Jeeps. The soldiers were all armed with automatic weapons and sidearms.

"Really?" Judith smiled. She pointed to the Rebels. "Well, don't tell *me* Tri-states doesn't exist—tell them!"

FOUR

Before leaving the reception center, each member of the press was handed a pass marked: VISITOR—PRESS. It was dated and signed by Roisseau.

"Don't lose those passes," he cautioned them. "You people don't have permanent papers with prints, pictures, and serial numbers. Our equivalent of social security."

"Why are those papers necessary?" a reporter asked.

"We've given asylum to many so-called criminals from bordering states. Some of the police from those states have tried to come in after them, undercover, slipping in without our knowledge. They didn't make it, but it did force us to go to a permanent ID."

"I don't . . . quite understand." Judith looked up from the pamphlet she'd been reading. She was very interested in this state. "What kind of so-called criminals?"

"As you have probably read, or heard, our laws are different from yours. Very different. In other states, if you were to shoot a punk trying to steal your car, your TV set, or whatever, you would be put in jail and charged. Not here. There is a full investigation, of course—we're not animals—but we do believe that a punk is a punk, and that a person has the right to protect what is his or hers from unlawful search or seizure. Using any authorized weapon."

387

"How many children have been shot?"

"None. Our children are taught, not only in the home, but in public schools, the difference between right and wrong—as we see it."

"You said authorized weapons . . . ?"

"Rifle, pistol, knife, hands, fists, feet . . . whatever is available. Our citizens"—he smiled—"do not possess nuclear weapons."

Barney shuddered. He had discovered how swiftly events could occur in this state. All over a little joke.

"Explain those permanent IDs," Roisseau was asked.

"Each ID is numbered, the same number is on the person's bank account, driver's license, home title. That number is placed in a central computer bank. Along with the number is placed the person's vital statistics. It's very easily checked and almost impossible to hide an identity."

"What comes next, Sergeant: tattooing at birth?" It was sarcastically put.

Barney resisted an impulse to tell the reporter to please watch his mouth.

Sergeant Roisseau smiled patiently. "No, sir, it's past 1984. Your government is the one who turned on its law-abiding, taxpaying citizens, not ours."

"What is the penalty for carrying a false ID?"

Roisseau's eyes were chilly as he said, "It's unpleasant. I hope you all have a nice stay in our area. It will be as nice as you make it."

A member of the armed forces of Tri-states rode in each van and bus. As they pulled out of the reception center, a soldier rose and faced Clayton Charles's group.

"My name is Bridge Oliver. During the ride to the

governor's house, I'll try to answer as many questions as possible and show you some points of interest.

"Coming up on your left is the first emergency telephone on this highway. You'll find them every four miles on every major highway in the Tri-states. They are hooked directly to an army HQ in whatever district the motorist is in, and each phone is numbered. Pick up the phone, give that number to whomever answers, state the nature of the problem, and someone will be there promptly."

"That isn't anything new," a reporter said. "It's been tried before in other areas . . . before the bombings. Vandals usually ripped the phones out. Destroyed them."

"Sir," Bridge said, "in other states, punks and hoodlums were—and probably still are—pampered and petted by judges, psychologists, counselors, and petunia-picking social workers. Vandalism, in your society, under your laws, is accepted, more or less, as part of a young person's growing up. We do not subscribe to that theory. As you have been told, and will be told a hundred times more during your stay here,"—until you get it through your goddamned thick skulls, Bridge thought—"crime, lawlessness, *is not tolerated here.* Our children are taught that it is wrong. They are taught it in the homes, in the schools, and in the churches."

The same reporter who had asked about tattooing at birth, now asked: "What do you do when you catch them, shoot them?"

Barney looked out the window while Judith busied herself with a notebook.

Bridge held his temper in check. Ben had told his people to expect sarcasm and, in certain instances, open hostility from some members of the press.

"No, sir," Bridge said quietly, "we don't shoot them. I would like all of you to understand something. Some of you—maybe all of you—seem to be under the impression that we here in Tri-states are savages, or that Governor Raines is some sort of ruthless ogre. You're wrong. We're all very proud of what we've done here: jobs for everyone who wants to work; our medical system; elimination of poor living conditions; but we're also somewhat of a law-and-order society. Not as you people know law and order, true, but we're not monsters.

"We do a lot of things quite differently from what you people are accustomed to. But that's all right, because it works for us."

"That's all very good, Mr. Oliver. And, I suppose, commendable, to your way of thinking. But I would still like to know what happens to the kids when they're caught. Just for having a little fun."

"Fun?" Bridge questioned. "Fun? Is destructive vandalism your idea of fun?"

"It certainly isn't a criminal offense."

"Isn't it? What's the difference between stealing a great deal of money or ripping out a piece of expensive equipment that might save someone's life?"

The reporter shook his head. "I don't intend to argue the question with you. It still doesn't answer my question."

Bridge sighed. "After they've all been warned, repeatedly, not to commit vandalism, and taught it in the schools, we attempt to find out why they would do so. Is it because of their home life? Are they abused? Do they have a mental problem? We try to find out and then correct the problem. But they will also work while we're doing that: painting public buildings or working for the elderly, picking up litter—which, if you'll observe, we don't have much of—public-service work of some kind. But they'll give us twenty dollars of their time for every dollar they destroyed."

"That's rather harsh, don't you think?"

Bridge shrugged and tried not to smile. He knew their way of life, their philosophy, would not be understood by many of the younger members of the news media. About half of the newspeople now converging upon the Tristates area were in their thirties, the products of the permissive '60s and '70s, which Bridge knew, only too well, was a time of poor discipline in schools, disregard for law and order, a downgrading of patriotism, morals, values. One could blame the time, but not wholly the individual.

"What about the police?" a woman asked. "I haven't seen any."

"We don't have police," Bridge said. "We have peace officers. And really, not many of them." He smiled, attempting to put the people at ease. "Here," he tried to explain, "the *people* control their lives. We have very few laws, and they are voted on *by the people* before they become laws. A fifty-one/forty-nine percent for and against won't make it here. It's got to be much clearer than that. That may be a majority in your system, but not here.

"Living here is very simple on the one hand, and very difficult—if not downright impossible—if you're the type of person who likes to spread malicious gossip, if you're lazy, if you like to browbeat others. If you're inclined to cheat and lie . . . you won't make it in this society."

391

"What happens to them?"

"Well,"—Bridge grinned—"you start spreading lies about somebody in this society, you're liable to get the shit beat out of you. It's happened a few times."

"And the law did what to the parties involved?"

"Nothing," Bridge said flatly. "I don't know of anyone, male or female, who doesn't gossip; that's human nature. Just don't make it vicious lies."

"I'm surprised there hasn't been any killings, if that's the kind of laws you people live under. If you want to call it law, that is."

"There've been a couple of shootings," Bridge admitted. "But not in the past three or four years. We're all pretty much of one mind in this area."

"Who shot whom, and why?" Clayton questioned.

"One fellow was messin' with another man's wife. He kept messin' with her even though, as witnesses pointed out, the woman told him, time after time, to leave her alone. She finally went to her husband and told him. The husband warned the man—once. The warning didn't take. The husband called the man out one afternoon; told him he was going to beat hell out of him. Romeo came out with a gun in his hand. Bad mistake. Husband killed him."

The press waited. And waited. Finally Clayton blurted, "Well, what happened?"

"Nothing, really." Bridge's face was impassive. "There was a hearing, of course. The husband was turned loose; Romeo was buried."

"Are you serious?"

"Perfectly. I told you all: this is not an easy place to live. But that's only happened three . . . yes, three times since the Tri-states were organized. There is an old western saying, sir: man saddles his own horses, kills his own snakes. And if I have to explain that, you'd better turn this bus around and get the hell out of here."

The bus driver chuckled.

The press corps absorbed that bit of western philosophy for a moment . . . in silence. Clayton broke the silence by clearing his throat and saying, "Let's return to the people controlling their own lives, if we ever indeed left it. Elaborate on that, please, without the *High Noon* scenario, if possible, and I'm not sure you weren't just putting us on about that."

"I believe that Sergeant Roisseau told Mr. Barney Weston that this is a one-mistake state and he'd had his—right?"

Barney felt his face grow hot. "Mr. Oliver, maybe I was out of line, but I just got mauled and humiliated. Don't you think that's going a bit far?"

"Would you do it again?" Bridge asked.

"Absolutely not!"

Bridge laughed. "Well . . . you just answered your question."

"Mr. Oliver?" Judith said. "Are you taking us on a preselected route? I've seen no shacks or poor-looking people. No crummy beer joints. No malnourished kids. Nothing to indicate poverty or unhappiness."

"I'm not qualified to speak on the unhappiness part of your question. I'm sure there must be *some* unhappiness here. But I can guarantee you there is no hunger or poverty. We've corrected that—totally."

The newspeople had just left an area—America— where people were still dying from the sickness caused by the bombings: cancer-related illnesses from radiation sickness; where people were starving and out of work;

where gangs of thugs still roamed parts of the nation; where the sights of devastation were still very much in evidence. Now, for Bridge Oliver to tell them that here, in the Tri-states, there was no poverty, no hunger . . . that was ludicrous.

"Oh, come now, man!" Clayton's tone was full of disbelief. "That is simply not possible."

"Perhaps not in your society, but it certainly did happen here. You'll be free to roam the country, talk to people. The only hungry people you'll find in Tri-states will be those people who might be on a diet."

"Well, would you be so kind as to tell us just how you people managed that?"

"By ripping down any slum or shack area and building new housing, and not permitting a building to deteriorate. We have very tough housing codes, and they are enforced. . . ."

"I can just imagine how," Barney muttered, his face reddening at the laughter around him.

". . . We have no unemployment—there are jobs going begging right now. We're opening factories, little by little, but the process of screening takes time; it's long and slow. As I've tried to explain, it takes a very special person to live in our society. We won't tolerate freeloaders, of any kind. We have no unions here, and will not permit any to come in. They are not necessary in this society. You'll see what I mean as you travel about. Our economy matches our growth, and wages are in line with it. Wages are paid commensurate to a person's ability to do a job, and a person's sex has nothing to do with it. It's equal pay right down the line. There is a minimum wage for certain types of work, but I defy you—any of you—to find a sweatshop anywhere in the

Tri-states. The people won't stand for it."

"That doctrine is somehow vaguely familiar," a reporter said.

"If you're thinking socialism or communism, put it out of your mind; you haven't got your head screwed on straight. I'd like to hear you name any communist country—ever—where the entire population was armed—to the teeth! No, none of you can. Believe me, if the people living here ever decide they don't like the government, they've damned sure got the firepower to change it. But they won't. Because, as I've told you, we like it this way.

"Now in terms of wealth, it would be very difficult for a person to become a millionaire—not impossible, but difficult. Taxes get pretty steep after a certain income level. But if a person is poor, it's that person's own fault, and he or she can blame no one else. But, it's as I said; we don't have any poor people."

"And no rich people."

"That is correct."

"Number of churches here," a woman observed. "Is attendance mandatory?"

"No!" Bridge laughed. "Where in the world are you people getting these off-the-wall questions?"

"But you people do place a lot of emphasis on religion," Judith said. "Right?"

Bridge shrugged. "Some do, some don't. Hell, people! Prostitution is legal here."

The newspeople all looked at each other, not believing what they had just heard.

"Well," Clayton Charles said, "I'd certainly like to get into that."

The bus rocked with laughter.

"I didn't mean it that way!" the chief correspondent said, his face crimson.

Judith shook her head. "I'm . . . still very confused about this area. I just witnessed a young lady—a teenager—beat up a grown man with nothing but her hands for weapons, and you people obviously thought it perfectly all right for her to do so. It's obvious you are teaching your young that violence—in some forms, and incidents, I suppose—is acceptable. Yet, I have only to look out the window to see that your society is religious. You people claim to have completely obliterated hunger, poverty, and slums. . . . That's the height of compassion. Yet capital punishment—so we've been told—is the law of the land. Tri-states seems to be, at least to me, a marvelous combination of good and evil."

"We agree on the definition of one word, but not on the other," Bridge replied. He found himself, for some reason, liking this reporter; he believed she would report fairly. "Here in our society, we have, I believe, returned to the values of our forefathers—in part. Much more emphasis is placed on the rights of a law-abiding citizen than on the punks who commit the crimes.

"There is honor here that you don't have in your states—that you haven't had in your central government for decades. You people still want it both ways, and it won't work; I'm amazed that you can't see that. We believe our system will always be worlds apart from yours. We set it up that way."

"Then where does that leave Tri-states and the rest of America?" he was asked.

"In a position of separate but workable coexistence."

"But that violates the entire concept of *United States.*"

Bridge glanced at the bus driver, the man who would

soon be moving into the area. The driver smiled and shook his head.

He understands, Bridge thought. Even if the others don't. "I suppose it does," Bridge said. "But that is not our problem. And it's yours only if you make it a problem."

He sat down and turned his back to the reporters.

The town of Vista lay quiet and peaceful under a warm early summer sun. People tended gardens and mowed lawns. Kids played along the sidewalks and yards, their laughter and behavior reminiscent of an age long past. No horns honked, no mufflers roared, no huge trucks rumbled about. Trucks, unless they were moving vans, were forbidden to enter residential areas. The only exception was pickups. Unless it was an emergency, horns did not honk in Tri-states. Straight pipes, glass packs, and other such adolescent silliness were banned. There were lots of sidewalks—all of them new—to walk upon, and there were bike paths for the pedalers. Speed limits were low, and they were rigidly enforced.

A contentment hung in the air; a satisfaction that could almost be felt, as if everyone here had finally found a personal place under the sun and was oh, so happy with it. A mood of safety, tranquillity, and peace surrounded the area.

To the newspeople, that was unsettling.

The buses and vans parked in front of a split-level home on the outskirts of town. In the two-car garage, there stood a pickup truck and a late-model (the last year automobiles were made), small station wagon. Parked in the drive was a standard military Jeep with a whip antenna on the rear and a waterproof scabbard on the right front side. The flap was open, exposing the stock of a .45-caliber Thompson SMG.

"You people are certainly careless with weapons," a reporter remarked.

"Why?" Bridge looked at him.

He pointed to the Thompson. "Someone could steal that."

Bridge shrugged. "Everyone in this state, male and female, over the age of sixteen has an automatic weapon and five hundred rounds of ammunition assigned to them, also a sidearm with fifty rounds of ammunition, three grenades, and a jump knife. Why would anyone want to steal an old Thompson?"

"Well, goddamn it!" The reporter lost his temper. He quickly checked it. "There are children, you know." Being from a large city—that no longer existed—the reporter's knowledge of firearms was limited to pointing his finger and making "bang-bang" noises.

But Bridge was under orders to be patient. "Sir, do you see that metal object on the top of the weapon, just above and in front of the stock? The stock is that long, funny-shaped wooden thing. You do? Good! That is a bolt lever. When it is pulled back, locked in position, as it is now, that signifies the weapon is void of ammunition. In Tristates, any ten-year-old would know that."

If looks could kill, Bridge would have fallen over.

A young man wearing starched and creased tiger-stripe field clothes suddenly appeared by the side of the garage. He wore buck sergeant's stripes and carried an automatic assault rifle, much like the Russian AK-47/AMK.

"Who is *that?*" a reporter asked.

"The governor's driver and bodyguard. Badger Harbin," Bridge said. "Don't make any sudden moves around him until he gets used to you."

Badger looked at the growing mounds of equipment and then at the men whose jobs it was to set it all up. He pointed to the rear of the house.

"Take it all around there," Badger said. "There are tables and chairs and plug-ins. If any of you are armed, declare it now."

"None of us is armed," Clayton said. Then with a smile, he added, "What's the matter, Sergeant, don't you trust us?"

"No," Badger said shortly. He stepped to one side, allowing them to pass.

The crowd was ushered onto the patio, then seated. Badger stood by the side of the sliding glass doors leading into the den. "When the governor and Mrs. Raines come out," he said, "get up."

"Young man," Clayton said acidly, "we do have some knowledge of protocol."

Badger grunted his reply and Judith laughed at her boss's expression.

None of the newspeople knew exactly what to expect of Governor Raines. But some of the younger newspeople had a preconceived image of a military man who would be dressed in full uniform, dripping with medals, armed with at least two pistols, and possibly carrying a swagger stick, tipped with a shell casing. When Ben and Salina appeared, most were mildly astonished.

Ben was dressed in blue jeans, a pullover shirt, and cowboy boots. Salina wore white Levi's, a blue western shirt, and tennis shoes.

They shook hands all around while flashbulbs popped and cameras rolled, many of them directed at Badger, who scowled appropriately. For half an hour the press corps sipped coffee or cold drinks and munched on hors d'oeuvres.

"I'd like to take some pictures of you two together," a photographer said to Ben and Salina, "and of the house. Do you mind?"

"No," Ben said, after looking at Salina and receiving a slight nod of agreement. "Fire away—figuratively speaking, of course." He smiled.

Out of the corner of his eye, the photographer noticed Badger's hands tighten on the AK-47. Badger made many of the press people very nervous.

The camera crews wandered around the house, taking pictures of this and that: the home, the lawn, the garden, the neighborhood. Governor Raines was a hero to many Americans, having stood up to the government, formed his own state over its objections, and now governed the only area in America, and probably the entire world, that was free of crime and poverty. That much had leaked out of Tri-states. Practically anything about the man, his family, and his way of life would be of interest to someone.

After a short time, an informal press conference was under way.

"Before the questions start flying," Ben said, "I'd like for you all to meet my daughter, Tina Raines. She works part-time at the western reception center. The one closest to Vista." He turned just as Tina opened the sliding glass doors and stepped out.

The press was silent for a few moments, looking at each other, putting it all together. Each waited for the other to ask the first question. Finally, Judith did. "We were at that reception center, Governor. How many Tina

Raineses are there in Tri-states?"

"Only one that I know of," Ben said. "I gather from your expressions you were there when Tina had her . . . small altercation with one of your colleagues."

Barney looked at the ground, thinking: of all the people I pick to get cute with, I pick the governor's daughter. Great move, Weston. Super timing.

"You know we were there," Clayton said.

"Yes," Ben agreed. "Not much goes on in this area I don't know about."

A photographer from the World News Agency was snapping away as Tina walked out onto the patio. He took two quick shots of her and smiled.

"Hello, again," Tina said.

"You're a very lovely young lady," he complimented her. "Very photogenic."

She blushed, then sat down beside her mother, on the patio, just behind and to the right of where Ben stood behind a podium.

Ben looked at the press people. "One word of caution before we begin. Be careful what you print, broadcast, or ask about people living here in the Tri-states. We don't have scandal sheets here; yellow journalism is not allowed."

Barney tore several sheets from his notepad and crumpled the pages, thinking as he did so: if I ever get out of this wacko state, I'll never come back!

"Governor—General; what do we call you?" a reporter asked.

"Either one. Ben—whatever. We're not much on pomp here."

"All right, Governor. But that's a pretty stiff warning you just handed us. What *can* we report on here?"

"Anything you see, as long as you present both sides of the issue. Isn't that fair journalism?"

What it's supposed to be, Judith thought. But seldom is.

"Oh, come on, Governor! People are opinionated no matter how hard they try not to be. Reporting objectively has been a joke for decades."

Clayton smiled outwardly at the reporter and inwardly in admiration for Ben. He had gone back and read as many of Ben's books as time would allow before coming to the Tri-states. He said, "I recall you writing, Governor, that the press enjoyed sending a black man to report on KKK meetings and an avowed liberal to report on the National Rifle Association's yearly strategy meeting. You haven't changed much—if any. I also remember your writing that the press is stacked with liberals and not balanced with conservatives and middle-of-the-roaders."

"I still feel that way," Ben said. "You people are supposed to be neutral, but you're not. You haven't been for decades."

"I'd like to debate that with you sometime."

"Maybe. I'll give you a reply when I see what you've reported about us."

Each man gave the other a thin smile of understanding.

"General," Ben was asked, "for the record, sir, just what are you people attempting to accomplish in this new state?"

"We are not attempting. We *have* created a society where the vast majority of citizens—I'd say between ninety-five and ninety-eight percent—are content with the laws they live under."

"Constitutionally?"

"According to our constitution, yes."

"A gunpowder society, void of human rights."

"That," Ben said, "and pardon my English, is pure bullshit. Law-abiding people have every right *they* voted to give themselves."

"General, do you believe the United States could be a world power if dozens of groups like yours splintered off to form their own little governments?"

"Since the bombings, there are no world powers—anywhere. With the exception, perhaps, of the United States. Yes, I believe the U.S. could be built back into a power. Tri-states has not broken with the Union—just with many of its laws.

"I have written to President Logan, telling him we will pay a fair share of taxes to his central government—and it is his. Our share won't be much, since most of the money will remain here, doing what we feel is right and best for the citizens of Tri-states. We will not ask the federal government for anything, and we will not tolerate their unrequested interference. We will fly the American flag alongside our own flag; we will live under the American flag, and if necessary, fight for it, as a friend and ally. Our borders will be open for all to pass through.

"However, there are certain things we are *not* going to do. We are *not* going to give up our weapons or disband our army. We are *not* going to change our laws to pamper thugs, punks, and social misfits who cannot or, as in most cases, will not live under the most basic of laws. We are *not* going to be ruled—totally—by a distant government in Virginia, or abide by the mumblings of your Supreme Court. Make no mistake about this, too, ladies and gentlemen: we are fully prepared to fight for our freedoms and our beliefs—right down to the last person."

Ben tapped the podium with a fist, rattling the microphones. "Now let's clear the air on a few more points. When we pulled into this area, it was chaos—that's the best one could say about it. The people were confused, disorganized—and that disorganization was partly the fault of the people, but mostly the fault of the federal government. The federal government wouldn't allow home militias without their so-called 'guidance.' But the federal government wasn't in here helping the people. We were. The federal government didn't send in doctors, food, medicines. We did it. We did it all, and did a damned good job.

"You won't find one person in this state suffering from hunger. Not one! We've eliminated it; wiped it out in less time than it takes some bills to get out of committee in your Congress. Your government has been attempting to wipe out hunger for decades, with only partial success. Think about that. Write about that. That says a great deal for our system.

"When we got here the elderly were living—most of them—in squalor. Existing might be a better word. Their possessions had been taken from them; they were neglected; and utterly terrified in their own homes, living in fear of punks and thugs and slime you people have, for years, been moaning and sobbing over. Hell, what else is new? Old people have been living in fear for their lives for decades, but you people haven't done anything about it, except moan and sob about the rights of street punks. We rounded up the punks, shot or hanged them, and helped the elderly put their lives back in order. Now, if that makes me a dictator or a man lacking in compassion, as has been written about me, then I'm proud to be just that.

"And, for your information, most doors in the Tri-states aren't locked at night, or at any other time. The lock on my back door doesn't even work, and hasn't for four years. That's got to tell you something about the way we live; the peace we all feel here. And we are at peace here, wanting trouble with or from no one.

"While you are here, by all means visit our hospitals and research centers and day-care centers and community centers and villages. Talk to anyone you wish to talk with. Visit our schools and see what we've done. Then compare what you see with what you've just left—out there"—he pointed—"in your *United States*.

"Visit our planning offices here in Vista, see what we've got on the tables for the future. You'll be surprised, I'm sure. But don't just report on a society that comes down hard on criminals; one where they are not pampered at taxpayer expense. For once, just once, you people report on both the good and the bad; weigh the rights of decent people against those of criminals. But by all means, do report that the life expectancy of punks is very short in the Tri-states."

A reporter raised his hand. "Governor, all you say may be true—probably is true—I'm not disputing your word. It's easy to see that you and your people have done a great deal of good in this area, but the fact is, you stole all the material you brought into this area. That's something you can't deny."

"I have no intention of denying it," Ben said. "We took from dead areas, transplanted what we took here, and put those materials to use. You people could have done the same—but you didn't. You people left billions and billions—probably trillions of dollars worth of valuable materials to rot and rust, and do absolutely no one any good at all. That is the crime."

"Governor"—Judith stood up—"on another topic— or maybe, really it isn't—on the way here, Mr. Oliver said you don't have police, but peace officers. Would you explain the difference and why their powers are limited?"

"Peace officers keep the peace," Ben said simply, and with a smile. "And folks out here—myself included— seem to prefer the name to cops. As to their limited powers, I'll try to explain, but here is where we veer off sharply from your society and its laws.

"First, and lastly, too, I suppose, a person has to *want* to live here. You'll hear that a dozen times before you leave. We are not an open society. Not just anyone can come in here to live. I have no figures to back this, but I would be willing to wager that probably no more than one out of every ten people in America could live under our laws or the type of government we have. Hucksters, shysters, con men, ambulance-chasing lawyers, cheats, liars . . . those types cannot last in this society. *Everything* is open and aboveboard in this state. Some of those types have tried to live here. We've buried a few; most left.

"Our laws on the books are few, and they are written very simply and plainly. Our laws are taught in our schools, our young people are brought up understanding the do's and don't's of this society. Any person with an average intellect can draw up a legal document in the Tri-states, and it will be honored in a court of law simply because the people in this state are honorable people. That sounds awfully smug, but it is the truth. Here, a person's word means as much as a written contract. That's why so many people can't live in our society. And here, as strange as it seems to you people, all this is working. Working because of one simple, basic fact: one has to *want* to live here.

"Our peace officers don't have much to do other than occasionally break up a family fight." He smiled. "And yes, we do have domestic squabbles here. Or they might issue a traffic ticket; occasionally have to investigate a shooting or a theft. But those are very rare. The army is constantly on patrol, so they pretty well take over most law-enforcement jobs in a preventive manner, so to speak. We've found their presence to be a deterrent."

Barney looked at Badger and could damned well understand why that would be so.

"Now as you probably realize by now," Ben said, "in the Tri-states, it is not against the law to protect yourself, your loved ones, or your property. That is written into our constitution just as it is in yours . . . but we enforce it. And there have been killings and woundings. All justified under our laws.

"Now, I'm going to tell you something all of you will find very difficult to believe. But it is the truth. The Tri-states take in approximately three hundred and thirty thousand square miles of territory. Per capita, we have .025 percent crime. I don't know how in the Lord's name a society could get any lower statistics than that. We've had one mugging in the Tri-states in the past two years."

"What happened to the mugger?"

"Twenty-five years at hard labor," Ben said calmly.

"Twenty-five years!" a reporter jumped to his feet. "My God, General Raines—what kind of laws do you people have in this state?"

"I just told you. Tough ones."

Several of the press people shuddered. Some smiled in disbelief.

"We have very tough drinking laws in this state," Ben said. "And they are enforced *to the letter*. No exceptions. If you doubt that, take a drive up to the state penitentiary and ask to speak to a Mr. Michael Clifford; he was our secretary of finance until two years ago. He got drunk one night and ran over a young girl. She was badly injured. Mr. Clifford is serving a ten-year-to-life sentence. Had the girl died, the charge would have been murder. Not manslaughter—murder. And he would have spent the rest of his life in prison, at hard labor. No probation, no parole.

"We are not a teetotaling society; we don't care if a person gets stinking drunk in his or her own home. That's not our business. Just don't drive drunk.

"There are bars and lounges all over the Tri-states. But none outside of a town limit, and there is a two-drink limit, or a three-beer limit. It's all on an honor system: no cards to punch, no undercover people sneaking about. And so far, it's working. There again, we have to go back to what has been preached to you people since you got here. One has to *want* to live in this type of society. And not everybody can."

Juno chose that time to wander out onto the patio, take a look around, yawn, and then drop to the ground and go to sleep. He was getting old, almost nine years old, and blind in one eye, but still a beautiful animal.

"That's a wolf," someone whispered.

"Malamute," Ben corrected. "I found him in Georgia, years ago. Or rather, he found me. Juno's harmless, for the most part. Just leave him alone; that's all he asks."

Ben smiled. "That's all *we* ask here in the Tri-states."

"Governor . . ." A woman rose. "I'm an atheist. Could I live in this area?"

"Of course; but your children would still be taught the Bible, our creation, in public schools—and there are no other kinds of schools. And won't be."

"Suppose I don't want my children subjected to that superstitious drivel?"

"Then you could leave."

"That's it?"

"That's it."

"Your form of government is not very fair, General." She slurred the "General."

"It's fair for the people who choose to live under it. And that is what Tri-states is all about. And I'm beginning to sound redundant."

"You stress the Bible, General," she retorted, "but it seems to me there is a definite lack of compassion in this state. And I really can't correlate the Bible with legalized prostitution."

Ben had taken an immediate dislike to the woman. Bad chemistry, he supposed. "*I* don't stress the Bible, lady. We have great compassion for the old, the sick, the homeless, the young, the troubled, the helpless, those in need. Our system is such that no one needs to steal. That is why we are so harsh with lawbreakers. The churches are for those who wish to attend. The whorehouses are for those who would like a quick piece of ass."

Behind him, Salina suppressed a groan and Tina giggled.

The woman sat down, angry.

Half of the press people laughed, the other half frowned at Ben's loss of composure.

"Some would say you have a cult here, Governor."

"No." Ben shook his head. "I'd have to argue that. I was afraid of it, I will admit. At first. But we have no clear and fast ruler here. I *know* the people of the Tri-states would fight and die for their system of government. I am equally convinced they would not blindly die for me. That's the difference. All of us are the architects of the system—not just me."

"What does it take to move into this state?" Judith asked. Her colleagues looked at her in surprise. She sounded as if she meant the question for personal reasons.

"There has to be a job for you, and you have to want to move in very badly. You have to agree to become a member of the standing militia, and to support the Tri-states' philosophy—war or peace."

"You suppose there might be a job for me?" Judith asked.

"I would certainly imagine so. We've opened a number of radio stations and installed a number of TV stations. In our check on your people, you came out very high. You're a fair reporter in all aspects."

A reporter jumped to his feet. "What do you mean: a check on us?"

"Just that. You were all checked by our intelligence people before coming in here."

"How? I mean . . . well, how?"

Ben smiled. "That, son, is something you'll never know."

The Tri-states had a fine intelligence-gathering network with sophisticated computers and databanks. Their microwave equipment was the finest in the world. Dozens of technicians, formerly employed by the CIA,

NASA, NCIC, the FBI, and others, worked for the Tri-states' military—both inside and outside the state. They had taps into many computers around the nation.

"Are you interested in joining?" Ben asked the young woman. "I believe your mother and father were killed by burglars, before the war—were they not?"

Judith nodded. How had he discovered that? "Yes, I am very much interested."

"Are you out of your mind?" her boss whispered. "What are you trying to prove?"

Judith shrugged her reply.

"You people prowl around for a few days," Ben said. "We'll meet again for more questions and answers." He wheeled about and walked into the house, Salina and Tina behind him.

Badger blocked the way, the AK-47 at port arms. And the first press conference in Tri-states' short history was over.

FIVE

"Dr. Chase and Legal Officer Bellford are waiting for you people downtown," Badger informed the press corps. "Tell your drivers to take you to district HQ. It's just a couple of miles from here. That way." He pointed. "There are vehicles waiting for you—Jeeps."

"For free?" a reporter asked.

"Sure," Badger said. "Why not? You thinkin' about stealin' one?"

The man laughed. "After what we just heard about your form of justice?"

Badger smiled. "Yeah. That's something to think about, isn't it?"

The auditorium in the Hall of Justice building was large and comfortably furnished. Charles Bellford and Chief of Medicine Lamar Chase were waiting for them.

Dr. Chase did not particularly like the press—those from the outside—but he agreed to meet with them. His dislike was evident with his opening remark.

"Let's get this over with," he said. "I've got important things to do."

"You don't consider meeting with us important?" he was asked.

"I consider it a waste of valuable time, and cannot see

that anything constructive will come from it. You each get one question directed at me." He looked at the reporter who had asked about the importance of the meeting. "You've had yours. Next?"

The reporter sat down, muttering. "I don't believe this place."

"Dr. Chase, how do your medical facilities differ from those of the . . . outside?"

Chase smiled. "Good question, son. I can sum it all up in one statement, then get the hell out of here.

"We have the finest research center in the world here in the Tri-states. I should know, I helped steal most of the equipment."

The room echoed with laughter.

"Our facilities are excellent, and seventy-five percent free to the public. The state pays the first seventy-five percent, the patient the remainder, and that can be paid by installments or by a state loan. But no one is denied medical care—ever.

"We have doctors from the outside begging to come in here. Here, a physician may not become wealthy, but he or she will, in most situations, work regular hours. Ob/Gyn people are exceptions. We don't have malpractice suits in the Tri-states. Not as you people know them. A doctor might amputate the wrong leg and get sued—he should be sued. But it has to be something major for a lawsuit in the Tri-states.

"Here, doctors see patients who need to see a doctor, well-trained paramedics take care of the rest. That eases the load quite a bit. You people could have done the same had not the majority of your doctors been mercenary and the people they served sue-happy.

"We have the finest organ bank in the world. I have

preached for years that it should be against the law for a person to be lowered into the ground with precious organs intact. That is not permitted here in the Tri-states. Every part of the human body we can use, we take at the moment of death."

"The patient has no choice in the matter?"

"None."

"Death with dignity, doctor—is that allowed in this semireligious society?"

"I'll let the sarcastic 'semireligious' part of your question slide, sonny. I am not a religious man, personally. Yes, euthanasia is allowed in this society. And it's nobody's business but the patient's—as it should be anywhere. Not all doctors agree with it, naturally; we have diverse philosophies in this society just as you do in yours. Those doctors that don't like the idea don't take part in it. But the right to die, with or without dignity, is a personal choice and right. And no one else's goddamned business." He walked out of the room.

"Very blunt man," someone observed.

"But a compassionate one," Charles Bellford said.

"Mr. Bellford, you used to be a federal judge. You don't look like a judge now."

Bellford was dressed in ranch pants, western shirt, and cowboy boots. He smiled. "I don't have all those lofty decisions to hand down here, Mr. Charles. I'm a rancher/farmer first, legal officer second. Lawyers and judges don't have much to do in the Tri-states."

"Sir . . ." A reporter stood up. "I don't mean to appear ignorant . . . but I just don't understand your system of justice here. Surely you have decisions to weigh."

Bellford shook his head. "I realize this state must come as a shock to most of you. But I have very few decisions to ponder. The people we allow in here are almost always amazed at how smoothly our system runs. It almost runs itself. And it's easily explained: we simply brought the law back to the people.

"You see, I believe—and have for years—that the legal profession tried to keep the law, and themselves, on a plane far above the average person's level of understanding. And they—we—did it deliberately. Gods on high, so to speak, uttering pronouncements in a verbiage beyond the grasp of the nonlegal-educated majority. It was arrogant of us, and that is not the way it is done in the Tri-states. Governor Raines believes that lawyers perpetuate lawyers. I agree with him.

"Our trials are different from those on the outside, but I assure you, one and all, they do not make a mockery of justice.

"You see, we don't believe it's fair or just for the state—as in your system—to throw millions of dollars, highly trained investigators, and fine legal minds into a case, when the defendant is left out in the cold with one attorney and all the bills. That is not justice for all. Even if the accused is proven innocent, beyond the shadow of a doubt, in your system, many times he or she is ruined financially and publicly humiliated—by the press. We just don't believe that is true justice.

"There are no fine points of law here; no tricky legal maneuvering; no deals; no browbeating of witnesses. If a question cannot be fairly answered by a simple yes or no reply from the witness stand, we allow that person to elaborate. Or, one of the judges may stop the witness and take him or her into chambers, along with the attorneys; they'll hash it out there." He laughed. "You can all see I'm rusty with legal jargon. And so very happy about it.

"As you all know, polygraph and PSE machines are much more accurate than, oh, say ten years ago. And they are used in every case in the Tri-states. Every case. If they leave any doubt, we use drug-induced hypnosis. But a case will seldom go that far."

"What if I don't want to be subjected to that type of treatment?" he was asked.

"You don't have a choice," Bellford replied. "By your very refusal, you're admitting a certain amount of guilt. Look, we're dealing, in some cases, with human life; certainly with careers, with families, with dignity, and we want to be certain the right person is punished. And I know, and you people should know, that eyewitnesses are notoriously unreliable. I wish we had a case being tried somewhere in the Tri-states so you could all see our system in action."

"Sir . . . are you telling us that in all of the Tri-states, you aren't trying someone?"

"That is correct. Sorry."

"That's impossible!"

Bellford laughed. "Perhaps incredible—to you people—but certainly not impossible. Sociologists, psychologists, psychiatrists, and social anthropologists have been preaching for years that the death penalty and harsh laws would not be a deterrent for criminals. Many people believed them; I never did. Our society proves they were wrong. One day a week—this day—I come in in the afternoon to hear cases. I usually read a book to pass the time. Obviously, we are doing something right."

"But you are selective as to the caliber of person you will allow to live in the Tri-states?"

"Oh my, yes."

"Then how do you know harsh laws would work in the

other states?"

"I don't. But you don't know that they won't, because you people have never tried them. Probably never will. But that's your problem; we've solved ours. Understand this: in the Tri-states, murder, kidnapping, armed robbery, the selling of hard drugs, and treason, are all punishable by the death penalty. And lesser crimes—and that is a paradoxical statement—are still treated in a very harsh manner."

"Your system of justice does not allow much leeway for human error, Mr. Bellford."

"More than you might realize, sir. We have counselors ready and willing to talk with anyone who might have a problem—twenty-four hours, around the clock. And our people do use them. We do not have a pressure-free society. But it's as close as we could come to it."

"Be that as it may, Mr. Bellford. I don't think I'd like to live in your society."

"Your choice," the reporter was informed. "And ours."

Barney and his crew drove through the countryside as the press scattered over the thousands of miles of the Tri-states. They admired the neat, well-kept homes, the tidy fields and meadows, and the open friendliness of the people. No one seemed to be in any great hurry to get anywhere, and the press people realized then that the pace was indeed slower in the Tri-states. They were invited into homes by people they did not know, for coffee and cake and pie and home-baked bread. Homes were open, with doors unlocked; keys left in the ignitions of vehicles.

"Don't let a good boy go bad," one of Barney's crew

said sarcastically. "I always did think that was a bunch of shit. Good boys don't steal cars. Punks steal cars."

Barney glanced at him. "I never knew you felt that way, Jimmy."

"You never asked me."

Toward the end of the second day, Barney and his crew stopped to sit in silence for a time, digesting all they'd seen.

Barney sighed and shook his head. "Ted, we haven't seen one shack in two days. I have seen no signs of poverty. I have not seen anyone who looked poor or unhappy about anything. Why is everyone so contented in this wacko place?"

"Because they have what they want. I couldn't live here; I'll admit that. I like to whore around too much." He grinned. "I'd get shot for fooling around with someone's wife. O.K., so I couldn't live here—I haven't been invited, have I? But these folks like it here. Hell, why doesn't the government just leave them alone and let them live the way they want to live. They're not *forcing* their way of life on anyone. It's none of President Logan's business."

Jimmy said, "I agree with you, Ted. But I'll admit something: I'd like to live here. Man, these people have something good going for them."

Barney glanced at him. "The death penalty, Jimmy? Hard laws? I never knew you felt that way."

"You never asked me."

Charles Clayton and his crew pulled to a halt at the northernmost edge of the western part of the Tri-states. They had been following a chain-link fence for miles. The fence had stopped abruptly, turning straight east. Inside the fence was a desolate-looking stretch of almost barren land, cleared and stripped of most vegetation. It looked to be about a thousand yards wide.

"Looks like a no man's land," Clayton said, gazing at the second and third fences in the open area. "I'm beginning to understand why they have so few police. Once a person gets in, he can't get out! The entire damned place is a jail."

The minicam operator consulted a booklet. "This is the strip, as it's called. Jesus, can you imagine the wire it took to build this thing?"

"Warning signs every few hundred yards," Clayton said. "I wonder if that area inside is mined?"

A military Jeep pulled up beside the van. It had driven up so swiftly and silently it startled the men. The two soldiers were dressed in tiger-stripe field clothes, jump boots, and black berets. Armed with pistols and automatic weapons, they were neither hostile nor openly friendly—just curious.

"Something the matter?" one asked.

"Are you police?"

"No, army patrol. Border security."

Clayton nodded. "What would you do if I had an urge to walk around in there?" He pointed toward the strip. "Just climb the fence and go in there?"

"Nothing," the soldier replied blandly. "You're an adult; you can read the warning signs. If you want to run the risk of getting hurt or killed in there, that's your business."

"So it is mined," Clayton said.

"That's the rumor." The soldier lit a cigarette.

Clayton did not see the wink that passed from one soldier to the other. The area was not mined, but could be

419

in a very short time.

"You people take death and injury very casually," Clayton said.

"No," the soldier contradicted, "not really. We love life, love freedom. That's why we chose to live here. We just figure any intelligent man or woman would have enough sense or respect for warning signs to keep out of any area marked 'Keep Out.'"

"There is still the matter of small children," Clayton said, his face hot and flushed.

"Yes, that's right. That's why we're here, sir. But our kids are taught to respect warning signs, fences, other people's property, and things that don't belong to them. How about your kids?"

Clayton glared at him for a moment, then smiled. "I have been properly chastised, soldier. Thank you."

"You're sure welcome, sir." The driver put the Jeep in gear and drove off.

Clayton sighed. "This is a tough one, people. I don't know how I'm going to report it. What they've done is bring it all back to the basics. That's all it is. The simplest form of government in the world. But goddamn it!" he cursed. "It's working!"

The press roamed the Tri-states, top to bottom, east to west for a week, some of them trying their very best to pick it apart and report the very worst. They talked with a few people who did not like the form of government, the harsh laws, and death penalty. Some people felt they had a right to get drunk and drive—they could drive just as well drunk as sober. They had a right to bully and browbeat. Laws were made to be broken, not followed.

But do you obey the laws in the Tri-states? they were asked.

Goddamned right! You'd better obey 'em in this place.

Has anyone mistreated you?

I got punched in the mouth one time; called a man a liar. Busted my tooth—right here—see it?

But when the talk shifted to hospitals, general health care, nursing homes, day centers, rescue squads and other emergency services, employment, working conditions, housing, recreational areas, and day-to-day living . . . well, that was kind of a different story. Yeah, things are pretty good, I guess.

The press picked the state dry; then, in an informal meeting among themselves, talked of what they'd seen and heard.

"There is gun law here."

"Anybody seen anyone get shot?"

No one had.

"There is no hunger here, and most people seem content."

"A person can get shot for stealing a car."

"But no slums or inadequate housing."

"I can't figure out whether dueling is legal here, or not. I think in a way, it is."

"The medical care is the best I've ever seen, available to all."

"Capital punishment is the law of the land."

"But there is full employment and the wages are good. This state is full of craftsmen who are proud of their work."

"There sure isn't any crime."

"Of course, there isn't. Everybody packs a goddamned

gun! Would you steal if you knew you were going to get shot for trying or hanged for the actual crime?"

"It's a dictatorship."

"No, it isn't. Governor Raines was elected by the people. I don't know what the hell it is. The only thing I know is . . . it's working."

"General," a reporter said, "we've been here a week, looking around, asking questions. I can't speak for the others, but if this is your concept of a perfect society— you can have it, sir."

The Raineses' back yard. Not as many press people as before; a full quarter of them having made up their minds—one way or the other—and left to file their stories.

"We're not striving for a perfect society. That is impossible when imperfect human beings are the architects. We just want one that works for us; for the people who choose to live here.

"No, we're far from perfection. Even within our own system there have been instances of injustice. No one will make any excuses for it except to say we've fought ignorance and prejudice and superstition . . . and I believe we've beaten it. Some of the people, who couldn't take our form of government, left—and we bought their lands and property from them; we didn't steal it—they had sat on their asses and done nothing but bitch and complain and criticize everything we were attempting to do, at the same time taking advantage of our food, medicines, and other help. They could not understand— or refused to understand—that black and white and red and tan and yellow all bleed the same color.

"There is no discrimination in the Tri-states, and there

is no preference for color. Any person qualified to do a job can do it. If a person is not qualified, the job goes to someone else. You have all interviewed the lieutenant governor and the secretary of state; you all know they are black. The woman in charge of central planning is Sue Yong. Mr. Garrett, the chief law-enforcement officer in the Tri-states is a Crow Indian. So on down the line. It would be grossly unfair to accuse us of being racially biased, but we are very selective."

"Then you admit your form of government could not work in the other states, Governor?"

"Oh, it *could* work, but it would take a lot of education and a lot of conforming to make it work. But I'm not concerned with the other states. Just this area.

"Let's wind this down and get it over with. Our bank interest rates are low—lower than they've been in the United States for almost twenty years. We have full employment, almost zero crime. Our pay scale is excellent, and we do it all without the threat of unions hanging over the businessman's head."

"Do you plan to keep unions out?"

"Yes."

"How?"

"By allowing in only those people who don't want something for nothing. Profit-sharing is law in the Tri-states; which is one of the reasons it's difficult for anyone to become a millionaire. Large factories are owned by the men and women who work the factories. We have very fair labor/management practices. Businesses offer excellent fringe-benefit plans. Our Fair Labor Practices Board—which is headed by a woman, by the way—is constantly checking to see that management pulls its share, and God help them if they are not. Sexual discrimination and sexual harassment *will not* be found in the Tri-states. That's why some hotshot executives who moved in here from the cities moved out about a week after they got here.

"Job descriptions are defined from A to Z, and getting the boss his coffee, picking up his laundry, and looking after the family cat while he's on vacation are not part of an employee's job. I'm hitting the high spots, but you all get the overall picture.

"We have grievance committees in every shop, every factory, every business. Retirement plans are mandatory: business pays a third, labor pays a third, the state pays a third. Funds are transferrable from job to job, and there is no hassle connected with it. The same could have been done in the United States forty years ago.

"No one—repeat, *no one*—works six months out of a year then lays up on his or her backside drawing unemployment the other six. We'll find people jobs the same day they lose or quit them. They might not like them, but they'll work them or get the hell out."

"How about taxes—are they high?"

"No. They are low, really, and we can keep them that way because our revenue goes to things other than fine new jails, federal grants and programs, make-work projects, investigating the sexual habits of a grubworm, and pork-barrel boondoggles. And we've done it without creating a monster bureaucracy." He smiled. "That sticks in the craw of Logan.

"It is very true that we have broken away from the Constitution of the United States—to a degree—but we haven't broken away from it any further than your government has in the past thirty years. The only difference was in direction. Your government went left, we went right."

"Mr. Raines, the federal government in Richmond declares what you've done is illegal, and they will eventually stop you. I'd like to hear your views on that."

"Well, sir," Ben said, "I'd be very interested in hearing just *how* they plan to stop us. The only way they possibly could do it is through another war, and they'd have to kill off every man, woman, and child in the Tristates. That's the only way.

"We intend to live in peace as long as we're left alone. But"—Ben smiled, a wolf's baring of teeth that touched each member of the press, sending an eerie tingling up and down the spines of all present—"the man who issues that order to wipe us out is a dead man."

The press waited, stirred, looked at each other.

"The Tri-states is broken up into districts," Ben said. "Each district has a team of five men and women, all volunteers, all highly trained. Only a very few people know their identities. They are called zero squads because that is the odds of their coming out of their assignments—zero. They might be able to complete their assignments in a week; more than likely it will take some months, but they will complete their assignments, believe that.

"To declare war on us orders have to come from the top: the President, the House, and Senate. When, or if, that order comes down to destroy us, the president, the VP, any member of the Joint Chiefs of Staff, and any representative and senator who voices approval of the plan . . . will die."

SIX

All the members of the press but one came to their feet in a roar of outrage. To break away from the Union was one thing—a bit daring, glamorous. But to plan and carry out mass murder was quite another; unthinkable—in their minds. Only Judith remained seated and calm in the midst of the uproar in the Raineses' back yard, a faint smile on her lips—a smile that could be taken as admiration. Governor General Raines had taken out quite an insurance policy on the future of the Tri-states, and she had no doubt but what he meant every word. She was finding the prospect of living in the Tri-states more exciting with every minute.

Badger was on his feet, swinging the AK-47 toward the newspeople, anticipating a rush toward the governor. Juno was standing, snarling. Ben calmed them both with a quiet voice.

"You can't be serious?" A young reporter yelled the questioning statement. His tone betrayed his shock and outrage. "That's murder!"

Ben waited for the din to settle and the press people to return to their seats.

"And," Ben said, "if the federal government moves against us, bombing and killing people, isn't that murder? Perhaps you people would prefer the term 'war'? If so, I'd like to see where you draw the line between war and murder."

"Some of the people your zero squads might kill, Governor, could possibly have had nothing to do with any war against the Tri-states. Have you considered that?"

"Neither will the very young and the very old of the Tri-states," Ben countered. "But they'll die just the same. Have you thought of that?"

"Suppose they are given the opportunity to leave?"

"Suppose they like it here?"

"Mr. Raines, is the size of your army secret?"

"No. Everyone in the Tri-states is part of our armed forces. They all know their jobs and will do them without hesitation."

"That doesn't tell me the strength."

Ben smiled. "Several divisions."

"General, what do you think your chances of survival are in the Tri-states?"

"I have no idea." He did. "As I have stated, all we want is to be left alone."

"The federal government has never had a very good track record for doing that," a reporter observed.

"Yes," Ben agreed. "How well I know."

The press left, all but Judith, who stayed on and became a resident and news director for a TV station.

Tri-states settled back to run itself: smoothly, quietly, profitably, and very efficiently. A dozen companies—major industrial conglomerates—had slipped quietly into the Tri-states and set up shop.

Those who came to the Tri-states, to live and to work, had many things in common: the desire to live and let live; the need for as much personal freedom as is possible in any society; the wish to give a day's work (as a craftsman) for a day's ample pay; respect for the rights of others.

There was room to relax in the Tri-states, room to breathe and enjoy life. Here, no one pushed.

America—the other forty-seven states—slowly returned to some degree of normalcy. Tourists were out and traveling in those areas that were not hot or forbidden.

Hesitantly, shyly at first—for the Tri-states had taken more than its share of bad press—a few tourists came in. But the Tri-states limited their numbers, after making certain they understood the laws of the nation. Then more people discovered the area was a very unique and quiet place to visit—if one stayed out of trouble. The Tri-states offered to the family unit a quiet vacation, with good fishing, good food, and honest surroundings, with no fear of crime.

The criminal element stayed far away from the Tri-states. Word had quickly spread in the newly organized underworld that to fuck up in the Tri-states meant a noose or a bullet—very quickly.

There were many things different, unique, and quite experimental about the Tri-states. One reporter called it right-wing socialism, and he was correct, to a degree. But yet, as another reporter said, "It is a state for all the people who wish to live there, and who have the ability to live together."

In the Tri-states, if a family fell behind in their bills, they could go to a state-operated counseling service for help. The people there were friendly, courteous, and openly and honestly sympathetic. If that family could not pay their bills because of some unforeseen emergency, and if that family was making a genuine effort to pay their bills, utilities could not be cut off, automobiles could not be taken from them, furniture could not be repossessed. A system of payment would be worked out. There were no collection agencies in the Tri-states.

As Ben told a group of visiting tourists, "It is the duty and the moral and legal obligation of the government—in this case, state government—to be of service and of help to its citizens. When a citizen calls for help, that person wants and needs help instantly, not in a month or three months. And in the Tri-states, that is when it is provided—instantly. Without citizens, the state cannot exist. The state is not here to harass, or to allow harassment, in any form. And it will not be tolerated."

"No!" President Logan said. "For the last time, I will not send any person from this good office to talk with the illegal governor of an illegal state. No!"

"Hilton, the state is a real state," Aston reminded him. "The people are real. Their economy is booming."

"I will tell you what I intend to do. I intend to denounce the Tri-states as illegal and politically non-existent in the eyes of the United States Government."

"And?"

"What do you mean?"

"What next—troops?"

"Perhaps. I've discussed it with General Russell."

"Hilton, for God's sake!"

Logan ignored the VP's pleas. "I think we should first concentrate on the rebellious Indian tribes. Get them back in line and off stolen property."

"No, Hilton—good Lord. What harm have they done?"

"We can be thankful for one thing: the niggers didn't get organized. Not really. I'll let Jeb Fargo and some of his people spearhead the drive to crush the Indians. I really never knew they were so military." He looked at his VP, not understanding the horror in the man's eyes. "Aston, we've got to pull this nation back together. General Russell tells me we're almost strong enough to break the back of Raines's Rebels."

"Hilton, let Ben Raines have his state; let the Indian have his land. I just don't want any trouble."

Logan laughed. "You're worse than an old woman, Aston. Do you look under your bed for ghosts at night?"

"I'll forget you said that."

President Logan stood up, walking from behind his desk to place his hand on the VP's shoulder. "I'm sorry, Aston. My remark was uncalled for. I do need and value your help and friendship."

"Hilton, do you think Raines was joking about those assassination teams? The zero squads."

The president laughed. "Why, of course—don't you?"

"No! I think we've been warned to leave them alone. I sure as hell don't think he was kidding. Review his record, Hilton, both as a soldier in the U.S. Army and as a mercenary." He looked up at his friend and boss. "Hilton, I'm worried, and so are a lot of other people around Richmond. Raines wasn't kidding; he meant every word he said. Let them have their state."

"Gun law, Aston? No. I won't tolerate that."

"Gun law is a phrase dreamed up by the press. They have courts and laws."

"This is the United States of America, Aston. *United!* Those Rebels, white and red, have broken from the Union to form their own little nations. I intend to see they pay for that."

The VP felt a cold, sluggish chill move in his guts, almost as a premonition of doom. "We'll all pay for it, Hilton. Bet on it."

The United States, for the most part, was recovering quickly. Nine years had passed since the nuke and germ holocaust. The people had adjusted to the fact that several major cities were gone, and there were areas they could never visit, or their children, or their children's children. People had adjusted to the relocation and were rapidly picking up their lives . . . and once more listening to the rumors of war coming out of Richmond.

Tri-states had opened a number of radio stations within its borders, all operating on a twenty-four-hour basis, with enough power to cover the Tri-states. The formats were varied, from all news to rock and roll to classical, something for everyone's tastes.

The telephone company had approached the Tri-states' communications people, asking, please, could they have some of their equipment back? In return, Ma Bell would allow a hookup with equipment in the Tri-states.

Tri-states could now communicate with most of the other states.

Then, as the rumors of war became stronger, the central government of the United States began getting tough with its people.

First came legislation reestablishing government controls over the lives of people; balloting as a means of seeking the support of the people, was rescinded and the people were now told how they could live their lives. Then came more legislation controlling the ownership of firearms—all firearms. Rifles and shotguns were to be turned in, or forcibly taken from citizens. But Americans recently had had a war on their soil—and they had toughened. When the final roundup of long guns began, as before, resistance groups began forming.

Ben knew the government was deliberately saving the Indian nations and the Tri-states for last. The Indians and the Rebels would fight the longest and the hardest for their freedoms.

In less than six months, the federal government had broken the backs of most new resistance groups, seizing thousands of rifles and shotguns in the process, and had reestablished control over the lives of the people in seventy-five percent of the nation.

But there were still many guerrilla units fighting, hard-line holdouts who would fight to the end against total government control.

It was winter in the Tri-states, the temperature in the twenties and snowing. The phone rang in the outer offices of the governor general.

"Governor . . ." Ben's secretary buzzed him. "It's President Logan."

Salina had come to have lunch with Ben and she smiled at his wink. "How about that?" he said with a grin. "That's the first time in nine years Logan has officially acknowledged our existence." He picked up the phone, calming the flashing light.

"Good morning, Mr. President. How are things in Richmond?"

"Cold," Logan replied. "And wet." He paused for a moment, then blurted, "I'd like a meeting with you and your staff. If we are to recognize your . . . state, there are a number of things we'd better discuss."

Two thousand miles away, Ben sat numb, knowing the Tri-states' time had come. For he knew Logan would only welcome the Tri-states into the fold if certain conditions were met, and the people of the Tri-states would never allow that. But Ben had to buy some time.

"Are you still there, Raines?"

"Yes," Ben replied slowly. "Why the sudden change of heart, Logan?"

"A great many reasons, Raines." The president's hatred slithered through the long lines like a snake. "Some of which will not be to your liking."

I'll bet that's a fact. "When do you want to meet?"

"Next Monday. Ten o'clock, eastern time. Here at the capitol."

Ben started to refuse, to name an alternate site, neutral ground. But he rejected the thought, knowing the president could, if he was setting Ben up for an ambush, have troops anywhere in America in a matter of hours. He said, "All my people will be armed, including myself."

"No! That is totally unacceptable."

"Then the meeting is off," Ben said flatly.

"Do I have to remind you I am the President of the United States? My God, Raines—don't you trust me?"

Ben chuckled. "Hilton, you have got to be kidding. You were a closet bigot for years, using the minorities for votes only, and now your agents and troops are running around the country, knocking people in the head, taking their weapons from them. It's ten times worse than before the bombings. So, trust you—? Hell, no."

A moment of heavy silence. "All right, Raines, do it your way. Monday morning." He hung up.

Ben sat for a long time, watching Salina work her needlepoint. She lifted her eyes, meeting his. She said, "It's coming down to the wire, isn't it, Ben?"

"Yes. Logan will offer us impossible conditions, knowing we'll refuse. When we do, that will clear his conscience and he'll move against us."

"Those troops that have been quietly moving into position all around us?"

"Yeah. He's blocked us from helping the Indians. He'll take them out first." He looked at Salina. "Salina . . . I want you to get out of here, up into Canada. You're five months pregnant; by the time Logan moves against us, you'll be too fat to wobble, much less run. I—"

"What do you mean, fat! I resent that. I think I'm having a rather slim, beautiful pregnancy."

"That's not what I mean, and you know it. Salina . . . ?"

"No, Ben. I stay with you. End of discussion."

He knew further argument would be futile. He called for Pal and Cecil and Ike and others, telling them of the news, and of his suspicions.

"I agree," Pal said. "I'll put the country on low alert."

"You'll have to stay behind, Pal—both of us can't be gone at the same time," Ben said. "When I return, I'll go on the air with Logan's conditions. We'll leave it up to the people."

"They'll never accept anything other than what we have," Cecil said.

"Yes," Ben said. "I know."

They all left, leaving Ben with his thoughts.

Badger had been waiting in the outer office, as usual.

When the group left, he strolled in without announcement, as usual.

"What's up, General?"

"Want to go to Richmond next Monday?"

"Not really. I like it here. But if you go, I go."

Ben laughed. "Badger, one thing I've always admired about you is your bubbling enthusiasm."

Badger sat down, cradling his AK-47 across his knees. "Yes, sir," he said solemnly.

The three jets, formerly corporation jets—state airplanes, now—flew in formation toward Richmond. In the center jet were Ben and Salina, Cecil and Lila, Ike, Voltan, Steven, and Badger. In the other jets rode two teams of Rebels. Ben's personal teams. Eighteen men and six women.

All regular Rebels were good at their jobs, experts, but these twenty-four were among the best—or worst, depending upon one's point of view. They were, for the most part, silent as they blasted through the air, for to a person, they all knew war was just around the corner.

At the field in Richmond, they were met by VP Addison, several aides, and a dozen secret service agents. Ben suspected there might be a full brigade of troops lurking about the airport, and that thought amused him. He shook hands with VP Addison and grinned.

"No brass bands playing? No red carpet? No throngs of cheering people?" Ben asked. "My, you people don't like me very much, do you?"

The VP stared into Ben's eyes. "I don't like what Logan has planned, Raines. It wasn't my idea."

"I know it. And that will be kept in mind."

A half-hour later, they pulled into the drive of the new

White House. The weather was dismal in Richmond, and Ben didn't expect Logan's welcome to be much better.

Badger stepped out first. "Wait here, sir," he said to Ben. The bodyguard walked up the steps of the White House and stationed himself beside one of the huge pillars. The secret service men on duty held their hands away from their sides, to show him they had no intention of reaching for a gun.

"Just keep that thing on safety," they requested.

Badger nodded.

Standing beside the limousines, an aide muttered, "The president is not going to be terribly thrilled about that man and his machine gun." He glanced at Ben. "What do you think is going to happen, sir? Do you believe we're planning an ambush, or something?"

Ben looked at the aide. Without smiling, he said, "I wouldn't be a bit surprised."

A piece of old verse popped into Ben's head:

> Then you're ready to go and pass through with the bunch,
> At the gate at the end of things.

"Some gate," Ben muttered.

"I beg your pardon, sir?" an aide asked.

Ben shook his head and walked up the steps.

SEVEN

The visitors from the Tri-states were ushered into the White House, taken upstairs, and seated in the president's office. The contingent of Rebels remained downstairs, having coffee and chatting with the secret service agents; both groups attempted to make the best of a nervous situation.

The press was very much in force, snapping pictures and asking questions.

Logan made his entrance, strolling in all smiles and cordiality. The head of the Joint Chiefs was with him. Ben immediately distrusted the general. Russell had been a major in Vietnam; a politicking, ass-kissing coward.

"Ladies and gentlemen." Logan smiled. "Welcome to the White House. So nice to see all of you."

And if you expect us to believe that, Salina thought, you're a bigger fool than you look. But she smiled in return.

Ben shook hands with Logan and smiled a grim smile at General Russell. The two men immediately understood each other's position; Ben realized that while America had a president, Logan shared the power with the military. Ben knew then why free elections had been postponed year after year. The military was setting up to take over total control of America. The rumors his intelligence people had intercepted and decoded were true. But Ben also knew there was discord among the military; not all commanders wanted the military involved in government, and the troops were taking sides . . . quietly.

The silent message in General Russell's eyes was easy to read: Play along with me, Raines. Take my side.

Ben minutely shook his head and the general smiled and fired a silent dispatch: You've had it, Raines.

Ben returned his unspoken reply: When you try, General—you're a dead man.

The messages concluded, there were a few moments of small talk about nothing at all until Mrs. Fran Logan gushed in, all smiles and southern hospitality, for everyone except Ben. She was very cool to Ben. She hesitated for just the smallest second before shaking hands with Cecil (it rubs off, you know), but then breeding took over and she gallantly took the offered hand, fighting back an impulse to wipe hers on her dress. A few moments later, the ladies left, much to the disgust of Salina and Lila. In the Tri-states, all government meetings were open.

"Gentlemen," Logan said, "we have a great deal to discuss—shall we get on with it?" Without waiting for an answer, he ordered coffee sent in. There was quiet in the large room until the aide poured the coffee and left. General Russell stood across the room, away from the seated party from the Tri-states.

"If you wish to rejoin the Union, Raines," Logan said, "it can be arranged."

I just bet it can, Ben thought. "What's the catch?"

Logan smiled and General Russell laughed aloud. The President said, "Absolutely no diplomat in you whatsoever, right, Ben?"

"Lack of diplomacy is just one of my many virtues. I'll ask again: What is the catch?"

"Straight from the hip?"

"Shoot."

"Your dictatorship has to end."

"There is no dictatorship in the Tri-states. I was elected by popular vote."

Logan waved away his words as if they had not been spoken. "You must fall in line with the other forty-seven."

"No way."

"You must open your borders, allowing any person who so desires to live in the Tri-states."

"No way."

"Your laws must conform with the rulings of our Supreme Court."

Everyone from the Tri-states laughed openly at that.

Logan flushed, then said, "The gun law must cease."

Ben placed cup and saucer on a coffee table. "Here is what we will and will not do, Logan: I will not tolerate your federal police coming in and setting up in our area. Our system of government works for us, and that is all that matters. No gun control; no flower-plucking, sobbing social workers telling us how to deal with punks. And no mumblings from *your* Supreme Court."

"Raines, I'm offering you statehood in return for a few concessions." He glanced at General Russell, then swung his gaze back to Ben. "You know, of course, what is going to happen if you refuse?"

Ben's stare was cold. "And you know what will happen if you wage war against us."

Logan laughed. "I don't believe you have those . . .

zero squads."

But VP Addison looked worried.

Logan said, "You must know we have the power to crush you like a bug. We didn't for a while; I'll admit that. But now we do."

"Yes, you probably do, Logan," Ben said. "But all you'll accomplish is a civil war, and it will, in all probability, tear this country apart."

"Raines, you've done some good things out there—I won't, can't, deny that. I could even find a place for you on my team. I could use you. But your state has to fall in line."

"Absolutely not."

"Then the Tri-states is through." Logan said it maliciously.

"Are you going to give the orders to kill all the tiny babies and all the old and sick, Mr. President?" Cecil asked. "We have the good life, free of crime and red tape, and you just can't stand that, can you?"

Logan flushed, but kept his mouth shut. Addison felt sick at his stomach. General Russell smiled.

"Logan," Ben said, "I came here with a hope of working some . . . type of arrangement with you. To live peacefully. Different ideologies, certainly—it's a different world, now—but still with some hope we could get together and live in peace. But your concept of peace is infringement on the personal liberties of law-abiding, taxpaying citizens. I'll never tolerate that system again—never. Logan, those zero squads are real. They exist. You know what is going to happen to you if you start a war with us, and to every member of Congress who agrees with your plan."

"I will unite the states," Logan said. "And I will

restore proper law and order. We cannot exist separately."

Cecil smiled. "You mean, you won't let us exist."

Logan ignored the black man. He glared at Ben. "I'm going to destroy your state, Raines."

"You've been warned, Logan."

"I don't believe in fairy tales, Raines. Good day."

Back home, Ben went on the Tri-states' radio and television, telling the people of the events in Richmond. Anyone who wanted to leave was warned to get out immediately.

A few left, most stayed. They began gearing up for war.

President Logan ordered a state of emergency and ordered all airlines and trucks and buses to cease—at once—any runs into the Tri-states. Phone service was cut—jammed. Troops set up roadblocks on the borders of the Tri-states and refused to allow any resident of the United States to enter the area. The Canadian Government cooperated only half-heartedly with Logan's requests to seal off their borders; Ben and his people had gotten along well with the new Canadian Government. But in the end, it went along with Logan.

The freeze was on.

"I'm asking you again, Salina; pleading with you. Get out while there is still time." Ben looked at the set of her jaw and never asked her again.

The central government of Richmond began dropping leaflets all over the Tri-states, urging its citizens to revolt against Ben, to leave.

A number of citizens of Butte built a huge sign on the outskirts of town, built it of rocks painted white, flat on the ground, the sign was immense, its seven letters telling the pilots exactly what they thought about the contents of the leaflets.

FUCK YOU

"How long can we last?" Ben asked his department heads.

"Medically speaking," Dr. Chase said, "years."

"We have food enough for years."

"Fuel enough for years."

"Ammunition enough for years."

"It won't be years," Ben told them. "They'll wipe out the Indians first, knowing we can't move to help them because we're blocked in here. They'll hit us in mid-spring, after all the snows are gone. The weather will be perfect fighting weather—cool. Troops move better in that kind of weather.

"All right, mine the strip; enlarge it, pull it in a couple of miles at least. Turn it into hell. Munitions factories go on twenty-four-hour shifts effective immediately. We've got about ninety days before the balloon goes up."

As Ben had predicted, the government of the United States decided they would give the Indians their comeuppance.

"The reservation lands will always be yours," the federal agents told the Indians. "However, any land you seized following the war goes back to the government, and to the people . . . if we can find them."

"Why?" the Indians questioned.

"Because it doesn't belong to you."

"It belonged to us a thousand years before you people got here. Look, we just want to live like decent people,

442

at's all. There is plenty of land for all."

"Your suggestion will, of course, be taken into consideration. However, during the interim, you will have to return to your reservations."

"No."

"I beg your pardon?" One does not ever say no to a federal agent—unthinkable. How impudent!

"No. We're staying where we are."

"Then I'm afraid we'll have to take action to move you and your people."

A smile greeted those words. "Look around you, federal man. Tell me what you see and hear."

The federal men tensed as they heard the snicking of levers pushing live ammunition into gun chambers. They heard the rattle of belt-fed ammo being worked into weapons. They saw the determination of these people to stand and fight for what should have been theirs years before—*was* theirs years before.

"This land is our land," the Indians said. "You'll have to kill us to move us."

When the first troops went in to move the Indians, the Indians did not fire the first shot. Instead, they tried to reason with the commanders. But the troops had their orders and the Indians had their pride.

When the first shot was fired against the Indians, Ben knew any early victories they achieved would be short and hollow ones. For they were too few, and the troops were too strong.

And Jeb Fargo and his people were too full of hate.

Reports of torture and rape began filtering out and into the Tri-states. In some instances, Indians who had surrendered were lined up and used for target practice.

Girls as young as ten and eleven were raped; boys wer
sexually mutilated, left to bleed to death.

"And we're next," Salina said.

She was heavy with child.

Ben ordered every resident into service. He told ther
to put on their gear and prepare to fight, or to pack up an
try to surrender at the borders. No one left. The Tr
states was blacked out during the night.

Thousands of men, women, and teen-agers pulled o
field gear, took up arms, and waited for war.

"I told you the shit was gonna hit the fan." Ike smile
at Ben.

The Indians fought bravely and well with what the
had, but they didn't have a chance—not against long
range artillery and planes and Cobra gunships and Puff
and paratroopers and marines—those who chose to figh
that is, and quite a few did not.

The government, at Jeb Fargo's proddings, began it
policy of extermination, with the help of many Indian
hating whites in the areas.

There was no sense in it. There was ample land for all
and the land claimed by the Indians was not that large
But governments rule by fear, and they are always right
Governments must always live under that premise.

The fighting was bloody and savage and senseless. Th
only good coming out of it was the death of Jeb Fargo. A
the end, ragged and dirty and sick and hated, the Ameri
can Indians fought what most believed was their last figh
for their land. *Their* land. Most were hunted down an
exterminated. The poor pitiful few that remained wer
herded onto reservations and left.

The government had won again—almost.

For the government did not know that a company of regulars from the Tri-states was with the Indians. When the officer in charge of that detachment saw which way the battle was going, he pulled his men and more than a thousand Indians—from various tribes—out and into Oregon. There, they waited for orders from General Raines.

When the last bastion of Indian defense fell, Ben and his people knew they were next; their time had come.

The strip had been turned into an area of hell: mines, punji stakes, barbed wire, booby-traps. Foot soldiers could and would move through it, but it would be at a fearful price—while the nation's leaders sat back in Richmond, dining in comfortable surroundings and sipping wine from crystal goblets.

It always comes down to the soldiers.

Gen. Ben Raines called for a meeting with civilian and military leaders. "We're next," he told his people. In his hand he held a communiqué that had been hand-delivered to the eastern border by government messenger. "Congress has voted to enter into war with us if we do not surrender within twenty-four hours. They say because we have formed an illegal state, and aided the Indians in their fight against the central government, we are traitors and must be treated as any other power attempting to subvert or bring down the democratic government of America.

"If any of you want to pack it in, I sure won't blame you. I know we don't have a chance in here, and we are too many to run. We'll hold out for several weeks—six max. Then we've had it."

No one left or spoke.

"All right, here it is. We still have some holes the

445

troops don't know about. Most of the women with small children didn't want to leave, but they had to. Some of them have made it out." He shuffled his booted feet. "Most of them didn't. Start the others out immediately with guides and supplies. If any of us get out of here, we'll regroup in Canadian sector five.

"Get your people into position and booby-trap everything you leave behind. *Everything*. Poison the water. Turn everything into a lethal weapon—a death trap. I want these sons of bitches to remember these next few weeks. You all know the drill. As soon as government troops touch the soil of the Tri-states, we move into guerrilla tactics. No prisoners." He turned to Voltan. "Bridges wired to go?"

"Yes, sir. We'll set timers as soon as our people cross them."

"I don't want a bridge left standing in the Tri-states. Not one."

"Yes, sir."

To Dr. Chase: "How about the people in the hospitals?"

"Some of them just cannot be moved and they refuse to surrender. They've asked that weapons be left by their beds. I have done so. We're painting red crosses on the roofs of the hospitals. Maybe they won't be bombed."

"I wouldn't count on it," Pal said.

"I'm not."

"Cecil, did the zero squads make it out?"

"Yes, sir. They are all awaiting the signal to go."

"All right, people." Ben shook hands with his friends. "Good luck and let's go."

EIGHT

Keep it; it tells all our history over,
From the birth of the dream to its last;
Modest and born of the Angel of Hope,
Like our hope of success it has passed.

Maj. Samuel Alroy Jones

The commander of the federal forces, Maj. Gen. Paul Como of the United States Army, lowered his binoculars and turned to his aide. Dawn was just splitting the eastern sky with beams of gold. The men stood on the east side of the Tri-states' Idaho border.

Como cursed. "Goddamn it, I stood on every border of his state for a week." He spoke through clenched teeth. "I've seen the same thing each day: nothing! Not one sign of human life. No smoke, no movement—nothing. Oh, this is going to be a bloody bitch!"

Brigadier General Krigel walked up, catching the last of Como's statement. "You know the response they gave to our leaflets. What are we going to do about the civilians and the hospitals and the nursing homes?"

"There are no civilians in the Tri-states," Como said shortly. "The entire populous is an army." He would rather not think about the rest of Krigel's question, for it was because of that the Air Force had refused to bomb the

Tri-states; the military was decidedly split over war with Ben's people. "What's the latest on aerial recon?"

"They started out at ten thousand feet and moved down to five hundred. There has not been a shot fired at any of them. We have not had one hostile move against us from the residents of the Tri-states. There are warm breathing bodies in there—everywhere—but we don' know if they are friendly, hostile, young, old, male, or female."

Como sighed heavily. "The bridges all around the state been cleared?" He knew they had not.

Krigel cleared his throat. "No, sir. The Navy SEAL have refused to go in. They say they won't fight against fellow Americans. Some of those people in there were SEALs."

"I don't give a good goddamn what they *were!* I gave orders for the SEALs to clear the bridges. I ought to have those bastards arrested."

"Begging your pardon, sir, but I would sure hate to be the person who tried that."

Como ignored that, fighting to keep his anger under control. He glanced at his watch. "All right, then—the hell with the SEALs." He glanced toward the east. Much lighter. "Get the airborne dropped."

"The drop zones have not been laid out, sir."

"What!"

"Sir, the Pathfinders went in last night, but they all deserted and joined the Rebels. To a man."

"*What!*"

"They refused to lay out the DZs. Sir, they said they won't fight fellow Americans, and anyone who would is traitor."

"Goddamn it!" Como yelled. He pointed a finger a

Krigel. "You get the airborne up and dropped. Start the push—right now. You get those fucking Rangers spearheading."

Krigel shifted his jump-booted feet. The moment he had been dreading. "We . . . have a problem, sir. Quite a number of the residents of the Tri-states . . . were . . . th—"

"Paratroopers, Rangers, marines, SEALs, AF personnel." The CG finished it for him. "Wonderful. How many are not going to follow my orders?"

"About fifty percent of the airborne have refused to go in. No Rangers, no Green Berets, no SEALs. About thirty percent of the marines and regular infantry refuse to go in. They said, sir, they'd storm the gates of hell for you, with only a mouthful of spit to fight with, but they say these people are Americans, and they haven't done anything wrong. They are not criminals."

The news came as no surprise to General Como. He had discussed this operation with General Russell, during the planning stages, and had almost resigned and retired. But Russell had talked him out of it. Como was not happy with it, but he was a professional soldier, and he had his orders.

Krigel said, "General, this is a civilian problem. It's not ours. Those people in there are Americans. They just want to be left alone. They are not in collusion with any foreign power, and they are not attempting to overthrow the government. Paul,"—he put his hand on his friend's shoulder—"I still get sick at my stomach thinking about those Indians. Granted, *we* didn't do those things, but we were in command of the men who did—some of them. It was wrong, and we should have been men enough to have those responsible for those . . . acts shot!"

449

General Como felt his guts churn; his breakfast la
heavy and undigested. He knew well what his friend wa
going through; and Krigel was his friend. Classmates a
the Point. But an order was an order.

Como pulled himself erect. When he spoke, his voic
was hard. "You're a soldier, General Krigel, and you'l
obey orders, or by God, I'll—"

"You'll do what?" Krigel snapped, losing his temper
"Goddamn it, Paul, we're creating another civil war. An
you know it. Yes, I'm a soldier, and a damned good one
But by God, I'm an American first. This is a nation of fre
people, Paul? The hell it is! Those people in the Tri-state
may have different ideas, but—"

"*Goddamn you!*" Como shouted. "Don't you dar
argue with me. You get your troopers up and dropped—
now, or they won't *be your* troopers. General Krigel, I ar
making that a direct order."

"No, sir," Krigel said, a calmness and finality in hi
voice. "I will not obey that order." He removed his pisto
from leather and handed it to General Como. "I'n
through, Paul—that's it."

General Como, red-faced and trembling, looked at the
.45 in his hand, then backhanded his friend with hi
other hand. Blood trickled from Krigel's mouth. Krige
did not move.

Como turned to a sergeant major, who had stoo
impassively by throughout the exchange between the
generals. "Sergeant Major, I want this man placed unde
arrest. If he attempts to resist, use whatever force i
necessary to subdue him. Understood?" He gave the
sergeant major Krigel's .45.

The sergeant major gripped General Krigel's arm and
nodded. He didn't like the order just given him. He'd

een a member of an LRRP team in Vietnam—back when
e was a young buck—and the idea of special troops
ighting special troops didn't set well with him. American
ighting American was wrong, no matter how you cut it
p.

"Yes, sir," the sergeant major said, but he was
hinking: just let me get General Krigel out of this area
nd by God, we'll both link up with Raines's Rebels. Us,
nd a bunch of other men.

General Como turned to his aide, Captain Shaw. "Tell
eneral Hazen he is now in charge of the Eighty-second.
et his troopers dropped. Those that won't go, have them
laced under arrest. If they resist, shoot them. Tell
eneral Cruger to get his marines across those borders
nd take their objectives. Start it. Right now! Those
roopers should have already been on the ground."

Shaw nodded his understanding, if not his agreement.
he young captain was career military, and he had his
rders, just as he was sure Raines's people had theirs.

"Yes, sir." He walked away. "Right away, sir."

General Como blinked rapidly several times. He was
ery close to tears, and then he was crying, the tears
unning down his tanned cheeks. "Goddamn it," he
hispered. "What a fucking lash-up."

The first few companies of marines and their
pearheaders, the force recon, hit the edge of the strip
nd died there. The area had been softened up with
rtillery and heavy-mortar fire, but Ben's people were in
unneled bunkers, and when the shelling stopped, up
hey popped.

The marines established a beachhead, or, in this case, a
ecure perimeter, taking the first three thousand yards.

They always take their objective—that's why they are marines—but the price was hideous. Neither side gave the other any mercy or quarter. For every meter gained that morning and early afternoon, the price was paid in human suffering.

The Rebels of the Tri-states waited until the paratroopers were on the ground and free of their 'chutes before opening fire. Those were Ben's orders, and the only act of mercy shown on either side. The first troopers to hit the DZs were killed almost instantly, raked with heavy .50-caliber machine-gun fire . . . or blown to bits with mortar fire.

By evening of the second day, the government troops were well inside the Tri-states' borders, coming in from north to south, east and west, hoping to trap the Rebels in a pocket. But Ben's people had reverted to guerrilla tactics and scattered; they had no group larger than battalion size, and most were platoon or company size. They hit hard, then they ran, and they booby-trapped everything.

The government troops who stormed the Tri-states soon learned what hell must be like. Everything they came into contact with either blew up, shot at them, bit them, or poisoned them. The older men thought they'd seen war at its worst in 'Nam, but this surpassed anything they'd ever experienced.

Earlier, the medical people in the Tri-states had discovered packs of rabid animals and captured them, keeping them alive as long as possible, transferring the infected cultures into the bloodstreams of every warm-blooded animal they could find. The day the invasion began, the animals were turned loose all over the area. It was cruel. Isn't war always?

The government troops began their search-and-destroy missions. They entered hospitals and nursing homes and found the patients had been armed. The very old and sick and dying fought just as savagely as the young and strong and healthy. Old people, with tubes hanging from their bodies, some barely able to crawl, hurled grenades and shot at the special troops. And the young men in their jump boots and berets and silver wings wept as they killed the old people. Tough marines cried at the carnage.

Many of the young soldiers threw down their weapons and walked away, refusing to take part in more killing. It was not cowardice on their part—not at all. These young men would have fought to the death against a threat to liberty; but the people of the Tri-states were no threat to their liberty. And the young troops finally learned the lesson their forefathers died for at Valley Forge: people have a right to be free, to live and work and play in peace and personal freedom—and to govern themselves.

Many of the young troops deserted to join the Rebels; officers publicly shot enlisted people who refused to fight against a group of citizens whom they believed had done no wrong.

The universal soldier syndrome came home to many of the troops: without us, you can't have a war.

And the children of the Tri-states, they fought as well. Some as young as twelve, stood and fought it out with the American military . . . wondering why, because they thought *they* were Americans. They hid with sniper rifles and had to be hunted down and killed. No compassion could be shown. A battered and bleeding little girl might just hand a medic a live grenade and die with him.

Rightly or wrongly, Ben's orders to school the young

of the Tri-states in the tactics of war had been driven home. They had been taught for nine years to defend their country, and that is what they were doing.

The hospitals finally had to be blown up with artillery; they were unsafe to enter because the patients were armed and ready to die. Everywhere the U.S. fighting men turned, something blew up in their faces. With thousands of tons of explosives to work with, the Rebels had wired everything possible to explode.

Tri-states began to stink like an open cesspool. The troops had to kill every warm-blooded animal they found. There was no way of knowing what animals had been infected—not in the early stages. The government troops became very wary of entering buildings, not only because of the risk of a door being wired to blow, but because the Rebels had begun placing rabid animals in houses, locking them in. A dog or a cat is a terrible thing to see come leaping at a person, snarling and foaming at the jaws.

The troops could not drink any of the water found in the Tri-states. Dr. Chase had infected it with everything from cholera to forms of anthrax.

There were no finely drawn battle lines in this war; no safe sectors. The Rebels didn't retreat in any given direction, leaving that area clean. They would pull back, then go left or right and circle around, coming up behind government troops to harass and confuse them, or to slit a throat or two. For the Rebels knew the territory, and they had, for nine years, been training for this. And they were experts at their jobs.

The bloody climax came when the government troops could not even remotely think of taking prisoners; they could not risk a Rebel, of any age or sex getting close to

454

them. Then the directive came down the chain of command: total extermination.

For many, this was the first time for actual combat. The first time to taste the highs and lows of war. And there are highs in combat. The first time to take a human life; and all the training in the world will not prepare a person for that moment.

Sometimes in combat, the mind will click off, and a soldier will do the necessary things to survive without realizing he is doing them, or remembering afterward. Rote training takes over.

Fire until you hear the ping or plop of the firing pin striking nothing. Make an easy, practiced roll to one side; quickly slam home a fresh clip; resume firing position, always aiming for the thickest part of the enemy's body, between neck and waist.

Your weapon is jammed. Clear it. Cuss it. Grab one from a dead buddy. Fire through the tears and the sweat and the dirt.

Sometimes a soldier will fire his weapon until it's empty and will never reload, so caught up in the heat and the horror of combat is he. Pull the trigger over and over; feel the imaginary slam of the butt against the shoulder; kill the enemy with nonbullets.

The yammering, banging, metal against metal makes it difficult to think. So you don't. The screaming, the awful howling of the wounded and the yelling of the combatants blend into a solid roaring cacophony in your head. An hour becomes a minute; a minute is eternity. God! will it never end? No! don't let it end; the high is terrific, kind of like a woman moaning beneath you, reaching the climax.

One soon learns the truth: you didn't climax, you shit your pants.

When did it start raining red? Thick red.

Suddenly, you become indestructible. *They* can't kill *you*. Laugh in the face of death. Howl at the reaper. A man running for cover is decapitated by a fluttering mortar round that sounds like a bunch of quail taking off as it comes in. The headless, nonhuman-appearing thing runs on for twenty more feet, flapping its arms in hideous silence. How fascinating. Look at it run. Fall down. Lie still.

A man is crawling on his hands and knees, gathering up his guts, trying to stuff them back into the gaping hole in his belly. He falls on his face, shivers, then screams and dies. Good. At least that shut the son of a bitch up. His guts are steaming in the cool air.

There is the enemy. Shoot him. Bring the rifle to your shoulder, sight him in—God! it's a *her!* Too late, you've pulled the trigger. Good hit. You know it's a good hit, 'cause the cunt falls funny, kind of limp and boneless.

The thought comes to you: how long has it been since you had any pussy?

Shit, man! What a time to be thinking of that!

Turn to say something to your best buddy, just a yard from you in a ditch. Discover that what you thought was red rain is really blood. A lot of blood. He's still alive, but the blood is really gushing out . . . in long spurts. You want to be sick, but here is no place to be sick; not enough time to be sick. Besides, you'd have to lie in it. You smell the stink of shit. Realize it's your shit—in your pants.

Your eyes smart from the smoke of battle and the sting of sweat. Wipe your face and dig at your eyes with shaky hands. You'd better get your shit together, 'cause here comes the enemy, almost on top of you.

There is that dude from Bravo Company, the one you never really liked 'cause he used to brag about all the pussy he got. He won't get any more. Took a slug right between the eyes; all that yuk leaking out.

Abruptly, too quickly, the enemy is all around you and you're mixing it hand-to-hand. This is stupid! The enemy looks just like you. His mouth is open, his eyes are wide with a combination of fear and excitement, and he is dirty and smells bad. Just for the smallest of a split second your eyes meet. Each brain sends the same message: This guy is going to kill me!

You're off your knees (How did I get on my knees? What the fuck was I, praying?) and out of the ditch. Your legs support you. Shaky, but you're going to be all right. You're going to make it. You're going to live!

Squeeze the trigger. Goddamn it! the weapon's empty. Slam the butt of your rifle into his balls and he screams and doubles over, puking. Bring the butt down hard on his neck, hear the neck pop. He's through. A fresh clip in the weapon. Shoot him to be sure he's dead.

You turn in a crouch, trying to suck air into your lungs; can't get enough air. There is another Rebel. . . . He's just killed . . . what's his name? Guy from third platoon. You notice the strangest things: the Rebel needs a shave. Rush over to him while his back is turned. But it's almost like slow-motion. Force your bayonet into his back, feeling the hard resistance as the blade pushes through muscle and passes bone. It's not as easy as in the movies. It's always so clean and glorious in the movies. Don't remember fixing the bayonet on the lug. What difference does it make? The Rebel is screaming and jerking and twisting in pain. Oh, shit! The blade is stuck in his back. Christ! Pull the trigger and blast the blade free.

How in the hell did you get on the ground, flat on your back? Am I O.K.? Feel yourself with your hands—timid hands. Jesus, don't let my balls be gone.

"Get up, you yellow son of a bitch!" a sergeant is yelling. Is he yelling at me? Damn, Sarge, I didn't get down here deliberately. The sergeant takes a slug in the back. Musta gone right through the spine; he falls funny. You can't remember his name.

Get to your feet to face the enemy. What is this, a replay? You just did this.

Some guys have captured a woman Rebel; pulling the pants off her. Aw, come on, guys! She's screaming something while they rape her. That's not right. We're not animals, guys.

"Want some pussy, Jake?"

They're talkin' to you, stupid. "No."

Someone is screaming. A Rebel.

"Beg, you mother-fucker!" someone tells him.

"Go to hell!" The Rebel shouts his reply.

The old man has said no prisoners. So the Reb is shot. But he didn't have to be shot there. He's screaming.

Look around you. Is it over? Yeah—almost. Holy MotherofGodJesusFuckingChristAlmighty: look at the bodies. All the blood and shit. Oh, God—the sergeant is walking around the area, shooting the wounded Rebs in the head. Someone tells you your squad leader is dead. You were a corporal; now you're a sergeant. Battlefield promotion. Somehow it doesn't seem like much of a big deal. You want to say: "But I don't want it!" Then suddenly there is a .45 in your hand and you're stepping through the gore and the pain and the moaning and the

458

5 is jumping in your hand, ending the screaming.

No prisoners.

On either side.

That woman Reb is still screaming. They're hurting er. "Fuck her up the ass!" someone shouts, laughing. Get a little brown on your pole."

You walk away from the sight and sounds. You could op them; you're a sergeant; but you don't want to lose ce with the men, not this early in your promotion. hat the hell? She's only a Rebel. The enemy.

Now the enemy is dead as you walk through the near-uiet battleground. But that woman is still screaming ay back there, across the meadow. Wish to hell she'd ut up.

A Rebel is still alive, shot hard in the chest. He's oking up at you, defiance in his eyes. You shoot him in e head.

Look . . . don't blame me. I'm just following orders.

Now, all the enemy is dead, and it's too quiet. omebody say something. But everybody you look at verts their eyes. Guys are breathing too hard; somebody osses his breakfast, puking on the ground. Someone else s praying. You think God is listening after all this shit?

"It's too goddamned quiet!"

You spin around. "Who said that?"

Nobody will answer.

A Rebel is moaning. You point to him, then look at one f your men. You hear your voice say: "Shoot him."

"Right, Sarge."

Bam!

The sound is so *goddamned* loud.

There is a guy from your platoon, kneeling, holding a iny blue-colored bird in his dirty hand. The bird is dead.

459

Everybody gathers around to look at it. There isn't
mark on the bird. No blood. Seems funny to se
something without any blood or dirt on it. Wonder wha
killed the bird?

"Hey, Sarge?" someone whispers. "You know what?"

"What?" Your voice sounds funny. Old.

That woman is still screaming, faintly, hoarsely.

"We won."

NINE

By dusk of the thirty-fifth day, the heaviest fighting was behind the government troops. The pincers had closed, and most of the Tri-states was secure. But the price paid for victory had been cruelly high.

Juno was dead, shot a dozen times, but only after the aging animal had killed a major, tearing out his throat.

And now the government troops had to be content with mopping up; combat troops can testify that mopping up can be awful. It is a sniper's bullet; a booby-trap; a mine; a swing-trap with sharpened stakes set chest high; a souvenir that can cost you a hand, or a leg, or a life.

Major General Como was dead, shot through the head by a thirteen-year-old girl wielding a pistol she had taken from the body of a paratroop captain. The girl was taken alive, raped repeatedly, then shot.

It has been written that there is nothing in the world more savage than the American fighting man.

Como's replacement, Major General Goren lasted only two weeks. He opened the center drawer of a desk in what was to have been his HQ, a cleared secure building, and five pounds of nitroglycerine and nitrocellulose blew him open and spread him all over the room, along with a colonel and his sergeant major. The charge was timed with a delay fuse: open the drawer ten times and the charge was still dormant; on the eleventh, it would blow.

Mopping up.

In a mountainous, heavily wooded area, west and north of Vista, HQ's company of Tri-states' Rebels prepared to fight their last fight. Most of them had been together for years: Steven and Linda, James and Belle, Cecil and Lila, Al and Anne, Bridge and Abby, Pal and Valerie, Ike and Megan, Voltan and Nora, Sam and Pam, Jerre and Jimmy Deluce; and Jane Dolbeau, Tatter and June-Bug and their husbands . . . Ben and Salina. And a hundred others that made up the company. The kids with them should have been gone and safe by now, but they'd been cut off and had to return. It was now back to alpha, and omega was just around the corner, waiting for most of them.

There was a way out, but it was a long shot.

Ben sat talking with the twins, Jack and Tina.

"Jack, you've got to look after Salina, now. I'm going to split the company and lead a diversion team. I think it's our only way out." He patted Jack's shoulder. "I'll be all right, son; don't worry about me. I'll make it. I'm still an old curly wolf with some tricks up my sleeve."

"Then you'll join us later?" Tina asked, tears running down her cheeks.

"Sure. Count on it," Ben said. He shook Jack's hand and kissed Tina. "Go on, now, join up with Colonel Elliot. I want to talk with your mother for a moment."

Salina came to his side, slipping her hand into his. They were both grimy from gunsmoke and dirt and sweat. Ben thought she had never looked more beautiful than during her pregnancy; she had stood like a dusty Valkyrie by his side, firing an M-16 during the heaviest of fighting.

She said, "We didn't have much time together, did we, Ben?"

"We have a lot of time left us, babe," he replied gently.

She smiled; a sad smile. Knowing. "Con the kids, General. Don't try to bullshit me."

"Yeah," Ben said ruefully. "Yeah, I wish we'd had more time." He kissed her, very gently, very tenderly, without passion or lust. A man kissing a woman good-by.

Salina grasped at the moment. "Is there any chance at all?"

"Not much of one, I'm afraid." He leveled with her.

She tried to smile; then suddenly began to weep, softly, almost silently. She put her arms around his neck and kissed him. "I do love you, Ben Raines." She smiled through the tears. "Even if you are a honky."

"And I love you, Salina." He fought back the tears to return her smile. "Now you step 'n' fetch yore ass on outta here, baby."

And together they laughed.

Ben helped her to her feet, gazed at her for a moment, then walked from her to join the group he was taking on diversion. Abruptly, without warning, the silent forest floor erupted into blood and violence. A platoon of paratroopers, quiet and deadly, came at the Rebels; the peaceful wood turned into hand-to-hand combat.

Ben flipped his old Thompson onto full auto and burned a clip into the paratroopers, bringing down half a dozen. Salina screamed behind him. Ben spun in time to see her impaled on a bayonet. Her mouth opened and closed in silent agony; her hands slowly crawled snakelike down her stomach to clutch at the rifle barrel, to try to pull the hot pain from her stomach. She screamed as she began miscarrying the dead child, for the bayonet had driven through the unborn baby.

"Jesus Christ!" the trooper yelled, as he saw what he had done. He tried to pull the blade from her belly. But the blade was stuck. He pulled the trigger—reflex from hard training—and blew the blade free, sending a half-dozen slugs into Salina, throwing her backward from the force.

Ben jerked his .45 from leather and blew half the trooper's head off, just as Salina collapsed to the ground, her hands working at the bloody mess that was once her stomach.

Ben was at her side as his Rebels, offering no mercy, took the fight to the troopers. The troopers were outnumbered and fighting against white-hot rage. They died very quickly; the Rebels took no prisoners.

Ben gathered her into his arms, knowing there was no chance for her to live. She was fading quickly. "I love you, Salina."

She looked up at him and smiled for the last time. "Sorry 'bout the baby, honey. But with our luck it would probably have been a koala bear."

She closed her eyes and died.

Ben tried to rip away the heavy load of grief that saddled his shoulders and clutched at his heart with cold fingers. He shook away dozens of emotions as he knelt beside the only woman he had ever truly loved. He touched her face, closed her eyes, smoothed her hair, kissed her still-warm lips. He fought his way back to reality.

Dr. Chase pulled him away from Salina's body and knelt down for a moment, cutting at her maternity slacks with a knife. He covered her with a shelter half and rose to face Ben. "Boy," he said. "Perfectly normal. All his fingers and toes. Her complexion, your eyes. Bayonet

464

went right through him."

Ben nodded. "Let's go!" he shouted. "There is no more we can do here. Help the wounded and let's move it."

Ike touched his arm. "Ben . . ."

"We don't have time to grieve, buddy. Later."

The Rebels drifted silently into the forest, taking their wounded, leaving their dead; Salina and the boy lay among the still and the quiet and the dead. Ants had already begun their march across her face. She lay in a puddle of thickening blood, one hand on the arm of her dead child.

The Rebels split up, the first two squads not making it past the edge of the northern border of the strip. A forward observer spotted them and called in artillery. None escaped the deadly hail. Another group walked into an ambush; only a few escaped. The kids lay like pebbles on a beach, their broken and smashed bodies a grim reminder of the vindictiveness and power of government. A half a dozen Cobra gunships spotted another group and came chopping out of the sky, strafing them with rocket and machine-gun fire.

A few moments before dusk Ben's group came face-to-face with two companies of government troops.

Jimmy Deluce was caught in a murderous crossfire and died on his feet, cursing the enemy.

Jack had regrouped with his father and now left Ben's side to help a friend. Jack was almost cut apart by M-60 fire. Tina lobbed a grenade into a machine-gun nest and finished it off with a burst from her M-10.

Sam Pyron watched his wife shot dead, and the West Virginia mountain boy rose to his feet, screaming his outrage. He walked toward the soldiers hip-firing an AK-

47 and cursing them. He took more than a few with him into that long good-by.

Ben took a slug low in his left side, the slug traveling downward, bouncing off his hipbone, the force of it knocking him against a tree, stunning him. A concussion grenade slammed him into darkness.

Ben was spared the sight of Pal taking a .45 slug through the head. He did not see Valerie torn apart by automatic rifle fire. He would be informed much later that Pal and Valerie's children had run into the line of fire trying to get to him, and had been cut to bloody ribbons.

Voltan died. Megan was taken alive and raped, then shot. Al, Abby . . . many, many more died. Lila walked in front of a Claymore and was blown into tiny bits. James Riverson helped carry Ben out of the forest and across the border, the big man walking and weeping. His Belle was dead, and so were their kids.

By the time darkness fell on the now nonexistent government of the Tri-states, not many Rebels had escaped. Less than three thousand had made it out. But Badger and dozens more had escaped weeks before, and headed underground.

The zero squads.

TEN

Senators Richards, Goode, Carey, and Williams were having a drink before their usual Thursday-night poker game in Richmond. They would never get around to playing poker, and it would be their last drink before death took them behind her misty curtain of sunless eternity. They all felt safe, knowing that three secret service agents were guarding them. The agents were there, but they were very dead, cut down by silenced .22 automatics.

Williams jerked up his head, the fresh drink in his hand forgotten. "Did any of you hear anything?"

Carey laughed. "Relax, Jimmy. You don't really believe in those so-called zero squads, do you?"

Sen. Jimmy Williams ran nervous fingers through thinning hair. He did not reply. Outside, a late-summer storm was building; heat lightning danced erratically and thunder rumbled across the sky, almost an ominous warning in cadence.

Senator Goode leaned forward. "Jimmy, it's been over three months since the Tri-states' defeat. Ben Raines is dead. Eyewitnesses have reported it. If anything was going to happen, don't you believe it would have occurred by now?"

"No." Williams spoke. "I don't. We allowed the

women and kids to be killed—slaughtered like animals
Just like we did the Indians. They're going to get us
We're dead men and don't even know it."

Senator Richards looked up into the gloom of the
darkened hallway. "Oh, no!" he shouted. "Oh, my God!'

The senators looked first at their colleague, then into
the faces of hate and revenge and death. Standing in the
hallway stood two men and a woman. They held silenced
automatics in their hands.

Goode fell forward on his knees and began to pray. A
self-professed "good Christian man," Goode had been
the first to vote for war against the Tri-states.

Carey's face turned shiny from sweat and a trickle of
spit oozed from a corner of his mouth. He began to rub
his hands together and lick at his lips.

Richards dropped his drink on the carpeted floor. His
eyes were wide and he urinated in his shorts.

Only Williams remained calm. "I knew you people
would come," he said. "I told them to leave you alone.
was against fighting you."

"We know." The woman spoke. "And because of that
you'll live. And the Tri-states will live again, too
Remember that."

"Yes. Yes, I will." Williams bobbed his head up and
down.

The automatics began to hum their dirges. Richards
Goode, and Carey jerked onto the floor and died. The
assassination team left as quickly and quietly as they had
arrived. They had a lot of work ahead of them.

Williams sat for a long time, looking at the cooling
bodies of his friends. His eyes grew wild and he soiled
himself. The telephone rang and he ignored it. He began
to giggle, childlike. The giggling changed to laughter and
he howled his madness as blood vessels burst in his head

He fell to his knees on the floor and cried and prayed. A massive pain grew out of his chest—a huge, heavy, crushing weight. He screamed, his heart stopping its beating. He died.

General Russell called for more coffee. He was working late in his office. A sergeant brought him a fresh pot, poured a cup, and opened a packet of sugar, stirring it in.

"Will that be all, sir?"

"Yes," Russell said. "You may leave." He tasted his coffee, added more sugar, and took another sip. He would be found the next morning, dead, his system full of poison.

Dallas Valentine and the first lady, Fran Logan, lay moaning and thrashing on the bed, both of them reaching for the final pinnacle of climax. Neither of them heard the door swing open. They were enjoying mutual climax as the Rebel with the silenced submachine gun sprayed them with .45-caliber slugs, turning the silk sheets red with blood.

The Rev. Palmer Falcreek answered his telephone. A voice said, "Let he that is without sin cast the first stone."

"What the hell did you say?" Falcreek said.

"I said"—the voice rang in Falcreek's ear—"open the drawer in the middle right of your desk, you semi-sanctimonious mother-fucker!"

"How dare you speak to me like that!" Falcreek raged. He jerked open the desk drawer and half the house blew apart as the heavy charge was detonated.

Senator Higley worked late in his office. The storm

didn't worry him and neither did the myth of the zero squads. He left his office at nine-thirty. Halfway down the steps of the Senate office building he sat down abruptly, twitched once, then slowly rolled down the steps, the hole between his eyes leaking blood and gray matter.

Senator Pough stepped out of his porch for a breath of cool night air. He heard a thump and looked down. Between his feet, on the porch, lay a hissing white phosphorus grenade. Pough had only a few seconds to feel panic, attempt to run, and scream just once before the grenade exploded and seared him to the house.

Rep. Carol Helger answered the donging of her apartment doorbell and took a twelve-inch bayonet through her chest. The young woman who shoved the heavy blade into her spat on the still-writhing body, left the blade in her, and quietly left the building.

The zero squads were busy that stormy, revengeful night. Very busy. The final tally was thirty-one senators and seventy-four representatives dead. Twelve cabinet heads dead and the entire Joint Chiefs were also wiped out. A few zero squad members made it out of Richmond to rejoin the eastern-based Rebels. Most died in shoot-outs with the police. Only one zero squad member had not worked that night of terror. He slept soundly in a motel room three hundred miles from Richmond. He had only one person to kill.

Badger Harbin was to kill the President of the United States.

Richmond went into a panic. No one could possibly

guess at the number of assassins roaming the streets, killing at random. Innocent men and women were killed by federal agents and police during raids on suspected Rebel sympathizers. Martial law was declared. The police were federalized. It was the beginning of America's first true police state.

President Logan smiled and leaned back in his leather chair. He was very pleased with the way things were going. Seven weeks since the awful assassinations, and the country was settling down. He had rid himself of a cheating wife and accomplished his life's dream: he had an iron grip on the country. The previous night he had dreamed of being crowned king of America.

Yes, Logan smiled, things were sailing right along. And, best of all, that damned Ben Raines was dead. That damned troublemaker was finally dead and through.

Or was he? The president frowned at the thought. His agents swore that Raines was dead; swore they'd shot him and a young blond woman who was with him. Said they saw them fall out there in Washington, up near the British Columbia border.

"Damn it!" Logan swore. Why hadn't they made more effort to retrieve the body and bring it back with them? Put the stinking, bullet-riddled carcass on public display, to show people that when the government says do something, by God this is what happens if you don't follow orders.

The president stood and stretched. He walked out of his office and up the hallway. "Get my guards," he told an aide. "I'm going for a walk."

Logan tried to take a walk every morning at ten o'clock, rain or shine. He had missed his walk the past few days because of meetings and was irritable because of

471

it. Now he would have his walk.

His last walk.

Outside the new White House, as it was still called, across the street in a public park, a young man sat, feeding the birds and the squirrels, enjoying the cool breeze of fall; a handsome young man, in his late twenties or early thirties. He looked very much the part of a highly successful executive, dressed in the height of fashion. He'd drawn the attentions of a dozen ladies strolling. The young man had smiled at them, then ignored them. Seemingly preoccupied with the time, he kept looking at his wristwatch.

Ben Raines gazed at the reflection of his face and upper torso in the still waters of the little creek in northern Idaho. He said, "Lord, man, you look like you've been dissected and rejected."

Ben was now in his fifty-third year, completely gray. His face was lined and tanned; body still hard, eyes old.

"No . . ." A voice spoke from behind him. "Never rejected. Not by me."

Ben turned, smiling, to look at the woman who had stood by him during the past very bad months. She returned the smile.

"At last count there were nine bullet scars in your hide." She touched one of the newer scars, pink and dimpled. Her touch became more intimate as she moved her hand from his shoulder to his chest, touching her lips to his mouth.

"I have a meeting in an hour," he reminded her.

She grinned. "General, there may have been a time when you could last an hour. But not since I've known you."

Together, they laughed.

In the small park across from the White House, Badger Harbin put his hand on the briefcase. He had heard the newscast, some weeks back, that Gen. Ben Raines was dead. Badger wanted very much not to believe that. And a part of him did not. Gen. Ben Raines, Badger knew, was a hard man to kill.

The attaché case under his hand was ready. In that case he had carefully prepared and packed ten pounds of C-4 plastic explosive, to be detonated electrically, activated by a tiny switch located under the handle of the briefcase.

Badger smiled. It was similiar to the grin of the Grim Reaper.

Vice President Addison stood in the president's now-empty office and fought a silent battle within his mind. The president had been his friend for more than thirty years. But Hilton had done so much twisting and changing in his social and political philosophy over the last years . . . Aston felt he no longer knew the man, and he was ashamed of himself for remaining silent at some of Hilton's outrages toward humankind.

Aston had been sick at his stomach for a week after the slaughter of the Indians, and for longer than that after Tri-states was destroyed. There had been more than slaughter in both places: rape and torture confirmed. Hilton had brushed that news aside.

"Traitors," he had said, and would speak no more of it.

The president's own doctor had come to Aston, telling him of his strong suspicions that the president was rapidly approaching the point of being a madman. Aston didn't want to believe it. But . . .

"Yes," he muttered to the silent office. "His mind is sick."

Aston then made up his mind: he would have that meeting with the members of Congress who felt the country was heading in the wrong direction. Certain military men would also be present. They would pool their ideas and thoughts, try to work something out. A bloodless coup, perhaps? But it would be difficult, for some units of the military, a lot of national guard and reserve units, and nearly all the newly federalized police supported Logan and his dictatorship.

Aston mused: Logan is no better than was Ben Raines. Actually, he grimaced at the thought, Logan is a lot worse.

Yes, Hilton was sick.

Aston paced the carpet, thinking: My God, how did this great nation ever come to this? What did we do over the years that was so wrong?

"We drifted away from the Constitution, you idiot!" he said aloud. He moved to the president's desk. There, he seated himself and cursed.

He picked up the binoculars that Hilton used to study the faces of people who walked past the White House. He adjusted the glasses until he had Hilton in focus, striding across the lawn, toward the fence by the sidewalk. Lifting the glasses, he caught a movement across the street, in the park. He studied the young man as he moved slowly onto the painted crosswalk leading to the sidewalk in front of the fence. The young man carried an attaché case.

Aston suddenly felt he was having a heart attack. His chest hurt, he had trouble breathing, his head felt light.

"My God!" he yelled to the empty room. "That's the bodyguard. General Raines's bodyguard."

He grabbed up the phone, punching a button for a line.

He ignored the light signifying the line was busy. He punched another. Busy. Cursing, he ran from the room.

Outside, the guard had unlocked the gate, allowing the president to step through to the sidewalk. He was alone except for his contingent of secret service agents, some feet behind and ahead of him. One stood by his side, street-side. The president noticed a well-dressed young man walking toward him. The young man smiled; a nice, open, friendly smile, and Hilton returned the smile. Hilton wished everybody would like him. He only had the country's best interests at heart. Hilton suddenly felt very good. It was a beautiful fall day.

"Paul, call that young man over here." President Logan gave his last order.

When the secret service agent hailed him, Badger punched the button trigger of the deadly attaché case. It would blow in thirty seconds.

"Sir!" a secret service man called to VP Addison. "What's wrong, sir?"

"Stop them!" Aston said, gasping for breath.

"Stop who, sir?"

Aston rushed past the man, ran down the steps. In his haste, he stumbled, rolling down the steps, gashing open his head, cracking his skull. He was flung into darkness. The secret service men ran to help him.

"Hello, there, young man," President Logan said to Badger. "Lovely day, isn't it?"

Badger grinned as he finished his silent count of twenty. He stepped up to the president, the force side of the attaché case toward Logan. "General Raines sends his compliments," Badger said. And just before the heavy charge blew them all over the White House lawn and into history, Badger added, "You rotten son of a bit—"

EPILOGUE

Reflect how you are to govern a people who think they ought to be free, and think they are not. Your scheme yields no revenue; it yields nothing but discontent, disorder, disobedience; and such is the state of America, that after wading up to your eyes in blood, you could only end just where you began; that is, to tax where no revenue is to be found, to— my voice fails me; my inclination carries me no farther—all is confusion beyond it.

Burke—first speech on conciliation with America

Ben looked about him, but he was not really seeing the several hundred men and women that made up his personal contingent of the western-based Rebels. No, his mind was far away. He was seeing Salina in the dim light outside that motel—he could not remember exactly where it was. So long ago, he sighed, but yet, only yesterday.

And now, his sigh deepened, I am past middle age, and she is dead, rotting in a forest. And my son—dead—as are all the others who fought and died for what they believed.

On both sides, he carefully, reluctantly, reminded himself.

General Krigel had his eastern-based Rebels ready to go, as did Conger in the mid-north, Colonel Ramos in the southwest, and General Hazen in the midwest.

Now, in the swamps, the mountains, the deserts, and the badlands and woodlands, many of the marines and paratroopers and SEALs and Rangers and Green Berets and Air Force personnel and regular infantrymen who had refused to fight anymore against the Tri-states, and had deserted, were gathered, awaiting Ben's orders to go. The Rebel dream had not died; it was as strong as before. Whether it would bloom as a beautiful child, or become as evil as a cancer, only time and history would know.

And now, it was time: Ben would give the orders and guerrilla warfare would once more shake the country, and possibly, the rebuilding world.

Again.

God! He was so weary of fighting.

Ben shook away his thoughts of things and people past and dead and said, "Badger completed his assignment. Logan is dead. VP Addison is hospitalized in a coma. Many military units are in revolt against the government; some others want to take over the government, continuing Logan's dictatorship. It's time for us to make our move toward rebuilding our dream of a free state."

Ben looked at the men and women around him: at Ike, sitting on a log, his right boot off, looking at his big toe sticking through a hole in his sock; at his adopted daughter, Tina, cradling a CAR-15 in her arms; at Jerre, who stood by his side. At the Indians who had waited for his return; at Judith, reporter-turned-warrior; at James, ever calm; at Cecil, Ph.D. with an AK-47 in his hands; at Dr. Chase, at least seventy, and still as tough as a mountain goat—and just as ornery.

Ben had to smile. The people who surrounded him were of all persuasions and races: black, white, red, yellow, tan, brown. At least here, he thought, the color line is broken. But God, at what cost?

"Dad?" Tina pulled him back to the present, then lost him as Ben turned his eyes to the valley that stretched before them.

There were mountain peaks far in the distance. A gentle haze lay over the area. It was so lovely and so lonely in its peacefulness, so quiet and beautiful.

Once again, Salina slipped into his thoughts, and his heart ached for her. He felt no guilt for his feelings. Jerre knew he was, and would always be, in love with Salina. At least a part of him.

He stood up from the rock he'd been sitting on. Ben was tired, but he knew he could not let it show. Could never quit.

He looked at his Rebels, the people ready to die for what they felt was right. He buckled his web belt, adjusted the canvas clip pouch, and picked up his old Thompson.

"All right, people," he said. "Let's do it."